Renegades among the Tumbleweeds

Hewitt Freiburg

authorHOUSE®

AuthorHouse™ LLC
1663 Liberty Drive
Bloomington, IN 47403
www.authorhouse.com
Phone: 1-800-839-8640

This is a work of fiction. All of the characters, names, incidents, organizations, and dialogue in this novel are either the products of the author's imagination or are used fictitiously.

© 2014 Hewitt Freiburg. All rights reserved.

No part of this book may be reproduced, stored in a retrieval system, or transmitted by any means without the written permission of the author.

Published by AuthorHouse   08/05/2014

ISBN: 978-1-4969-2874-0 (sc)
ISBN: 978-1-4969-2875-7 (hc)
ISBN: 978-1-4969-2876-4 (e)

Library of Congress Control Number: 2014912954

Any people depicted in stock imagery provided by Thinkstock are models, and such images are being used for illustrative purposes only.
Certain stock imagery © Thinkstock.

This book is printed on acid-free paper.

Because of the dynamic nature of the Internet, any web addresses or links contained in this book may have changed since publication and may no longer be valid. The views expressed in this work are solely those of the author and do not necessarily reflect the views of the publisher, and the publisher hereby disclaims any responsibility for them.

CHAPTER 1

Japanese businessman, Katsutoshi Ohno, sat at his desk looking at the package he had just been given by his assistant, Eisen Shakura. It was a DHL delivery from Cardiff University, so he knew it was from his Welsh friend, Professor Dafydd Smith, whom everyone called 'Daf.'

He had known Daf for over 50 years. In 1959, Katsutoshi, whom only Daf was brave enough to call 'Kat,' had begun graduate studies at Cambridge. He had just turned 21. Daf was a year ahead of him and almost three years older; he had taken Kat under his tutelage, helping him polish his English among other things.

He remembered Daf teaching him the English version of the tea ceremony. It was so different from the Japanese version, the *cha no yu*, but also a ritual. Daf had been a good teacher. He looked at all things "English" with a keen eye—being Welsh allowed him to see the little nuances that he and Kat then learned. Daf's goal had been to be more English than the English when he was among them. He had come close, but he was still Welsh. And Kat definitely was still Japanese.

Both men loved history and art; Daf had studied Medieval Wales, and Kat had studied European art as it grew into the Renaissance. Many experts felt the Renaissance was the rebirth or revival of the arts which, they said had declined over time since the magnificence of the Greek and Roman eras. To them, it also meant the freeing of art from religion. Kat had chosen to focus on religious symbols in art of the 13th century—on the cusp of the Renaissance. He considered Renaissance art to be a new configuration of religious art and he embraced the traces of Byzantine that remained. He had often called on Daf to help him understand the Catholic iconography; it was a subject that Daf, even though a Catholic rather than an Anglican, had trouble with as well. As Daf would explain, very few Welsh, Catholic or Anglican, ever actually went to church.

In 1963, when Kat was 24, his father died. Kat's father had given him his interest in Western art. His father also had pulled strings to get him accepted at Cambridge. So Kat accepted that he had to return to Tokyo to take over the family business started by his grandfather and continued by his father.

Kat believed that his early success with the company came primarily from capitalizing on his English schooling. The Americans were focused on reindustrializing Japan as a bulwark against Communism in Asia. An English-speaking Japanese industrialist schooled at Cambridge was just what the Americans wanted. Over the years, he became a very wealthy man, growing the small manufacturing plant started by his grandfather in the early 1900s into a major provider of parts to Yamaha, Kawasaki, Suzuki and then, in 2000, to Subaru as well.

It wasn't a bad business—one could argue there was some art and beauty in it. After all, Yamaha had been making pianos for many years before deciding to build motorcycles, hence the tuning forks on its logo. And Suzuki had once made weaving looms. Even Subaru had taken a Japanese constellation as its name and incorporated its stars into its logo. The Japanese saw six stars in the Subaru constellation. The ancient Greeks called it the Seven Sisters or Pleiades after the seven daughters of Atlas; they concocted some story about one of the sisters running off as they too could see only six stars easily. He would have Eisen find him a picture of the Greek version of the Pleiades.

Now, decades later, Kat had a fairly significant collection of Western Art of his own, courtesy of his family's company and the wealth it had generated for him. Kat would always be thankful for that. He no longer could remember any regrets he may have had so long ago about coming home from Cambridge.

Although Kat was now 75, he still went to his office every day. His son, Michel (actually Michelangelo, named after Michelangelo Merisi da Caravaggio of the Baroque era, not after Michelangelo di Lodovico Buonarroti Simoni of the High Renaissance and *Pieta* fame), was now running things. Michel was doing well, so Kat tried to stay out of the way. Besides, an Italian art historian recently had found the image of a horned devil in the clouds of a Giotto fresco in the Basilica of Assisi. Kat now was busy re-evaluating a paper on the iconography of Giotto he had done decades ago. He hoped to have a new paper ready for publication at the end of May.

Kat looked at the DHL package again. For many years now, he and Daf always met somewhere at least twice a year. These days they preferred meeting in London–Daf could take the train in from Cardiff. After getting his doctorate at Cambridge, Daf moved to Cardiff University, where he taught Welsh history. Daf had a very popular column in the local paper which had run every other Saturday for years now. It was entitled 'Famous Welshmen.' Kat always greeted Daf with the question, "have you run out of Welshmen yet, Old Man?"

Now, Daf was emeritus and he had turned the column over to his students, retaining only the right to veto the students' choices or make corrections. Kat thought for a few minutes–it had been almost a year since they last met in London and he hadn't spoken to Daf since October. Well, that needed to be remedied.

Kat opened the package. Inside was a short letter from Daf's long-time secretary, Margery Short. Her letter said that Dr. Smith had died on December 24, 2012. Kat felt tears welling in his eyes, but he fought to control his emotion. He sat for a minute, and then continued reading. Her letter also said that Dr. Smith had directed that, on the day he was buried, December 29, 2012, she was to send Kat the sealed envelope that was in the package with her letter.

He reread Margery's letter. Daf also told her to mail two more packages five days after he was buried–the delay would give Kat time to review the first package, before he was inundated with two more. As that would be January 3, the last two packages would come from London since Margery would celebrate New Year's Eve there with her sister.

Kat stood and walked over to the east window of his office. As he looked down 53 floors to the busy Tokyo streets, he focused his thoughts on his dear friend. After a few minutes, he sat down again and opened the envelope from Daf. Inside he found an old document and Daf's hand-written translation of the document. He also found a neatly typed letter from Daf dated December 15, 2012 at the top. It also had hand-written dates of December 16 and 17 added. He started with the letter.

December 15, [Hand written after the 15, *"16 and 17 DS"* was inserted] 2012

Cardiff, Wales

Dearest Kat,

If you are reading this letter, it is because I have finally given up on fighting old age and have moved on to some peaceful place—or, nowhere—either is fine with me. I have enclosed an 'old' document as a gift by which I hope you will remember me. I am hopeful that perhaps the love of history that we have shared since our early days at Cambridge will entice you to determine whether the document is real. I, of course, will no longer be available to help except to the extent of my annotation of the document, which is included in this package.

I came across the document, which is written on parchment in an old version of Welsh, in a small London gallery. It caught my attention because of the vanity of seeing a reference to my own name, Dafydd, in the text. I was able to translate it and then annotate it for you. However, as I have now had a minor heart attack, which again, if you are reading this, has likely contributed to my demise, I am asking you to take over what hopefully will be an interesting project.

[Here in the right margin of the text, Kat saw a handwritten note which read: *"I believe the document dates somewhere in the range from the early 1300s to the early 1600s. The language is appropriate for that time period. The parchment looks old, but you should check the ink etc., to see if it is a modern forgery. I have not quite finished the annotation, as you can see, but I think you should have enough to complete my project. 16/12/12 DS"*]

The document's author, Dafydd ap Talog (you call me 'Daf' so I will call this man 'our Daf'), says he sailed from Llandrillo-yn-Rhos, which is better known today as Rhos-on-Sea. I will refer to it as "Rhos" herein. The date seems to be March 13, 1308, but, much as I would like that to be true, it looks like it may have been tampered with—a better date, based on a reference in the document, would be about the first decade of the 1600s. Our Daf is a seafaring Welshman and this document purports to be a record that he had stamped at Rhos by port officials before sailing from there. It tells where and when he was going. It also should have had a second page recording when he got back, but that is missing, so he may not have returned. When you read where I believe our 'Daf' went, you will agree that the 'when' needs much more research. I don't think whether he got back matters as much as 'where' he went and 'when.' As an aside, I was able to trace our Daf's family name back to about the eleventh century. Going forward, it seems to be absent after about 1620, so he is not my relative.

> [Here in the left margin and onto the back of the page of the text, was another handwritten note which read: *"Don't confuse Rhos, which is on the sea as the name says, with the tiny inland city of Llandrillo in Denbighshire near the River Dee.*
>
> *I have been too weak to travel to Rhos this month as I had planned. I did, however, speak briefly by phone with the harbormaster there. He said that it sounded like I had a simple ship record that used to be filed with the port when the ship returned. He also said that if there were records of ship sailings from that time, they would have been transferred to the National Library of Wales or possibly the National Archives a long time ago. By the way, the 'Llandrillo' part of Llandrillo-yn-Rhos derives from the sixth century Celtic saint, St. Trillo. His tiny little church is still there in Rhos. I read somewhere that it is the smallest church in England. 17/12/12DS"*]

Our Daf was the navigator for a ship that he says was captained by a Portuguese man named Joham Alvares Diaz Ovelho. Ovelho's ship came to Rhos from Tomar, Portugal. He and his shipmates stayed there for the winter. Our Daf doesn't say much about Captain Ovelho, his ship (other than that it is a well made Portuguese vessel) or the Captain's crew of 13 men. Our Daf does say that the ship had come to Rhos three times before. Also, there were an additional twenty men in Daf's crew, so that's either thirty-three or thirty-five men, depending upon whether he is counting himself and Captain Ovelho. What he says after that should get you interested.

To end the suspense, I believe the ship's destination probably was Port Royal, which is on the Bay of Fundy side of present day Nova Scotia. I base this, in part, on our Daf's statement that they are sailing to a settlement far north of what he calls 'Madoc Landing' (see below) and, more importantly, what appears to be a latitudinal reference (annoyingly, he doesn't name the settlement, but Port Royal is the closest and oldest). Port Royal was established by the Frenchman, Champlain, in 1605. That is a basis for not believing the

1308 date—there was nothing there in the 1300s. As I will explain later, I believe that a storm that our Daf mentions actually pushed him west so that he landed on the Maine (a US State) side of the Bay of Fundy across from Port Royale. You are probably thinking I am senile about now, but bear with me.

[Here, in the right margin and onto the back of the page of the text, was another handwritten note which read: "*When you get the map (a separate package), you will note that it is probably signed by Captain Ovelho, but part of his signature is missing. Again, do look carefully at the date on our Daf's document. It is possible that someone has modified the year as the parchment near the '3' looks possibly to have been scraped ever so lightly. I hope that is not the case, of course. The map has a similar 1300s date, but that and the signature could be faked as it is on an edge where the map is otherwise blank. Of course, the whole map could be a fake. I guess I will never know. 17/12/12DS*"]

A Welsh legend says that in the 1100s, the Welsh Prince, Madoc ab Owain Gwynedd (sometimes seen as Madog), sailed from Llandrillo-yn-Rhos to North America (that is more than 300 years before Christopher Columbus). Although there is much speculation about where our Prince went ashore in the States, many suggest that he landed somewhere on the East Coast near the Carolinas and then traveled north. However, I also have been told that there is a plaque commemorating the landing of Prince Madoc in Mobile Bay. The plaque is on the wall of the Fine Arts Center of the South in Mobile, Alabama. Oh, the Prince had a half brother or something named Dafydd, so mine is a rather common name.

We Welsh take the legend of Prince Madoc very seriously. In the 1950's, while a sea wall was being built in Rhos at Penrhyn Bay, the remains of an old stone harbor were found. That old stone harbor was right where legend said our Prince Madoc set sail for America in the 1100s. There is now a plaque at the site as well. That one commemorates Madoc's embarkation. If you go to the Rhos website, you can find directions to the plaque—I would say send me a picture if you get there, but then, we know I won't be here.

Before you laugh too hard, the Madoc legend was used by the English to argue that since Prince Madoc had come to North

America in the 1100s, the English could claim that North America was theirs and not Spain's. This shouldn't surprise anyone—there is evidence that the Norse traveled to 'Vinland' well before Columbus. Leif Erikson supposedly wintered in Newfoundland in 1001. But you know all of this about the Vikings. Nevertheless, if you go forward with this project, look at the 'Vinland Map' and the controversy regarding carbon dating to determine its age—you may find it useful.

One last comment on Madoc—the literature is full of stories about stray Welshmen mixing with the Indians. I remember your excitement at finding those aquatints by Karl Bodmer. They were made from sketches Bodmer did while accompanying Prince Maximilian Alexander Philipp of Wied on his North American expedition in the 1830s. As I recall, your favorite Bodmer was *Idols of the Mandan Indians*. There is a legend that Madoc went up the Missouri River in the US and settled in with the Mandans (he never came back to Wales after he left on his second journey). The American artist, George Catlin, who also painted the Mandans, thought they were Welsh. He reported that the Mandan 'bull' boat was similar to our Welsh coracle. They both look like round tubs. Obviously, Catlin had heard the rumors about our Prince. I'm not sure this is relevant, if possibly even true, for the task at hand.

[Here in the left margin of the text, was a handwritten note that said 'see back' and on the back the note read: *"As historians, we sometimes do not know where to stop, so I add one last little tidbit. Martha Bulloch Roosevelt, the mother of U.S. President Theodore Roosevelt and the grandmother of Eleanor Roosevelt, had a brother named Irvine Stephens Bulloch. Apparently, Brother Bulloch served in the Confederate Army (they lost in that Great Civil war of the United States). As he was not given amnesty after the war, Brother Bulloch lived out his days in Liverpool, but died at Llandrillo-yn-Rhos. I have heard that his sword is in the Confederate Museum in Liverpool. That is another damn thing I will not see before I die. 17/12/12DS"*]

Now for the good stuff: Captain Ovelho was carrying a special cargo. Our Daf described it as a small wooden box or maybe boxes. I can't tell for sure whether 'box' is singular or plural as the page is torn there. I doubt you'll find a fortune, but then, you already have one. Also, three members of Ovelho's crew were there to guard the box[es]; our Daf calls them the "Guardians."

7

You will receive one or two more packages from me. One will have the old map I mentioned and a summary of another document that I found in some materials of a colleague here. That colleague had been studying medieval shipping routes by using port logs and other materials to demonstrate the early use of latitude. He would laugh himself silly, though, if I told him that I was using a latitudinal reference to verify the legend that the Welsh got to America before Columbus. Obviously, I won't be telling him. I have made notes with all of my thoughts as to my use of latitude in finding the landing site. Those will be in one of the next packages—I am not quite done with them yet.

I believe that if you review what I send in conjunction with the map, you will understand how I decided where you should look. As I mentioned, I have narrowed it down to an area in the US State of Maine. For reference, I will include my map of present-day Maine in the second package with the old map. A rock prominence with petroglyphs should serve as a more specific marker. I would say let me know your thoughts once you get to the spot, but given the timing of this letter, that will not be possible.

As an aside, I stupidly contacted the London gallery again. I asked where the owner had obtained the material and whether he had, or had sold, any other similar pieces. He immediately offered to buy my two pieces back at a fair profit. He has been quite the nag ever since. He even came here to Cardiff last week, but I was too ill to see him. He won't know I sent his pieces to you, so I don't think he'll bother you, Old Man. If he does contact you, be on guard. I found some information about him on the Internet that suggests he has been implicated in some shifty dealings. He has never been caught though, so perhaps he was in the wrong place at the wrong time…more than once.

[Here in the space to the right of the closing, Kat saw one last note: *"The dealer is Richard Prenbryer, of Prenbryer and Co. He deals in what I would best call Biblical era antiquities, which to me usually means those little oil lamps with menorahs imprinted on them; that is primarily what he had in his shop. I have never had any interest in them. So, while waiting for my friend, who does like those oil lamps, I found a pile of old documents. The document with my name in it was on top of the pile. The map was just under it, so, feigning disinterest,*

I bought it and the map—not sure why they were even in his shop. He wasn't in the shop that day, so I couldn't ask him. 17/12/12DS"]

Yours ever truly,

Daf

PS–I do hope you take on this project. You may hit a dead end or the documents may be fakes, but then again it may be one for the Welsh! And, since it will be you who confirms that we were in America before Columbus, it may be one for the Japanese as well. Please give my best to Eisen. He has always been most helpful to me.

PPS–Please get Eisen to help. He is probably languishing away with nothing to do except bring you tea. You will need someone to travel with anyway. As old as you both are now, you probably look alike. I once told someone that he could tell you from Eisen by the way you spoke English—you with a proper English accent and poor Eisen with an American one. But it wasn't true; I could always recognize you without a word, dear Friend. Hopefully, you would say the same of me.

Kat sat staring at the letter. He felt tears welling up in his eyes again; he again fought them back. So many times in the last six months, he had determined to go see Daf. Now, it was too late. The letter itself read like many of their old conversations. Those could veer off in any direction as they regaled each other with facts. He would so miss talking with Daf.

Kat reread the letter. Was this truly something that Daf thought might be real? Kat knew very little of Welsh history other than what Daf had told him over the years. Daf had never told him anything like the Mandan Indians in America being Welsh. It could be interesting to prove that the Welsh had indeed been in the Americas before Columbus, but Kat was an old man, now. He certainly had no idea how to find the site, but then if Daf left enough information, maybe it could be done. He and Eisen would become treasure hunters.

He chuckled to himself remembering a story a Japanese American friend had told him about getting in trouble at her school in Hawaii. The day's lesson was about some European treasure hunter named Balboa. Her teacher said Balboa discovered the Pacific Ocean in the 1500s when he crossed the Isthmus of Panama and there it was. She raised her hand to correct the teacher by pointing out that her Japanese ancestors had known where the Pacific Ocean was long before the 1500s. How stupid could this Balboa be? Kat wondered if he had ever told Daf that story.

Kat picked up Daf's document. He could make out letters here and there, but he certainly couldn't read Welsh. He then read Daf's annotation. Simple enough—he could see why Daf may have been interested. It was not just the name "Daf," but also the cargo, the passengers and the destination. But how would Kat ever find something like that in the United States? He wasn't sure that he would even be able to find a small box on his own estate, let alone one buried for over 700 years. That map had better be pretty good.

Kat chuckled to himself. Even on his deathbed, old Daf was trying to make the Welsh famous, but Welshmen living with the Mandan Indians before Columbus?

Maybe he would try to reach Daf's secretary. Kat looked at his watch—it was 10:15 a.m. Tokyo was nine hours ahead of Cardiff, so it was only 1:15 a.m. in Wales. He would have to wait until tonight to try reaching her. No, he would have Eisen do that—it would give Eisen something to do.

He rang for Eisen to come in. Eisen was a year older than Kat, but Eisen too still came to work every day. He had no one to care for him or to care for. His wife had died childless almost four decades ago and most of his family had died in World War II. So, Eisen just kept working for Kat's company. Actually, it was Kat who now paid Eisen's salary—the company had retired them both five years ago. Kat still had an office though and Eisen still had access to everything. They would retire together when they were ready, Kat often told him. Well, this might show Eisen he had another year or two to work for Kat before they both had to sit at home all day.

"Yes, Ohno-san?" Eisen asked with a slight bow as he came in to Kat's office. "Here is your tea," he said as he set the tray down.

Kat smiled, the damn old Welshman was right. Eisen did mostly bring him tea these days. Poor old Eisen, Kat also had told him to drop any honorific when addressing him after they retired. Eisen just couldn't do it—at least it was only 'Ohno-san' now. "Eisen, we have a small project at hand. This package was from our dear friend, Daf," Kat said.

"And how is Smith-san, sir?"

"He is dead, Eisen. Apparently, he died on December 24. I will miss him," Kat said.

"We are all reaching that age Ohno-san," Eisen said in almost a whisper. He too would miss Smith-san. "What is the project and how can I help you, sir?"

"First, I want you to find that gentleman in Zurich who authenticated the Gaddi correspondence that I acquired last year. Tell him I have another document for him to authenticate. See where he will be next week. Also, I assume that Daf was buried in Cardiff, but would you call Daf's secretary, Margery, later today so we can be sure? I want to pay my respects to Daf—we can make a visit to Zurich a part of the trip."

"Yes, sir, of course," Eisen said. He was saddened to hear about Smith-san, but the idea of a trip was overriding his sadness. He enjoyed travel as much as Ohno-san. Also, it would be interesting to finally meet Margery—he and she had been responsible for their bosses' 'get-togethers' for many years now, but they had never met in person. "When would you like to go, sir?"

"There must be a memorial or something. Find out when it is, and if it is soon, we will attend the memorial and stop in Zurich on the way back. Also, Daf says there should be another package or two coming. Have you seen anything else?"

"No, sir, but today's deliveries haven't been distributed yet. The first delivery is at 11:00 a.m., so that will be about twenty minutes from now. The second one is at 4:00 p.m."

"When did this one arrive?"

"That package came in on Friday, January 4, after you had left. I held it locked in my drawer until you got in today."

"Good. Call 'Receiving' and ask them to do a special delivery to my office if anything comes in from Europe. Do find out if there is a memorial—we will want to attend that, Eisen. Also, we may need to visit the United States. How long would it take for us to get visas?"

"If we only go to Great Britain and Switzerland, our business visas should still be good, sir. I am not sure about the United States. I will check on that and look for the second package now. It's too early to call Ms. Short—let me see if there is a posting about a memorial on line. Do you need anything else?"

"No, you and I have a lot to do. Thank you, Eisen. Please call me at home after you talk with Ms. Short," Kat said hesitating. Then he added, "Daf said to thank you for all of your help over the years. You know he was forever grateful when you got his wife, Beca, and her friends out of Ethiopia. It was when Eritrea invaded, right?"

"Yes, sir," Eisen answered. "That was back in 1998, I believe. She was there on behalf of Amnesty International or some group like that, which wasn't welcomed by either side. They were never in any real danger, though, as they were in Addis Ababa. As I remember, most flights had been cancelled, but we got them out to Rome without much difficulty. They made it home from there. She died the next year, didn't she?"

"Yes, it was a bad time for Daf. She died from an aneurism, so it was unexpected. Well, we will visit Beca's grave as well when we are there, Eisen. She was a good person."

"Indeed she was, sir. Very kind as well," Eisen said.

"Daf told me you should help on this project, so here is Daf's letter for you to read," Kat said as he handed the letter to Eisen. "Supposedly, a map is coming in another package. Daf refers to a 'Vinland Map' that I am not familiar with. Can you check into that for me, please?"

"Of course, sir," he said trying not to look surprised that Ohno-san had just handed him a personal letter from Smith-san. "I will see what I can find."

"Just what this 'Vinland Map' is would be good," Kat said. "Apparently, it is old so maybe see if there is any information on how it was dated."

"Yes, sir," Eisen said as he started to leave.

"Oh, and one more thing—Daf says that an American artist, George Catlin, believed that their Mandan Indians were Welsh," Kat said drawing Eisen back into his office. "I have seen Catlins before. I think they are liked for their historical perspective, as I recall them being somewhat sketchy. Anyway, the Mandans are one of the American tribes that he painted. They were a popular subject—I have a print of a Mandan burial by Karl Bodmer, a German somewhere. I will have to find it. See if you can find a picture of the Catlin painting of the boat Daf mentions in his letter, please."

CHAPTER 2

The two additional packages from Daf came that afternoon—this time they came from London. Eisen retrieved them from the mail room when the call came at 3:00 p.m. that they came in. He knew Ohno-san would be anxious to get the packages. And, after being permitted to read Smith-san's letter, he was anxious as well. Maybe 'stunned' was a better word…nothing like that had ever happened before.

"Ohno-san, I believe these are from Ms. Short. They were shipped from London."

"Ah, it's only 3:10 p.m.; you must have picked them up yourself. Excellent," Kat said as he reached for the packages. "Daf said there might be a third one; this is very good. Ms. Short was on vacation in London with her sister, Eisen."

"Yes, sir. I also checked the Internet. Dearest Smith-san did die on December 24, 2012. He was buried in Cardiff on Monday, December 29, 2012. That was the day the first package was sent. The Cardiff University website says there is a memorial on February 1. I will confirm that when I speak with Ms. Short."

"Then we will plan on that. We must pay our respects," Kat said. He then remembered that many years ago, he had anonymously funded the Chair occupied by Daf at Cardiff University. "Please also check on the endowment for his Chair—we will want it to carry his name now," he added.

"Yes, sir," Eisen said. "I will commence arrangements later today. Also, I looked into the 'Vinland Map.' Shall I report?"

"Yes, Eisen," Kat said. "Please do."

Eisen began slowly. "I found a 2005 article on the Internet called 'The Vinland Map—Some 'Finer Points' of the Debate,' by J. Huston McCulloch. I have a copy of the article here for you. It is a good summary. The map purports to be mid-15 century; it shows some of North America, including the portion the Vikings called 'Vinland.' Its importance, if real, is that it pre-dates the Christopher Columbus 'discovery' by at least 50 years. Based on my brief reading, the conclusion seems to be 'old parchment, new map.'"

"Old parchment, new map," Kat repeated, smiling. "Sounds like a warning from Daf all right. We will keep that in mind, if we proceed."

"I also saw a reference to a 1507 map called the Waldseemüller Map; it's the oldest known map to show the Western Hemisphere as a separate continent and the name 'America.' I'm not yet sure if it is relevant, sir."

"Good job, Eisen. And Catlin?"

"I printed copies of a couple of the Catlin Mandan paintings, including one of the Mandan bull boat," Eisen said handing Kat the copies. "I also printed a Mandan bull boat by Karl Bodmer. The boats look like round tubs, just as Smith-san said. The description says a bull boat was made by covering a framework of willow poles with raw buffalo hides. They must have smelled if the skins were raw."

"Excellent," Kat said looking at the reproductions after putting on his reading glasses. "Oh, not that the skins smelled," he added without looking up. "I meant the reproductions here. Bodmer is certainly the better artist."

"Yes, sir. I also found a quote from Catlin's 1841 book, *Letters and Notes on the Manners, Customs and Condition of the North American Indians*," Eisen added as he pulled the quote up on his iPhone. "Catlin says, 'From the striking peculiarities in their personal appearance, in their customs, traditions, and language, I have been led conclusively to believe that they are a people of a decidedly different origin from that of any other tribe in these regions.' The quote's on that last page I gave you, sir."

"We shall see how far we can take this. Are you game, Eisen?" Kat asked looking at Eisen over his reading glasses.

"Absolutely, sir," Eisen smiled. "I will call Ms. Short and Dr. Gruber to get information. Hopefully her cell will work in London." Eisen knew that

Ohno-san had been looking for a project. Ohno-san was happy that his son, Michel, was doing so well with the business, but it left him with nothing to do. Now, he had a project and he would include Eisen. It felt good to be busy again.

"Ah yes, Dr. Gruber. Hershel, right?"

"Yes, sir."

"I am glad you were able to find his information—I was having trouble recalling his name. I will look through these materials tonight. We can talk about scheduling tomorrow morning. I will be in at 8:30 a.m."

"By the way, sir, making a round boat by stretching skins over rods from a local tree and waterproofing it with the tree's resin is quite common around the world," Eisen added. He was anxious to work with Ohno-san on this project and to travel again. Even if it were a hoax as Smith-san hinted, it could be interesting.

"It is good for us to be skeptics, Eisen," Kat said. Daf was right, it would be good to have Eisen helping him—he was an excellent researcher.

"Anything else, sir?" Eisen asked.

"No, I am going to work through these new packages. Tell my driver I will be ready at 5:15 p.m."

Kat opened the first of the two new packages. More of Daf's notes were in it. There was no map though, so he assumed it was in the other package. As Kat read Daf's notes, he began to smile. This might just be doable. Daf still believed that his Welsh mariner hadn't returned from the trip with Joham. But with the information provided by Daf's additional notes, it seemed a good bet that he had landed in Northern Maine. The more difficult issue would be whether he landed as early as the 1300s.

He opened the other package. On top was a short note from Ms. Short saying that she had thrown in an extra page of handwritten notes dated December 23, 2012. The notes were almost illegible, but, as Mr. Ohno's name was at the top of the page, she thought the page should go to him. Kat looked at it and then set it down. Those notes would take some deciphering—Daf never did have good hand-writing.

He then opened the sealed package that was also inside. There, on top of the materials, was the map, if you could call it that. He started to despair—it was in very bad shape. But then he saw the second document in the pile from the package. It was a beautifully enhanced copy of the old map. Under the map and the enhancement, was another letter from Daf as well as the present-day map of Maine that Daf had promised.

December 21, [Hand written after the 21, *"22 DS"* was inserted] 2012

Cardiff, Wales

Dearest Kat,

I will not be able to finish the notes I had planned to enclose with the map. However, based on everything I have now seen, for the rest of my days, I will remain certain that it shows a site in Maine.

[Here, there was a handwritten note in the right margin which read: *"I repeat in my defense, I could not pass up a document with my name on it. 22/12/12 DS"*]

When I first saw the map, its lower left and upper middle were barely discernible. That may be why Prenbryer, the dealer, didn't realize what he had, particularly since the Welsh document with it was rather short and, superficially, the content was boring. Also, how many people can read old Welsh? However, I then realized that an enhancement of the map by any of the numerous techniques we have today might pop out more detail.

[Here, there was a handwritten note in the left margin which read: *"Richard Prenbryer's shop is just off Saville Row. Contact Jennifer Sitwell at Cardiff if you need help translating the Welsh. 22/12/12 DS"*]

I contacted Eilat Shiloh, an excellent restorer who is now at Cambridge, our *alma mater*. She worked with me one summer before doing her doctoral work at Ben-Gurion University of the Negev and the University of Southern California. That summer, we thought we had found a previously unknown copy of the 9th century *Book of Aneurin* in the attic of an old house in Swansea. The material had substantial damage from a leak in the roof. Eilat was able to recover a fair amount of text that had been unreadable. Unfortunately, the recovered text proved that the material was only a copy of the *Book* that was done 300 years later than the only previously known copy.

When I called Eilat about the map, she offered to meet me in London, but I was already too ill to travel. She had me send her the map. She promised to see if she could digitally enhance it. When she got a break the first week of this month, she brought me a beautiful enhancement of the map (perhaps she also came to pay her respects to a dying man). You now have that map enhancement in your hands. I personally made the notes, adding what I knew from our Daf's Welsh document. My best guess is based primarily on where our Daf's ship would have 'hit' the North American Coast after the storm he mentioned. My guess is supported by an annotation of what I think are latitudinal references in our Daf's log and on the map.

As you may know, there would have been no accurate measurement system for longitude in the 1300s. Longitude is dependent upon accurate time keeping. That doesn't happen until the 1700s. An interesting point, one which I would love to pursue had I the time, is that latitudinal references were relatively common early on. If it wasn't too cloudy, you could use something as simple as a cross-staff to measure the angle between the horizon and the North Star to see how far south of the North Pole you were.

While I cannot tell you how Daf and Joham got across the Atlantic, I can estimate where they landed, based on that latitudinal reference. Our Daf gives the latitude to the second (roughly, one degree is about 70 U.S. miles, a minute is 1.2 miles and a second is .02 miles or about a 100 feet–remember Old Man, you'll be in the States, so none of this dividing by ten stuff). He also said they sailed for 69 days, but I don't know the speed, so that didn't much help.

The latitude reference hits a very nice little spot near Machias Bay on the coast of Maine. It's about 60 to 70 miles due east of Bangor and south and west of Port Royal across the Bay of Fundy. That is a nice coincidence, as Bangor also is a tiny city founded in Wales around 540 CE. It is one of the oldest bishoprics in Great Britain. Anyway, the log seems to indicate that our Daf and his friend Joham were coming around the tip of Nova Scotia to Port Royal (my guess). They hit a storm that pushed them across the Bay of Fundy into the Machias Bay area (as it is in Welsh, you have to trust me that they went into a bay for shelter).

Our Daf, or whoever drew that map, wrote a second latitude in the log indicating where they encamped west of Machias Bay. They built a shelter on a hillock on that latitude inland about 1650 US feet from the western shore. Look for the hillock. Last but not least, the map seems to show a box buried 3.3 US feet due north of the rock outcropping with the petroglyphs (see the mark; either there is only one box here, or they are buried one on top of the other). The petroglyphs are drawn in a corner of the map. The rock outcropping itself was 132 US feet due south of the shelter; the petroglyphs may be above and across from what we think might be a small stream. Use Eilat's map—she did a great job.

> [Here in the left margin was another 'see back'—on the back was yet another of the handwritten notes. *"Sorry, Old Man, but we didn't go metric until 1965 and then only half way; we think the measure is in rods (16.5 US feet), chains (4 rods or 66 feet), and feet (about 12.1 US inches). Since you will be working in the US, we converted everything for you. As an aside, Hipparchos, a Greek astronomer, proposed a latitude/longitude method for describing places with exactitude around 150 BCE. He also invented trigonometry. Another Greek astronomer, Eratosthenes, calculated the Earth's circumference to within 300 miles in the Third Century BCE. It seems that everyone except Columbus knew that the Earth was round. Alas, schoolchildren do still learn that brave Columbus sailed off to what could be the edge of the Earth. And, thusly, Christopher Columbus 'discovered' that the Earth was round. By the way, Columbus had a compass, an astrolabe (a primitive sextant) and a cross staff on board.*
>
> *NOTE: A correction, Columbus did know the Earth was round. He disagreed with others about its circumference—he thought the Earth was much smaller and hence, India much closer. 22/12/12DS"*]

That should give you a good go, Old Man—sorry there was no longitude then. As I said in my last letter, I do hope you involve Eisen in this project. He is such a gentle man, but so intelligent. Tell him I have enjoyed my conversations with him over the years. He too needs one last adventure—hopefully this dying Welshman will be remembered for giving one to the two of you.

Best of luck to you both! Perhaps we will meet again in another world, but I doubt it.

Yours ever truly,

Daf

PS. We recently featured Thomas Jefferson as one of our famous Welshmen last year. Some say that he asked Lewis and Clark to search for pre-Columbian evidence of the Welsh in North America, but I doubt it. Why would Jefferson want to give the Brits another leg to stand on so soon after the Americans' little revolution? Even if he did ask Lewis and Clark (actually I think the story is that he asked Lewis not Clark) to look, and they did find something, surely Jefferson would have told them to erase any such evidence. Anyway, as I believe I mentioned, the Brits, specifically Sir Francis Bacon, used the Madoc legend to support some of their claims in the New World. The reference I found was in his *History of the Reign of King Henrie the Seventh*, published in 1622. Lest you scoff, the Captain of the Mayflower (which sailed in 1620 from Plymouth in England to new Plymouth in America), was purportedly Welsh as were a fair number of his Pilgrim passengers. Oh, in case you are still wondering about my sanity, I did some more research. Sagadahoc is in Maine–it is also known as Popham Colony. The date though....

The letter ended there. Kat picked up the enhanced map. If you knew the location the map was showing, it could well show you where the box had been buried. The 'iffy' part to him was concluding that they landed in this Machias Bay. Kat decided that he and Eisen would keep this project on a 'need to know' basis for now, just in case Daf was pulling his leg or overly optimistic. He did not want his son to learn of this in case it was pure folly.

Daf probably knew that Kat and Eisen would enjoy this project even if it did turn out to be a hoax. Kat's eyes focused on a little stick-figure picture in the corner that Eilat had inked in. He realized that the picture must be the rock art on the outcropping that was drawn there. Well, that might help if they did get close with Daf's 'latitude.' Kat picked up the letter again, realizing that it would be his very last communication from Daf. He sat thinking for a minute and then buzzed Eisen again.

"Yes, sir?"

"Ask our counsel here if we have a law firm that can look into a small property acquisition in the States for me. Use Utamaro, he is one of the less offensive ones. I want to move quickly on something, so ask him to call me before I leave tonight. That's in a short while, so butter him up, please. You are good at that; tell him it is a special favor for me."

"Yes, sir," Eisen said. He knew he couldn't ask why Kat wanted the property, although he hoped it was because he had just received Daf's map. That was probably hoping for too much though. "If I'm asked, do I know where the property is, sir?"

"We'll leave that for another discussion," Kat said as he started to hang up. Then he realized Daf would think he should share the map with Eisen. "Eisen," he said. "Are you still there?"

Yes, sir."

"As you know, my plan is to see if you and I can find Daf's box," Kat said. "Obviously, we do not want anyone to know that we may be chasing butterflies. Utamaro will believe you if you tell him you don't know where the property is or why I may want to acquire something in the States. He wouldn't expect me to say much about a private matter."

"Of course, sir, I know nothing about it," Eisen said and then hung up. He was again pleasantly surprised. Ohno-san was going forward with the project and, more importantly, it was sounding like he really would involve him. He hadn't been this happy in years. Being busy was part of it, but trying to ferret out a hoax with Ohno-san, this couldn't be better. He loved research projects, but now they were few and far between. He was beginning to think there might not be any more…and now this, a gift from dear Dr. Smith.

CHAPTER 3

Kat picked up the notes that Margery had included. After a little work deciphering Daf's handwriting, he figured out that they were annotations to the Welsh piece he received earlier. It read like a debriefing of the journey to Maine:

> Six men died in a storm off the coast as they had tried to make land. On a hill from which they could see the shore, the men who survived built a (lodge?) for shelter while they repaired the ship. They tried to head out again, but the seas were so rough that they had returned to shore within a day after fighting to stay afloat from [swamping?]. When they got back to shore, more repairs were needed. On the fifth day, they were attacked by Indians while doing the repairs. A dozen more men were killed. Among the dead were the three Guardians who had come with Joham to guard the box[es]. Joham, who had been wounded, and our Daf and the remaining men, headed south to spend the winter. Our Daf's information ended there.

Kat stopped for a minute, and then continued reading; he could hear Daf's voice as he read.

> At least the three Guardians stayed with the box[es]– Joham and his men buried them and the box[es] near the rock outcropping. I'm voting for 'boxes'–that should keep you busy. You might well find some dead Welshmen or Portuguese nearby, as well, Old Man.

That was the last of dear Daf's information. What happened to them? Did they all die? Kat would have Eisen see if there was anything to the south that they might head for.

He picked up Eilat's map—although Daf suggested there might be more than one box, he only saw one spot marked. Perhaps Daf was right, and they were buried vertically on top of each other. Although the map Daf sent was signed, it was only a partial signature. It did look like 'Joham Alvar' as Daf said, but the rest of the signature would have been in one of the areas on the edges that were missing. He wondered why Eilat hadn't included the signature in her enhancement. He wished he could call Daf to ask, but alas, that could not happen.

As he continued to stare at Eilat's map, he realized that what at first looked like water stains, actually might be crude topographical markings. There were semi-concentric markings with numbers on them in four places. He would have to check—if the markings were purporting to show elevations, it might be an anachronistic element evidencing a hoax. With Eilat's drawing in the corner, you could see the petroglyph on the rock outcropping had a moose and three men who seemed to be dancing. Was it possible that the petroglyph might still be there? The phone rang, startling Kat. He regained his composure immediately and answered.

"Hello, sir. This is Utamaro, General Counsel for the Company. I understand you need a lawyer for a real estate transaction in the States. Is that correct?"

"Thank you for calling," Kat said slowly as he gathered his thoughts. "I have a very dear friend who needs to acquire a specific property there. It is a little complicated. She knows where the property is, but not what it is used for currently. I will buy it initially, perhaps through a subsidiary, and hold it until she wants it transferred to her. I will not know pricing or anything else until I know more about its current use and owner. So, how might I find that information, as a first step?"

"Well, sir, all of the States have very good information about land ownership and usage. It should not be too difficult if you have the location. Do you have more information to convey to our US counsel? Perhaps your friend's name would help."

"The property is in the State of Maine, but I am not presently at liberty to explain this in great detail. I asked for you, Utamaro, because I would like to keep this confidential," Kat said. "The property has sentimental value to my friend—it was owned by one of her ancestors, and she wants it to come back into the family. I do not want anyone to know that I have agreed to do this for my friend. And she does not want her name to be disclosed. Oh, and this is a personal matter, so please keep track of that—I will need to reimburse the Company. Who is our US counsel?"

"It is Hartley, Marin, sir," Utamaro said. He wasn't surprised that Ohno-san wouldn't share the name of his female friend, but he figured it had been worth a try. "If the property is in Maine, I would suggest using their Boston office."

"Okay, please contact them to see if they can represent us. As I said, we will transfer the property to her later, so they have no need for my friend's name now."

"Yes, sir," Utamaro said. "Shakura told us we might use a subsidiary of your US real estate company."

"That's fine, and did Eisen also tell you that I would like to keep our names out of this for now?" Kat asked.

"Yes, sir, he was very clear about that," Utamaro said.

"Good, I should have the location soon, but there are a couple of issues I need to resolve before we proceed," Kat said.

"I understand."

"I may be going to the States as early as the end of the month, so please see what Hartley would need."

"I will contact them as soon as they open, sir. And, again, the name of your friend or her trust shouldn't appear anywhere. Is that correct?"

"Yes, that will be taken care of between me and my friend when we know that the property can be acquired," Kat said rather curtly. Kat knew Utamaro would love to know who the lady friend was so he could spread a little gossip. He had found men to be worse gossips than women sometimes. "Thank you for seeing to this, Utamaro. I will be in at 8:30 a.m. tomorrow, if you have any questions."

"Yes, sir," Utamaro said chuckling to himself. It was odd that Ohno-san himself was dealing with this acquisition, but then it sounded like he had a lady friend of some sort. That must be why Shakura had said that Ohno-san had asked specifically for Utamaro to handle this because of his 'discretion.' Utamaro wished he had been able to wheedle out the woman's name, but Ohno-san seemed to know he had been fishing for that. Oh well, Utamaro hoped he was that lively when he was Ohno-san's age.

Kat sat looking at the phone. He hoped this little story about a lady friend didn't get back to his son. He looked at his watch, and then rang for Eisen again.

"Yes, sir?"

"Eisen, tell my driver I will be 15 minutes late and then come in, please," Kat said. "We will catch up on the project." He sat thinking for a minute, giving Eisen time to contact the driver. Kat's father must have hired Eisen in about 1961–Kat had known Eisen almost as long as he had known Daf. Eisen had learned to speak English from the American soldiers stationed in Japan after the War. His knowledge of English secured him a position as an aide to a senior member of the Ministry of International Trade and Industry. When that member died unexpectedly, Kat's father had convinced Eisen to work for him. When Kat's father died, Eisen had been assigned to Kat–that was 1963. Kat and Eisen always tried to speak English with each other for practice in those early days. They were both quite proficient, even if poor Eisen never did lose his American accent.

"I notified the driver, sir," Eisen said, bowing slightly as he came in. Kat had told him many times that it was no longer necessary to bow, but old habits were indeed hard to break.

"I need an expert on old maps," Kat said. "Not whether they are authentic, we will talk to Dr. Gruber about that, but how one goes about finding out the exact location shown on a map. This particular map supposedly shows a place in the United States that is too old to have street names. In fact, that is specifically what I need–an address for a property shown on a very old map of an area in one of the States. I would prefer someone here in Tokyo. See what you can do. Keep my name out of it for now and don't tell them it is Maine unless you think they can do something for us."

Kat sat for a minute after Eisen left. It occurred to him again that perhaps this was a parting practical joke played by his friend Daf. Well, hopefully he would find out before he spent too much money. He put some of his Giotto research in his briefcase; he would work on that at home. Before he left, he asked Eisen to track down his friend, Florencio. He wanted Florencio to find him a graduate student at I Tatti to help him with some of the Giotto research, a letter in Latin, specifically.

CHAPTER 4

On Tuesday morning, January 8, Kat was in at 8:30 a.m. He spent a couple of hours reviewing a reference for his Giotto paper, and then at 11:30 a.m., he called for Eisen to come in.

"Yes, sir," Eisen said.

"An update, please."

"Ms. Short confirmed that the Memorial for Daf-san will be on Friday, February 1 at 1:00 p.m., in Cardiff. Ms. Short sent your invitation last week, but it has not yet arrived. I told her I would confirm whether you would attend after I had spoken with you."

"Have you made arrangements then?" Kat asked.

"Yes, sir, subject to your approval, I have made arrangements using Japan Airlines, not your jet–is that correct, sir?"

"Yes, Eisen–that is fine."

"Since the Memorial is on February 1, we can fly to London on January 30 and have a car take us to Cardiff on January 31–it's about 2 hours and 30 minutes. If you wish, the car will take us on to Rhos on February 2, and then back to London. We would stay in London February 2 and 3. Dr. Gruber will be in Zurich after February 3, so we would take a flight to Zurich in the morning on February 4. He would like for you to have dinner with him on Monday, February 4. If not, he will keep dinner on the 5th open. His assistant also is holding the morning of February 6 open in case there is more to discuss. He is tied up during the day on the 5th. We have a flight to

Tokyo on the 6th. I have the Dorchester in London, St. Davids in Cardiff, and the Alden in Zurich.

"Eisen, be sure that Dr. Gruber understands that you will be with me for any meetings or meals," Kat said. "The flight from London to Zurich is short, so we should be able to make the dinner on February 4. Since we will have time in Zurich on the 5th, I will visit a couple of galleries. Move our London flight to January 29. I may want to set up couple of meetings in London on January 30."

"I will have a car at your disposal, in London and Zurich, sir."

"Good. Anything else?" Kat asked. He was anxious to do some reading on carbon dating today.

"One more thing, sir," Eisen said trying to hide his excitement. "This afternoon I will be getting additional information from Dr. Kuniyoshi, the owner of KAS International Cartography. It's here in Tokyo. I think he can help with your map, at least he says it may be doable, based on what I told him. He said we had a fair amount of useful information. He may actually be able to find the area you are looking for."

"Doable? That's excellent–I assumed it would be a long shot to locate our site from what we have."

"Yes, sir, I did as well. I asked the owner for references. He had me speak with an archaeologist working here in Tokyo this morning. The archaeologist and his team were trying to find a site in the Miyagi Prefecture that was mentioned in an old Edo period document from about 1450. Kuniyoshi's team was able to pinpoint the spot for them."

"And Kuniyoshi thinks he can do something like that in some rural spot in the United States?"

"Yes, sir, especially if the spot is undeveloped. Given the amount of detail that 'Google Earth' has on the States, as well as data from accessible topographical libraries, he may be able to find your site. He can even buy time on one of the satellites and look at the terrain, if need be. We are using a dormant subsidiary of your US real estate company as cover right now, sir. I told Utamaro that we were still confirming information on your friend's property. I hope that was okay."

"Eisen, that is excellent news," Kat said. He was surprised that Eisen had managed to get so far so fast. "About the map, that is. I have the enhanced map here—you can give that to KAS. We might as well make copies of everything that Daf has sent us. Make a set for each of us. Put a spare set and the originals in my vault."

"Yes, sir," Eisen said as he got up to leave. He still needed to arrange for a confidentiality agreement and a contract with KAS.

"One more thing, Eisen," Kat called as Eisen got to the door.

"Yes, sir?"

"Please arrange for us to have dinner with Ms. Short after the Memorial. Oh, and I will be out tomorrow and Thursday." Kat thought he saw Eisen smile as he left the office—hopefully it was because of dinner with Ms. Short.

Eisen had everything lined up with KAS by noon the following day. He had received the KAS contract by email. He had an attorney in Utamaro's group, whom Eisen knew personally, review it. He knew the guy wouldn't ask too many questions. Only a few changes had to be made. A secretary of the entity they were using signed the confidentiality agreement and contract. The signed agreements as changed and the enhanced map went to KAS that afternoon by runner.

CHAPTER 5

Eisen was waiting for Kat when he got in on Friday morning. "Good morning, sir. We are set to arrive in London on January 29. We will be at the Dorchester for two nights—the 29th and 30th. We will travel to Cardiff by car on January 31. We will stay for two nights at the St. Davids. Ms. Short remembered you like the restaurant there, so she made a dinner reservation for the three of us at the hotel for the evening of the February 1. A limo will take us to Rhos on the 2nd and then on to London. We'll stay at the Dorchester that evening and on the 3rd. We have a morning flight to Zurich on the 4th. I have booked rooms at the Alden in Zurich for the 4th and 5th. We will come back to Tokyo on February 6th."

"Excellent, Eisen," Kat said. "I would like to visit Dr. Blair at the National Gallery on January 30—see if we can have lunch. Also, I will meet with Dr. Stuart; tea perhaps—he has been doing some research for me on that Giotto project."

"Anything I should send Dr. Stuart in advance, sir?"

No, I don't think so, but ask me again as we get closer to leaving. Have you spoken with Florencio yet?"

"Yes, sir. He will call you on Monday at 8:00 a.m. our time—he is on vacation until then, but he has a graduate student for you. Her name is Artemisia Boccioni.

"And she can help with some medieval translations?"

"Yes, sir. She is a specialist in Medieval Greek and Latin."

"Excellent, arrange for me to talk with her. Too bad she doesn't read Medieval Welsh."

"Yes, sir. By the way, when we are in London, I thought I might stop by Prenbryer and Co., to see what it's like. What do you think?"

"Yes, perhaps," Kat said.

"I also have an oral report from KAS," Eisen said.

"Already?" Kat asked. He hoped it wasn't bad news, but then Eisen had booked the tickets and he was smiling.

"Yes, sir, I hinted that this was a private project for a very important person, and that there could be a small bonus if they were successful quickly. I hope you don't mind, sir."

"What is it, Eisen? What does the report say?"

"The formal report with satellite pictures and a map showing where they believe the site is will come next Wednesday," Eisen said. "KAS had some difficulty locating the site because the coastline has changed and the sea level is different. However, the information you gave them on the possible latitude was very helpful. They found a map of the Maine coastline done by a Portuguese explorer in 1525 and one done by the English in 1527. Using those maps, a later map, your map and the latitude designations allowed them to get very close, especially since the area is still undeveloped."

"Close enough to find it?" Kat asked.

"Yes, sir, they think so," Eisen smiled. "They identified a site west of Machias Bay in Washington County, Maine. I looked at a website for petroglyphs in Maine and it says that the area is well known for rock art dating back about 3,000 years. In fact, there are over 500 of them at nine sites in the area. The local American Indians there are the Passamaquoddy Tribe. Most of the glyphs apparently are animal figures that appear on shale ledge outcroppings. KAS has arranged for a local surveyor to look for the petroglyphs that are shown on Eilat's enhancement."

"But a specific site?" Kat asked.

"Yes, sir," Eisen said again. "Apparently, there was a fair amount on Google Earth; they supplemented it with private satellite time. There is some kind of United States Navy radio installation a few miles away at Cutler, Maine. Luckily, it was far enough away, that there was no interference. Also, a nearby branch of the University of Maine is documenting the petroglyphs of local Indians in the area."

"So, we might really have petroglyphs?"

"Yes, sir. So far, we know the land does not encroach upon University or Indian lands or the Naval Base. There is also conservation land in the area, but the property is not part of it. They cautioned though, that only a title report from a US title company would be dispositive for ownership. They expect to hear from the surveyor on Monday."

"Bring me the report when it gets here. We will sterilize it–take out everything, except the location. Then you can take the information to Utamaro. I want a buffer around the site, so we will need more than just the land where the rocks are."

"Yes, sir. I will see if KAS can make a recommendation."

"As you know, Utamaro thinks that I want to buy it for a friend–a woman friend, Eisen. You are to be consulted for any questions…you are to be involved, but neither of us is to be named, if possible. Feel free to embellish my fictional 'friend,' if need be."

"Does she have a name, sir?"

"No, Eisen, you do not know her name. Let's make her the wife of an old friend from my days at Cambridge. Her family is English, but it had a branch in the States. That way, if my son hears this 'rumor,' he will not be too concerned. Our stories do not have to be elaborate. The simpler they are, the less chance for us to make a mistake. It is my business and it will be purchased with my funds."

"Yes, sir. If Utamaro asks, do you or your friend want to visit the site?"

"That's a good question, Eisen," Kat said thinking for a minute. "No, not yet. Tell Utamaro we have other travel plans now, I suppose if necessary, you can tell him we are going to an old friend's funeral. My friend knows the property; she probably won't visit it before I buy it. Meanwhile, we will go visit Dr. Gruber; I should see if these documents are real before I go traipsing off to the US. It's always possible that dear Daf picked a spot in Maine, and then faked this map and the story just to send us off on a last adventure. Well, we've already started, so let's see what the lawyers can do."

"Yes, sir."

"Excellent job, Eisen. Excellent."

CHAPTER 6

Kat and Eisen left for London on the 29th as planned. Kat had the Welsh piece and the map with him. The property in Maine turned out to be 30 acres of private land. It had been owned by a widower who lived in Bangor. When he died in early 2011, the property went to his two children. Because the land was not on the seacoast, neither of them wanted it. They planned to sell the property or perhaps donate it to a land trust, but nothing had been done. Kat's story for the sellers was that the property would be used as a site for a corporate retreat. Utamaro himself had assured Kat that the transaction could close by the middle of March, with the main issue being confirmation of clean title. Even better, Kat would get 30 acres for a very reasonable price.

When Utamaro sent the title work to Eisen, he mentioned that there had been a temporary easement for an archaeological dig on the property. The site of that dig was near where the petroglyphs should be, but all work had ceased when the prior owner died. The archaeologist was a man named Jonathan Christiansen from the University of Pennsylvania.

The plan was to buy the property if Dr. Gruber was able to confirm the age of the documents. Eisen would then contact Dr. Christiansen and ask him to restart his work. The story would be that they wanted a little brochure on the petroglyphs for visitors to their corporate retreat. They would ask him to look at the site near the petroglyphs first so that they could have the brochure ready for their friends.

Kat and Eisen arrived in Cardiff on January 31, as planned. The Memorial was short, as Daf would have wanted. After the Memorial, Margery went over to say hello to Mr. Ohno and Eisen. She had spoken with Eisen many times, including the day before, but had never met him or Mr. Ohno. Although there were almost 100 people at the Memorial, only four were Asian. She had met Mr. Ohno. So she assumed that the slightly taller man was Eisen.

"Good morning Gentlemen," Ms. Short said bowing her head ever so slightly. Neither man looked as old as Dr. Smith, even though they had to be about his age. Spry too, traveling all this way from Japan.

Eisen, indeed the slightly taller man, took a step forward, bowed and said, "I am Eisen, Ms. Short. I assume you know Mr. Ohno." On the phone, he had enjoyed their conversations. Perhaps because he and Margery shared a love of Agatha Christie movies, he had imagined her as being a rather dowdy old Brit, rather like Margaret Rutherford, who played Miss Marple in *Murder Most Foul*, but maybe with glasses. He was pleasantly surprised—she didn't look that old, even though Eisen knew she was in her mid-60s. Eisen thought she looked more like Helen Hayes in *Murder with Mirrors*, only much younger. She did have reading glasses hanging around her neck, though.

Ms. Short, or Margery, depending upon who was present, had convinced Eisen to start watching the Agatha Christie movies five years ago, when he mentioned that he couldn't sleep, but was too tired to read. She suggested that he first watch the movie version of *Death on the Nile* even though she was a Miss Marple fan and *Death on the Nile* was Hercule Poirot. He had now seen all of the Poirot movies as well as almost all of the Poirot TV series with David Suchet, many of them more than once. He chuckled to himself—who would have thought even a month ago that he and Ohno-san would be searching for a lost treasure with a real archaeologist. Hopefully, there would be no murders. At some point, when Ohno-san approved, he would have to tell Margery about this adventure.

"It is so nice that you both came all this way to pay your respects to Dr. Smith," Margery said. She was happy to finally meet Eisen in person; he was as cute as he sounded. "I have an envelope for you, Mr. Ohno," she said handing him a letter addressed to Dr. Smith. "It was delivered to Dr. Smith the day before he died. I told him the return address and he said he was too tired to deal with it. He told me to keep it for you. I guess he knew you would come to pay your respects, sir. Anyway, when Mr. Shakura called to say that you were coming, I decided to hold it for you rather than send it off to Tokyo."

"Who is it from?" Kat asked, looking at her rather puzzled.

"It says 'Prenbryer and Co.,' but I don't know who that is," she said. "It has a London postmark and it is addressed to Dr. Smith. As you can see, it says 'Personal,' so I didn't open it. I also have a small cardboard box that Dr. Smith left for you. It was too cumbersome to bring with me, so I left it back at the University. Are you staying long, sir?"

"No, unfortunately we are due in Zurich the day after tomorrow. You have a box for me?"

"Yes, it's on my desk—I will send it round to your hotel later today," Ms. Short said. "I'm sorry. Maybe I should have tried to bring it with me. Is that all right?"

"Yes, of course," Kat said. "Would it be easier if Eisen picked it up?"

"Do you have time, Mr. Shakura?" Margery asked. "As I mentioned, it's a small cardboard box—not very heavy. I'm afraid I can't tell you anything more, I don't know what's in it."

"Please call me Eisen," he said as he winked at her. They had been on a first name basis for many years now—just not in front of their bosses. "Perhaps I can go to your office with you now to pick it up."

"Yes, that would be perfect, Eisen," she said. "I planned to go home from here before meeting you both for dinner tonight, but if we go back now, I will stay to do more work. Then I can stay home tomorrow."

"Will you be staying on at the University, Margery?" Kat asked.

"No, I had planned to retire last June, but then Dr. Smith asked me to stay on through year end when he said he too would retire. He began getting weak in late October. They think now that he may have had a minor heart attack then, but he did so hate doctors, that he never went in. In early December, he had a bad heart attack. On December 23 he had a stroke and then he was dead." Margery had stopped now to regain her composure.

"We will all miss him," Kat said.

After a minute, she continued. "My last day now is at the end of February. Actually, I only have a few more things to do before I am done at Cardiff altogether. Dr. Smith's post-doc is working with a new assistant to transition Dr. Smith's research. Honestly, I don't know where they got this new woman. She came up from London—doesn't seem to do much work, just poking around at things. Says she's learning the job—well, that's for the post-doc to deal with. Eisen, I just need to say hello to a few people. I will meet you back here in about 10 minutes."

"Before you go, is Mrs. Smith buried nearby?" Kat asked.

"Yes, they are together again in that crypt over there. It's her family's crypt—the Llewelyns, one of the old Celtic families."

"Thank you," Kat said. "We will see you tonight at dinner." Eisen handed Kat two roses he had bought at the hotel as they walked over to the crypt. Kat touched the plaques of Dafydd and Beca Smith. He then set the roses down on the ledge in front of the plaques and walked back to the waiting car. Eisen went off to wait for Margery.

Eisen and Margery headed for Margery's desk when they entered the History Department's building. As they turned the corner toward Dr. Smith's office, Eisen saw her desk in front of him. Just as he was wondering to himself how Dr. Smith could have tolerated such a messy woman, Margery gasped.

"What is it, Margery? Are you okay?" Eisen could tell from her look that she wasn't. As she started to answer, he realized that she wasn't messy—her desk had been ransacked. Drawers were open, the trash bin was tipped over and Dr. Smith's office door was ajar.

"Eisen, can you see if Dr. Smith's office is okay?" Margery looked at him pleading. "I will call security. Someone has made a mess of my desk here."

Eisen went in to Dr. Smith's office. It wasn't much better. All of the cabinets and desk drawers were open. Those with locks had been pried open. Eisen went out to see if he could help Margery, who was now in tears.

"What is the name of the new assistant?" Eisen asked as two security guards arrived.

"Kate Parker," she answered.

"Mrs. Short, what happened?" one of the security guards asked.

"I don't know for God's sake. I just returned from Dr. Smith's Memorial—this is what I found. It was fine when I left this morning. I checked the lock on Dr. Smith's office before I left as I always do. Now, the door is open. It's a good thing we decided to come back," she said looking at Eisen.

"Is anything missing?" the other security guard asked.

"How would I know?" Margery snapped. "As I said, I just came back with Mr. Shakura—this gentleman—so that I could give him that cardboard box there that has been ripped opened. Dr. Smith wanted his friend, Mr. Ohno, to have the box. This is what we found. The box was sealed tight when I left."

"Where is the new assistant, Ms. Parker?" Eisen asked. They all turned to look at him. "Where is the new assistant, Ms. Parker?" he asked again. "Did she have a key to Dr. Smith's office?

"Yes, but not to the locked cabinets or drawers," Margery answered.

"The door shows no evidence of tampering, but the locked cabinets and drawers have been pried open," Eisen said.

By now, at least half a dozen people had come to see what was happening. Eisen assumed that the tall, very thin man was the post-doc as Margery ordered him to go into Dr. Smith's office and see if he could tell whether anything had been taken.

The local police arrived—they had been called in as this was not something that had happened before. Eisen heard Margery telling the police that the only thing she couldn't find on her desk was her calendar—she still hand wrote appointments in it rather than doing them in the University's system. He then heard her ask, "Where is that stupid new assistant, Ms. Parker? Is someone looking for her?"

An hour later, Eisen got back to the hotel with the opened cardboard box. Margery had insisted that he be allowed to leave, but even then he had been kept for some time—the police kept asking him why, if he was there to pick up the box, his name wasn't Ohno. When they finally realized that the new assistant had disappeared, they decided that Eisen could leave. Remembering that Margery had stayed with a sister in London for the New Year celebration,

Eisen suggested that she return there for a few days. They were trying to decide how to determine what had been stolen when Eisen left.

Eisen handed Kat the opened cardboard box when he got back to the hotel. He explained why the box was open. He then left Kat so that he could confirm arrangements for the next few days.

CHAPTER 7

The cardboard box contained mostly old pictures of Daf and Kat. The one on top was a picture of Daf, Kat and their wives taken some time in the 1960s. Kat stared at the picture for a while before remembering that it was taken when they had all met in San Francisco. The note on the back said it was taken at Seal Rock. Kat and his wife, Yoshiko, were there on business—Yoshiko had to be with him at the cocktail parties. Daf and Beca were there because Daf had just given a lecture at Berkeley. He put the picture in his wallet.

The second picture had the four of them in front of Carol Doda's Condor Club. He would never forget the two-story neon sign on the Condor Club—it was a very well-endowed woman, probably Carol Doda herself. The woman's nipples were showing and they had flashing red lights on their tips. Ms. Doda supposedly was the first woman in the US to dance topless. Given that it was the US, none of them believed that.

Daf and Beca went to one of Ms. Doda's topless dance shows. Kat and Yoshiko couldn't bring themselves to go with them, so they walked to the cable car and rode it down Powell to Union Square. They ate a block south of the Square at Omar Khayyam, a little Persian restaurant on the corner of Powell and O'Farrell. 'Carol Doda,' he thought. She certainly wouldn't shock him today.

The four of them rented a car and drove over the Golden Gate Bridge to the Muir Woods. Thinking back, Kat was almost certain those Sequoias couldn't have been as big as he remembered, but they were magnificent. It was 50 some years ago—perhaps they had grown in his memory, but then again, perhaps they had shrunk. As that drive had proved that Daf could drive on the right side of the road, they toured the American West by car for ten days.

The drive took them down Route 99 through Central California to Los Angeles, then over to Arizona on Route 66, made famous by an American TV show of the 1960s. The road could have taken them all the way to Michigan Avenue in Chicago, but they only had ten days in the US. It had proved to be barely enough time. They detoured up to the Grand Canyon and stayed overnight at El Tovar on the South Rim, then drove down past Flagstaff to Tucson, where they stayed at the Arizona Inn.

The West was much bigger than they had imagined, but they had a specific goal. They wanted to see Tombstone, the 'Town too Tough to Die,' made famous in yet another American TV show, *Tombstone Territory*. It was an easy drive from Tucson—maybe 80 miles.

He could read the sign behind them in another picture. The four of them were standing in front of the tiny office of the *Tombstone Epitaph*, the newspaper made famous by that old TV show. But it was like looking at strangers or, at best, long lost friends whose names you could barely remember. He assumed Daf had sent him the box for that reason—they had journeyed a very long way since the pictures were taken. Of course, he was now the last one. He thought perhaps he would fashion an 'epitaph' for himself at some point soon. It would be something like the one he had seen at Tombstone's Boot Hill Cemetery those many years ago:

> "HERE LIES LESTER MOORE
> FOUR SLUGS FROM A .44
> NO LES NO MORE"

He loved that epitaph.

CHAPTER 8

There were tears in Kat's eyes as he put the Tombstone picture of the four of them back into the box. He had loved Yoshiko...she had always been there for him. She had a master's degree in comparative literature when they married, but she gave it all up to become the perfect wife for Kat's position as head of the company—and to raise Michel. It was a different time—Daf's wife, Beca, taught Greek and Latin at a boys' school in Cardiff. A woman teaching at a boys' school was considered quite an anomaly, but after the War there had been a dearth of teachers who knew both languages. She found out years later that she had been paid less than half the amount that her male counterparts received.

Kat broke from his thoughts when he realized he still hadn't opened the letter from London that Margery had given him—enough of these tears, a sure sign that he was getting very old. He opened it and found that it was a short letter from Richard Prenbryer, the London dealer Daf mentioned. He called Eisen's room after he read it. "Eisen, please come in. I have the letter from London here." When Eisen came in, Kat handed him the letter.

December 20, 2012

Dear Dr. Smith,

After trying to reach you several times by telephone, I was finally advised that you are quite ill. Thus, as a courtesy, I am contacting you by post. When you in were in my shop on September 4, 2012, my aide sold you two old documents that technically were not for sale. They were simply in my shop for consideration and the owner would like them back. I have enclosed a check for the amount you paid plus a 50%

bonus for your trouble. I will arrange to have the materials picked up for transfer if you will give me a call (my card is enclosed).

Sincerely,

Richard Prenbryer

"What do you think, Eisen?" Kat asked when Eisen had finished.

"Two things, sir. First, it seems clear now that Dr. Smith really did find these as he said. He didn't fake them to send you off on a wild goose chase."

"Yes, I believe you're right, Eisen. And the second thing?"

"I think Dr. Smith would like for you to see where the map leads, sir," Eisen said. "Once you have done that, then perhaps you will return the documents to Mr. Prenbryer, if he confirms they are his. Your obligation to Dr. Smith would be fulfilled, I believe."

"Thank you Eisen. We will do just that, then," Kat said smiling. "Could you see that the check is returned? Keep the card, please. At some point we will need it to return the documents to Mr. Prenbryer, if he can prove provenance."

"I will mail the check back from here, sir," Eisen said. "With that funny business yesterday, I don't want to make it easy for him to trace anything back to us. I think I should forego visiting his shop as well when we return to London."

"Yes, I don't know that we would find anything there. We aren't detectives," he said.

"No Sherlock Holmes and Dr. Watson, for us then?" Eisen asked with a wry smile.

"No, we would spend far too much time deciding who was who," Kat chuckled.

As Eisen left, he was thinking that seeing Ohno-san chuckle made him happy, but nervous. Eisen wasn't used to seeing Ohno-San even smile—not after his wife died. Well, that made two of them—he assumed Daf would have been a member of that club as well.

As dinner began that evening, Margery was still quite shaken by the day's events. She was even more shaken when Eisen, with Kat's permission, told her to be wary of the dealer, Richard Prenbryer. Eisen then deftly proceeded to engage Margery in helping him explain to Ohno-san why they both liked Agatha Christie.

"So," Kat said, "I like this dapper Mr. Poirot. However, he seems a little too full of himself to have survived so long. You would think at least some crook in London would have made him a prime target."

"Well, perhaps they are all too busy knocking each other off," Margery said. "Ms. Christie isn't shy about multiple murders, you know."

"She's also not shy about murdering off characters that you like or making them the murderer," Eisen added.

"I'm not sure I like this idea of getting everyone into one room and then disclosing which of them has done the dreadful deed. I do like the idea of everyone being a suspect or having some dirty little secret. Eisen, perhaps you and Margery would consult and determine which one I should read first. It sounds like you've read or seen them all."

"Not quite, Mr. Ohno," Margery protested. "Eisen shall we take this on then?"

"Of course, madam," he answered. "But you have had quite a long day; we should get you home."

CHAPTER 9

The driver picked up Kat and Eisen early the next morning to take them to Rhos on Sea. They were a little nervous traveling through this tiny Welsh seaport; it couldn't be everyday that two old Japanese men drove through in a limo.

Their first stop was at the 'heavily restored' St. Trillo's Chapel that Daf had mentioned. The Chapel was built in the sixth century on the site of a pre-Christian well. It was indeed small—it could seat only six parishioners at a time. But so was the town; there were probably no more than 5,000 inhabitants by Kat's estimate.

Eisen had picked up a pamphlet on St. Trillo at the inn where they had lunch. "Ohno-san," Eisen said to get Kat's attention. "This pamphlet says that 'St. Trillo was a contemporary of Saint Deiniol of Bangor.' Didn't one of Smith-san's letters say that Bangor was a town in Wales?"

"Yes, in fact Daf said it was a nice coincidence that our spot was near Bangor, Maine. Find out why 'Bangor' was the name selected for this tiny town and the one in Maine, Eisen."

Eisen gave the driver the directions to the Madoc seaport that he had printed from the Rhos-on-Sea website. It said "[e]xit the [St. Trillo] Chapel and continue west for another mile and in the garden of 'Odstone,' the last house before the Rhos Golf Course, you will come to the place from where the Welsh Prince Madoc is said to have sailed to find America, 300 years before Christopher Columbus."

They found the plaque. It said simply, "Madoc ap Owain Gwynedd sailed to America from the nearby port in 1170." Eisen took a picture of Kat by the plaque. They had not expected anything, but at least they saw the plaque.

After leaving Rhos, they headed for London. On the way, Eisen looked up "Bangor." "It's a little complicated, sir. Bangor, Maine was named after an old hymn by William Tan'sur, who was from England, not Wales. Bangor, the town in Wales, is a university town. The word means an enclosure, like a pen, surrounded by a wattle, which is a woven fence. I'll see if I can find anything else, but it looks like they liked woven fences."

"That's good though, Eisen. Having a Bangor here in Daf's Wales and a Bangor in Maine is merely a coincidence. We can sleep well tonight."

CHAPTER 10

The Zurich flight on Monday, February 4th was delayed, so Kat and Eisen went directly to the hotel after Eisen confirmed that they would meet Dr. Gruber for dinner the next evening. Before dinner with Dr. Gruber the next day, Kat went to his galleries. Eisen elected to go first to the Museum Rietberg to see its two finely carved Buddhist bodhisattva figures, Jizô and Kokûzô, from the Kamakura period. His mother was a Buddhist before she married. The religion she taught him was Shinto though, with a fair amount of Buddhism added to the mix.

In the afternoon, Eisen went to the Landesmuseum to see if the Swiss flag was analogous to the flag of the Knights Templars—something Dr. Gruber had told him. The Swiss flag had a square-sided white cross in a red background, while the Templars' flag usually was depicted as a red cross on a white background, with the shape of the cross being slightly different as well. He had seen at least one image of a 'Templar' flag with a red cross on a white background; so, to him it would remain unresolved for now.

Eisen and Kat met back at the hotel before dinner. Kat informed Eisen that he would have Dr. Gruber date only the map. Kat would have the other document dated only if the map seemed authentic. He didn't want Dr. Gruber to see the other document and realize that Kat might be on a wild goose chase. As Eisen already had made copies of the map, they would leave the original with Dr. Gruber. They would not give Dr. Gruber Eilat's enhancement.

At dinner that night, Kat paraphrased what Daf's letters had said about the map. He didn't disclose s where he had obtained the pieces. He did tell Dr. Gruber that a colleague had warned him that the date and signature on the map might have been altered. Dr. Gruber indicated that he would need about two weeks.

With the business discussion behind them, the discussion turned to art. Dr. Gruber asked, "So, why haven't we seen you at the Zurich International Art Fair? By the way, please call me 'Hershel,'" he said.

"Thank you," Kat said. "You know Eisen well from prior discussions regarding your work for me. As for me, my friends call me Kat, since Katsutoshi is far too long. The Zurich Fair and Art Basel are a little too contemporary for me. As you may recall, I tend to prefer the late medieval to early Renaissance. Zurich has always seemed too old or too new for me."

Ah yes," Hershel said. "We do have wonderful antiquities available here from time to time as well. I though, tend to like the modern…a little change from what I do all day," he laughed.

"Yes indeed," Kat said. "I am thinking of a little change, too. I may visit the auctions in New York this year." Kat was remembering another trip to the American West, in the 80s he thought. He and Daf had flown from LA to Jackson's Hole, Wyoming to visit Yellowstone National Park. As with the Grand Canyon in Arizona, they were stunned by its abject beauty. It was at Yellowstone's Mammoth Hot Springs Hotel that Kat had first seen reproductions of works by Thomas Moran.

Kat remembered showing Daf the Morans, thinking he might be interested since Moran was born in England in 1837. Moran moved with his family to the States and became one of the best landscape painters ever, if not the best, in Kat's opinion. Daf, of course, had used the occasion to remind Kat that he was Welsh, not English. Kat had thought many times about acquiring a Moran, but then discipline would take over his senses. Daf would needle him sometimes for being so 'stiff.' He would then say, "Buy that Moran, Old Man!"

"And what are you looking for?" Hershel asked.

"I'm not sure that I am actually looking," Kat started. "Sotheby's and Christies both have American art auctions in late spring each year. I may look for an American Luminist like Thomas Moran or Sanford Gifford. Or maybe a later artist like Winslow Homer," Kat said a little surprised at himself. He corrected himself, "no, not Winslow Homer. I have only seen a couple of Homers, like *Sunlight on the Coast*, that approach the luminosity of Gifford or Moran. Maybe I'll find a Hudson River School painter like Bierstadt. He was a German like you, Hershel." Kat turned to Eisen and winked, having just called Hershel a German. "Of course, I would really like a Moran, but I won't get my hopes up," he added.

"I am actually Swiss," Hershel said. "I do know Winslow Homer, I think of him more as an action painter with figures—like his men at sea. I don't know Moran or Gifford. I'm afraid I don't know the Americans much at all, unless they are 1945 or later. A Clyfford Still I would know, for example. Unfortunately, most of those are in an American museum in Denver, I believe."

"Well," Kat started, "Gifford and Moran both traveled in the Western United States in the 1870s after the Americans' great Civil War. At some point, I believe both of them were with expeditions that reported on geological wonders of the West like Yellowstone. However, most of Gifford's paintings are of New England and the East Coast of the United States. They are beautiful renderings with the light being handled beautifully. But Moran—he returned to England to study the works of J.M.W. Turner, another favorite." Kat loved the way Moran used light. It was not just representational; it reflected a mood—like a storm, perhaps. "In some way, it was like being there," Kat said. He turned to Eisen. "Can you find a picture for Hershel?" Eisen nodded—he had already pulled up *Grand Canyon of the Yellowstone* to see what Ohno-san was talking about. He handed his iPhone to Hershel.

"That is spectacular," Hershel said looking at the iPhone. "But it's a far cry from your collection's focus...I would think more of Cimabue, or perhaps Giotto or Gaddi. In fact my last project for you related to Taddeo Gaddi, did it not?"

"Yes, indeed," Kat said smiling. "But, Giotto...Vasari told a great story about Giotto. When Giotto was a boy studying with Cimabue, he painted a fly on the nose of a face Cimabue had done. It was so perfect, that Cimabue tried to shoo it away, thinking that it was real."

"That's great," Hershel said laughing.

"Yes, but sometimes one's focus changes, no, one's focus expands, and a new wonder becomes important. It was that way for me with Thomas Moran, although honestly, I hadn't thought of him for a while. Gifford is good in a different way. Eisen, show him a Gifford now, please."

Eisen pulled up a page on Sanford Gifford. It showed him in a military outfit. Looking at the page, Eisen saw that Gifford had fought for the North in the United States' Civil War. He knew Hershel liked photography. "Here is a photograph of Sanford Gifford in the 1860s; he was a Union soldier in the US Civil War," he said handing the phone back to Hershel. "You can also 'click' on some of his paintings below that image."

"Eisen, that is a great picture," he said. "I am a photography buff–do you know that the word 'photograph' means drawn with light? The word supposedly was coined by Sir John Herschel at about the same time as Louis Daguerre announced that he had developed the first practical photographic process. That was in 1839, if I remember correctly. Herschel spelled his name incorrectly though. I see no need to add that 'c' into the equation," he laughed. "The photographers were making an image formed by a pinhole camera or a camera obscura into a permanent image. This image is very pleasing–it doesn't say who took it though; I'll have to track that down. Thank you," he said, handing the iPhone back to Eisen.

Kat gave Eisen a nod of approval. "Now, Hershel," Kat said, "Eisen was showing you the site so you could see a Gifford painting. You must see at least one by Gifford, so you can compare his painting to Moran's."

"Yes, yes, of course," Hershel said, taking the iPhone back from Eisen. "Ah, *A Gorge in the Mountains*, the treatment of light is splendid."

"Gifford also did a number of Civil War scenes as well," Eisen said as he showed Hershel an example. "Ohno-san, is Frederic Church one of your favorites as well? I have just found a painting of a tattered flag called *Our Banner in the Sky* that is attributed to him."

"Yes, but I don't know that one. *Rainy Season in the Tropics* would be one to look for, Eisen. May I see the 'flag' please?" As he was looking at the Church painting, he asked Hershel, "How did you get interested in photography?" He then looked over at Eisen and said, "This Church is interesting; find where it is Eisen."

"I became enamored with photography when I did graduate work at the University of Chicago," Hershel said. "I learned conservation there. Then I branched into authentication work so that I could join the family business. But photography is my love.

"Eisen, we will have to look more at photography," Kat said.

"One of my greatest joys was working on recovery conservation of some early daguerreotypes of soldiers going off to fight in that Civil War," Hershel continued. The pictures came from a home in one of the Chicago suburbs. They had been damaged in a flood–what a job!" he laughed. "Anyway, there were more than 5,000 photographers in the States by the time of their Civil War. I think it was the first war documented by photography."

"So, there must be quite a record," Eisen said.

"Indeed, the war made photography very popular. Soldiers on their way to battle would leave a photograph behind for the family–most of the daguerreotypes I worked on were those small portraits. However, even though they had advanced from the camera obscura to plate-glass negatives which allowed them to print their images on paper, it was still an extremely cumbersome process. Can you imagine hauling your dark room with you in a wagon to a battle site? They say there were so many glass plates left at the end of the War that they were often used as green house window panes."

"I know very little of that Civil War," Kat said. "Perhaps Eisen and I can learn more about it through its photographers."

"I will make suggestions. By the way, the camera obscura has been around since at least the 5th or 4th century BCE," Hershel said as he beckoned for the waiter to pour more wine. "I think Aristotle or Euclid described it first. The Chinese claim that it was described by a Chinese scientist even before that, but unfortunately, I do not remember his name."

"When I visited San Francisco many years ago, there was a room-sized camera obscura set up at a spot on the Coast," Kat said reminiscing again. "The Cliff House, I believe. Yes, that's where it was, the Cliff House at Seal Rock." He smiled to himself, thinking of the picture in his wallet. "It was quite a detailed projection, but we've drifted, Eisen. Can you show Hershel another Moran on that gadget, please?"

"Perhaps you might look again at the Moran site I showed you," Eisen said. "It mentions a photographer named Jackson who, like Moran, accompanied the Hayden expedition to the American West in the 1870s. Would he have been one of your Civil War photographers as well?"

Hewitt Freiburg

"Yes, indeed–William Henry Jackson," Hershel said as he took the iPhone from Eisen. "Brady was the best known of the Civil war era photographers, but my favorite is probably Gardner, a Scot who worked for Brady. Of these Luminists, who is your favorite, Kat?" Hershel asked.

"It's definitely Moran and his painting *Big Springs in Yellowstone* is probably my favorite. On another day, though, I might say it was *Green River in Wyoming* or *Grand Canyon of the Yellowstone.*"

They finished the evening with a 1956 vintage port.

CHAPTER 11

It was Wednesday, April 17, 2013, and Susan Graves had been in her office at Peale, Curtis and Blume since 6:30 a.m. It was still cold in Chicago, but at least the sun was up now. She looked at her watch–it was already 8:30 a.m. She had just finished reviewing a list of issues to be resolved for the Eastland deal. Eastland was complex, requiring a merger as well as market placements of debt and equity and it was due out Monday. Unfortunately, the Eastland accountants had now found a revenue issue that was holding up the pro forma financial information. Her client, Evergreen Securities, the underwriter, was concerned that the numbers would be worse than expected–they needed to see those pro formas.

Susan had been at Peale, Curtis for almost thirty years now, working her way up through the firm to partner. She still liked the excitement of pulling everything together in time to hit the market. She especially liked complex deals that kept her busy. They were like solving a puzzle, where the solution was everything coming together to hit the market at the right time. She needed to be busy; when she wasn't, she felt like tumbleweed, rolling along a deserted landscape with no purpose. She had seen way too many tumbleweeds; she hated feeling like one.

Susan walked down the hall to the conference room where the Eastland documents were being assembled. Wilhelm Galianos, a fifth year associate, was there reviewing documents. He had done a fair amount of work for Susan over the last five years. She had him running the deal, more or less, as she had just recommended him for partner. Firm politics meant that he would never know she had recommended him–assholes, she chuckled to herself.

"How's it going?" Susan asked.

"It doesn't look too bad. We still need that draft of the pro formas, though," Wilhelm answered.

"Give O'Keefe Hopper a call—it's getting late in the game. Come to my office a few minutes before our call at 11:00 a.m.," Susan said and then headed back to her office. She stopped at the desk of her assistant, Jane Butler. "Any sign of that draft I edited for the Big A?"

"It hasn't come back from typing," Jane said. "It will be another hour. The Big A hasn't called yet either."

"Thanks. Tell him I died if he calls. The damn thing was a mess—it took time to fix." She walked back into her office and closed the door. She looked at her watch—almost 9:00 a.m. She went to the window and, for a few minutes, watched the people 40 stories below streaming into the Loop from Union Station. She would watch them streaming back to Union Station in eight hours when their day was over.

Jane had been with her for almost ten years now. She knew the work and was good at ferreting out personnel issues that floated around the office from time to time. Susan wasn't naïve, but she often got so wrapped up in a deal…Jane made sure Susan knew the gossip, especially when Susan needed staffing for a deal. Women partners, still very much in the minority in big firms like Peale, Curtis, still had difficulty getting staffing for their deals. Susan's solution was to volunteer on difficult issues; she was pretty good at solving them. That was how she became the Big A's captive—he came to her to fix things. Big A was head of her group…being at his beck and call kept the amount of shit she had to shovel down to a minimum. It did mean long hours, though, and it didn't stop her male partners from trying to steal her associates.

Susan sat down and began rummaging through the piles on her desk. She was looking for Elaine Pagels' book, *Revelations: Visions, Prophecy, and Politics in the Book of Revelation*. She bought the book after hearing Pagels interviewed on NPR a while ago, but only began reading it Friday while she sat on a plane in New York, waiting to come home to Chicago. She liked Pagels' argument that the Book of Revelation was essentially a well-disguised historical rant rather than prophesy. John of Patmos, the author of Revelation, was describing the horrific events of his world which should have led to the expected second coming.

They got the Roman Empire and Nero, the 'Beast' of Revelation 13:18, instead. The King James Version of the Bible, translated from Greek, said the Beast's number was '666.' Numerologists readily translated '666' to mean Nero. If the legends were correct, Nero was indeed a beast. One legend was that when Rome burned in 64 CE, he blamed the Christians. As punishment, Nero used Christians as human torches at night to 'light' his gardens. That alone earned Nero the title of 'Antichrist.' There wouldn't be a second 'Antichrist' for almost another 1,500 years when Luther would get that designation from the Catholic Church.

Fear of the number, '666,' even had a name—Hexakosioihexekontahexaphobia. In Chicago, the address of the old Furniture Mart was changed from 666 to 680 Lake Shore Drive, when it was converted to condos. She picked up her phone to see if Marta was in the office today. Marta loved trivia, so today's trivia would be that Arizona changed the Arizona portion of Route 666 along the New Mexico border to Route 191—they thought there were too many fatal accidents to be coincidental.

Before she dialed, her eye caught sight of the draft Eastland analysis—she should give it another look before the call at 11:00 a.m. Marta and Pagels would have to wait. Susan reminded herself that this would be her last deal. Although she originally planned to take a three month sabbatical beginning on July 1, last week she realized that she was done—she wouldn't come back. She sat for a moment staring at the analysis while wondering why she hadn't quit sooner. Her husband, Steven, had sold his company a year ago; they could travel more and focus more on other interests. They did love to travel, but she worried whether travel could supplant the excitement of a complicated deal.

It would be nice to have more time—no more half day trips to Guatemala City to see a museum. A week in Eastern Turkey would be nice, she thought. They could start in Istanbul, with dinner at Tughra in the Ciragan Palace, then head for Urfa. Some said it was the ancient city of Abraham; Ur seemed more likely, though. They would buy peppers in the Urfa market, then go on to Nemrud Dag. She had always wanted to see for herself if the colossal head of Antiochus at Nemrud Dag really did look like Elvis Presley.

Susan also would spend more time in Tucson. She grew up there on a ranch started in the 1870s by her father's great grandparents on his mother's side. When her father died in 1984, she and her sister donated all but ten acres and a life estate in an old cabin for Pete, the foreman, to a conservancy. Her sister had no interest in the ranch, so Susan bought her remaining share. The old ranch house was on the acreage she kept. But it wasn't the old house Susan wanted, it was the view of thousands of saguaros running up the hills and into Caliente Canyon from its back porch. She would never tire of that view.

She looked at her watch—it was 9:30 a.m. She read and answered some new emails and then went back to looking for the Pagels book. She found it under a stack on the credenza. Luckily, there was a bookmark where she had left off. She set Pagels by her phone where she could find it later. As Susan picked up the Eastland analysis, Jane knocked on her door and then poked her head in.

"Are you expecting Dr. Cahokia?" Jane asked.

Susan looked up from her book. "Who?"

"Caught you daydreaming, didn't I?" Jane chuckled. "Anyway, the receptionist just called—Dr. Eusebius Cahokia is downstairs at the Security Desk. I don't have any appointments for you today. You just have the status call at 11:00 a.m. and a meeting at 2:00 p.m. with Wilhelm."

"Eusebius Cahokia isn't a real name. And I'm not expecting anyone today or tomorrow—this deal has to close," she grumbled. "Is that all he said? It is a man right?"

"Yes, it's a man," she said. "The receptionist had Security spell the name, so she's positive. Maybe he's an old Indian you met at the Cahokia Mounds. You were just there last month on your way to St. Louis."

"Very funny...we did climb Monk's Mound, though. It was built by the Mississippian mound builders of Cahokia. You can see Saarinen's Gateway Arch in St. Louis from the top, since it's just off I-55 on the Illinois side of the Mississippi."

"You told me...Cahokia was larger than London in 1250 CE," Jane said. "By the 1400s, Cahokia had pretty much disappeared. I do listen to you sometimes...so, maybe a very old Indian?"

"No one should have that name. Eusebius was a famous fourth century Biblical historian. And of course there was Father Eusebio Francisco Kino, a Jesuit missionary to the Southwest. So, someone could name a kid Eusebius, but Cahokia as a surname is nonsense. This is either a joke or the guy's a nut who changed his name for some goofy reason. You know I won't be happy if he thinks I am too stupid to know it's not a real name...."

"You could be a Cahokian," Jane said. "That highly caffeinated drink that they got through trade with the Aztecs, would give you a nice buzz. As I said, I do listen–sometimes. With your coffee fixation, the caffeine reference must have gotten my attention."

"It's not a fixation–it's a need," Susan countered. "That area of Illinois is the horseradish center for the world. Maybe he should have called himself Eusebius Horseradish."

"So, shall I bring him up here or say you are in a meeting?" Jane laughed. People in the office sometimes wondered how Jane could stand working with Susan as she was demanding and did have a temper. Jane, though, always found Susan to be quite entertaining. Besides, the tirades usually occurred when she was alone in her office–just a way of letting off steam, while she tried to figure out how to fix a problem that someone had created. And Jane had taught history at a Chicago high school for 30 years before she came to Peale, Curtis–she was used to tirades, so she could deal with Susan's. Despite teaching, she still loved history too.

Susan looked at her watch again. It was only 9:45 a.m., so she had a little over an hour. "Well crap, so much for my break–I'll just go downstairs and see who he is. It's a fake name, so he won't have an ID–I'll let this guy get away with the charade for a few more minutes. I hate games like this. It better be good …Eusebius Cahokia," she grumbled as she headed for the door. She liked puzzles, not games.

"Don't forget your status call at 11:00 a.m.," Jane said.

"This can't take long. It's probably someone we know who is just stopping by. If I'm not back in twenty minutes, call my cell so I can wrap up. Oh, see if Wilhelm got that draft from O'Keefe. I'll go see what this stupid Dr. Cahokia wants."

These days, no one could get upstairs unless they were on Security's list. This was a pain in the ass, but if she didn't go down to Security, Jane would have to authorize this Dr. Cahokia to come upstairs. Then, it might be difficult to get rid of him. So, Susan went downstairs to the Security Desk.

There were three people waiting. She didn't recognize any of them. Odd, she had expected to see someone she knew, chuckling at his Cahokia joke. But then again, Susan always had been bad with faces and names—hopefully this Dr. Cahokia wasn't someone she should know, but didn't recognize. She went over to the Security Desk and said, "I'm Susan Graves from Peale, Curtis. Which one is Dr. Cahokia?"

"Dr. Cahokia is that man over there—with the beard and mustache, Ms. Graves."

"Thanks," Susan said.

The man she saw was well dressed, not as a businessman, but more like a professor. His sports coat even had patches on the elbows; the patches were smooth leather, not suede—that was a sartorial distinction. No tie—that was good with the sports coat; casual should be carried through. And he wasn't wearing loafers—that would be too much. He did indeed have a beard and mustache; both were nicely trimmed, too. Susan guessed that he was maybe 65, based on the reading glasses around his neck and his graying hair. Maybe he was a professor from her grad school days. He certainly wasn't a law school professor—he looked a bit too rugged as if, despite his dress, he had been outside too much. He did look sort of familiar. The mustache—oh well, there was one way to find out. She walked over to him.

"Dr. Cahokia, I'm Susan Graves."

"Ah, Susan," Dr. Cahokia said as he reached out to take her offered hand. "You look pretty much the same after 30 years, but I doubt that you remember me."

"Thirty years is a long time. I'm afraid I don't recognize you or your name, sir," she said, trying hard not to stare at his mustache. "Although…," she hesitated before continuing, "given the combination of Eusebius and Cahokia, you certainly would think that I would have at least remembered your name."

"If you have a few minutes, I can refresh your memory."

"Okay, I have reserved a conference room upstairs. You'll have to show an ID and sign in at Security."

"Um, rather than take all that time, why don't we just have coffee there in that little coffee shop," he said pointing to the restaurant off the lobby. "I could use a cup."

"That's fine," Susan said as she thought to herself, "aha, he doesn't have a stupid 'Cahokia' ID." Of course, she would have been stumped if he had. She had a few minutes, so she would see who this guy was even if she did have to play along for now. "I apologize, but I will have to take a call shortly. I have maybe 20 minutes."

CHAPTER 12

When they were seated, Susan asked, "Do you have a card? Here is mine." Given her problem remembering names, she liked to have a business card sitting in front of her to refer to if need be. In this case, she just wanted to see if this Dr. Cahokia actually had a card with this name on it.

"I'm sorry, I don't. I promise I won't take too much of your time, but I need to explain some background to clarify why I've come to you. This isn't a social call," Dr. Cahokia said, "although I have often thought of you and Steven."

The waiter came over to take their order. "You're back," he said smiling.

"I am," Dr. Cahokia said. "I guess I'll have another cup of coffee."

"Coffee for me, too," Susan added. This Dr. Cahokia apparently knew Steven as well.

As the waiter left, Dr. Cahokia said, "I had a cup of coffee here before asking for you. I was trying to gather my thoughts so that I could be succinct."

"I'm sorry, but I really don't recognize your name. Are you a friend of my husband, Steven?"

"Well...," he started. He sat looking at his hands for a minute and then looked at her and said, "I'm not sure where I should begin...," but then he stopped again and stared into his coffee cup.

Susan always had a hard time being patient. Obviously, the man was trying to formulate what he wanted to say, but Susan wanted to finish reviewing the draft analysis before her call and maybe read a few more pages of Pagels. She waited patiently for a minute, and then decided to prod him. "Sir," she said to get his attention. He looked up at her, so she continued. "I suppose it's possible that you were given the name Eusebius, but it is virtually impossible that your surname could be Cahokia. The inhabitants of Cahokia disappeared in the early 1400s. So, who are you and how did we know each other 30 years ago? Is Cahokia some sort of adopted name that you use?"

"Let me end the suspense," he laughed nervously. "I used a pseudonym because I thought it would pique your interest enough to see me. It seems to have worked, since you are here."

Susan looked at him wryly and said, "Thanks, but what can I help you with?"

"It's nothing legal...," he said. "I just didn't want to sign in and all that—so, I figured this way you might come down here to talk. I wasn't sure you would remember me—I'm Jonathan Christiansen."

"Dr. Christiansen?" she said looking at him.

"Yes, I was one of your graduate professors. You and Steven took an elective seminar from me on Clovis at Penn; I was a fresh new Assistant Professor then. I think that's why I got assigned the Clovis seminar—the old guy who taught it died and I was too young to object. As I said, I don't have a legal issue, but I do have a problem that I'm hoping you and Steven can help with."

Susan looked at him again. He didn't look like their old professor from so many years ago. But then she and Steven had left graduate school around 1980, so it was over 30 years since they had last seen him. He definitely didn't have a beard then. Crap, she thought, he did have that same funny little mustache—amazing how it hadn't helped her recognize him. "You are J.M.J. Christiansen, then?" she asked. "We enjoyed your seminar—but that was the last semester we were at Penn. That was a very long time ago."

"Yes, indeed I am and it has been too long. I'm also much older, now."

"We are all much older," she said. "I do remember you and your initials because they are 'JMJ'," she said. "Steven always referred to you as 'Jesus, Mary and John.' And I remember the mustache, but you didn't have a beard, did you?"

"No, I grew it about five years ago, and please call me Jon. The initials stand for 'Jonathan Matthew James.' Matthew was my paternal grandfather and

James was my maternal grandfather. 'Jonathan' was pulled from the air I guess. By the way, I still have my silver bullet with the JMJ inscription. I remember showing it to you. I don't remember why though...oh, I remember, you teased me for having two middle names. You don't have one at all, right?"

"I remember that bullet! And no, I don't have a middle name," she added. She was more relaxed now, knowing who he was. "Some of my favorite Presidents had no middle name–George Washington, Thomas Jefferson and Abraham Lincoln, for example. I asked my dad once why I didn't get one. He said it was just one of the many things he and my mom couldn't agree on. So, I guess you haven't used your bullet on any werewolves."

"You know, killing a werewolf with a silver bullet may come from the *Beast of Gévaudan*; it's a story about a wolf that terrorized the French countryside in the 1700s," he answered. "The 'silver bullet' part likely was added to the story in the 1800s. Peasants who believed that werewolves could only be killed with a silver bullet would take the extra precaution of inscribing the JMJ initials on their bullets. God knows where a peasant would get the silver," he laughed.

"I've never heard of your 'Beast' before," Susan said. At least this is entertaining, she thought.

"That bullet is still my good luck charm," he said. "The 'JMJ,' does stand for Jesus, Mary and John–at least that's what the Jesuit I got it from told me. But that was in the 1960s, when I was graduating from high school. It has worked for me so far, but...well that can wait. I know you are short on time."

"Jesus and Mary are obvious as the 'J' and 'M,' but, the second 'J' is not. The minority say it is Joseph or 'John the Baptist.' I think most say it is John, of the Gospels. But that Gospel never says John, only the 'Beloved Disciple. That means it might be Lazarus and not John. Oh, crap, I don't know.... Anyway, why are you here in Chicago? You're still at Penn?"

"Yes, of course. I apologize for the false name. I struggled to find an appropriate first name. When I saw that Eusebius had written the first history of the Christian Church in the Fourth Century, I thought the name might pique your interest. You were both biblical archaeologists when I knew you. I picked Cahokia because, of course, you live in Illinois and I am a Native American archaeologist. Rather clever, don't you think?" he asked.

Susan looked at him, doing her best not to seem like she was staring. He was a lot older, granted that was natural. She would have recognized his name, but there was no way she would have recognized him—even with that mustache. "Rather clever indeed, Dr. Christiansen," she finally said, laughing.

"Susan, do call me Jon."

She always enjoyed Jon, as she was to call him now. He could talk for an hour without ever getting to a point. You didn't really care because he imparted so many facts. Nevertheless, today was a busy day, so she asked, "Why are you here, Jon?"

"Well, I have two problems. I'll start with the more recent one—one you probably can't help me with," he said and then stopped.

"And that is…?"

"Well, I will explain that in a minute. I recently reopened my primary site in Northern Maine. It's east of Bangor, near the coast. I have a little work shed there where my students and I store our tools. We are focused on the Wabanaki in the late Archaic Period. The translation of Wabanaki is quite beautiful—the 'People of the Dawn,' or 'those living at the sunrise' or 'the East.'"

"That is beautiful. The Archaic Period is when?" Susan asked.

"Technically Archaic refers to maybe 4,000 to 10,000 years ago. My focus is on the more recent end of that period—about 4,500 years ago. Paleo, which is roughly 10,000 to 16,000 years ago, would include your Clovis spear points. They were used around 12,000 to 13,000 years ago."

"They are beautifully made," she said. She smiled to herself remembering how she had convinced Steven to take Jon's 'Clovis' seminar as an elective before they packed up and went to law school. "You don't find Clovis in Maine, do you?" she asked.

"Why do you ask?" Jon sounded irritated by her question.

"I remember you saying that there was a debate over whether Clovis spread to New England—so I thought I would ask if it had been resolved. Is it a stupid question?"

"Well, remember, I'm not a Paleo expert, but there is no solid evidence of Clovis in Maine," Jon said. "Clovis is found primarily in a triangle-shaped area, with points in southern Texas, eastern Washington and western New York."

"You probably said the same thing 30 years ago, too." She did love the Clovis points. The Field Museum had a beautiful collection of them; she often went to look at them—it was like visiting a favorite painting.

"I didn't mean to discount your question," Jon said. "There is a site in Maine where they may have found Clovis evidence. Personally, I am leaning heavily toward the 'probably not' side." He stopped again.

"I always thought of Clovis as maybe the first example of rapid adoption—like cell phones today. Within a short period, everyone has them. That explanation would obviate the need to figure out how use of a specialized spear point by a tiny band of Paleo-Indians could spread so far in a very short period of time. But then, why did it disappear almost as quickly?"

"Maybe they had eaten all of the mammoths," Jon laughed.

"I've dragged Steven and a friend all over the Southwest visiting Clovis sites. I took Steven to the Clovis, New Mexico site while we were still in law school. The points themselves are what I really love, such beauty in a technological advance."

"The points were first characterized in the 1930s in the Clovis area," Jon said. . "It's also now pretty much settled that there are pre-Clovis cultures in the Americas. In fact, some are suggesting that humans were in North America well before the last ice age ended—as much as maybe 30,000 or more years ago. I'm not comfortable with those oldest dates and where we are, there would be nothing like that."

She did still love archaeology and she did have almost an hour—this was just like old times with Dr. Christiansen. "No Clovis—too bad," she said mostly to herself.

"There is just no evidence that suggests it," he said looking at his cup. He looked up and said, "You know that the Clovis points are often found in conjunction with mammoth kills right?"

"Yes, that's like the Murray Springs site southeast of Tucson," Susan said.

"Well, in 1959, during excavations for a mall in Maine, they came across some bones. Everyone initially thought they might be from a mammoth. Then someone remembered that there had been an old circus elephant in the area in the early 1800s—I think it was 1816. 'Old Bet' was the elephant's name. They decided it was Old Bet, so they closed up the site. They did send a rib to a museum, though. It turned out that it was a mammoth, but it probably died naturally. The rest of that mammoth is now under the parking lot at the mall. That may be as close as we get in Maine."

"I will have to look up Old Bet and this circus in 1816," Susan said making a note.

"It's a sad story, but for another time," he said.

"Hmm," Susan said tapping her iPhone to see what time it was. Fifteen minutes had already gone by. She had better focus. "You said you wanted to talk to us about something?"

"Yes, and having no Clovis in Maine is sort of my first problem. Susan, there was a small conference in Bangor on Monday. The topic was the Archaic Period of the Wabanaki—I filled in for a speaker who was ill. Since I was in Bangor, I decided to drive over to my site after the conference. I figured I could poke around for a few hours. We have Spring Break this week, so nobody was there. I was looking, well let me backtrack a bit."

"Monday, two days ago?"

"Yes, April 15. I should mention that my site is on private property. When the landowner died in 2011, his children yanked our permission to be there. I think they were planning to subdivide the property, but ultimately they sold it, lock, stock and barrel to someone just this past February. The new owner called me out of the blue in early March and invited us back. I didn't want him to change his mind, so we started right away. We have been back there now for almost four weeks. He even gave us a small grant to help us re-open our site and a separate grant to start one nearby where there is a rock outcropping with petroglyphs."

"Why did he buy it?"

"This new owner says he's planning to build a lodge on the property, sort of a retreat I guess. He wanted us to work by the petroglyphs first, so I focused on that with one of my interns. My son and his friend had some free time, so they came up and re-gridded my old site. We began the dig at both sites when the ground started thawing; of course we had to plat it out first anyway. Then we had our mid-semester break."

He had paused again, so Susan prodded him with, "And?"

"And now there is this…anyway, I will be retiring at the end of this year. I will be 69."

"I thought you were younger than that," Susan said. This is my last year as well, but I'm 56. I haven't actually resigned yet, but I will when my current deal ends. Steven was only 54 when he sold his company. I'm not sure why I have stayed in law this long. I used to think it was fun—the deals I work on are like putting puzzles together, but now…," she paused.

"I heard that you both had done very well, so I was quite surprised to find you were still working. Good for me though as it was easy to find you," Jon said. "I found you both on the Internet. Steven went into business right?"

"Yes, he left his law firm around 2007 to start a company around an invention he had been toying with since his undergrad days. He started college in science, like me," Susan said chiding herself for helping to change the subject. "He sold the company for a fair amount. Now, he's doing biblical research on a full time basis. It was our hobby when we were undergrads—I didn't meet him until graduate school, you know. Now, he has time to truly focus again. My job is to question his conclusions and identify areas that I think require additional factual support."

"I do sort of remember that."

Susan's cell phone rang. It was Jane. It was 10:05 a.m.

"Susan, sorry to call a few minutes late, but you got a call from the Eastland attorneys." Jane said. "They cancelled the 11:00 a.m. call. They have a slightly bigger accounting issue than they thought. Actually, they want you in New York tomorrow for a 1:00 p.m. meeting. They'll work on it today and then discuss it tomorrow, when you're all in the same room."

"Damn, I was just in New York last Friday," Susan said. "Did they say what the issue was?"

"They would only say that they want you and Evergreen to be there," Jane said. "I have you on the American flight at 7:00 a.m. tomorrow. Would you prefer to go out tonight?"

"No, I have a lot to do here anyway–no sense trying to do it in a hotel," Susan said. "Tell Wilhelm I would like him in New York with me tomorrow–also ask him to call the associate at O'Keefe Hopper to see if he can get any more information on Eastland. Oh, and have him call Evergreen. Any sign of the draft from typing?

"I checked just now before I called you; they're on the second half, but it'll be another half hour," Jane said. "I started the proofers on the half that's done, so that will speed it up a bit. Oh, you also had a call from the Big A; he wants you to talk to him about his deal."

"Well, I can't do that until the document comes back from typing," Susan said. "Remind me to call him when I get back. I'll ask him if he can type. Sorry, put me on the 7:00 p.m. back here to Chicago tomorrow night. Just in case we have to be there Friday as well, can you see if there are rooms at the Pierre?"

"Already did," Jane said as she hung up.

"I'm not doing any more deals!" she grumbled to herself. She didn't like the Eastland deal, which made it a good one to finish on. She didn't even like the name–Eastland was the name of a passenger ship that sank in 1915 in the Chicago River, drowning many of the passengers who had just boarded. She chided herself; the names were the same, but it was inappropriate to link the two–even subconsciously.

Susan checked her watch. At least now she would have more time with Jon. She looked over at him. He did look worried, but about what? "I'm sorry, I slipped out to see you, but I am in the middle of a large transaction, so I have to take calls from Jane, my assistant."

"I'm just glad you were in," he said. "It may seem stupid that I didn't make an appointment, but as I mentioned, I wasn't sure you would see me. You're a big corporate lawyer now."

"Not 'big,' but I am a corporate lawyer. And you…you are married right? You mentioned a son."

"I was married when you took my class—my wife was one of my graduate students. She left me decades ago—married another professor and went on to get her PhD. She left him too, so I don't feel too badly," he smiled. "I have one son, Scott. We had him when I was 35 and she was 24, so he is 33 now—I probably had him, too, when you took my class."

"Do you have any grandchildren?" Susan asked. She hated pleasantries; she was never quite sure that she was doing them correctly. She wasn't as bad as Steven, though. He usually flat out refused to even try.

"Actually, no," he answered. He sat for a minute and then added, "My son is now Father Bartolome. He did his undergraduate work in Boston at Shawmut College. He started his graduate work there, too. It was quite a surprise when he entered a Franciscan seminary after his first year of graduate school. Scott said he wanted to atone for something—our treatment of the Indians maybe. That was, um, about 10 years ago, though. Sorry, I still can't get used to calling him Father Bartolome."

"So, is he an archaeologist, too?" Susan asked.

"Yes, he's worked off and on for years at a site down by Portland on Cape Small. It's maybe 175 miles south of me. When he was young, I told him how Thomas Jefferson had excavated an Indian burial mound in Virginia in 1784. He thus became America's first archaeologist. Father says that got him interested. We aren't too close anymore. The Church became his family and God his father—I hope He's done a better job than I did," he laughed.

Susan saw the sadness that came over Jon, but she didn't know what to say. It must be painful—in a way he had lost his son.

Jon interrupted her thoughts, "he does come by to talk about archaeology sometimes. We drifted apart many years ago—after his mother left us. I turned to my work and I guess he turned to the Church. He's a good archaeologist. I am very proud of him. He and his friend, Clay, who's also an archaeologist, are helping me re-open my old site. Oh, I told you that already."

"I worked with a couple of Franciscans in Jerusalem at the end of my first year at Penn. They've done a great deal of archaeology in the Middle East," Susan said.

"Well, the Abanaki Indians of New England are my son's real love; they are descendants of the Wabanaki. He's focused on the period just as they began interfacing with the Europeans. He tolerates my older stuff, but just barely. I have to admit that it is interesting—the Abanaki were meeting European fishermen at least as early as the 1500s. They met Verrazano in 1524, but it was not a friendly meeting. Then Jesuit missionaries from France tried to convert the Abanaki, and, of course, Champlain met them near Mount Desert Island in 1604. As I said, Scott's site, the Abanaki one, is on Cape Small."

"So he's still working there?" she asked.

"Only once in a while, now...he also helps out sometimes at a Verrazano site near there. Anyway, my son the Franciscan will be teaching the Jesuits here in Chicago this coming fall. He'll teach a class in archaeological techniques at Loyola. He's also planning to take a few classes."

"Loyola?" Susan said to herself as she tried to figure out why Jon's son would go to a Jesuit school. She had no idea how the different orders interacted, and mostly didn't care, but she did like to understand how things worked. "Is it because the Jesuit missionaries were friendly to the Indians?"

"Good guess, but he says it's time he learned Greek. I really don't know too much about his plans other than that it will somehow have to involve Native Americans. Scott took his name from Bartolome de las Casas, a Dominican historian who fought for the rights of native Indians in the 1500s. Father's namesake even went before King Charles V to plead for them. He had his faults, though. Some say that he urged the Spanish to use Africans instead of Indians as slaves. It's interesting, Bartolome's father, Pedro de las Casas, was on Columbus' second or third journey to the New World. Pedro's son became a Jesuit and fought for the Indians. Oh, and Margaret Truman confused Bartolome with his father, Pedro. She used the name Bartolome de las Casas as the person who sailed with Columbus in *Murder in the Library of Congress*. As I said, it was his father, Pedro, who sailed with Columbus."

"Really?" she caught herself again encouraging Jon to wander. "But Jon, tell me why you are here," she said while making a note to look up Bartolome de las Casas. She had read the Margaret Truman mysteries many years ago—she would check that, too.

"I'm getting there—bear with me," he begged. "I'm at the two sites now as often as possible—three days a week sometimes to get as much done as my schedule permits. Plus, I really needed to be back out digging and I need to publish on my old site before I retire."

Jon was rummaging in his bag—he pulled out a small gold box of Godiva chocolates. As he took a chocolate from the box, he looked a little sheepishly at Susan. "Sorry," he said. "I am addicted to chocolates, would you like one?"

"No thanks. My mother liked Frango Mints," she said. She pictured her mother sitting in the garden of her Chicago home, reading a mystery and eating her mints.

"They are delicious, too," he said. "Anyway, as I said, Father's primary site was on Cape Small near the Lost Colony of Popham. It was also called Sagadahoc Colony, which is from the Abanaki word for the confluence of a river and the sea. Popham was founded in 1607, about the same time as Jamestown. Apparently, they weren't ready for the extreme winters, so they packed up and went home to England in 1608, but not before building the *Virginia*, the first ship built in North America."

Susan chuckled. "This is the wrong continent for me, but I've been to Popham. We have friends in Phippsburg. Popham was 'lost' because people forgot where it was after the settlers went back home to England. It wasn't like Roanoke, where the whole colony of English settlers disappeared. That's all I know of Popham."

"Well, my son's site is near Popham. There are late petroglyphs near Popham—that's one reason he's there. Rock art sites often are adjacent to canoe-navigable water on particular kinds of bedrock outcrops...our new site is similarly located. The rock art at his site is only a few hundred years old, though."

"So recent?" she started. "Oh, that's a dumb question. There's a Charles Russell painting of an Indian standing on a horse doing a petroglyph—I think I saw it in Indianapolis."

"Yes, it's in the Eiteljorg Museum. So, if you see a horse in a petroglyph in the Americas, you know it can't be older than the 16th century, when the Spanish re-introduced the horse. Father Bartolome's site was especially interesting because they periodically found evidence of early homesteads—a small foundation and a hearth with a few pieces of pottery—things like that. Unfortunately, they've had a lot of trouble with treasure hunters around those outlying sites. It was so bad in one area, that he thought the looters had used a backhoe."

"What would they look for with a backhoe?" Susan asked.

"Who knows," Jon said. "Anyway, some of the outlying sites had been abandoned quickly—possibly trouble with the Abanaki—or they just gave up and went home with the rest of Popham. They found one site where some valuables had been hidden. Actually, they were more like keepsakes possibly buried by a settler who left them behind when the call came to return to England—or, maybe the settler just died without telling anyone about them. Last year, when Father was helping at his old site, he stumbled upon some settler materials near the main dig on Cape Small. They weren't in good shape and they weren't Indian, so they were sent on to the college. When Father went back to the area this year, it was one that had been vandalized."

"And now?" Susan asked. She hoped that he was getting closer to why he was here.

"As I said, Father Bartolome does love Maine. I think he's volunteered at most of the sites on Cape Small. He was at that 'Verrazano' site I mentioned last week—they are trying to find evidence that Giovanni da Verrazano met the local tribe there in 1524. The chief archaeologist there is a friend of Father's."

"It's a beautiful bridge," Susan mused.

"What? Oh, the Verrazano-Narrows Bridge in New York City. Yes, indeed it is. Here, I brought a map to show you. My site is right there—just off a quiet little harbor called Machias Bay. Go west and there is Bangor—go east across the Bay of Fundy and you hit Nova Scotia. Champlain founded Port Royale more or less east of Machias Bay in Nova Scotia. Father's site, actually he just volunteers there now, is down there, near that spot on Cape Small," he said, pointing. "You can see it's not far from Phippsburg. It's the site that was damaged. The Verrazano site I mentioned is just there, I think. He volunteers there, too."

Susan did love maps, but now they had been talking for 35 minutes and she still had no idea what he wanted. "Jon, why did you come to see me?" she asked.

CHAPTER 13

"Well, I have been chattering away, haven't I," he said.

"I'm enjoying it–like old times." It wasn't Pagels, but it was interesting. Since she now had a little time, this wasn't a bad way to spend it.

"To make a long story short, I have come across two, no three, things at our site. The one I think you can help with requires a biblical scholar," he said. Susan was now looking at him with that skeptical eye–just like old times he thought–he knew he had her attention. "At least, I need help in seeing if what I found is real or planted–and that requires someone who can read Greek and Hebrew," he continued.

"Planted as in a hoax?"

"Yes, I found a damn box with some very old looking documents at the new site. I think they are in Latin and possibly Greek and Hebrew," he said. "You and Steven came to mind because you always had a truly critical eye in looking at things–and you're honest. In some ways, I think that was why you, in particular, were always getting into hot water," he laughed before pausing to recollect his thoughts. "Most importantly, I figured you two would still know Greek and Latin from grad school."

"Steven still does, probably Hebrew too. I can read only Latin these days," she said. "But a Hebrew document in a box? Where did you find it–I mean how old is the box? Is it maybe an old Torah?"

"Wouldn't a Torah be rolled? These are pages."

"Well, I should...," she caught herself before volunteering to look. "Yes, a Torah generally will be rolled."

"Susan, the documents look very old, but I don't know why the box is there. I trust you and Steven—I enjoyed your thesis about requiring doctrinal teachings to be consistent with historical facts. Your argument that organized religion was inconsistent with the teachings of Jesus and the historical record is what really set them off. More importantly, you didn't back down." He started to chuckle, but then he paused again.

"That was a long time ago," Susan said. "I think I upset a major donor." She was surprised that he knew that much about them. "Anyway, we both left and went to law school," she added waiting for him to get started again. She decided to fill the gap, "the teachings encompass a beautiful philosophy—feeding those who are hungry, for example. The trappings added by organized religion are not only inconsistent with those teachings, but there also is no basis for them in the early Christian writings. 'Original sin,' is another example. Would Jesus really hold an innocent child responsible for the sins of a parent? Oh, and infallibility of the pope didn't come in until the 1860s. Sorry, it still bothers me."

"It confirms you are still that student I knew so many years ago," Jon said. "Your advisor, Dr. Livingstone, was a good friend of mine—he was very sad to see you and Steven leave, even if you did attack his religion."

"We heard of his death after his funeral…he was very patient with me. Anyway, I didn't attack religion per se," Susan added defensively. "My thesis only analyzed what could be supported and what could not. In fact, nothing in Christianity was concrete, even the Gospels, until the time of Constantine. Actually, Constantine was more Steven's area—he thinks Constantine was orchestrating to be the embodiment of the second coming."

"You and Steven are atheists…," he said slowly. "People say that is such a sad view. We are all alone…," he said almost to himself.

"Not everyone needs religion, Jon," she said quietly. "We still need to act as if we are all one and lead an ethical life. Even an atheist must focus on perfecting the soul. That's from Socrates, or at least what Plato has him say. Atheists must be good people here on Earth, not because they will be rewarded in Heaven, but because it gives life a meaning. A Gnostic might say 'what you seek is within you.' Of course, Genesis 1:27 says we were created in God's image."

Jon cut her off, "Well, the 'God' of the Old Testament is rather...," he stopped and then, after searching for the right word, he added, "mean."

"Yes, incomprehensively so," she answered. "So maybe being his image is what causes all of the strife on Earth," she laughed.

"As many times as I have read the Old Testament, I have never been able to resolve that," Jon said.

"Anyway, religions are best as philosophies of how to live, but then the leaders dumb them down so they can manage their flocks. Even that would be okay if they didn't preach so much hatred and ignorance. I mean refusing to teach evolution...I sometimes wonder how they can be so stupid, but then...," she stopped and shrugged her shoulders. "Even the Catholics eventually accepted Galileo—science is not a damn belief."

"Well, I will demur as my son is now a Catholic priest. At least he joined the Franciscans—they are more humble. He is like that—a good person. I must confess, though, I have made him agree never to say 'my son' to me."

"Sorry, I was babbling, wasn't I?"

"No, no, please. This is exactly why I am here. I'm sorry, but it is hard to explain what I have found. So, Steven agrees with you?"

"Steven focused on showing that many Christian concepts could be traced to other religions. The Romans were good at that...they would absorb enough religion of a conquered land to keep the people happy. In a similar fashion, Constantine used Christianity to unify his realm. That meant, though, that Constantine had to standardize it; there were a lot of competing ideas out there. With Christianity having only 'one' God, Constantine was better off than the Roman Emperors. From Augustus Caesar on, the Emperors were gods during their lifetimes, but they competed with all of the other Roman gods. Christianity fixed that for Constantine—there was only one God and Constantine was God's appointee. Now, what did you find in Maine?"

"This is difficult," he said.

Susan decided she would give him another minute—then maybe he would talk just to shut her up. "By the way, the 'Word of God,' has been modified more times than you can imagine. Even the authors aren't definite. For example, the author of the Gospel of John identifies himself only as the 'one whom Jesus loved the most.' It probably was attributed to John much later than it was written; some people believe the author was Lazarus because he, not John, was called 'beloved.' Of course, the Catholics and Protestants have different books in their Bibles and Revelation wasn't added until after the time of Constantine."

"But then, again, that is why I looked you up," Jon added.

Susan looked at him—he looked so nervous. "Jon, Steven and I left grad school over 30 years ago. Now, it's your turn—why are you here?" Susan sat thinking for a minute as she waited for Jon to say something. They had been away from academia far too long for him to seek their expertise. Maybe he was just here to ask for more funding—sometimes it was awkward, especially if you show up unannounced after 30 years. Well, she would ask; maybe it would start him up again. She took a sip from her just refilled cup of coffee and then asked, "Jon, are you looking for funding?"

"No, no," he objected. "As I said, the property owner has given us two nice grants. I just want you and Steven to look at the documents that I found in the box at my site. As an American Indian specialist, I never learned Greek, I haven't used my Latin since high school, and I am not even sure what I saw is Hebrew. Just tell me at least if the materials are gibberish."

"It must be something a settler buried," she said.

"I hope so. As I said, we just began at the new site a few weeks ago. We generally dig down until we find no more evidence of habitation and expect none. Our donor agreed to a plan for the new site that was similar to the one that we would continue at our old site."

"So?"

"I was delighted to be back. My site showed a lot of promise before we had to shut down in 2011, so I figured if I did a good job at the new site, the new owner would then let me finish the old site. My plan was to run the two pretty much in parallel. First, we platted the new site and then we started a test trench. We immediately found a crystal buried only a bit under the surface ...contamination from some New Ager. You know what that does."

Susan hesitated, then said, "Yes, but if it was only a surface intrusion, how would that disturb your region of interest?"

"Luckily, it didn't," he answered. "At first, I worried that the new owner buried it there, since he had told us where to dig. When I reported it to him, though, he was as irritated as I was. So, my intern put up a sign telling the crystal owner to call me if he or she wanted it back," he chuckled, "and we continued."

"Okay, the crystal is no big deal. But the box—for God's sake, it must be an old settler. I mean, Hebrew?"

"The soil was undisturbed under the crystal," Jon protested. That was a good sign as we didn't expect anything there for at least another half meter, based on our other site. But then, when we got a little more than a foot deeper, there was another disturbance—the box. It was right there in my damn test trench."

Susan's cell phone rang again. "Crap! Excuse me for a second, Jon," she said. "It's Jane again."

CHAPTER 14

"I'm sorry for these interruptions, but I have a little more time now, so please continue," Susan said. She didn't tell him that the call was to tell her the principals were revamping the deal. They would work through everything today and tomorrow in New York, with the lawyers coming in now on Friday. It meant that her weekend would be ruined, but she would be free tonight—no sense reviewing materials that might no longer be relevant.

He looked relieved as he continued. "The good news, I guess, was that the box was below the undisturbed area under the crystal. It was above where we would typically begin finding habitation artifacts—charcoal and things like that. It was far enough down to connote at least 400 to 700 years ago." He paused again.

"Jon, we have been here almost 45 minutes," she said thinking to herself that 400 years ago would be the 1600s.

"My intern and I were the only ones there—it was getting close to the end of the day and we had already cleared the damn crystal a few days earlier."

"Just you and the intern?"

Yes, when my intern hit the box, I was devastated. I was going to just put it in the shed with the damn crystal and forget about them. It was a wooden box partially covered with something like pitch or tar. But then, I decided I decided to take the stupid box home with me and look at it over the break; I took the crystal, too. We weren't planning to go back until April 25, because of mid semester exams and then Spring Break this week."

"And this was when?"

"It was about ten days ago, April 8, to be exact. I was busy with exams and then I was asked to give the talk in Bangor so I had to prepare for that. I didn't get a chance to look at the box until last week end. It was wood, with a metal hinge and hasp. When I finally got the hasp cleaned enough to open the box without damaging anything, I saw that the hasp had a date of 1307 stamped right in its center. As you can imagine, then I was really angry. I knew that the crystal was planted, but the box was a conundrum," he said shaking his head. "That damn date on the box is why I went back to my site Monday after my talk in Bangor."

"The hasp says 1307?" she asked as she leaned forward to look at him more closely. "How did you know it was a date and not just some identifying number? Couldn't it be an old box buried recently?"

"It has 'A. *Domini*' engraved after it. Western Europe began using 'Anno Domini' in about the 800s, so it is plausible that this is a date on the hasp. Again, my first thought was that the new owner had planted both the box and the crystal. It was confusing though, because the crystal was barely below the surface. Knowing it was contemporary, we continued below it into undisturbed soil. As I said before, the top of the box was below undisturbed soil at a level that could have been anywhere from about the 1300s to 1600s."

"Did you have the wood of the box dated?" Susan asked.

"Not yet," Jon said. "We did radiocarbon dating of hearth char we found at our old site before we lost our permit. We haven't yet calibrated that radiocarbon age to tree ring data, so it's an estimate. However, I am comfortable with the range. We have an approximate date at the new site, because the fire char at our original site is at about the same depth. Because of the proximity of the two sites, the layer tells us when the box was buried, not necessarily how old it is. We are fudging a bit, except that it has to be at least as old as where it was buried when it is under an undisturbed layer."

"So, this box and the dated material at the old site were at similar depths and therefore you could approximate when the box was buried?"

"Yes, that's a simple way to put it. And we were at the new site because of the petroglyphs. As I said, he wanted a little brochure for visitors to his lodge, once it was finished. What could I say other than that we would do a test trench at the new site?"

"He told you where to dig?" She was surprised, that was never a good sign.

"Not exactly," Jon responded looking a little hurt. "He asked us to survey a small area at the base of the petroglyphs to see if anybody had been 'camping out' there while they did the petroglyphs. To clarify, I hit the box in the test trench we were digging for that purpose. It's not far from our old site."

"Do places where there are petroglyphs ever have evidence of habitation?" Susan asked.

"The petroglyph makers do 'camp out' sometimes. I mentioned the waterway nearby and the site's kind of sheltered; that's good for habitation. Susan, look, he just asked us to do a little work there because of the petroglyphs. It seemed like a reasonable request—and he was funding it."

"So, who is this new owner?" Susan asked.

"I have only dealt with him by email," Jon said slowly. "Oh, and two very short telephone calls. His lawyer in Boston handles our logistical questions—gates, keys and things like that. I send the owner's representative, Joaquin Samovar, updates every week by email. I didn't find him on the Internet. It may sound foolish, but I was so excited to have a chance to finish up and publish on my old site before I retire that I didn't really ask too many questions."

"Well, it's suspicious. He tells you where to dig, and you find a crystal and then a box," she said. "He called you because you had worked nearby in the past?"

"He saw an article about the possibility of Clovis coming from Solutrea in the *New York Tribune Herald*. That got him interested in the petroglyphs on his new property," Jon said. "As an aside, the theory rests on tool similarity between the 'Solutreans,' whose major site is in France, and the Clovis. But there's at least a 5,000 year gap between the European pieces and North American pieces, not to mention the distances and lack of evidence on the purported route. That's just too great much archaeologically for me."

"Maybe the Clovis found them and copied the points they left behind," she started, but then stopped. He didn't need another distraction. "How did he find you?"

"Apparently, some of the people in town remembered me. I was there for several years off and on before the site was closed. We ate at local restaurants, stayed in their motels, you know."

"So, you went back."

"Yes, of course, I went back. As part of the deal, I agreed to do a little work by his damn petroglyphs and write a brochure. He was very reasonable. He assured me he wasn't expecting me to find anything, certainly no Solutreans or Clovis. That was good–it meant he wasn't some sort of nut. He saw the article and though it would be nice to have an archaeologist look around. Again, there is no clear evidence of Clovis in Maine. Before you comment, I know that absence of evidence is not proof of absence."

"Okay, then you found the box. It contained Latin, Greek and maybe Hebrew documents, so you came to us, right?"

"Yes. But before we leave Clovis, I guess I should just tell you–this damn box isn't my only worry. On Monday, when I went in the shed at my site to get my favorite trowel, I found a damn spear point that looked like it might be Clovis. It was wrapped in a cloth sitting on the shelf behind some of my tools–my trowel, specifically. Susan, it's not funny."

"Sorry, but are you really saying that you found a box dated 1307, a crystal and a Clovis point in Maine? Good work, Jon!" She was finding it to be pretty funny.

"You can have the crystal. I think the Clovis point is a damn fake and someone chipped away at its surface. The fluting is wrong; maybe it's Folsom. And the box–who knows? I guess it does sound rather ridiculous, doesn't it?"

"Well," she laughed, "it kind of does, Jon. I can understand the crystal. I've heard of 'New Age' crystals being buried at sites in the Southwest. And maybe it's just an old box buried by a Pilgrim. But someone really stuck a fake Clovis point in your shed? Sorry, I didn't mean to laugh, but it must be a prank by one of your students."

"I don't think so. I was asked to do the Bangor talk on short notice, so no one expected me to be up there Monday–everyone is away. I'd like to think my students were playing a trick on me, but they wouldn't drive all the way to Maine during Spring Break to do it. I was the last one to leave the site, in case you're thinking my intern did it after I left. And where is the damn thing from?"

"Maybe it is real…it isn't stolen is it? Could somebody be trying to discredit you? If not a student, I guess I would think about someone who has a grudge against you."

"Susan, I just don't know—I am at wits end. I um…," he hesitated, and then continued. "I do not want to lose this donor's money because I keep finding these ridiculous things. He was upset when I reported the crystal. If I tell him that now I have found a fake Clovis point and a box buried almost 200 years before Columbus, he may decide the site is too contaminated."

"Is it, Jon?" she asked.

He hesitated and then said, "No."

"It's really only the new site by the petroglyphs, so, it's better to know now." Susan stopped—Jon had his head in his hands. "Jon, let's go through these one at a time. They could be three isolated occurrences. You found the crystal just under the surface near the petroglyphs, right?"

"Yes," he said resignedly.

"How easy is it to get to the petroglyphs?"

"It's not very difficult if you come up the little stream by canoe, which some people do in the summer. You can see the petroglyphs from the stream. They're about 25 feet above the bank—steep, but doable."

"Okay, it's plausible that some New Ager was paddling upstream, saw the petroglyphs, scrambled up the bank to the petroglyphs and buried a crystal—right? It wasn't at your original site, so it could have been done twenty years ago for all we know. We've all heard stories about New Agers doing that."

"Yes," he said, "we have."

"And the box—just because it says 1307, doesn't mean it was buried then. Someone could have buried an heirloom or something in the 1600s—that is what the layer corresponds to right?"

"Yes, it's about 1300 to 1600."

"And you said Verrazano was in Maine as early as 1524?" Susan asked.

"Yes, but the documents…?"

"I haven't seen them yet, Jon. They could be heirlooms that were faked hundreds of years ago; lots of things were faked in the Renaissance. Ancestors might have passed them down unknowingly. There are so many possibilities…I guess we do need see them before hazarding a guess."

"And the spear point?"

"Well, that's a puzzle–if it's a fake, that's one thing. Even if it's real, Clovis or Folsom, it can't be from either site."

"My students know that. They also know our plan only anticipates about 3,000 to 5,000 years ago, with a focus on around 4,500, but no deeper. It just could not be from these sites."

"Okay, any sites in the area that might be old enough?"

"Well, of course, some tribes, like the Passamaquoddy, believe they have been in Eastern Maine and Western New Brunswick for over 12,000 years. Putting that in perspective, our test area trench is only at the 1300 to 1600 level, as you know. We haven't even re-opened our old site, yet, but even our target level is about 9,000 years above Clovis. That would be roughly 13,000 years ago, depending upon the area," he said. "I just don't think there is any Clovis material in Maine. Again, absence of evidence does not necessarily mean…but I know I am using up your time. Do you have a question? You're pondering something."

"Well, the spear point must be a prank…. But could someone really fake the burial of the box?"

"I don't think so, but then who put the damn spear point in my shed? And that crystal…."

"Forget the crystal, Jon—a canoeing New Ager left it and will call you if they come back to get it. The Clovis piece, um, we'll send it off to an expert and turn it in if it's stolen…we need to know what it is. So, let's focus on the box."

"The point is the box has 1307 marked on it. I believe the documents in Greek and Hebrew may be significantly older than the box. I don't know about the two in Latin–they don't look as old as the others. Couldn't you and Steven just see what they say?"

"Maybe...," Susan said slowly.

"Susan," he said, interrupting her, "I don't know what I have. When I opened the box, I found what I believe is an oilskin wrapped package. Inside that, there were several documents that were between two wooden book covers I guess you would say, but the wood is covered with leather. It has an embossed design on it, but I'm not sure if it represents anything."

"Are the documents bound in like a book?"

"No, they were wrapped in a silk-like reddish cloth and laying between the wooden covers. There was a cord tied around the covers."

"And they're all parchment?"

"I think so, but I haven't seen a piece of parchment since graduate school. Maybe, well, I don't even know if parchment was still used in the 1600s. And, of course, neither I nor my son can read Greek, if that's what it is. I am nervous about asking my colleagues–what if it's gibberish?"

"We could find that it's an ancient language on parchment and it is still a hoax...," Susan started.

"Susan, the box has been buried for a long time–I had to clean off a fair amount of build up on the outside before I could even get it open. I mentioned that there was a sealant on the outside; that kept the contents pretty well preserved. It won't take you and Steven long to look at them."

Susan was puzzled–why would someone of Jon's stature bring these to her or Steven? They weren't experts, so he couldn't expect them to authenticate the stuff. Had he faked the documents or was he being duped by someone? She certainly wouldn't bet on Steven missing a fake. Of course, a well done hoax could be interesting. And it could be a good exercise to see if anachronistic words were used. She wasn't worried about the crystal or the spear point, but the documents...what were they? "Jon, you've been at Penn for so many years...."

He interrupted her again, this time he was clearly exasperated. "Susan, I just want you and Steven, people I trust, to tell me what you think," he said. "What is that look? What are you thinking?"

"Sorry, I was just thinking how dangerous it would be to suggest something that is outside the realm of accepted thinking…like a box of Greek documents buried in Maine before Columbus. There's a woman, Dr. King, from the Harvard Divinity School, who just experienced that. She gave a presentation on a small Coptic fragment that included a reference to Jesus' wife, recently. The current belief is that he wasn't married, so she was not well received even though she said the fragment could be a fake and only suggested that the writer may have thought Jesus was married."

"Was he married?"

"The fragment is indeterminate. There is circumstantial evidence for a 'wife.' For example, since Jesus was a Jew, given the customs of the times, it would be very controversial for him not to be married."

"Yes, well then, perhaps you see why I came to you, and not my colleagues."

"Maybe," Susan said smiling to herself. "I once asked a priest if Jesus was a Jew like his parents. He told me that because of the Immaculate Conception, it didn't matter that Mary and Joseph were Jews–Jesus came from God."

Jon groaned and then said, "What if this is another Piltdown man?" He looked at her as if he were pleading for her to make it go away.

"My mother loved that story," Susan said. "It was such an elaborate hoax that some people thought Sir Arthur Conan Doyle was behind it. When was it, 1910?"

"It was 1912, and it took 40 years for people to accept that it was a hoax. The skull was a combination of man and ape, but not the right way. Anyone who questioned it was laughed off until it could no longer be ignored. Susan, help me please."

"Crap Jon, they still aren't sure who the Piltdown perpetrator was." Susan was torn–this might be interesting–but then it might make all three of them look ridiculous. Like Jon, she had absolutely no desire to get mixed up in any controversy

"I know," he said shaking his head. "I probably should have told you this before…I um, voted against a colleague for tenure recently. I wasn't the only one, but I've heard that he knows how I voted and that he's out to get me. My fear is that he planted the box and maybe the spear point and the crystal. I found out because Father's friend, Clay, knows him."

"There really is someone out there?" she asked. She was stunned. "And you are just telling me now?"

"I don't know who told him how I voted, but as I said, Clay knows the guy. My colleague told Clay that he would get even."

"Well, crap, somebody really could be setting you up," she said. "Let's go back to our analysis. We'll get an expert to see if the spear point is real and, if it is, whether it has been reported as being stolen. That should be simple; we should do that immediately. Now, as for the box–my guess would be that it is an old box buried at a later date."

Jon looked at Susan. "Okay," he said half committed. "Who can we send the point to?"

"Let me think…it has to be someone neutral, of course, in case there is some sort of subterfuge here. Um, we have a friend at a museum, but I should ask Steven about sending it to him." She would send it to Bob Pitt if Steven agreed. She was intrigued by the description of the documents, but wasn't convinced that Jon hadn't concocted the whole thing. She took a breath, and then said, "Jon, unfortunately, I am in the middle of a transaction, so even though I like Maine…."

"Susan, I brought the documents here to Chicago," he broke in. "The damn spear point too."

CHAPTER 15

"You brought the documents and the spear point with you?" she asked looking at him. He didn't even have a brief case. "Where are they?"

"I put the documents in a safe deposit box across the street at the Chase National Bank when I got here yesterday afternoon. I didn't want them in my room at the hotel–I wouldn't have slept at all. Before I left Philadelphia, I was able to read a little of one of the Latin documents, the one that I call the 'attestation,' because it is signed by someone named Joham Alvares Diaz Ovelho. From what I could read, he got something in Tomar, Portugal; I assume it was the box. There's a date, but I couldn't make it out."

Susan looked at her watch. She had been jabbering for well over an hour and it turned out everything was right across the street. Should she send Steven for a look? They both learned Greek and Hebrew in graduate school and, of course, they started Latin in high school. Steven could still read all three with ease, but she could read only Latin now. Steven had liked Jon, so maybe he would look at the materials for old time's sake or something like that. He wouldn't be happy if she sent him on a wild goose chase, though.

Susan still didn't quite believe Jon's explanation. Would he really prefer that she and Steven, rather than a colleague, tell him that this was a hoax? It made no sense that he would come to them after 30 years. On the other hand, maybe a little project like this would ease her back into the archaeology world she loved...she was retiring after all. Well, there was one way to find out–she would bite.

"Jon, I have to get ready for a meeting in New York. What if Steven met you tomorrow morning at Chase to take a look? I'll call him to see if he will be free," Susan offered.

"I need to go back to Philly tonight—I'm on a 7:15 p.m. flight. Can't one of you come now?"

Susan could see that he was anxious, almost wringing his hands. "I really can't, but let me check with Steven," she said.

"Tell Steven we can talk first over lunch," he said. "I'll buy. After that, I can show him the documents."

"I need to use the restroom, so I'll call Steven on my way," she said as she stood. "I'll be right back." She wanted to see these documents, too. It would be a pain waiting to hear about them from Steven. Maybe she could meet them for coffee after she finished with the Big A. As for the spear point, she would ask Steven about sending it to Bob Pitt at the Arizona State Museum. She called Steven.

"Hello," Steven answered.

"Good morning," she said as she continued to walk to the restroom. "Do you have anything planned for today?" she asked.

"No...is anything wrong?" Steven asked.

"Just because I call you during the day, doesn't mean anything is wrong—you are up right?" she asked.

"Yes, I have been reading that book you got me on the Temple Mount," Steven said. "Why did you call?"

"Do you remember Dr. Christiansen, the guy who taught our Clovis seminar?"

"Dr. Christiansen—from Penn?" he asked.

"The same," she said.

"That was a long time ago. Why are you bringing him up now—did he die or something?"

"No, he's sitting here at Rivers Restaurant with me—he's quite alive. I just left him for a few minutes to call you. He has found some box at a site in Maine. He isn't sure if it's a hoax, but it has a 1307 date on it. More importantly, he says that when he unsealed the box, it had documents in it. He thinks they are written in Greek and Hebrew. He looked us up because he is too embarrassed to show them to his colleagues without knowing what they are. Oh, there's also a cover letter in Latin—and, um, a fake Clovis spear point and a crystal. Jon thinks they may be planted because he voted against a rival for tenure."

"You're joking—he just popped in out of the blue after 40 years and…," Steven said. "Dr. Christiansen? A crystal? Susan, that's ridiculous!"

"Yes, dear," she said. "He totally agrees. You remember him, Steven. He wasn't a crackpot…in fact, I remember him as being a pretty thorough and knowledgeable researcher. He's here and he wants us to look at the documents from the box. I have to go to New York again tomorrow or Friday, so I've offered you up—he will buy you lunch. And it's only been a little over 30 years ago, not 40 years, dear. I didn't even know Marta 40 years ago; we were only 16 then."

"You have to go to New York? You were just there last Friday," he protested.

"Yes, but maybe not until Friday. I would like to see the documents, but I can't really spare the time right now. I have the damn Big Asshole waiting for me. Look, just take Jon to my club for lunch and see what you think. If he convinces you it isn't a waste of your time, go to Chase and see what he has."

"Well…," he hesitated. "The box is 1307 CE, not BCE, right?" he asked.

"Of course it's not BCE, Steven," she said shortly. "We are talking about a box with that date stamped on it sitting somewhere in Maine for a few hundred years. Actually, I will qualify that—he said the hasp on the box had a 1307 date on it. It still shouldn't be 1307 CE in Maine for God's sake."

"But then why would he look us up—that's almost a 1,000 years after anything you or I could possibly care about," he said. "Susan, don't you think this is kind of fishy?" he asked.

"Kind of fishy? It's very fishy, but he says the documents are old and they're in Greek and Hebrew. He knows we can read those languages—you can anyway. Oh, and he has a Clovis point —which, if real, is probably stolen. He is very nervous—Jon thinks this guy he voted against is trying to trip him up before he retires. Consider it a free lunch and let him talk," she said. "Then go look, tell him they're fakes and send him home."

"You have to pay–it's your club. Besides, even if I can read the documents, it won't mean they are old. They could be on old paper, but written yesterday...."

Susan cut him off. "Yes or no? I have to get back to work. I've been with him since about 10:00 a.m."

"Okay, tell him I'll meet him there at noon, that's 25 minutes," Steven said. "Why are the documents at Chase?"

"He brought them here so that he wouldn't have to convince us to go to Maine or Penn I guess. He didn't want to leave them in his hotel room so he took them to Chase. I may be able to join you for coffee in a while, but right now I have documents of my own to review." She hesitated for a moment and then asked, "Just to be sure, you didn't send Jon here as a joke did you, Steven?"

"You know I don't waste my time on stupid things. Tell Jon that I will meet him in the dining room on the third floor of your club. I will call you after I have seen what he wants to show us," he said. "And, by the way, you are retiring after this deal."

"No shit!" Susan said.

"How will I recognize him? Does he look the same?"

"I didn't recognize him at first, but it's been 30 years. He still has that funny little mustache, but he's added a beard. So, look for someone with a funny mustache and a beard. Be nice to him even if they are fakes, unless you think he faked them. Remember to call me–I will tell Jane I am expecting your call."

"Sweetie, I doubt that you would recognize anyone you hadn't seen in 10 years," Steven chuckled. "Nevertheless, you should have recognized him with that damn mustache–as I recall, it looks like the one David Suchet sports as Poirot, doesn't it? Surely you remembered that?"

"I told you I did, but not right away. Hmm," she stopped for a minute to think. "You're right, it does look like David Suchet's 'Poirot' mustache, but Suchet wasn't doing Poirot until sometime in the 2000s. So, I don't see how that would have helped. Also, Jon didn't have a beard when we took his course."

Renegades among the Tumbleweeds

"Even so…," Steven started.

"Yes, well ask him about the fake Clovis point he found," she said cutting him off. "Oh, and if we want to see if it's a fake, we'll send it to Bob Pitt," she added and hung up before he could respond.

Susan called Jane and asked her to get a lunch reservation for Steven and Jon on her way back to the table. Dr. Christiansen was on the phone. He hung up when he saw her. "Sorry," he said. "That was my son, Father Bartolome. He wanted to know where I was."

"Perhaps we will meet him at some point," she said, looking at his mustache. Crap, it looked like there was even a touch of wax on it. "Steven will meet you for lunch. My assistant has made a reservation down the street for noon. Is that okay?"

"You can't join us?"

"No, I really do have to get back to work. Steven will go to Chase with you and then we can meet for coffee. There's a Starbucks there. It's the main Chase office, right?"

"Yes, that was handy for me," he said.

"Handy for me as well–almost across the street," Susan said. "Does your son know you have brought the documents here for us to look at? You said he is working at your site."

"He's helping at my old site in his spare time. He doesn't know about the box or the spear point yet, so I didn't tell him I was coming here to see you," he said. "I'm sure he would think I am overreacting about the box. Maybe I'm a little more sensitive than he, but I didn't want him to get wrapped up in any nonsense if the wrong person got wind of this and went to the press. Besides, he is visiting his friend in Boston, so I didn't want to bother him with this."

"Why…," she started to say, but Jon raised his hand for her to stop.

"There have been Templar rumors all over the Northeast for many years. For example, there is the Westford Knight carving in Massachusetts, which supposedly depicts a medieval sword carved around 1400 CE. As for the sword carving, the Peabody Museum says it is nothing more than glacial scratches and weathering marks. I am just too old to be a part of a controversy like that. So, I came to you," he added chuckling.

"Well," Susan stopped for a second, not sure what to say. Knowing about the tenure guy, she now better understand his concern. But flying to Chicago? She stood and said, "This has certainly been an interesting chat. I'll have Jane arrange a private room at Chase where you can show Steven the documents."

As Susan walked out of the restaurant with Jon, he turned to her. "Thank you for seeing me," he said as he clasped her arm. "I'm so relieved that you and Steven will look at the documents for me. I didn't bring the box or the leather bound cover, only pictures of them, but they're also in the safe deposit box. Thank you, Susan," he said again.

"Jon, one more thing—I would like to send the spear point to Bob Pitt at the Arizona State Museum. Is that okay?"

"Bob? Yes, of course, that's an excellent idea. Tell him I said hello. We worked together twenty some years ago on a big project in west Texas." He reached in his pocket and pulled out a handkerchief. For a minute, Susan thought he was going to wipe his eyes. "Here, send this damn thing to Bob," he said handing it to her. "No, please don't unwrap it in front of me—I don't want to see it again."

As Susan went back to her office, she was trying to dissuade herself that she had seen tears in his eye. "Must be allergies," she thought. "What an interesting mess."

CHAPTER 16

Steven called Susan at 1:20 p.m. She had just spent over an hour with things for the Big A. "What's up?" she asked.

"I am going to look at the documents now. Jon gave me the safe deposit box key and a power of attorney that the bank had him fill out and sign. It authorizes us to open the box," he said.

"He's not going with you? He didn't tell me about any power of attorney," she said puzzled.

"He forgot to tell you," Steven said. "He did a power of attorney at Chase because he wasn't sure you would be in today. He figured if he left the power and instructions, at least one of us would be curious enough to go to Chase. He's gone back to his hotel to lie down before he checks out. His flight home to Philadelphia is at 7:15 p.m. He told me to get a head start."

"So, he's just leaving the documents here with us?" she asked.

"Yep."

"What do you think about his story, Steven?"

"Well, it still sounds fishy," Steven said. "But then, it sounds like someone has gone to a fair amount of trouble. I understand that he doesn't want to get caught up in a 'scandal' as he put it, but he doesn't see how someone could have faked the burial of the box. Of course, it could be a real box but fake documents." He stopped for a minute then asked, "Would he fake something like this when he's so close to retirement?"

"Does Morton Smith ring a bell, Steven?"

"Whoa, good point, Susan!" he said. "But I don't think Jon has the expertise for this."

"What about this new property owner who funded him?" she asked. "Could he have some ulterior motive? Maybe he bought an old box and some old, fake documents and buried them, damn it."

"I asked Jon that. He is nervous because the box was where the new owner wanted him to dig, but he insists that the box was below a fair amount of undisturbed soil. So far, Jon's only told the owner about the crystal. Apparently, only an intern was present when he found the box," he said. "Oh, am I right that he gave you the spear point?"

"Yes, I have the damn spear point. I want to send it off to Bob Pitt tonight. He can see if it's stolen. Can you call him?"

"Why me?"

"You know Bob better. Also, did Jon say why the property owner picked the spot?"

"Well, there are petroglyphs there," Steven said. "The guy is planning to build a retreat on the land. He wants a brochure on the petroglyphs for his guests."

"That's pretty much what Jon told me," Susan said. "We can compare notes tonight to see how consistent he is. Have you seen a picture of the box? I forgot to ask him if there was anything other than the date on the hasp. I spent too much time chatting and not enough asking questions—that's what happens when I have too much time on my hands."

"There are photographs of the box with the documents. Jon documented it closed and open, of course," Steven said. "Oh, and the leather cover, he has a picture of that, too. It's embossed with an insignia that I don't recognize and the number 1267."

"Do you think it's a date?"

"I'm not sure what else it could be. Of course, if the insignia identifies some organization, 1267 might be when it was established."

"Email me a picture of the insignia," she said. "Anyway, it has to be an old box brought over by early settlers. Jon did say the layer was maybe 1300 to 1600, so the date could just mean they used an old box to bury something important a few hundred years ago. It could even be an old family heirloom brought over from Europe. It doesn't necessarily mean it was buried there 600 years ago."

"Since we're guessing, maybe they'll be medieval forgeries…that would still be pretty interesting. Or, maybe it's something Joseph Smith missed…," he laughed. "Or, maybe they are the writings of some unknown prophet–we can start a new religion with these documents, the same way Smith started the Mormons."

"Steven, just get over to Chase and look," Susan said. She had to get back to work. More importantly though, she wanted to know what those documents were. She knew Steven would sort them out in his methodical way.

"I didn't say I wasn't at Chase. I'm already here, in a comfy little room, waiting for Sarah to bring me the safe deposit box. Jon should be here shortly. Can you grab coffee with us around 3:30 p.m.?" he asked.

"I think so," she said. "Let Jane know what room you are in at Chase so I can find you if you aren't at Starbucks. And remember to call Bob and warn him about the spear point. If he won't look at it, Jon has to take it home tonight–I do not want it here if it might be stolen."

"Yes, dear," he said as he hung up.

CHAPTER 17

It was 3:10 p.m. Susan had called the Big A when she hung up with Steven. Unfortunately, she ended up spending over an hour with him going over the changes she had made—at least he thanked her. As usual, mum was the word on who fixed it. Then one of the O'Keefe Hopper partners called to tell her Eastland's year end numbers weren't going to be anywhere near as good as they had projected. At least she wasn't going to New York tomorrow—it was definitely pushed back to Friday. She hadn't heard from Steven since 1:20 p.m., but that was normal when he got wrapped up with something. It would be interesting to see what kept him so engaged. Susan walked out to Jane's desk. "I am going to meet Steven for coffee over at Chase. I will be back in about an hour."

"Steven called ten minutes ago. He said not to bother you until you surfaced. He is in room 1402-D at Chase. He has coffee there for you, so don't go to Starbucks," Jane reported. "He gets a brownie point for calling, right?"

"I guess so—maybe two brownie points. I just figured he got wrapped up and forgot to call me. If anyone needs me, have them call my cell. You have a flight for me on Friday now?" she asked.

"Yes, same flights only one day later. Oh, did Marta reach you? You had your private line forwarded to me for a while…," Jane added. "She wants you to call her."

"I'll stop by her office on my way out," Susan answered as she was putting on her coat.

"I need to leave by 6:00 p.m. tonight," Jane said. "I have you in the pool, so you can turn the documents again, if you want."

"I won't need anything tonight," Susan said. "Oh, can you get a small FedEx box ready for me? I want to send something to Dr. Robert Pitt at the Arizona State Museum in Tucson."

"Will do. So, is it 'C' as in Cahokia?" Jane asked.

"It's definitely 'C,' but not as in Cahokia. He figured I would at least go see who he was with that name," Susan said.

"It worked, huh?" Jane asked.

"Yep. He's getting me out of the office on a cold day in April. A bit of the pressure is off, but I will still need to be in New York all day Friday. Is Wilhelm ready to go?" Susan asked.

"He is on your flight Friday morning. Go, or it will be time to come back. Oh, and you need to talk to him. He wants to know if he can come back Saturday rather than Friday. I got you each a room at the Pierre, just in case."

"Tell him he can do anything he wants as long as the work gets done," Susan yelled back. "Thanks! Oh, and I will catch up with him tomorrow in the office."

"Wait, did you get a card—do you want me to just put 'C' in the system?"

"No card, he is just an absent minded professor. Bye," Susan said as she headed for the elevator. She pulled out her iPhone to see if 'brownie' points were tied to the Brownies who were junior Girl Scouts. "Crap, nobody knows." She put her iPhone away and started to push the elevator button, when she remembered Marta. Marta's office was down a floor—Susan would stop for a minute to see what she wanted.

Susan met Marta Krejci in 1974, when they were freshmen at the University of Arizona. Susan was majoring in chemistry and Marta in Slavic languages. Someone said Marta came to Tucson because she loved horses, so she offhandedly invited Marta out to her dad's ranch. She didn't think more about it until Marta found her in the library and asked when she could go. It caught Susan by surprise—Marta might like horses, but she looked more like the 'dressage' type than a rancher. She was in a sorority, after all. But Susan felt obligated, so she invited Marta to come out for a weekend in February.

With the visit settled, Susan had a new set of issues. As usual, she had no idea where her dad was, so she had Pete, the foreman, get a guest room ready at the house. He volunteered to air out the cabin in case they stayed out there to watch the great horned owls; it would be a full moon. Then she worried about Pete, who was in his 80s. What if the old fart had a heart attack when he saw Marta—she was sorority girl beautiful. As the weekend got closer, Susan convinced herself that Marta's 'visit' was some sort of practical joke. She thought about canceling, but Marta kept calling to ask questions.

They still laughed about it sometimes—Marta so wanted to go, but she had never actually been on a horse. Even worse, Marta's only experience of the 'wild' had been a week long summer camp in Wisconsin.

Marta did learn to ride a horse, but that first time they drove the old pick-up to the cabin. Susan smiled to herself, remembering that Pete and her dad called the cabin the 'outhouse.' It had running water and a bathroom, but not much else. It was a good introduction for the sorority girl.

Marta shared Susan's love of the Southwest. They would take off for some archaeological or historical site whenever they could. Or, Susan would pick an old back road to go looking for wild life. One of Susan's favorites was the four plus hour drive over the old Reddington Pass road and then along the San Pedro River to Benson. Arizona sycamores and cottonwoods lined the river the whole way. You ended up just north of Benson near the Singing Wind Bookshop.

Susan went to graduate school at Penn to study biblical archaeology in 1977. She realized in her junior year that analyzing inks on ancient documents to create acceptable standards for dating, was less exciting than reading the actual documents. When Susan met Steven at Penn, Marta was already doing graduate work in London. All three of them ended up in Chicago for law school in 1980. The Graves went to law firms. Steven, who, had majored in biophysics as an undergrad, had gone to an IP firm and Susan to Peale, Curtis and Blume where she went into corporate work. Steven left his firm twenty-five years later to help found the company which he had sold last year. Marta parlayed her knowledge of Slavic languages into a job with the NSA. She was there for eighteen years.

The Graves didn't see Marta much during her NSA years as she was stationed in Europe. Sometimes, if Marta was going to be in a city that they all liked, they would all meet for a museum spin, an archeological highlight or dinner.

Marta had a few travel restrictions, though—she could meet them in Beirut, but she couldn't cross into the Beqaa Valley with them to see the temple complex at Baalbek. She never confirmed their suspicions, but they figured it was because Baalbek was near Hezbollah headquarters. But then, Susan and Steven never knew what Marta did at the NSA other than traveling a lot.

When Marta left the NSA, she joined Senator Hinderman's staff in a function related to the Senator's position on the Select Committee on Intelligence. When the Senator decided to retire five years ago, Susan convinced Marta to join Peale, Curtis in the firm's advocacy and government affairs group. Susan always considered the group to be glorified lobbyists, but since someone had to do it, it might as well be Marta. Although the group was based primarily in DC, Martha insisted on living in Chicago, so she was often in the Chicago office. DC was only a two hour flight, so she always could be there on short notice.

They never met either of Marta's two husbands. The first was a co-worker at the NSA. It lasted for a little over a year and ended amicably by mutual agreement. Her second husband died in a plane crash in Nigeria while Marta was working for the Senator. That had hit Marta very hard—the Graves didn't see her for a year. Then, one day, Marta asked them to meet her in Mexico City to see a Frida Kahlo show at the Bellas Artes, and everything was back to normal. Now they were all betting on when, not whether, there would be a third husband.

Susan had once heard someone at a DC bar steal a line from Raymond Chandler to describe Marta. He told the barman there's '…a blond to make a bishop kick a hole in a stained glass window.' Marta was still stunning after all these years—even though she was a brunette and the guy those many years ago was a drunken idiot. Susan never had the guts to ask Steven, but he probably would describe Marta much the same way even today.

"You rang?" Susan asked as she knocked on the door sill of Marta's office.

"Yes, I was looking for you. I hear you are going to New York again," Marta said.

"Jane tell you that?"

"No, I can never get squat out of Jane. I ran into your boy, Wilhelm. He is going to New York tomorrow, so, it must be with you," Marta said smiling.

"They will shoot you if they hear you calling associates boys or girls," Susan said. "Wilhelm's probably 30 years old. New York has been pushed to Friday."

"He's 31."

"I was close," Susan answered. "What's up?"

"I have to go to Berlin the last week in May. Can you and Steven meet me there? We could visit Nefertiti—I'll be staying at the Kempinski."

"I thought you were going to Seattle with us for the Herb Farm," Susan said. "No, I'm wrong, that's not until June."

"Do you think the Herb Farm might have some special huckleberry dessert on the menu then?"

"Huckleberries? Too much time on your hands today, huh? Anyway, they'd have to be frozen from last year since the best time to pick them is mid-August to mid-September when they are a deep purple and nice and plump. Trivia for you—the Yakima Indians say that huckleberries are the eyeball of their God."

"Then we could go to Yakima and pick them in September," Marta mused.

"Not me—I picked huckleberries with my parents when we used to vacation at Coeur d'Alene in Idaho," Susan said. "First, you find a rugged old mountainside where there's been a forest fire within the last five to ten years. Then, you fight your way through the new growth looking for them. There are bugs, bears and you name it."

"Susan, you love that...."

"Not anymore," Susan laughed. "And, Steven would never put up with it. It took a day to pick enough for a couple of pies. Then, you still had to make the damn pies." She remembered how her dad would keep her from wandering off by pointing to black stuff that looked like bear fur hanging from the lower branches of some of the shrub-like trees. "See, the bears have been here for their huckleberries. Stay near me," he would say. Susan was almost nine before she actually pulled some of the 'black fur' down. It turned out to be a type of moss that grew symbiotically on those shrubs. Years later, when she had been reminiscing with her mother, she found that her mother still thought it was bear fur. Susan's dad was probably laughing himself silly in his grave.

"Susan?" Marta said. "What are you thinking about?"

"They say the best place to pick huckleberries is in the Indian Heaven Wilderness. It covers a crest in the Washington Cascades west of Yakima. There are even more bugs there, actually mosquitoes, so I won't be going with you. Anyway, it's much better to eat them after someone else picks them and makes the pie."

"Okay, I'll hunt down a source for huckleberries so we can have some pie."

"We'll have to be nice to Steven, then. You and I aren't going to be cooking some dumb pie, huckleberries or not."

"I can be nice—for a while. So, how about Berlin?" Marta asked.

"I'd like to see the 'Throne of the Devil' at the Pergamon Museum again. Remember when you had to go through Checkpoint Charlie to get into East Berlin and Museum Island? Steven and I were there in 1989 or 1990, when the Wall was coming down, but Americans still had to use Checkpoint Charlie. We went to Prague for the first time on that trip too; we watched three guys load a statue of Lenin onto the back of an old pickup truck in some square and off they went. You were living in The Hague, I think."

"Probably."

"We do need to get back to Berlin," Susan stopped, if her deal didn't close, she'd be lucky to get away for the Herb Farm.

"Come with me," Marta said.

"If my deal closes…. I'm on my way to meet Steven, I'll ask him about Berlin," Susan said as she looked at her watch.

"I'll work on restaurants," Marta said.

"I have to run—I'm meeting Steven and someone at Chase in a few minutes," she added.

"What's at Chase?"

"I'll tell you when I get back...we're looking at something for an old professor and I'm late."

"Will you have any spare time in New York over the weekend?"

"Either no time or a whole lot of time," Susan said. "Anyway, I'm coming back Friday night. I have to go."

"Wait, where's my trivia?" Marta asked. "And what's with the cane? Your ankle again?"

"Oh, crap, some people say that a butcher named Sussman Volk served the first pastrami in New York in 1887. He got the recipe from a Romanian friend. Katz, of Katz's Deli, also claims to have been first," she said as she headed for the door. "And, yes, it's my damn ankle—the damp weather set it off again."

"What's the 'Throne of the Devil'?" Marta called after her, but Susan was already gone.

CHAPTER 18

Susan got to Chase at 3:40 p.m. Steven supposedly had coffee waiting for her, so she resisted the urge to buy a cup at Starbucks and went directly to the Chase security desk. When she got upstairs, she found Steven poring over a document with a magnifying glass.

"Coffee's over by the window," he said without looking up, before she could say anything. "There should be cream there as well."

"Hello, Sweet One. Where's Jon?"

"He hasn't shown up yet," Steven said. "I was going to call him, but then I realized I didn't know which hotel he was at."

"Well, that makes two of us," she said as she poured herself a cup of coffee and added the cream. "I'm surprised that he let you out of his sight. So, what do you think–anything of interest?" She walked over to him. He had brought not only a magnifying glass, but also tweezers and gloves to handle the documents. That was Steven–always prepared.

"Susan, I have been looking at this one here in Greek–it's the first one I picked up. Oh, the Latin cover piece with the Templar's signature is over there on the credenza, with the other Latin piece," he said pointing with a gloved finger. "Those were separate."

As Susan walked over to where Steven was pointing, she asked again, "anything of interest, Steven? Crap, why did you say 'Templar'? Does that mean this is a stupid 'Templar' hoax after all? Oh well, Jon did say that he was concerned about all the Templar nonsense going on in the Northeast. Guess he was right to worry."

"Susan, I did not necessarily say it's a hoax," Steven said calmly. "It may be, but I'm not sure yet. I just said 'Templar' to pique your interest. I didn't actually see anything that said 'Templar' when I glanced over it. I am focused on these now."

"And those are in Greek?"

"Yes, I have four Greek pieces and one Aramaic piece here. There also are three fragments, one in Latin, one in Hebrew and one in Aramaic."

"That's nice—no Templars. Should I look at the two on the credenza or the Latin fragment?"

"Ignore anything in Latin for now," he said. "Come look at these parchments— all but one of these were wrapped in those materials. The outermost wrapping is over there; it feels almost like silk. The inner one is next to it; it feels like oilskin. These three Greek documents and possibly the Aramaic one purport to be copies of older documents. At least that's what this top parchment says."

"Copied from what Steven?"

"Look here. This letter on top says that the copies with it were finished in 1267."

"Steven, that 1267 date probably ties to the insignia's 1267, if it's a date. Crap, did you send to me?"

"No, I got too busy. You may be right about 1267, but we need to research the insignia itself."

"That letter looks like Greek, but I can't read it— it's medieval, right?"

"Yes, the author says he wrote it in Cyprus in 1292. The ones underneath are Koine Greek." He looked up at her and said, "If these are fakes, they were done by an expert. I think that rules Jon out."

"Cyprus in 1292? That's not good."

"Why?" Steven asked.

"Legend says the Apostle Paul made his first missionary trip to Cyprus. St. Helen, the mother of Constantine, stopped in Cyprus on her return to Constantinople in 327, following her discovery of the Holy Cross in Jerusalem. She even left a piece of the Holy Cross at a Monastery there as well as some stupid cats. And, damn it, the Templars retreated to Cyprus after they lost Acre," she paused and then said slowly, "in 1291. What are these?"

"Helen brought the cats to rid Cyprus of its snakes. Anyway, I need to talk with Norman, Susan. This 1292 cover piece says these documents were carried out of Constantinople in early 1203 because of the problems at Zara. Susan, that's just before the Fourth Crusade sacked Constantinople—they sacked the Christian city of Zara first. They headed for Constantinople in 1203, and sacked it in 1204, as you well know."

"Out of Constantinople to where, Steven?" she asked. "Just a minute," she said as she walked to the window and set down her coffee.

"To the Sinai, Susan. Here, what does that say?" he said pointing to a clause.

"Steven, I can't read…oh, it says 'Monastery of the God-Trodden Mount Sinai.' It's the formal name of the St. Catherine's Monastery. Is that possible? Somebody brought these from Constantinople to have them copied at St. Catherine's. And then they took them to Cyprus?"

He sat in silence, staring at the Aramaic scrap on the table in front of him

"What are you staring at? We have two Latin documents, four recopied documents and a cover, anything else?"

"There are three fragments—the one in Hebrew is a text copied from the Old Testament—it's Isaiah 7:14."

"So, is Mary a young woman or a virgin in the scrap?"

"It just uses 'almah' or a child bearing woman; it never should have been translated as 'virgin' as used in the New Testament," Steven said without looking up.

"So, the 'virgin birth' interpretation is still only in Mathew and Luke. Paul says only that Jesus was born of a woman; and John says only that Joseph was the father of Jesus. What about the Aramaic one."

"It looks like a list of the Apostles," he said looking at her. "There's a Latin scrap, too. The author of this 1292 cover letter doesn't mention the scraps. He does say the first document was copied from papyri collected in the scriptorium at Constantinople. The other three are copies of letters on parchment, one is Aramaic and the other two are Greek. Apparently, these were important enough to have been copied at least once before they were finished in 1267."

"So, over the years, when they were recopied, it was exactly as written–in Koine Greek. Is that it?"

"Yes, I think so–who would do this as a hoax?" Steven said to himself. He looked at Susan and said, "I'm glad the 1292 letter is short, Medieval Greek is painful for me."

"Well, one of those Latin pieces is Medieval Latin, so we'll both have to suffer."

"Koine Greek, which evolved as words picked up by Alexander the Great in his travels came into common usage beginning around 300 BCE, hence 'koine' or common, is easier for me."

"You can't pinpoint when it morphed into Greek of medieval times; it continued to evolve like any language and phased out around 300 CE as Constantine was founding Constantinople."

"Constantine consecrated Constantinople in May 330 CE," he corrected her.

"Steven, it was a rough estimate. I know this history, remember? Constantine was born near Nis in modern day Serbia. My grandfather was born nearby in Montenegro, just like Nero Wolfe. God knows how he got out West to marry my grandmother in Tucson. Constantine died in Nicomedia in 337 CE. Stop correcting me and tell me what these are. And don't quiz me either."

"Sorry, Sweetie," Steven said. "Your grandfather probably was headed to Bisbee to work in the mines."

"Yes, dear, there are still a lot of Serbians and Monte Negrins there. Grandpa had several friends there, all with names ending in 'vich'."

"Anyway, if these are fakes, they're damn good, so it's making me nervous. What do you think?"

"Steven, for all I know, it could be gibberish," she said exasperated. "I can't read Greek anymore and I can't even pick out where the words begin and end in Koine Greek. Just tell me what the topic is…actually, let me be sure I understand. The four parchments were copied from copies of earlier documents—is that correct?"

"That is what the 1292 cover letter says. It also says that these three Greek documents and the Aramaic one are copies of ones that were written in the 'early days.'"

"How early?" Susan asked. "Is it early enough to pre-date Eusebius? I mean there were a lot of local Christian beliefs and documents floating around before Constantine had him standardize everything."

"The author says that like those who gathered these, they had a duty to preserve the words of those who were with 'Him.' I guess 'he' means Jesus."

"And the Aramaic one, too?"

"As I said, he treats that one a little differently, but reverently."

"We know that there was a lot of resentment when Constantine presided over the Council of Nicea," Susan started slowly, thinking as she spoke. "In his *Life of Constantine*, Eusebius says that Constantine ordered him to standardize the Bible and send fifty authorized copies out to the churches of the realm. Because those Bibles became the gold standard, other traditions were untenable. You know how that went over."

"The 1292 cover says one of the Greek letters was from Alexandria, one was from Caesarea, and one was from Rome. The Aramaic one was written in Jerusalem. Damn, if I had come across these 30 years ago, I might not have gone to law school. No, I would have been too poor to be sitting here."

"Wait a minute, if these were written around the time of Nicea, being about 325 CE, how are they the words of those who were with 'Him'? Steven, is this a hoax?"

"I don't know…whoever copied the Greek pieces either did them verbatim or was a very good storyteller. The copiers must have been scholars of some sort to be able to copy the koine texts and make sense out of them. I wonder how many times the texts were copied."

"So?" she asked.

"Well," Steven said hesitating, "what he actually says is that, for example, the Alexandrian gathered 'His' word from those who were taught. He then used those words as the basis for his complaint against Nicea. I guess it's sort of been passed down, and they used what has been passed down to disagree. For my part, I hoped this might be something like pieces of one of the fifty Bibles that Constantine had Eusebius dash off," he said.

"Very funny," she said. "So, since it's probable that neither the *Codex Vaticanus* nor the *Codex Sinaiticus* is a candidate, it's still true that one has never been found."

"Unfortunately, yes," Steven said calmly. "Nevertheless, these are pretty good. There are two letters written to Hosius of Cordova. As I said, this one seems to be from an Alexandrian."

"Hosius as in Constantine's religious advisor?" she asked. She was staring at Steven to see if he was kidding. He did look serious. "That could be interesting."

"The date is March something in 325 CE. That means it's shortly before the Council of Nicea. The Alexandrian is complaining about Constantine convening the Council. A couple of letters in the Bishop's name are hard to read. It looks like the name is probably Ammonius, but some of the letters are very indistinct," he said. "I'm not sure what else it could be, though."

"He isn't Ammonius Saccas who taught Plotinus is he?"

"No, and I can't say that this looks like Plato or that he is that old. There's also nothing about reincarnation."

"Good, I never was one for that, although knowing God through meditation is better than some approaches. So, is this 'Bishop' a supporter of Arius—an Arian?" Susan was interested now. Even if this was a fake, a well done one might be interesting. "If he is complaining, that should mean he's a follower of Arius rather than a 'trinity' guy."

"You will enjoy this—first he says he is simply head of his flock, he doesn't call himself a bishop. Ammonius says that Constantine has no authority to convene the Council. Then, he says the teachings of Christ are not debatable and cannot thus be decided by a body of Bishops elected by men. He then finishes by saying that Jesus said he was not God."

"The last part definitely sounds Arian, but Arianism is a little more complex," she said. "He would say that God, the Father, begat Jesus, the Son, so there was a time when there was no Jesus, thus making Jesus distinct from God the Father—not necessarily that Jesus wasn't God as well. Of course, there is scripture where Jesus says he is not…"

"I know, Susan. Of course, after Nicea, the Church's position was that God was always the Father, the Son and the Holy Spirit. So, their belief is that God is three distinct personages that are co-eternal and co-equal, indivisibly united in one essence. Most churches today agree."

"Yes, dear," she said. "I've always thought it was odd that these 'Trinity' guys, like the Catholics, prevailed over time, even though Constantine later reversed himself and decided to side with the Arians. I believe it was Eusebius' influence that brought Arianism back into favor with Constantine. There's also something about the 'Trinity' being too much like polytheism, do you remember who said it?"

"No, but I know the Mormons and some Quaker and Pentecostal sects don't accept the Trinity—anybody else?" he asked.

"There are the Unitarians, like my mom and Charles Darwin, and the Jehovah's Witnesses. The Witnesses certainly don't accept the Trinity. They say they have restored Christianity to its first century concept by removing non-scriptural doctrine, like the Trinity concept," she said. "You know what they think of organized religion and all of its pomp—and, for them, Jesus is sort of an intermediary between God and humans—he isn't God."

"Maybe I could be a Jehovah's Witness," he said.

"Shall I order you a copy of the '*Watch Tower*? They also say that an eternal hell would be totally inconsistent with God's love. I don't remember exactly how they get there, but it relates to "God is Love," from 1 John 4:8 and something in Jeremiah. Oh, and they say Christmas and Easter are based on pagan rituals and thus not Christian," Susan added.

'Well, they are right," he chuckled. "Susan, we'll have to see if our Ammonius is in Eusebius' list of Bishops who attended the Council of Nicea, which by the way, is where they agreed on a date for Easter," he said.

"I thought he said there shouldn't be 'Bishops,' Steven."

"Oops, you're right. I'll check into it a little more."

"I do remember some of this," she said defensively. "Apparently, better than some experts…I just saw something that said Eusebius of Caesarea baptized Constantine before he died. But since Constantine was on his way to battle the Persians when he got sick, he only made it back to his villa in a suburb of Nicomedia. An Arian local bishop, Eusebius of Nicomedia, baptized him there. Hannibal committed suicide near there, right?"

"Yes, when it was known as Bithynia," he said. "Or, was it–when did Hannibal die?"

"Around 181 BCE, so, it was Bithynia then. Hannibal took the poison he carried in his ring and died."

"See, you knew that; it's why you are still the only person I can be with…for more than a couple of hours," Steven said.

"If that 'more than a couple of hours' was a compliment, thank you, I guess. Anyway, there is only one place in the Bible that may reference the Trinity."

"Yes, dear, Voltaire said the clause 'Father, the Word, and the Holy Ghost' was added in Constantine's time."

"The clause is referred to as the Johannine Comma because it was added to 1 John 5:7. And Voltaire is probably wrong. Erasmus' New Testament, done in about 1520, was based on Greek sources. He excluded it from his first two editions because he said there was no Greek source for the clause. Then a Franciscan produced a source, so Erasmus relented and added it as a footnote to his third addition. It's pretty well accepted today that the Franciscan's source was a forgery. Many newer Protestant Bibles exclude the clause. I think it's still in the King James Version, though."

"Maybe...," Steven started.

"Steven, you don't really think these are real, do you?" Susan interjected.

"For now, I can only say that these are interesting enough that I can't reject them out of hand. But I've only been here for about two hours. So, which John wrote the first letter, 1 John?" Steven asked.

"Don't mess with me, Steven."

"I'm really not positive, Susan—this is a good exercise for us."

"Whatever," she said. "First, 1 John is written like a letter, but, unlike Paul's letter to the Romans, it doesn't have an addressee. There are several 'Johns' in the New Testament. The author can't be John the Baptist. There are fragmentary accounts of him throughout the gospels, which call him the 'forerunner of our Lord,' but no writings by him."

"There is John the Apostle, the Canonical John of the fourth gospel, John of Artemis, John the Evangelist, John of Patmos, Presbyter John, John the Revelator and John of Zebedee," Steven added.

"We know that John of Zebedee and his Brother James are Apostles. John the Revelator and John of Patmos are probably one and the same. And, of course, there is Titian's painting of Saint John the Evangelist on Patmos."

"We saw the cave on Patmos where John supposedly got his 'revelation,' while he was exiled there," Steven said.

"Yes, dear. Revelation is usually dated to around the mid-90s CE, although some of it may have been written earlier, possibly during or shortly after Nero's reign," Susan said.

"So...who is this John?" Steven asked.

"Well, some say that the three epistles of John may be written by two different authors. John I is attributed to John the Evangelist, but the author of John II and III calls himself 'ho presbyteros' which means 'the ancient' or 'the old.'

It was your Eusebius who distinguished Presbyter John from the Apostle John, I think."

"So...," Steven urged.

"So, some Christians believe that John of Patmos also was 'John' the Apostle and he wrote not only the Gospel, but also John I, II and III. We both know that's highly unlikely. If John of Patmos died around 100 CE on Patmos, then he couldn't be the Apostle John."

"Assuming Jesus was born during the reign of Herod the Great," he added.

"Yes, Steven. The consensus is that Herod died in 4 BCE. Mathew and Luke both say Jesus was born during his reign—so Jesus was born no later than 4 BCE. John and Judas Iscariot were the only apostles who died from natural causes—the other ten were martyred. But if the Apostle John died in Ephesus around the beginning of the second century and he was born about the same time as Jesus; he would be about 105. So, it has to be John of Patmos who also likely is John the Evangelist, John the Presbyter, and of course, John the Revelator."

"We've been to Ephesus as well. The Temple of Diana, one of the Seven Wonders of the World, is there, too," he said.

"Yes, dear. We've been to the Basilica of St. John in Selçuk, which was built by Justinian over John's tomb. The Basilica was modeled on Constantine's Church of the Holy Apostles. I give up—I would guess it is either 'John of Patmos' or a 'John' that we don't know. That's as far as I can go," Susan said. It drove her nuts when there was no definitive answer. "But seriously, do you think these may be real?"

"I'm not sure, of course," he said slowly. "I can certainly translate them. With some time and your help, we can determine where the language puts them and whether there are any anachronistic usages. I haven't caught anything glaring yet, though. I'm intrigued, but certainly not convinced."

"We should probably get the parchment dated...it is parchment, right?"

"Yes, everything is parchment."

"Well, we can't go to one of the Universities. I think that would be contrary to Jon's wishes. Marta might be able to get a contact from one of her former colleagues," Susan said.

"The Oriental Institute would be perfect, but we do need to honor Jon's request for now."

They both jumped when Susan's phone rang. It was Jane.

CHAPTER 19

"I'm sorry to bother you, but James Jameson at Jameson Properties just called. He says it's imperative that you call him immediately. He specifically asked me to track you down."

"Damn, what's his number?" Susan asked.

Jane gave Susan the number and then asked, "So, you'll you call him?"

"Yes, I'll do it now. Is it already 4:10 p.m.?" Susan asked.

"Yes; remember, I can only stay 'til 6:00 p.m. tonight."

"Thanks," Susan said and hung up.

Jon walked in with his suitcase as Susan was dialing. She hung up her phone. "Hi, Jon, I have to make a quick call," she said as she walked out to find another room to make her call. "I will be right back."

He mouthed 'thank you and walked over to talk with Steven.

CHAPTER 20

"Hi, James. It's Susan Graves. You called?"

"Susan, thanks for calling back. Is it true that Eastland is going to consolidate and go public?"

"James, I couldn't comment even if I did know," Susan said slowly.

"We haven't talked to them since they turned down our offer last year. We know they have a debt issue that should be raising its head right about now. We think we can sweeten things for them and make it easier," he said.

"Have you talked with them?" she asked.

"No, we've just heard the rumors about them and an IPO, but we haven't seen anything yet. I thought I would see what you knew," he said.

"Look, is it okay if I have Timothy Martin at Evergreen Securities call you? See what he says," Susan said.

"Does that mean we are right?" James asked. "They are crazy to try to go public, especially now."

"It means you should talk with Timothy," she said. "I will call him now. If I don't reach him, I will call you back," she said as she hung up. She had just been through a quizzing with Steven—she was in no mood for another.

She then called Timothy. "I have a new possibility for Eastland," she said.

"It can't wait until you're here in New York Friday?" he asked.

"No, I just got a call from James Jameson of Jameson Properties," Susan said. "He has heard rumors that Eastland is going public. I believe he has an offer to buy them pretty much ready to go. He would like to discuss it with you. You know Jameson has the funds to do this—James may want a couple hundred million of debt financing, though."

"They walked last year, so why now?" he asked.

"He believes that Eastland is desperate if it's trying to go public now. My guess is that he thinks they will let him save them the heartache of being a public company," she said. "Because of his negotiations with them last year, I'm sure he knows that goal is to buy out some long time investors and refinance some debt. He can do that, if the price is right."

"That would be nice—this is a tough one, you know. Can we be his bankers?" he asked.

"If you can get Jameson cheap debt financing, I would say yes, he'd be happy to have you," she said. "You need to talk to your internal ethics guys, though."

"Who would you represent?" Tim asked.

"Possibly no one," Susan said. "We represented him last year when he was looking at buying them. But then, we could have a conflict because we represent you in this deal—Eastland also might object, although I don't think there is a basis. If you decide it's serious, I will notify our ethics committee to see if we could do it by getting consents. That is if either of you wants us. I just emailed you his contact information."

"I'll call him now, but plan to be in New York Friday," Tim said.

"Okay, call my cell if you decide anything about Jameson," Susan said. She then called Jane. "Can you have someone on the ethics committee call me right away? My first choice would be Sandra Wainwright. And can you transfer me to Marta, please?"

Jane obliged and put Susan through to Marta.

"Any chance you could find someone to authenticate the age of some documents for us?"

"How old?" Marta asked. "And where's my trivia?"

"They could be as early as maybe first or second century CE." As Susan was saying the date, she realized that Marta was going to want to know what exactly she was doing. "Things that are equal to the same thing are also equal to one another," Susan added.

"Are you still at Chase?" Marta asked. "And what the hell do you mean by your last sentence–wait, never mind, that's Euclid, is that related?"

"Um, yes, I am still at Chase. We are in the Trust Department and someone has a bunch of old documents in a safe deposit box that we have been asked to look at," Susan said. "Euclid is your trivia for the favor. Sorry, I couldn't think of anything else."

"Call your friends at the Oriental Institute," Marta said.

"I can't. I need a non-university expert. It's a favor for a professor, so it needs to be off the radar. Hmm, I just thought of someone…anyway, let me know if you find anyone. It's kind of a rush."

"Do you want a language analysis or just materials? What exactly are you and Steven working on?" Marta asked.

"I'll stop by when I get back to the office," she said. "I'll tell you more then. Maybe I can drag Steven along."

"I need more trivia, then," Marta said.

"Crap, um, the first reference to a spy operation is in Numbers 13, when God directs Moses to send spies into Canaan. Bye." She had just hung up with Marta when her cell phone rang again. It was another Peale, Curtis number, so she guessed it was Sandra Wainwright.

"This is Sandra. Your assistant said to call you."

"Thank you. I have a situation that may develop quickly. May I give you the facts?" she asked.

"Something interesting, I hope," Sandra said.

"Well, we may get squeezed out, but we have at least one client who wants us to stay in the deal." Susan then described the issue and the time frame for when a decision would have to be made. Sandra was more hopeful than Susan that the firm could represent Jameson, if Evergreen agreed to get other counsel. Susan now had to wait for the decision; she never liked having something she needed to be out of her control.

As she was going back to join Steven and Jon, she saw Sarah coming.

CHAPTER 21

"Susan, we have to close up in 15 to 20 minutes, do you need any help?" Sarah asked.

"Sorry, I knew it was getting late. I saw Dr. Christiansen come in, so we can finish up. Steven will probably need to be here tomorrow," Susan said.

"Dr. Christiansen?" she asked. "He just left to catch his plane, but he signed the authorization to close his safe deposit box. I'll be back with the authorization for you and Steven to open the new safe deposit box in a couple of minutes."

Susan walked back to where Steven was and asked, "Jon left?"

"Yes, he was worried he'd be late for his plane with rush hour starting soon. He just came in to say we could reach him in his office tomorrow."

"And what's this about a new safe deposit box?"

"He wants the documents in one without his name on it. I took a picture of a few of these pages with my cell phone. Can you print them for me at your office?"

"A new safe deposit box?"

"Yes, Sarah is bringing documents to sign for the new box. She will need your ID. She already got a picture of mine. We need to think about getting these to a conservationist."

"By the way, New York is off until Friday," she added. "Why do we need a new box?" she asked, but Steven ignored her. "Stupid mustache," she grumbled. "Probably glued on–it's not grey enough."

"Maybe he dyes it," Steven said.

Sarah and her assistant walked in with the new safe deposit box and the document for signature. "Susan, can you give my assistant, Alice, your ID so we can make a picture of it?" Sarah asked.

"Of course," Susan said as she handed Alice her ID.

"Sarah, what did you think of Dr. Christiansen?" Susan asked as she and Steven signed the authorization for the new box.

"Well, I don't know," she hesitated as she wasn't sure why Susan was asking.

Steven looked up—he had already started putting things into the new box. "Don't mind Susan, Sarah. She just found out she has a free evening, so she's looking for trouble."

"Steven," Susan said exasperated. She turned to look at Sarah. "Sorry—it's been a long day. At least I'll be home tonight." She looked over at Steven; he was still carefully putting things in the new safe deposit box. Susan was glad that he did that part. Susan hated handling anything of value unless it was absolutely necessary. She had even once declined the offer to hold the skull of the 1.5 million-year-old Turkana Boy in the Nairobi Museum's Strong Room. The thrill was to see it, not to risk the possibility that she might drop it.

"Ms. Graves," Alice said still holding Susan's ID. "Here's your ID."

"Sorry, I must have been daydreaming for a second," Susan said as she took the ID back and put it in her pocket. "Steven, are we ready?"

"Yes, dear," he said. "Ladies, I'm done with the safe deposit box for today. Sarah, I will be back again tomorrow, probably mid-afternoon. I would like a room again, if possible. I wonder...might there be one with a window? I would like a slightly different light to read in."

"Alice, can you reserve one for Mr. Graves?" Alice nodded as she picked up the safe deposit box.

"Thank you Sarah. Thank you Alice," Susan said as she and Steven left the room. They rode down the elevator in silence.

CHAPTER 22

When they got outside, Susan said, "Let's go to my office first. I need to check in with Jane, and then we can go see Marta. We'll see if she's come up with any suggestions for authentication. I thought of David Siskin."

"David would be perfect, if we can find him," he said. "Don't forget, we need to send Bob the spear point."

"That's fine, but you should call Bob to alert him," she said as she walked over to the Security Desk to get Steven a pass to go upstairs. "Jane was getting a FedEx box ready when I left. I also need to print those pictures for you." They went through the gate and then, as they got on the elevator, Susan asked, "What do you think about all of this? Are we stepping into something we shouldn't?"

"It could be interesting, but it's too early to tell," Steven said. "Maybe it will be your first retirement project. Where is David?"

"I think he's teaching in Shanghai," she said. "Steven, even if that the language is appropriate, shouldn't we get the parchment dated?"

"That would be good," Steven agreed. "There's no use dating the material if there are anachronisms in the text. David would be great for the Hebrew and Aramaic text–I could use some help. Besides, he's Israeli, so he must have good experience at recognizing fakes too."

"Jane should have his card. We probably should clear it with Jon first, though. I told David to call Mary when he got to Shanghai."

Susan's cell phone rang as they walked off the elevator. It was James.

"Well Susan, good work. Tim is talking with Eastland now. If they are amenable to a sale, we will meet in New York tomorrow at 10:00 a.m."

"Hopefully, just you, Evergreen and Eastland, right?" Susan asked.

"That's right, principals only—and Evergreen," he said. "No lawyers tomorrow. Tim said to tell you to still plan to be in New York on Friday."

"I'm on the 7:00 a.m. flight Friday and then back to Chicago in the evening, I hope," she said. "So you might buy Eastland?"

"Actually, yes. By the way, a different group at Evergreen will do the financing we want. They can get other counsel, so I get you."

"Subject to my Ethics Committee decision—I asked for clearance a couple of hours ago, just in case," she said. "I better call and give them an update. Are you going to New York tonight?"

"I'm already in New York," he said. "That's how I heard the rumor. There are more loose lips in this city than Carter has little liver pills. I'm having dinner with my daughter, tonight. She lives here now. Anyway, I'll be here at least through tomorrow night. That way, I will be in New York on Friday if there is anything more to talk about."

"It's Seattle, right? Is she still with the *New York Tribune Herald*?" Susan asked.

"She is indeed with the *Herald*," he answered. "Too bad you aren't coming to New York until Friday. You could join me and Seattle for dinner tomorrow night."

"Well, it would be nice to see her again; it's been a couple of years. Tell Seattle I would love to grab a cup of coffee with her while I'm in New York Friday, if her dad doesn't keep me too busy," she said before hanging up.

"Anything new?" Steven asked.

"This may be a sale now. If so, we may or may not get kicked out of the deal," she said. "New York is still on, but it's still Friday, not tomorrow. If it's a sale, I could be done in a couple of weeks at most." She started to do a little dance, but thought better of it.

Steven kissed her head. "I hope it's a sale."

"Me too," she said as she picked up his hand and kissed it.

They headed for her office. Susan stopped at Jane's desk and told her she could leave. "Um, before you go, could you see if Marta has a few minutes to chat with me and Steven? We will stop by her office in about ten minutes."

After they sat down, Steven asked, "What should we tell Marta?"

Jane popped her head in. She had her coat on and was ready to leave. "Did you forget this?" She asked as she set the FedEx box on Susan's credenza. "Marta said she is free. She has an engagement today, but she will wait for you," Jane said. She left before Susan could come up with something else for her to do.

Steven asked again, "What should we tell Marta?"

"I'm thinking," Susan said. "Any suggestions?"

"Let's just tell her everything. It might be good to have her think about this," he said. "You and she can pick the crap out of this puzzle."

"Okay, but let's not name Jon for now. I don't want to betray his desire to keep this quiet, at least not yet. She will be quite happy when I tell her you wanted her opinion."

Steven's phone rang. He whispered to Susan that it was Jon calling. He talked for a few minutes. "Well, that's good, I guess," he said when he hung up. "Jon's at the airport. He said to make it clear that he found the 'Clovis' point in his shed and it's not from his site. He apologized for 'thrusting' the spear point on us, but he could barely bring himself to even look at it."

"Well, let's thrust this on Bob. If you call him now, I can get it off to him tonight."

"I tried earlier ...can't you?" he started.

"No, he's your friend. I do not want this damn thing here if it's stolen."

Steven reluctantly called Bob—he didn't mind once he was on a call, he just didn't like starting them. "All set," he said when he hung up. "Bob will look at it, but he's leaving tomorrow afternoon. He'll be out until April 23. He may not get to it until he's back. Now, you get to explain our project to Marta. All I know is that I want to spend some time with those documents."

"All right, let's go see her. By the way, did you make an inventory of the documents?" Susan asked.

"Actually, Jon had a list based on what he thought the language was. I started with it. I looked at each piece long enough to add a short description–basically, a key word or two. Then, I started reading the Ammonius letter, because it was on top," Steven said. "Oh, there's a little list I will bug you with later," he said smiling.

"Okay, so according to your inventory, there are the two Latin pieces and a Latin fragment, the Greek 1292 cover and the three copied letters, an Aramaic piece, an Aramaic fragment and a Hebrew fragment, right?"

"Yep."

"Get me the spear point so I can put in the FedEx box," she said. "It's in my top desk drawer."

"Susan, didn't you unwrap it? It's still in bubble wrap."

"I didn't want my finger prints on it. I just left it in bubble wrap. Jon carried it that way."

"Well, I am going to look at it, but I won't touch it. Why did he say it was Clovis? There's a chip in it. There's no oxidation or anything like that on the rest of the surface, so it may be recent. Maybe that's why Jon thought it might be a fake. Does he find projectile points at his site–would he be that familiar...."

"He said 'or something,'" she interjected. "I was bugging him about Clovis because he wasn't telling me why he was here. I don't think he meant it was Clovis–he said it looked like a damn fake, except that he doesn't swear. He did run our seminar on Clovis all those years ago, so he must know something. And, damn it, he just told you on the phone that it wasn't from his site. Wrap it up–we have to go."

"Susan, if it isn't from his site, why was it there?"

"I don't know. Wrap it up, we have to go or we'll miss Marta."

They headed down to Marta's office by way of the mail room where Susan dropped off the package for Bob.

CHAPTER 23

"Marta, dear," Susan said as she knocked on her open door. "Do you have a few minutes to chat with us? We know you have an engagement tonight, so we won't take too long."

"Are we going to talk about Berlin or why you were at Chase?" Marta asked. "Hello, Steven my love. Do come in."

"What is this about Berlin?" he asked.

"I got so wrapped up at Chase that I forgot to tell you that Marta's going to Berlin at the end of May. She can spare a little time with us if we want to go."

"Berlin would be fine, but tell Marta about Chase," he said.

"Marta, we need your help, right Steven?"

"Yes, dear."

"First, did you come up with any authenticators?" Susan asked.

"I will have at least one name by tomorrow morning," Marta said. "What about your friend? The one we met in Israel last year? Dan Siskin, right? He was nice…too bad he's married."

"Close, it was David Siskin," Susan said. "We are trying to find him. And he's divorced–lost opportunity there, Marta. He's supposed to be teaching for a year at Jiao Tong University in Shanghai. I asked Mary to look him up last month. I haven't heard from either her or David, so I'm not sure he's there yet."

"Mary Chen?" Marta snorted. "She is too far on the fringe–for me at least," Marta said again. "I'm still bound by certain, um, things, so I have to be careful."

"She's brave enough to sit with you," Steven chuckled. "Are you chicken, Marta?"

"She is very entertaining," Susan said. "She's damn smart, too."

"She would have to be over 100 for all of her stories to be true," Marta argued.

"Most of them are true–just not specifically about her. Sort of the way the Chinese mix up 'he' and 'she.' She mixes 'I' with 'someone else.' That's all," Susan countered. She enjoyed bringing Marta and Mary together from time to time; they started sparring the minute they saw each other.

Steven broke in. "Marta, Mary knows all of the best restaurants in Shanghai. Anyway, Susan, let's tell Marta about Chase. Do you have a few minutes?"

"To hear more about why you two spent an afternoon at Chase and want an authenticator?" she asked. "Are you nuts, Steven? I'm so bored this week…."

Susan gathered her thoughts for a minute. "Good, you can help us."

"We need a disinterested person; that would be you, Marta," Steven added. "And an authenticator."

"Well, then perhaps you would tell me why you need my help before I have to leave."

"Okay, an old archaeologist friend from our graduate school days visited us today. We hadn't seen him in years. Basically, he found some documents at his site and he wants us to translate them. Steven has looked at them and he thinks they may be written in the Greek used in the time of Constantine, meaning very roughly 300 CE. There also are documents in Hebrew and Aramaic."

Steven chimed in, "it's referred to as 'Koine Greek, with 'koine' meaning 'common.' It's an early precursor of modern Greek, which I know you can read, Marta."

"Well, I could twenty years ago; now, I can probably only sound it out because the Cyrillic alphabet is basically derived from the Greek alphabet, with some added sounds represented. It doesn't mean I still have enough vocabulary to understand it," Marta said. "Susan had a few years of Russian in high school and college, so that's why she found Greek so easy. Do you remember the first time we went to Athens, Susan?"

"That must have been 35 years ago—we had just finished our sophomore year," Susan said. "We didn't know any vocabulary then, so we had no idea of what anything other than a name meant. We were just sounding things out, but it was still kind of fun."

"I'm sure it was charming," Steven said glaring at both of them before he continued. "By about 225 CE, early Christian theological writings were often being written in Koine Greek, so, it's also known as Biblical Greek. The word 'biblios' in Koine Greek originally referred to a 'scroll' and then came to mean 'book.' Of course, 'biblios' itself likely derived from the Phoenician seaport, Byblos, because papyrus was exported to the Aegean from Byblos."

"One of the largest finds of papyri was at the Villa of the Papyri in Herculaneum," Susan added. "The library of Lucius Calpurnius Piso Caesonius was at the Villa; it was preserved when it was buried in the eruption of Mount Vesuvius in 79 CE. Lucius was Julius Caesar's father-in-law."

Yes, well if both the word usage and dating of the parchment are positive, there is a chance that we are looking at very old documents."

"Steven, we should just tell Marta how she can help. She has a date of some sort tonight." Susan saw Marta smile.

"Go ahead, Susan."

"Oh crap—I meant you, Steven. Anyway, Marta, the rub is that the documents were found buried in a box in the US. The box has a date on it, 1307 to be specific. Our archaeology friend brought the documents to Chicago; they seem to be on parchment and they look old. He has asked us to see if they're real."

"If he's an archaeologist, he must be at a university. Why didn't he just take these to someone there?" Marta asked. "It's Penn, right? You said it was your graduate school days. No, wait a minute. You really think you may have old parchment documents that were buried in the US in 1307? That's not possible, is it?"

"We've been asking ourselves that same question all day," Steven said. "Obviously, we think the answer is 'no'."

"Our professor is very nervous about this. The really fishy part is that there is a separate document written in Latin that is much later. It is signed by a Portuguese sailor named Joham Ovelho who is a knight, but hopefully, not a Templar knight. That alone would be enough to make a laughing stock of the professor. He's about to retire and says he doesn't want to get involved in some big controversy like Templars in the US. At least that's what he told us."

"Templars? Oh, for God's sake, doesn't that just mean it's all a fake?" Marta asked. "Why are you even thinking it might be real?"

"Well, because whoever faked the much older Greek documents did a damn good job of it," Steven snorted. "The piece I focused on reads like a document from the time of Constantine."

"There is no reference to a Templar anywhere in what we have seen so far," Susan said. "We are just afraid that someone will jump to that conclusion because Joham appears to be a knight and the date on the hasp is 1307. We do know that the Viking, Leif Erikson, made it at least as far as Newfoundland by about 1000 CE. Also, there was a study in Iceland that found mitochondrial evidence that an American Indian woman settled in Iceland around 1000 years ago." Susan loved the genetics of human migrations—this was a rare occasion when she could actually throw in a genetics tidbit.

"Damn it, Susan, what is mitochondrial evidence?" Marta asked.

"It's a way of looking at matrilineal inheritance," Steven said. "Iceland has a large genetic database of Icelanders. They found that an American Indian woman probably came back to Iceland with some Vikings about 1000 years ago and raised a family there. They knew it was a woman because they had used matrilineally–inherited mitochondrial DNA."

That's going to Europe—the wrong way, but somebody had to go get her." Susan said. "But the point is...," Susan hesitated. "There simply isn't any good evidence of a European presence in Maine before Columbus."

"If these documents are real, we think they must have been brought here by a Pilgrim in the 1600s," Steven said. "That pretty much has to be how they got here. And, of course, the box would have to be buried much later than it was made."

"So you want David to help you see if he thinks these documents are real? Steven if you have read them, what are they about?" Marta asked.

"Ask me later—I need David's help on the Hebrew and Aramaic ones. I also need more time with them. It's not hard to translate the words, but sometimes it's hard to understand what they actually mean," Steven said. "Maybe Susan will help me since she doesn't go to New York now 'til Friday," he added.

"Slow down," Marta said. "Who is this professor? Would I know him?"

Susan looked at Steven. "Our spy friend here will find out anyway, but I say we make her work for it. Is that okay?" Susan asked him.

"Your call," he said.

"Marta, the guy is only a few months from retirement," Susan said. "He's afraid that someone is playing a bad joke on him to get even. He suspects a colleague who was up for tenure but didn't get enough votes."

"Our guy voted against him," Steven added. "A friend of our guy's son told our guy that the colleague knows he voted against him."

"Now that makes sense. He comes to you because you will understand his problem and give him a good read confidentially."

"Precisely, Marta," Steven said. "He is a Paleo-Indian specialist; Susan had us take an elective seminar on Clovis with him 30 some years ago. Since we were studying biblical archaeology, it was pure folly—that may be why he remembered us. Anyway, he says he saw Greek and Hebrew, freaked and came to us."

"Archaic, Steven," Susan said. Rarely did she get a chance to correct Steven. "You know how I love those Clovis points at the Field Museum, Marta, but that wasn't his specialty."

"What, oh yes, you're right, Archaic," Steven said. "He was an interesting guy, so we used to talk with him after class—coffee sometimes. I think we probably even had dinner with him a few times. But to be honest, we haven't seen him since leaving grad school."

"Marta, this could be some type of scam," Susan said. "You know, somebody thinks they can get us to say something that's fake is real. But why us? I can't imagine that anyone would consider us as experts. I mean we left graduate school so long ago."

The only thing that ends up being logical is that, as Jon said, we can at least tell him if it is an obvious hoax, so he doesn't look silly," Steven added.

"Anyway, we do need to get someone to determine the age of the documents," Susan added. "However, I don't really want to explain this to someone who doesn't know we aren't 'crackpots.' As I'm telling you this, I'm feeling sort of stupid. I mean, it should be obvious that these are fakes, given where he found them."

"But it isn't," Steven said.

Susan hesitated for a minute, and then said, "Steven, maybe he found the box or the documents somewhere else. Or, maybe someone gave it to him and the Maine story is just a ploy. And we cannot discount that it was an old box—like an heirloom—buried by a Pilgrim in the 1600s—that's most likely, I guess. Marta, we need you to tell us if we are being stupid or missing something."

"Did you just give me another clue—Maine?"

"Yes, his site is in Maine," Steven said. "So far, the documents look good, too. I haven't seen any vocabulary that is anachronistic and the topic is very interesting."

"May I at least know this professor's name, for God's sake?" Marta asked. "I mean you have asked me to help."

"Not quite yet," Susan said surprising herself. "He is being very cautious; he didn't even want anyone to know he came here to see us. Steven, I think I want to analyze this a bit more—if it is a hoax, then we should be protecting him, right?"

"Well, based on what you have told me, I probably can figure it out," Marta said. "I'll just go to the Penn website and look for an old man with a site in Maine who is a Clovis expert."

"Whatever, at least I can say that I didn't tell you," Susan said trying not to convey her discomfort. She wouldn't correct Marta's premise that Jon was a Clovis expert.

As Marta started to respond, Susan saw Wilhelm raising his hand to knock on Marta's open door. Marta followed her gaze to the door. Susan could swear Wilhelm looked surprised to see her there, but why would he be coming to Marta's office unless he was looking for her. "Hello, Wilhelm. You've met my husband Steven, right?" Susan said to break the silence. She smiled; Wilhelm had recovered from whatever it was that had surprised him.

"Yes. Hello, sir," he said.

"Hello, Wilhelm. You can call me Steven. I understand you are going to New York Friday with Susan. I always hate being there when I am too busy to go to the museums. Are you here to see Susan or Marta?" he asked. Steven turned and winked at Susan. They were both sure that they had seen Marta smile.

Marta saved Wilhelm by stepping in to say, "I asked him to stop by. Someone said he was an art history major, so I had a question for him."

"Yes," Wilhelm said. "I was an art history major at Michigan," he said looking relieved.

"We know Wilhelm, and Marta does love art. Statues of Greek warriors, isn't it Marta?" Susan said as drolly as she could muster as she looked at Marta. She turned back to Wilhelm and said, "Marta knows every inch of the *Wounded Warrior* in the Met. It's a Roman copy of the fifth century Greek bronze."

"You, dear, were the one who dragged me all over Rome looking for statues of naked men bending forward, so we could compare their 'hangs' from behind," Marta countered.

Susan turned back to Wilhelm and changed the subject. "I know Jane told you we aren't going to New York now 'til Friday. Come see me tomorrow around 10:00 a.m. We can decide what needs to be done if this morphs into a sale. We should still be pretty close."

"I called the O'Keefe guy—he claimed he didn't know anything," he said.

"I've already talked to Sandra Wainwright in our Ethics Group about the possible change," Susan said. "Steven, are we ready?"

"Yes, dear."

"Marta, I'll talk to you in the morning, but remember, no information to get those names for us. In the meantime, we will look for David. Steven, I have to stop by my office, and then we can go eat."

"So, I guess somewhere in there, you told me I can't know who the professor is, right?" Marta said.

Steven answered, "Not for another day or two, Marta. We promised to keep this confidential. Besides, you'll figure it out on your own. Nice to see you, Wilhelm."

Marta started to say something, thought better of it, and said, "Susan, call me when you get in tomorrow. I may have those names for you and I want to hear more about Chase."

"Thanks," Susan said as she and Steven began to leave. "Remind me to tell you about the crystal the professor found and the stolen spear point that someone put in his shed."

"Stolen what?"

"Actually, that one we aren't sure about…see you tomorrow."

"Wait," Marta said. "I'm doing you a favor, so where's my trivia?"

Susan looked at her. "No trivia damn it. I'm hungry."

"Please," Marta laughed. "There, you know I don't say that often."

"You haven't been to the Sinai, but here's one related to our new project. Legend has it that Constantine's mother, Helen, ordered that St. Catherine's Monastery be built to protect the 'Burning Bush,' mentioned in Exodus 3.1. You can still see the bush there, it's just not burning anymore," Susan said.

"The Monastery actually was built a couple of hundred years later by Justinian in 550 CE. How's that?"

Steven added, "as Susan can tell you, the actual name of the Monastery is 'Sacred and Imperial Monastery of the God-Trodden Mount of Sinai,' with no mention of St. Catherine or St. Helen. Mind you, none of this actually was reported by Eusebius who, of course, was a contemporary of Helen and her son, Constantine. The story was later appended to the Latin translation of Eusebius' *Ecclesiastical History* done by Rufinus. Oh, and Susan thinks it might be a type of creosote bush."

"Thank you, Steven," Marta smiled.

"I'll throw in a Tucson tidbit for you," he said. "Tucson's Catalina Mountains were originally called the 'Sierra de la Santa Catarina' for St. Catherine; they were named by Father Kino in 1697. Then, between the early 1890s and 1902, they began to appear on maps as the 'Catalinas.' The name, Santa Catalina Mountains, became official in 1902. Of course, the Tohono O'odham call Mount Lemmon, the tallest peak, Babad Do'ag or 'Frog' Mountain."

"Thank you dear, but Susan told me that a very long time ago…so did you."

"We are off to Shaw's for dinner," Susan said as she grabbed Steven's hand. "The Tucson Historical Society has an old map where they are called 'Santa Catrina Mountains,'" she added as they left. "And Helen may have built a small chapel to St. Catherine, just not the monastery."

"What stolen crystal?" Marta asked, but it was too late—they were gone.

CHAPTER 24

"It looks like Marta has herself a new boy," Susan chuckled.

"I thought that might be why Wilhelm was so surprised to see you in her office. He must know you're friends…I guess he didn't expect to find you there. What do you think—a tryst or recruiting for the NSA?"

"I would bet heavily on a tryst being a part of whatever he was there for," Susan said. "You know she broke off seeing that guy we didn't like…the one who didn't like to travel."

"He was too ecstatic about medieval history for me. However, he was more age appropriate for her," Steven said. "Marta needs someone who likes what she likes, not just a night time pal."

"As far as I'm concerned, if Wilhelm isn't too tired to do his work, he can be her night time pal. She does get bored you know…and, he might actually be very entertaining. I hate to say it, but I don't really know him too well. Arthur was a hoot…," Susan added.

"She slept with him too?" he asked looking stunned.

"No, no, I just meant that I know Arthur better. You know Arthur is gay; that wouldn't stop Marta from trying, though. I just don't know Wilhelm that well," she said.

"That's a relief, I guess. And I do enjoy dinners with Arthur. Does he like his new job?" Steven asked.

"Yes, he does. Crap, it's never good to have an office romance, let alone with someone who is twenty some years younger than you. Plus, Wilhelm is up for partner. He'll have to be careful of jealousy and all sorts of things. I can imagine there would be a long line of men and women ready to have an evening with her."

"Are you jealous?" Steven asked.

"What on earth can they talk about? She has been everywhere and done who knows what. And he's only about 31," Susan added. "He had never been to New York when we hired him. He does learn fast though. Oh, I guess they wouldn't necessarily be having long conversations, either."

"But are you jealous?" he asked again.

"Oh, for God's sake, Steven—you're stuck with me. I mean, who else would be tracking down Templar documents buried in Maine? It was hard to find someone like you, actually, you may be one of a kind," she smiled. "I just hope Marta is careful. The guys here are pretty brutal—if nothing else, they will be pissed that she isn't after one of them. Then, because she has powerful contacts in DC, they will take it out on poor Wilhelm. She will have to let them do it, sort of a cost of war thing. Unlike you, she didn't have a successful business to sell, so she still has to work to maintain her lifestyle."

"She makes as much as you, right?"

"Possibly more in some years, Steven."

"Well, then she can afford to have a little fun. Besides, her mother has a ton of money."

"Maybe she likes the intrigue—sneaking around as she did in her old NSA days. If so, Wilhelm's in big trouble, I bet. He blew her cover…never mind, let's go eat." She was chuckling now—Marta got caught. "I was serious about Shaw's for oysters, since I have the night off now. Is that okay?"

"You know I would go anywhere for good oysters," he said. "Let's go—I want to relax, so I can plan out how to review this stuff."

"I really need to have this deal end, Steven. I hate being away from you for even a day. First though, I left those pictures I printed for you on the printer—we need to stop and pick them up."

"What if you just didn't go to work tomorrow? We certainly don't need any money; we can go out to the ranch for a while and sort out these documents," he said. But he knew the answer–Susan would never leave a client in the lurch like that. They would just have to wait until the deal ended. As usual, he knew nothing about what she was working on. He took her hand as they left her office. He did want her to quit.

"Good evening, Mr. and Mrs. Graves, same table?" It was good that Rafael, the Maitre d', was there. Susan got the reservation on 'Open Table' as they were leaving her office, but they needed Rafael for the table they liked.

"Yes, Rafael," Steven said. "I hope you have some good West Coast oysters tonight."

"And the raspberry pie, of course," Susan added. She was so glad that New York got pushed to Friday. She wouldn't have been home until about 11:00 p.m. Then, she would look for leftovers from what Steven, who would be in bed already watching a movie, had made himself for dinner. While she ate standing in the kitchen, she would go through the mail, then go to bed about midnight. She would leave for the airport by 5:15 a.m. to catch the 7:00 a.m. flight to LaGuardia. She was having dinner at Shaw's with Steven, instead.

"I'll send the waiter right over," Rafael said. "I know we have Hama Hamas tonight," he said before walking away.

"Steven, before we get to Jon, did you find that Thomas Jefferson quote I mentioned to you last night?" Susan asked.

"Yes, I did," he said. "'The day will come when the mystical generation of Jesus, by the Supreme Being as his father, in the womb of a virgin will be classed with the fable of the generation of Minerva in the brain of Jupiter,'" he read from his iPhone. "Almost three hundred years later and that day hasn't come yet," he added.

"Jefferson was too optimistic," she said. "People like religion as a religion, not as a philosophy. I think they need a 'cause,' or something to care about. You know...football on Friday night at the local high school and church on Sunday. Or, they need the 'hope' of something better–that is so sad."

"Well, John Locke once said 'the care of every man's soul belongs to himself.'"

"Steven, some people need the 'comfort' religion provides. Also, the philosophy behind what they believe is good, so maybe religion can help them find that goodness in their soul. And there are ministers, nuns and priests who actually do good works. On the other hand, having an organized system of pederast priests whom the Church protects is beyond despicable. And those mega-church ministers who get rich on peoples' miseries should be in jail. I mean, crying in front of a TV camera when they have been caught with a prostitute…trying to blame the prostitute."

"Calm down, Susan–it's your night off. And I do agree with you, religion itself isn't necessarily bad; it's the organized type that leads to all of the strife in this World. There isn't enough introspection–just greed and a desire for wealth and power. Ah, here's our waiter, have you decided what you want to order?" Steven asked.

"Hello, Agnes. My husband is trying to be funny, since we always order the same thing," Susan said.

"You do have to choose the oysters," Agnes laughed.

"A half dozen of the Hama Hamas and a half dozen of the Malpeques," Susan said. "Is that okay, Steven?"

"Only a dozen?" he asked knowing the answer.

"Yes, a dozen. I'll have a glass of the A to Z Pinot Noir," she said. "Steven, iced tea?"

"Yes, an iced tea, please," he said. He waited until Agnes left, and then asked, "Since I got your quote, does that mean you really will do a book on 'Freedom from Religion'?"

"Not really, I'm just weaning myself from 'Tetris,'" Susan said. "I do have hundreds of quotes from our early U.S. Presidents and a ton of notes. But I'd rather work with you on Jon's project."

"Any others from Thomas Jefferson?" he asked.

"I have some stored in my iPhone. How about, 'It does me no injury for my neighbor to say there are twenty gods or no god.' Or, 'Christianity is the most perverted system that ever shone on man.'" She paused as the oysters were being delivered, and then added, "Anyway, Carl Sagan once said that '...Jefferson attempted to excise the Pauline parts of the New Testament. There wasn't much left when he was done, but it was an inspiring document.' Let's eat."

"Jefferson and his brethren knew that a theocracy cannot coexist with a democracy," Steven mused. Egypt is a good example. They elected the Muslim Brotherhood, believing that it was the beginning of a democracy. But then the Brotherhood immediately began enacting religious mandates that doomed women unless they wrapped themselves up and hid in their homes. Christians too, since attacks on the Copts skyrocketed."

"It was just another type of dictatorship, except that only one religion as interpreted by one faction is permitted. These far right religious nuts are trying to do the same thing here. The Founding Fathers were saying government can't enforce a religious belief any more than it can favor one over another. If you let that happen, then all of a sudden you have schools that can't teach evolution."

"Kennedy had to convince people that he wouldn't let the Pope's desires trump what the people of the United States wanted," Steven said shaking his head. "He had to make it clear that his country was first, not his religion. Why was keeping one's religion out of government a big deal then, but not now? It's taken 2,000 years for Christianity to deviate from the original teachings; in only 300 years we have corrupted the brilliance of our founders."

"Too much sports, Steven, let's get back to Jon, so I don't get too irritated," Susan said as the entrées arrived. "If you send me a picture tomorrow, I can look at the Latin 'Joham' letter."

"Will you have time?"

"I think so," she said. "I will feel better if I can get comfortable with it. I do hope a Pilgrim brought the box here as an old family heirloom. By the way, did you look at Jon's pictures of the box? I was thinking maybe we could get Jackie Santanos at the tree ring lab to take a look if there are any tree rings showing."

"Jackie?" he mused. "Do you think she might?"

"Well, yes," Susan said. "She does like you, you know. Do you think it's doable from a picture?"

"I suppose it depends on the picture," he said. "If the pictures are good, she might be able to tell if it's brand new."

"If she asks, we'll say a friend found a box on his property in New England," Susan said. "That little white lie wouldn't bother you would it?"

"Not if you tell it," he answered.

"Did you leave the pictures at Chase?"

"No, I have the box pictures in my brief case. We can see if any of them show tree rings in the wood," Steven said as he pulled out the pictures. He gave half to Susan and began looking at the rest. "I think I might send a picture of the leather cover insignia to Dr. Alberts. I won't tell him where it was found, so the 1267 date won't excite him too much, but he might recognize the insignia."

"Good idea," she said when she finished her last sip of wine. "Did you bring the picture of the insignia?"

"No, sorry, I forgot. Look at this one—the rings are still visible and very well defined," Steven said.

"Steven, that's perfect. If we finish dinner by 8:00 p.m., we can stop at FedEx over on Michigan Avenue, and have it to Jackie tomorrow morning. What luck, I mentioned it as a long shot," she said.

"It still is a long shot—we can tell her it may be about 400 years old in a voice mail. Should we send her the originals?" he asked.

"I think so. We'll make a copy at FedEx. If they are good, we will send those. If not, we will send the originals. I'll put a return envelop in for her to use to return them, so the originals could be back here by Friday. Let me just make sure which FedEx offices are open until late - we don't use them as much anymore."

"How was the garlic shrimp tonight?" he asked as they got up to go.

CHAPTER 25

Marta chose La Luce for dinner that night with Wilhelm. It was her favorite Italian restaurant. She also heard Susan say they were going to Shaw's, so they wouldn't run into each other.

La Luce was like stepping back in time—something Marta enjoyed. It was under the Lake Street El, almost all the way to Ogden where the Lyon harp factory was still making harps. Susan saw the restaurant from a cab once many years ago—there was a bright red and green neon sign and a bunch of black limos parked out front. She thought it might be one of the Mob's old dinner hangouts, but called anyway to see if it was open to the public. It was now their favorite place in Chicago for Italian food. They never did find out why all the limos had been there that one night.

Marta couldn't begin to name all the restaurants she had been to with the Graves. Sometimes it was hard to convince people to go with them when they heard the address—like Milon in New York down by Alphabet City—Marta loved their cheese puri and spicy chutney. One of Susan's friends had 'found' it down around First Avenue and Fifth Street back in the '80s. The neighborhood was still "iffy" then, so much so that Susan often offered cabbies an extra $10 to take them there.

"So, am I in trouble?" Wilhelm asked Marta bringing her back to reality.

"For what?" she asked, a little irritated at being interrupted while thinking about food.

"Ms. Graves saw me come to your office...."

"Wilhelm, if you're in trouble, it's because you were supposed to meet me downstairs, damn it." Marta was truly irritated now. "I've known Susan for over 35 years and I've known Steven for almost as long. They are sitting at Shaw's eating oysters. I would be with them, except that you and I have a few things to discuss before your final NSA interview on Monday."

"Thanks for setting it up in Chicago," Wilhelm said. "I do need to be in the office for the Eastland deal."

"Dedication goes a long way. As for the Graves, they will spend five minutes deciding whether to order all West Coast oysters or half West Coast and half PEIs. They may then spend five minutes discussing why you came to my office. But probably not…Susan hates to speculate and Steven doesn't like personal things. So, they might just order their oysters and then continue discussing a very interesting project that someone asked them to do today," Marta said.

"If she thinks I am interviewing with the NSA, she may kill my chance at partnership," he said. "God knows what she would do if she knew…what should I do?" he asked.

"You should focus on things that are actually important; damn it, you should have asked me about the interesting project I just mentioned. Susan is leaving next month after the partners' meeting, assuming the Eastland deal is done by then. So, wherever you are then, she won't care," Marta said.

"You must be joking; she loves her job." Wilhelm couldn't imagine Ms. Graves with nothing to do.

"Yeah, I love my job too," she laughed. She beckoned to the waiter that it was okay to come over. She ordered her favorite, fried calamari appetizer, lasagna with the meatballs, and a glass of the Barbaresco. Wilhelm decided that he would have the veal–he followed Marta's lead with the Barbaresco.

When the waiter left, she started again. "Susan's philosophy was to work as hard as she could so that she could make enough money to do what she wanted. She said it was a teleological way to tolerate all of the bullshit she's put up with all of these years. She has plenty of money, now. So, if you were her, would you rather be getting on a plane at 7:00 a.m. Friday to go to New York and hear people bicker over how many millions they will get, or to Paris to see the new installation of the Louvre's Islamic collection?"

"I never thought of it that way," he said. "They call her a career-driven bitch around the office."

"That's stupid, but I also know that if you work with her, you end up damn well trained. Then I can send someone like you to the NSA."

"Her assistant, Jane, told me I was an idiot if I agreed with what they say."

"Good for Jane!" Marta exclaimed. "But do you…oh, never mind, you are too smart to say 'yes' to that one. Anyway Susan is fine with it," Marta laughed. "I know I have a bad rap, too–kind of a badge of honor."

"She knows?" he asked incredulously.

"Of course she knows." Marta was laughing now. "Jane says that my reputation here in the Chicago office is that I'm 'cold.' She said I shouldn't feel bad…they would come up with something worse, if I were here more."

"Seriously?" was all he could get out.

When Marta stopped laughing, she looked at Wilhelm and said, "You need to question things a little more. You do know she orchestrated your partner nomination, don't you?" Marta asked. "It cost her a lot politically."

"Mr. James told me I was being nominated for partnership," he said defensively. As Wilhelm said it, he realized that Mr. James hadn't actually said he had recommended him.

"Oh, for God's sake," Marta said sarcastically. "She had to agree to back that son-of…," Marta stopped mid-sentence. She needed to be a little careful–she liked having an office in Chicago. They left her alone because she opened lots of doors for the DC people. Nevertheless, a little tact might not hurt from time to time. She started over. "Susan had to agree to back a certain partner for the Board, among other things."

"Then, why didn't she tell me?" he said looking skeptically at Marta.

"Maybe I should rethink my NSA recommendation–you are a dumb ass. Susan had to horse-trade for the votes; hearing that you should make partner from your 'Mr.' James was part of the deal. So, he tells you and, when he asks you join his group, you do because you think that Susan didn't recommend you. She can live with herself by helping a dumb ass who did well make partner. That's the way it works, Wilhelm."

Wilhelm sat thinking. He knew some office politics, but the partners pretty much keep their issues to themselves. Once in a while you would hear something, but not like this.

"Oh, and when I said that the NSA needed someone, she said you might want an option. She's leaving anyway."

"Someone mentioned a sabbatical—is that it?"

"No, she is done."

"What about Jane?"

"Jane is 64 and she wants to work until she's 67," Marta said. "She'll work for the Graves, if she doesn't want to stay at Peale, Curtis. The Graves do have other lives outside of work. Personally, I hope they spend more time out at Susan's ranch."

"Ms. Graves has a ranch?" he asked incredulously.

"Yes, just outside Tucson," Marta said. "That's why Steven threw in the Tucson trivia for me. She only has about 10 acres now, but it was much bigger, something like 25,000 acres. We used to ride out to a cabin that her dad called the 'outhouse.' It was rustic, but it had running water. You could see more stars out there than I knew existed. I had never seen anything like it growing up here in Chicago. As I said, it's mostly gone now, but the stars and the birds are still there."

Marta remembered asking Susan if she could visit her ranch. Susan said they would look for phainopeplas along a wash where desert mistletoe had built up on the mesquite. She said the phainopeplas loved the mistletoe berries that came out in late winter and early spring. Marta had immediately looked for a picture. It was beautiful—jet black, with a red eye and almost a cardinal kind of top knot—'phainopepla' meant 'shining robe.' "Have you ever gone bird watching, Wilhelm?"

"No." He was having a hard time with this new information. He couldn't imagine Ms. Graves riding out to a cabin to spend the night looking at stars.

Wilhelm knew she had a degree in archaeology, but he always thought of her going to a major metropolis to try a new restaurant or see a museum. He could see Marta riding a horse off into any sunset, but Susan Graves?

"When I'm there, a whole new world opens, all of a sudden there are birds everywhere–the sounds alone are amazing. There are roadrunners, quail, doves, hummingbirds and my favorite, the phainopeplas, to name a few. Susan keeps a basin of water on the ground for one of the roadrunners. He is almost two feet long–just walks over and takes a few sips and then saunters back out into the desert. At night, you can hear the great horned owls calling back and forth across the canyon."

"I've never even been west of the Mississippi," Wilhelm said.

"Nor had I before I went to Tucson for college." She chuckled to herself; she and Susan met for coffee after Marta confessed that she'd never been on a horse. Susan's friend, a gay guy, was there with her–what was his name? He said he was there for 'support,' after Susan introduced him. That got Susan chuckling–Marta was braless when she entered college those many years ago. Susan composed herself, took another swig of coffee and then looked at Sebastian–that was his name, 'Sebastian.' All she said was "please." Sebastian called Susan a wimp, then turned to Marta and said, "Look girlie, Susan says that you'll beat yourself to death with those if you don't wear a bra on a horse." It turned out to be damn good advice.

"Do you go often?"

"Whenever I'm invited," Marta said. "I usually get out there only for the holidays. I was last there for Christmas, even though they are atheists."

"And you're Jewish."

"Yes, and I...well, maybe I'm agnostic. But I am Jewish whether I believe in God or not. Steven's parents were Catholic, he objects when Susan teases him that he was born a Catholic. I think Steven is correct. What with having to be baptized and all, you are not born a Catholic. But I was born a Jew, just like I was born an American. Anyway, you can still celebrate holiday seasons like Christmas," Marta said. "Time off is time off."

"And what about Tucson? I saw the movie, *Tombstone*, a few years ago. Does it look like that?"

"They probably filmed *Tombstone* in Tombstone. It looks pretty much the same today as it did a hundred years ago. Tucson is a modern city."

"Did they have cattle?"

"No, Susan's grandparents stopped ranching before World War II–they leased the land to a neighbor who had cattle. Her dad spent World War II at the University of Chicago and Los Alamos. He went back to the University of Chicago after the War where he met Susan's mom. They lived in Chicago until his parents died in an accident in the early 60s. They moved to the ranch, but then they divorced when Susan was ten, which would have been 1966. Her mom moved back to Chicago. Her dad moved to Seattle where an aunt had settled. Susan went with her dad, but by the time she was 16, she was spending most of her time at the ranch again, helping Pete run it."

"And who is Pete?"

"Pete was the caretaker; he ran the ranch. Susan handled the finances, and Pete's sister, Adele, who was a retired schoolteacher, made sure Susan got an education. I never met Adele–she died just before I met Susan. Her dad died shortly after she graduated from college. That's when most of the property went to the conservancy to cover estate taxes and pay off her father's debt. Susan carved out a life estate in the cabin for Pete. I miss Pete–so many stories. Ask Susan about the Red Ghost sometime."

Wilhelm was staring at Marta; he was sure she was toying with him.

"I don't think I ever knew Pete's last name," Marta said absently. She was lost in thought for a moment. Then she sang to herself, 'Cool water...'"

"What?" he asked.

"It's a song called *Cool Water*. An old guy and his mule imagine they see water in the desert. It was one of Pete's favorite songs. It's by Bob Nolan; he also wrote *Tumbling Tumbleweeds*, one of Susan's favorites."

"You met Ms. Graves in college?" he asked.

"We were freshmen," Marta said. "I was from Chicago, but I picked the University of Arizona because I had always wanted a horse–seems pretty stupid now. Susan was in my Russian class; I heard she was from a ranch. I saw her one day in the library; she always sat in the art section, so I went over and asked if I could see it sometime. It was better than I imagined. Those were her 'poor' days, as she would say. She lived on scholarships and what she could earn from...well, whatever."

"Whatever what?"

"She got Pete to start running bird outings up into the canyon. She also had some friends who worked on sites in Mexico and had access to whatever they wanted. She never admitted it, but I think she and Pete helped distribute what her friends brought back once in a while—probably where she learned to network so well. God knows what else she and Pete were doing. She told me once that Pete's motto was 'Do, don't whine'."

Wilhelm realized he didn't know much about Ms. Graves, but this was a little farfetched. "I just don't see her growing up on a ranch."

"Tucson was still pretty rural in the 70s. Pete had friends, old guys like him, who were still prospecting and living in old ghost town shacks. He would visit them sometimes; Susan would go with him if he was just dropping off some booze. After he died, she would take a fifth of Jack Daniels out a couple of times a year to one of the old guys who lived down near Dragoon—for Pete's sake, she told him."

"Now, I know you're joking."

"No, I'm not.... Susan once said that Pete taught her how to see the desert. She taught me and then Steven. I can still name at least a dozen chollas and prickly pears; those are the *opuntia* cacti. A line of palo verde trees and slightly denser plant growth in the distance—almost like a green line—means there's a river or wash there. When you get to it, you find an entirely different habitat. And when the summer monsoons roll in, the lightning is even more spectacular than you see here in Chicago. After the storm rolls through, there is a smell in the air released by the creosote bushes—scrubby little things, but such a wonderful smell after the rain."

Wilhelm was staring at Marta—he had never heard her being so personal. "How old was this Pete?" he finally asked.

"He was in his 80s when I met him," she said. "He was two and his sister, Adele, was seven when his family came to Arizona. His father worked the railroads, so one day in about 1890, the family just got on the train somewhere and got off in Tucson to start a new life. There were maybe 5,000 people in Tucson then. Pete said there were more cows than people. He didn't want to work the railroad like his dad, so he signed on with the old Empire Ranch when he was ten. Except for a stint in the Army during World War I, and two years working at the Arizona Inn, he was at the Empire Ranch until he was 50. That would be about 1938. That's when he went to work for Susan's grandparents and there he stayed.

"Susan always thought Pete would die somewhere up in the foothills. Instead, he died of a heart attack near the old cabin in 1980, just before we started law school. That would make him 91 or 92 when he died. He was still running bird outings up into the canyon when he died."

"So, you've been close friends for a long while," he said, not knowing what more to say.

"Closer than you can imagine, sweetheart. Some of those evenings in that cabin were pretty cold," she chuckled. She saw she had gotten a new level of interest out of Wilhelm. He was digesting what she had just said, but trying to maintain his sophistication and not ask questions. Susan would kill her if she knew that Marta was sitting here telling Wilhelm so much about her, but since Marta wasn't going to tell her.... She probably went too far with her last comment, but then Wilhelm needed to understand that people were seldom two-dimensional. If he was going to work for the NSA, he needed to be more observant of what was around him. Otherwise, they would stick him in some dull area of research.

"Well, I'm grateful that she recommended me," he said.

"She tries to do what is right," Marta said. Hopefully, Wilhelm meant what he said. But then, as Susan always said, "People can think what they want. In the end, you have to be able to live with yourself."

"And what about Mr. Graves?" he asked.

"Oh, crap, it's almost 9:00 p.m.," Marta said slowly. "This has to be the last little tidbit.... He and Susan both had a science background, but somehow they both ended up at Penn for graduate school studying biblical archaeology. I'll never understand why they did that, since they are both atheists. Anyway, I was in London for graduate school, so I didn't meet Steven until just before law school here at the U of C. She already had him, or I would have grabbed him. I would have divorced him within a year, though. He can be very witty and he is brilliant, but he is very high maintenance. He does take good care of her, though. I don't know how they could live without each other. I hope they never have to find out."

He sat thinking for a minute, and then said, "One more, what's with her cane?"

"The bank of an arroyo collapsed under her and her horse. She jumped clear, so her horse wouldn't come down on top of her, but broke her ankle when she landed. I guess it's more like an arthritic joint these days. God, I miss her damn old horse."

Wilhelm sat for a few minutes as he finished his wine. "She can really just walk away from here?" he asked.

"Yep, with her cane of course. Now let's talk about the interview while we finish dinner. Wait a second…I just need to send Susan a quick text message."

"While I'm being a dumb ass, what does PEI stand for," Wilhelm asked.

"Prince Edward Island, where there are several varieties of Malpeque oysters. Okay, we've wasted enough time with pleasantries, let's practice. I want these guys to think I recommended someone they would want. So, what skills can you bring to the NSA?" Marta was back to the business of Wilhelm's interview Monday.

CHAPTER 26

"Steven, I just got a text message from Marta," Susan said.

Steven could see Susan was chuckling. "What does it say? Did she think of an expert for us," he asked. He knew from Susan's chuckle that it was something else, but he thought he would ask anyway.

"No, it just says 'BOTH,' and it's all in caps," Susan said.

"Both?" he pondered it for a few minutes. Then he said, "Oh, I get it. That's not good. Your partners won't be happy with her if they find out she had Wilhelm hired out from under them…or, if he stays and they find out she is sleeping with him. I know she worked for the NSA in an atmosphere of risk taking, but that was more calculated."

"And it was years ago…at least they won't shoot her for this," she laughed. "I guess she knows what she's doing. It'll be easier if he goes to the NSA, so it moves outside the office. She can sell the NSA job in the office as a political move that's good for Peale, Curtis. Anyway, I'll have Jane try to find David."

They ordered two coffees and raspberry pie a la mode to share. "Here's your other coffee," Steven said as he passed Susan the coffee that had been poured for him. He didn't drink coffee, but always ordered one for dessert, so that Susan could have a steady stream of coffee. Waiters didn't always realize that she could down a cup like a shot. "Now, finish the pie," Steven said. "I want to get home and mull this over some more before I call Jon in the morning."

"Bob will have the spear point by 10:30 a.m. tomorrow morning, you know."

"It seems like it's a separate matter. I think Jon panicked because of everything else. It probably belongs to a student who picked it up somewhere. He or she may have put it behind Jon's favorite trowel for safety—you don't want to leave an artifact out in the open so that it can be stolen," he laughed.

"So, which documents did you take pictures of? I didn't look when I picked them up off the printer."

"I took a picture of the one I was reading; it's the letter from Ammonius in Alexandria to Constantine's advisor, Hosius of Cordova. He wrote it just before the Council of Nicea. He is arguing that Jesus did not say he was God. I also have the one written by someone in Rome complaining that the translation of Paul is incorrect. We were lucky they had the Hama Hamas tonight. Pretty good, huh?"

"They were delicious," Susan said. "So was the pie. We should go, did you pay?"

"All done," he said after he paid the check. "Off to FedEx?"

"Yes, the one on Michigan down by Madison is open until nine. I think that's closest," Susan said. "So, you think I just took some kid's spear point and shipped it off to Arizona?"

"Yep—and now we'll go ship the pictures of somebody's box off to Arizona."

CHAPTER 27

Susan was at work by 9:30 a.m. She had done her emails and checked voice mail in the cab on her way in. She was still waiting to hear from Sandra Wainwright and Evergreen. She had at least an hour, since the meeting with Jameson and Eastland had only just started. She decided to search the Internet for David Siskin. She should have called the Institute last night to see if he was still there. If not, someone there would know where he was. It was already almost 7:00 p.m. in Jerusalem.

As she logged on, the page opened to the Arts Section of the *New York Tribune Herald*. She had to find David, but she would just spend a minute to see what was happening in the art world. The Turner show would end soon; Constable was in the show as well, but they definitely would miss the show. She loved the American Luminists, but the British painter, Turner, 'the painter of light,' was always her real favorite. Maybe it was because some historians suggested he had cataracts in later life, which changed his perspective. Or, maybe it was that Thomas Moran had studied him. She liked Constable too, especially the stormy skies, his 'chiaroscuro of nature,' as he described the clouds and the sun....

She was interrupted by a rap at her door and looked up to find Wilhelm. "What's up?" she asked.

"Nothing really, just checking in," he said. "I left a message with my guy at O'Keefe Hopper this morning when I got in. He hasn't called back yet."

"We probably won't hear anything from the big guys for about an hour. I've already asked Patrick Mason in real estate to be ready to go tomorrow. Damn, I hate this waiting…you can get some 'brownie points' by asking Patrick if he needs any help getting ready."

"I'll check with him. Do you have a minute?"

"Of course," she said. He was still standing there, so she added, "Sit down if you have time."

He came in and sat. "Ms. Krejci said I should ask you a question."

Oh crap, Susan thought. What had Marta put him up to? Well, there was one way to find out. "Yes?"

"Who was 'Old Pete'?" He had decided last night that he would ask Ms. Graves this, so that he could gauge how much of what Marta told him was true. If Susan knew about this Pete, then maybe some or all of the rest was true.

"Old Pete?" Susan asked. Damn Marta, she must have been chatting away about something involving her. "Marta must have had too much time on her hands last night," she smiled. "She loves to tell stories; god knows how she makes them up so easily."

"Ms. Krejci mentioned your ranch in Tucson," he said.

"I'm sure you call her Marta, so you can call her Marta when you are with me," Susan said. So Marta had told him something about her—maybe trying to humanize her for Wilhelm. Susan did that for Marta when people told Susan that Marta was 'cold.' Marta just had to get to know you, and like you, before she would waste any effort—a lot like Steven in that way. What with the 'BOTH' email, and now this, it seemed pretty obvious that Wilhelm had overcome those hurdles with Marta.

"Sorry, Marta then," he said. "Do you really have a ranch?"

"No, I don't have a ranch," Susan answered. "Was that the question or was it about Pete?"

"Both really," he said bravely. "It didn't seem like you would have a ranch. Sometimes she tests my ability to tell if she is making something up. I am just checking to see if I passed her test."

"She does like to play. Steven and I do have a house outside Tucson where I keep most of my library. The house is on about ten acres at the base of the

Catalina Mountains, which I guess is what she meant. I inherited that from my dad and I inherited my love of books and archaeology from my mother and her father; they were librarians."

"But...,"

"We still call it a ranch sometimes, because it used to be much bigger. My great-grandparents had about 25,000 acres. It was a ranch then, but not big for Arizona. The old Empire Ranch in southern Arizona was a big ranch– it had over 1,000,000 acres. Sandra Day O'Connor's ranch near Duncan, Arizona had something like 200,000 acres. You were an art history major... did you know that in 1832, George Catlin said there should be a 'Nation's park, containing man and beast' out West? Anyway, Saguaro National Park is straight south of us."

"So, you *do* have a ranch?"

"We did until my dad died; I was the fourth generation. Unfortunately, when he died, I had to give most of it away. It went to a conservancy group, which bought it for enough to pay off all of my dad's debt. He could have paid off his debt if he had lived to be 100, but he didn't. As I said, we kept the house and a little land. Oh, and in Marta's defense, we still had the 25,000 acres when I met her. And Pete was our foreman, is that what she told you?"

"Yes, she also said to ask you about the Red Ghost," Wilhelm said.

"Oh, for God's sake–she must have been enjoying her wine, too. Anyway, Pete was a real old timer. He swore he saw some of the last wild camels in the desert when he was a kid, but I don't believe it," Susan said laughing.

"They don't have camels in Arizona," he protested.

"Not any more. I'll give you the short version of the 'Red Ghost.' It was an old cowboy tale about one of the camels imported to the Southwest by Jefferson Davis when he was Secretary of War under Franklin Pierce. There weren't many of them, so almost no one knew what they were." She looked nervously at her watch.

"I didn't mean to interrupt," he said when he saw her look at her watch.

"Checking the time is a bad habit…I need somebody to slap my hand to train me to stop," she said. "Anyway, Jeff Davis imported a herd of camels to Fort Davis in Texas. He figured they could handle heavy packs over long distances in the dry heat of the Southwestern deserts. They worked pretty well, but the Civil War came, the camel troops were disbanded and the men were sent back East to fight for the Union. The camels were let loose in the desert. Of course, after the War, the railroads expanded through the West. That pretty much obviated any need for pack animals."

Wilhelm sat there listening. He had been an art history major; he did love the history part.

"Had enough?" Susan asked.

"Not at all," Wilhelm said. "I know very little about the West and I haven't traveled much. As I told Marta, I've never been west of the Mississippi."

"Speaking of railroads, you can thank the South for the Transcontinental Railroad and its route from Omaha through Utah to Sacramento. Lincoln wanted that route, but the Southerners wanted a more southern route. When the South seceded, old Abe got Congress to approve the railroad along the route he wanted."

"It was approved during the Civil War?" he asked.

"It wasn't completed until about 1869, but it was approved in 1862. Sorry, I ramble sometimes."

"No, please—I love history," he said. "I guess I forgot that men like Davis and Lee held positions in Washington before the South seceded. So, you did mean Jefferson Davis, the President of the Confederacy, right?"

"Yes, and, by the way, Tucson was part of the Confederacy. Anyway, nobody knows how long the camels survived on their own, except that Pete swore he saw some even though he wasn't born until 1887. Personally, I think they came out of his whiskey bottle."

Wilhelm was beginning to see why Marta and Susan were friends.

"Pete was a great storyteller. When he told Marta about the Red Ghost, he had already gone around and put little tufts of hair from one of the neighbor's reddish brown cows in strategic places." Susan was having a hard time telling the story without laughing. "Marta…."

Jane poked her head in and asked, "Can you take a call from Mr. Jameson?"

She immediately got serious and said, "Tell him Wilhelm and I will take the call. Can you see if I might have given you a card for David Siskin?" she asked just before she picked up the call on speaker. "Hi James, any news?"

"Are you ready to come to New York tomorrow," James asked.

"Are you buying Eastland?" Susan asked.

"Indeed we are," he said. "I came in with an offer price this morning that's about 5% higher than our offer last year. Evergreen thinks Eastland will go for it. Given their accounting issues, his is an easier way to deal with that debt issue. You'll represent us."

"Wilhelm Galianos, who's been running the deal with me, and I will be there tomorrow, if we get clearance from my Ethics people," Susan said. "We're working on that." She looked at Wilhelm when she hung up. "Well, it sounds like we will still need to be in New York tomorrow, but you and I will become superfluous. Can you give Patrick in real estate an update?"

"Yes, of course," he said. "Anything else?"

"I don't think so. I need to get Sandra lined up and you need to go see Patrick." Susan sat back for a minute. She definitely would be able to quit now in a few weeks.

"Susan, I have something you want here," Jane said as she walked in and handed Susan a card. "You gave me David's card at some point. Naturally, I filed it, so I could find it."

"You found it? That's great."

As Wilhelm was leaving, Susan called after him, "Ask Marta why she screamed like a girl when she saw those tufts of cow hair. Tell her I will remind her, if she feigns amnesia."

"You'll get Wilhelm killed that way, Susan," Jane said. "I want the card back when you are done with it."

"Okay," Susan said, "back to work I go." She then called Sandra–things there looked good. She needed to let Patrick sit a bit, so that Wilhelm would talk to him first…that would show Patrick that she trusted Wilhelm. Then she would follow up with Patrick so his nose wasn't bent out of shape because she sent an associate to talk with him. First, though, she would track David down. She called Jane, who was back at her desk now, and asked her to see if Marta would be free for lunch.

It was almost 10:30 a.m. She picked up the phone to call the Hebrew Institute in Jerusalem, first. Crap, she thought, it was already 6:30 p.m. in Jerusalem. She would try to get David there, anyway. There was no answer at the Institute, but David still had a voicemail box there. She left him a message and then tried his cell.

"Shalom?" David said.

"David, it's Susan Graves."

"Susan, it's good to hear from you," David said. "Are you and Steven in Chicago?"

"Yes, we are, but where are you?"

"Well, you caught me in Tel Aviv today. I'm visiting relatives," he said. "I fly back to Shanghai next Friday, April 26. I'm teaching a seminar at Jiao Tong University there, but we have a break right now."

"I'm glad I found you," Susan said.

"I finally had coffee with your friend, Mary, in Shanghai couple of weeks ago," David said. "When she found out that I had been associated with Mossad…well, then we just bullshitted each other with more and more outlandish stories. I am going to dinner with her and some of her friends when I get back to Shanghai. How much is true?"

"Probably as much as yours, David," Susan laughed.

"Not much, huh?"

"Very funny—as far as I can tell, it's all true; it's just not always something she herself did. I suspect you do the same, right?"

"The quality of the story is what counts."

"I agree. Mary once said that she tells her stories with honor wherever they are from. I like that…and I love the stories, so I don't really care."

"I will continue to enjoy her and her stories then," David said. "And I will practice my own on her—it'll be a good exercise, she's damn sharp."

"David, Steven and I just had a very interesting project dropped on us. Someone brought us some documents that look to be very old. We would like to get them dated to see if they might be real. First, though, we want to see if there are any anachronisms or structural errors in the language. We also may need some help with translation, although Steven has been doing pretty well. Would you possibly have a little time to talk with Steven about it?"

"Paper, parchment or papyrus?" he asked.

"What?" Susan asked. She had just been distracted by a note Jane handed her telling her that Sandra was holding for her. "Oh, sorry, I got distracted for a second. I think it's all parchment," she said. "It's definitely not papyrus."

"I always have time for you and Steven, but I have even more time for parchment," he said. "Where is it from?"

"May I have Steven give you a call?" she asked. "Any time that works for you. I could tell you a bit, but then you would have to hear it again from Steven, and he has been working with the documents."

"Can you at least pique my interest?" David asked again.

"To make a long story short, an old friend came across a small stash of documents in an unexpected place," she said. "He came to us, because he thought we could tell him if they are fakes; he can't because he's a New World archaeologist. Steven thinks they are interesting enough that we should try to enlist your help. He says the language is holding up well, a lot seems to be Koine Greek, but he would like to talk with you as there is even one in Aramaic."

"Well, I'm heading to Shanghai next week," he said. "Do you have pictures you could send me?"

"Look, let me just have Steven call you. Do you have any time today? I know there are only a few more hours there…."

"Susan, you have a call waiting don't you…tell him to call me now, does that work?"

"David, you sure it's okay? I know you are with your family, but I also know Steven is anxious to talk to you," she said.

"I have been here in Tel Aviv for almost a week with my relatives. I am ready for an interesting conversation," he said reassuring her.

"Thanks, I will tell him to call you now. Maybe we'll see you in Shanghai," she said before she hung up. She then picked up Sandra's waiting call.

"Hey, Sandra," Susan said.

"Hi, I think we are okay on this, but do you have any problem if we get consents from Evergreen and Eastland?" Sandra asked. "I have a form drafted. I just sent it to you by email. It's short."

"Give me a second and I'll look at it. It is short, it looks fine. So, we need it from Eastland and Evergreen. Since we represented Jameson last year, should we get something from them as well acknowledging that we were representing Evergreen in this deal before it was a sale?"

"It won't hurt," Sandra responded. "Do you have any thoughts on getting signatures?"

"Hold on, let me get my associate, Wilhelm Galianos, on with us. He should be able to track down the signatures." She called Wilhelm and connected him to the call. "Sandra, I have Wilhelm on with me and I just forwarded your email to him. Wilhelm, we will need consents from Evergreen, Jameson and Eastland, if we are going to be in New York tomorrow. I'm going to run–I am late for a call." Susan completed an email to thank Sandra by the time she hung up.

CHAPTER 28

Steven called Jackie when he got up. There was a two hour time difference, so he left her a message about the FedEx and returning the originals. He then left Bob a message saying that they had sent the package as discussed. He would track down Bob's assistant later today.

Steven started on the 'Ammonius' letter again after the calls. He would get pictures of the two Latin documents for Susan when he went to Chase.

He decided to call Jon at 10:45 a.m. Chicago time which was in an hour, since Jon said he taught in the morning. He would go over his plan with Jon, and find out how often he wanted to get updates. It would take a good week to get an outline of each document and the fragments. He also would ask Jon if he could use David to help, although he wasn't yet sure that he would give him David's name. Susan and Steven both agreed not to tell Jon that they had sent a picture of the box off to Jackie yet.

The phone rang at 10:30 a.m. It was Susan. "Are you calling to tell me that whatever you are working on will be a sale, and you are ready to come home?" he asked.

"Pretty close," Susan said. "I should be done by the end of May, but we still have to be in New York tomorrow. If all goes well, I will pass the torch to the real estate group and be done. More importantly, I just spoke with David. Jane had his card—I guess I gave it to her at some point. He is waiting for your call."

"That's excellent!" he said. "Do you have time for me to tell you what I found this morning?"

"Yes, dear," Susan said. "I actually have some time until about 2:30 p.m. when I have to go see the Big A, but David is waiting for your call."

"Five minutes won't hurt and he'll forgive me when I tell him why I'm calling," he said. "I decided to spend some time with the second letter this morning. I am about half way through the 'Ammonius' letter, so I decided to spend a little time with the second letter to see if anything jumped out."

"And," Susan asked.

"And there was a reference to Hadrian," he said.

"Hadrian?"

"Yes," he said. "Actually, it is his Greek name, not the Roman, so it is Adrianos, of course."

Susan could tell he was having a hard time controlling his excitement. "But Steven, that would be, um, what, around 130 CE, right? That's almost 200 years before the Council of Nicea met. Is the letter that much older than the Ammonius letter or is it just quoting Hadrian?"

"It's quoting Hadrian. The letter is from about the same time as the Ammonius letter. It quotes where he says that devotees of Serapis called themselves Bishops of Christ and that those who worship Serapis are, in fact, Christians. Do you know the one I mean?"

"Yes, of course," she said. "I know the Hadrian bit, but why is it quoted in your letter?"

"This time, it's a letter to Eusebius. It also complains about Nicea; it argues that the 'Bishops' are making up Christianity. Actually, it complains that they are borrowing from the Pagan religions and suppressing the 'true' Christian teachings. It quotes Hadrian to make the point that there are few true Christians. For a finale, it says that Jesus never said he was the 'Sun' God."

"Steven, how on Earth would this letter end up in Maine in a box with a date of 1307 on it?"

"I have no idea," he laughed. "I imagine they were put in the box after 1307, and not in Maine. Someone brought them here later; how much later depends upon the reliability of Jon's dating of where it was found. But then, why did they bury the box?" he asked.

"Salem Witch hunts, maybe?" she suggested. "They didn't want to be caught with something complaining about Christianity, so they buried it. Steven, do you think these are real?"

"It's too early to tell, but it's plausible," he said.

"We both know there are a lot of very good fakes out there," she said.

"Yes, you already mentioned Morton Smith and the letter from Clement of Alexandria he supposedly found at the Monastery of St. Sabas," Steven said. "People still don't know if he forged the letter perhaps as a joke that got out of hand or if he found a real letter. Meanwhile, as with Smith's piece, the subject matter of our two letters is interesting."

"It also could have been forged in medieval times. Anyway, I still like the argument that the letter Smith found was 'too Clementine' to be written by Clement," she said. "Seriously, though, it might be interesting even if these are forgeries," Susan said. "Someone trying to get an enemy labeled as a heretic, maybe."

"Yes, dear. Anyway, this letter …can you help me translate it?"

"My Greek is too rusty–the best I can do is man the dictionary for you. I wish I could come do it now, but I have a bunch of crap to finish. How about the 'Templar' letter? My Latin is still okay. Can you email me a picture of either that or the other one that is Latin?"

"I can send you the Templar one, but it may not come out too clearly," he said. "There are a couple of spots where it is pretty well worn, but see what you can make out."

"I have some time to kill, so I will see how much I can read," Susan said. "And, I am coming home early again tonight; I hope to leave right after I meet with Big A. Steven, David is expecting your call. I emailed you his number while we were talking. Oh, send me the insignia."

"Okay, but just one more thing," he added. "The Latin fragment is a list of the Seven Churches of Asia."

"As in Revelations 2 where John of Patmos sees the 'Son of Man' walking among seven lamp stands, which are supposed to be the Seven Churches of Asia?"

"Yes, for whatever reason, just a list. Can you still name them?" Steven joked. "I have the list in front of me."

"You are stalling because you don't want to call David."

"I will call David as soon as we hang up," he answered. "But if you can't remember...."

"Damn it, Steven. They are named in Revelations 2 and 3; they are Christian communities living in seven Roman cities located on the Asiatic side of Western Turkey. The easy one is Ephesus–the church that had forsaken its first love. Then there is Pergamon–the church that needed to repent, Philadelphia–the church that had endured patiently, Sardis–the church that had fallen asleep, Smyrna–the church that would suffer persecution, and the last one, Laodicea–the church with the lukewarm faith. Is that seven?"

"Six. You need one more," he laughed. "All of the cities were located on ancient trade routes between the East and the West."

"I know where they are. Oh, I forgot the one we haven't been to, Thyatira–the church that had a false prophetess. And for a bonus point, Ephesus represented the apostolic or one true church founded by Christ, and Laodicea represented the apostate church that had departed from the faith of the apostles. How's that?"

"Good job, now I will call David," he said.

"I will see you soon," Susan said. "And email me the Latin piece you toad."

CHAPTER 29

Susan had just hung up when Marta came in. She was in a beautifully tailored sky blue suit with a cream colored silk blouse. No jewelry, Susan noticed… must have been a late night. Susan never could bring herself to wear anything other than grays and navies–blouses were either silk or softest cotton, but still either cream, white or a very light blue. She would sometimes get risqué and wear a sweater in a brighter color over the blouse, but that was mostly on weekends. "Nice color–stunning as usual."

"How sweet," Marta said. "Nice slate grey for you today. Any trivia for me?"

"Truffles are mushrooms that have evolved to grow underground," Susan said without thinking. "Did we have a nice evening?"

"Don't know, I wasn't with you," Marta answered. "So, truffles are mushrooms?"

"Yes, they release an aroma so that the pigs can smell them. The pigs dig them up, causing release of the spores, which then grow into more truffles," Susan added. "Global warming is affecting them though, so eat all you can. Do you have any names for me? I did find David. He was on break in Israel, so Steven is probably talking with him now."

"I have one name for you and one favor to ask in return," Marta said.

"Okay, who?" Susan asked.

"First the favor, then I'll give you the name," Marta said. "How's that?"

"Well, I probably don't have a choice, so go for it."

"I had dinner last night with Wilhelm," Marta started. "Don't give me that look, it was just dinner. I wanted to call around to see if I could find anybody for you, so I sent him home after dinner. He's interviewing with the NSA. I want you to ask him a question today when you see him."

"I didn't give you a look and you texted me the word 'BOTH' last night—in caps, I might add," Susan said defensively. "Perhaps you forgot he was there after dinner—you are getting old, you know."

"Oh, yeah, I did say 'BOTH,' didn't I? Anyway, he was getting on my nerves. May I please tell you the question?"

"I might not see him until after lunch," Susan said.

"Well, the sooner the better,' Marta said. "The question is 'when did Pete, your caretaker at the ranch, come to Arizona?'"

"Damn it! You were jabbering last night. Wilhelm already asked me if I lived on a ranch this morning. Then he asked me about Pete and the Red Ghost. Pete must have told me the Red Ghost story 50 years ago when I was a kid. Crap, I think I forgot to mention that they called it the Red Ghost because they would find tufts of red hair, and nothing else at first. Besides, camels are more brown—I never did quite understand that myself. I did manage to tell him you screamed like a girl though…."

"Susan, slow down," Marta said. "You've said 'damn it' or 'crap' at least twice now in about 5 seconds. That may be a record for you. I only told him that when we were younger, you kept me warm on cold nights at the cabin. I didn't tell him you still do sometimes or anything like that." Marta was having fun now.

"What? Damn it, damn it, damn it. You can't do that. Wait a minute, I kept you—oh forget it, damn it."

"Okay, you broke the record you just set."

"Marta," Susan couldn't think of anything else to say she was so irritated.

"I was trying to show him that you are multi-dimensional," Marta laughed. "And that I am pretty irresistible."

"Marta, you can't tell some kid here something like that. It's bad enough that you were weaving Pete into your nonsense, but…."

"Why do you care? You're leaving soon…oh, and you shouldn't call Wilhelm a kid. *They* might not like it."

"Touché, Marta. I guess there isn't anything I can do about it now." Susan never liked the idea of mixing work with her private life…it gave people too much power over you for stupid things. Marta, of course was an exception, but then Marta was in DC a lot and their work rarely overlapped.

"Wilhelm has a final NSA interview on Monday," Marta said. "This is to see how observant he is and to teach him that there may never be a stray fact that you don't need."

"Good for him, but this is stupid–and Pete was our foreman, not our caretaker."

"You have to be nice to get the name I have for you," she said.

"Marta, you know how hard that is….I kept you…damn it. I was a naïve kid from a ranch when I met you." Susan was glaring at Marta. She gave up after a minute, it was Marta after all. "Why can't you just ask him?"

"Because, coming from you will throw him off. Just ask him, okay? And as for being naïve, you were selling pot from the library, dear–and you were a quick learner. Actually, you probably already had lessons from that rancher you knew on the east side of Reddington Pass–Bess, right?"

"This better not be one of your tricks…."

"It'll take two minutes, Susan."

"I never sold pot from the library. I may have taken a few orders there, but I never sold it there. And I sent Pete over to service Bess, except then he sometimes wouldn't come back for a couple of days and Adele would get mad." The thought of Pete made her stop glaring at Marta. Pete, Adele, Bess, even her parents, were like ghosts now; they didn't seem real anymore…it was getting harder to conjure them up. "Damn it, I'll ask him after lunch. Where's my damn name?"

"There is a guy in Zurich named Hershel Gruber. He can tell you whether the parchment is old or not. He has impeccable integrity. He can do other things as well, like dating the ink used, if you need it. It is parchment right?"

"Yes, according to Steven...I just told David the same thing. I've only seen two pieces up close–those were definitely parchment."

"What's the difference?" Marta asked.

"Damn it, Steven just quizzed me–you know I hate that. And if you're trying to humor me, I'm not mad at you anymore, although I might be if I were staying at Peale, Curtis."

"I really don't know the difference," Marta said.

"Crap, parchment is animal skin and papyrus is reed, actually the pith of the reed. Papyrus originated in Egypt and was used as far back as the third millennium BCE. Parchment came in about 250 BCE, as a substitute for papyrus when for some reason I don't remember, Egypt stopped exporting it. It was perfected in Pergamon, where there was a library that rivaled the one in Alexandria. It differs from leather in that leather is tanned and parchment is treated with lime. Egyptians wrote on leather scrolls as far back as maybe 2500 BCE. The nice thing about parchment is that you can scrape it clean and reuse it. The reused parchment is called a palimpsest."

"That's the title of one of Gore Vidal's last books," Marta said.

"His memoir–perhaps he was trying to re-write some of his life, but it was still there under the surface. I wouldn't mind writing over some parts of my life–evidence of the original would still be deep down there–indelible unfortunately. Anyway, even when a parchment has been scrubbed clean, there are techniques today that sometimes can let you read what was scrubbed away. You know that Gore Vidal is my favorite author of fiction."

"Yes, and you know he's mine too," Marta said. "Do you remember how the 'Liar's Paradox' goes? I saw it first in one of his novels."

"It's '[t]his sentence is false,' right?"

"Yes, and...?"

"If the statement in the sentence is false, then the sentence is true, but that then contradicts the statement that the sentence is false."

"Perfect," Marta smiled. "If the statement in the sentence is true, it contradicts the statement that the sentence is false."

"One more tidbit–a very famous palimpsest was found by twin sisters at St. Catherine's in the 1890s. It was a fourth century portion of the New Testament on parchment–it's known as the *Syriac Sinaiticus*. A biography of saints had been written over it."

"I like it when you aren't crazy busy," Marta said. "You can be quite entertaining."

"That is so sweet, that I'll give you one more paradox. This one is from Socrates, who came up in a conversation yesterday. He said that because he knew he was not wise, paradoxically, it made him wiser than so-called wise men who thought themselves wise, because he was aware of his own ignorance."

"Yes, well anyway, I checked with some friends. Herr Gruber still does work for anybody who can afford it. We used him on a stash of historical documents stolen from a museum. It was years ago when I was stationed in Vienna. I've never met him, but he does have an excellent reputation. Does that make up for my indiscretion?"

"I still hate it when you have too much fun at my expense," Susan said. "However, I should be done here at the end of May, so I guess I don't care how many stories you tell. May I at least assume that Wilhelm won't be jabbering to others the way you jabbered to him?"

"I only tell the truth," Marta laughed. "If Wilhelm blabs, Jane surely will hear and then he won't get an offer."

"If he does blab, you're dead," Susan said. "So, does Herr Gruber's lab do radiocarbon dating?"

"Yes," Marta said. "Also, Susan, he owns the lab–if you would like, I'll make sure he knows that the source and result are confidential."

"All right, I have forgiven you—if there is no blabbing. It would be a pain if people thought I quit because you were telling stories about me, but if that's all you…oh never mind, that's stupid— who gives a sh…damn it, Steven is right—I do swear too much. Are we still on for Berlin?"

"Of course. Hmm, I'll have to count sometime—do you think you've ever hit a hundred swear words in a day?"

"Yes, it's a piece of cake when I'm around you. How do we reach this Dr. Gruber?"

"He goes to New York regularly, so you might be able to meet him there. Now, give me one more piece of trivia and I will leave you alone. Oh, I will email you his telephone number when I get it—I'm still waiting for that."

"Damn, how about 'alphabetizing documents for ease of location was originated in the Library of Alexandria, one of Hypatia's haunts,'" Susan said. "You know this isn't easy. I'm always worried that I have repeated one… Steven loves doing it, though, so you can always ask him for trivia."

"*Agora* was a beautiful movie," Marta said.

"The ending is sad though, Susan added. "Ignorance wins and Hypatia dies. Oh, I have a different one for you, more in keeping with our new project."

"Yes?" Marta asked waiting.

"There is a legend that says Helen, the mother of Constantine, sent dirt from Golgotha to Rome," Susan said. "It was strewn in the Vatican Gardens to symbolically unite the blood of Christ with that shed by thousands of Christians supposedly murdered at the behest of Nero. That one may be pertinent to our new project."

"Golgotha is?" Marta asked.

"It is the site of the crucifixion of Christ in Jerusalem. Some say she was in the wrong place," she stopped as Jane had just come in.

"Can you take a call from Jackie?" Jane asked.

"Of course," Susan answered. As Marta got up to leave, Susan looked at her watch. She called after Marta as she left, "Maybe I can take care of your assignment when I finish this call. Let Jane know if you have time to grab lunch around 12:45. Oh, and remind me to tell you about the '666' phobia." Susan picked up the call.

"Hi, Susan. I just tried reaching Steven, but I got his voicemail. I thought I would try to catch you as I am leaving this afternoon for a conference."

"Thanks," Susan said. "Could you make out anything from the pictures we sent you?"

"Well, it's generally impossible to do anything with a picture, especially one from a structure—Steven said it's a box, right?" Jackie asked.

"Yes, it supposedly is somewhere between 400 and 700 years old."

"I can't tell you much, except that we think it's pine. Since it's a box, it's probably *Pinus pinaster* or Maritime Pine. The pine is native to the western and southwestern Mediterranean area. It's an important timber source in France, Spain and Portugal even though 'pinaster' roughly means 'poor imitation of a pine.' I've asked one of our interns to see if she can get a date range for you, but don't get your hopes up. Check in with me when I get back on Monday."

"The Mediterranean…," Susan repeated. At least it wasn't from Maine. Then she realized that France or Portugal could tie to that stupid Templar legend.

"Yes," Jackie said. "That's the easy part. As I said, dating from a picture is almost impossible. It could be a few hundred years old, but certainly not a thousand years old. I wish I could tell you more, but I do have to run. Where did you find it?"

"We were told that it was found in Maine," Susan said measuring her response. "We are getting more information. The date range we gave you is based on fire char at the depth where the wood was found, the uncalibrated range is 1300 to 1600, plus or minus."

"Interesting…call me Monday. I'll see if we were able to do anything more. Are you coming to Tucson any time soon?"

"Probably not for another month," Susan said. "Come to Chicago some time…we owe you dinner."

"I will. Bring me the box; maybe we can tell you more. Bye."

Susan sat for a minute reflecting on what Jackie had told her. Finding wood for a fake couldn't be too hard, but someone certainly was doing this right. So far, there were no glaring errors or mistakes. That was pretty amazing. She decided to track Steven down…Wilhelm could wait. She found him at Chase.

"Steven, I spoke with Jackie just now," Susan said. "The wood may be maritime pine–she says it's a timber source in France, Spain and Portugal. It may be at least a few hundred years old, but not a thousand years old. She is pretty sure about the pine, but not at all about the date because it's only a picture. Damn it, I forgot to ask if she could have someone send the pictures back."

"I asked her to send the pictures back in my message. So, the wood is consistent with our Joham being in Portugal and Cyprus."

"Yes, I know," she said. "I was almost hoping it would be new wood from the US. It still doesn't rule out a box brought over by a Pilgrim. Also, Marta got us another contact. Did you talk to Bob, yet?"

"I told you–he might be in today but then he's out of the office until April 23. I also called Jon's office, but he's out until Monday. Apparently, he doesn't have Thursday classes. It's odd, because I could swear that's why he was going home last night. David, of course, wants me to meet him in Tel Aviv so I can show him what we have right away."

"Jon won't be in until Monday?" Susan asked.

"Apparently not," Steven said. "His assistant said he took this entire week off. She wouldn't give me another number for him, so I didn't leave a message. I found him on the Internet, and he is at Penn–there is a picture of him on the Penn site sans beard but with his mustache. I could not find any contact information for him, except the office number that I called and an email address."

"Damn, he said it's Spring Break, so maybe he forgot; that's why he was the only one at his site Monday."

We are only calling Jon to give him an update," Steven added.

"Well, then we just keep his name out of things, but go ahead with David and Dr. Gruber. He would expect us to do what he asked—see if these are a hoax, right?"

"Yes, that would be my plan," Steven said.

"When does David go back to Shanghai?"

"Next Friday he thinks," Steven said. "He's working on something for the Rockefeller—he was a little vague as always, so, he may get delayed a few days. I told him we would talk and get back to him tomorrow. Does he observe the Sabbath?"

"I don't think so Steven. By the way, Marta's contact, Dr. Gruber, lives in Zurich. He comes to New York regularly, though. I have to go; I have some stuff to do and I have a quick errand to run for Marta—a stupid one at that."

"I emailed a picture of the Ovelho Latin piece to you. Sarah has been very helpful here at Chase—she got someone to help me make copies too."

"Ah, I got it," she said. "Steven the text look pretty good—except on the edges. I will work on it as soon as I run Marta's errand. I will try to scan it by lunchtime."

"What has she got you up you now?"

"Wilhelm is interviewing with the NSA—she has me asking him a stupid question. I don't know what all she was blabbing about last night, but I have to see if Wilhelm remembers something she told him about old Pete, damn it."

"Oh, for God's sake—your foreman?"

"Yes, damn it."

"You have enough to do."

"Steven," she hesitated. "Can you come have lunch at our cafeteria about 12:45 p.m.? I think Marta will join us—she can tell us more about Dr. Gruber."

"Maybe…I'll call you if I get too wrapped up in this for lunch," Steven said. "It's 11:15 a.m. now; I will need food at some point."

"Do try—you can help me manage Marta. Come to my office, first."

CHAPTER 30

The ethics issue got wrapped up quickly, so Susan spent some time on the 'Joham attestation,' which had proved harder to read than she anticipated. Their Joham appeared to be stating that he had safeguarded the box just as they had thought. But it was odd—she was looking again at the word for box. It was clearly in the plural form, not the singular. Joham was referring to at least two boxes. He was entrusted to bring them to a designated site and there were three men with him. Could there be another box—or did the plans change? But why did Joham go to Maine in the first place?

The phone rang—it was Jane. "Sorry to bother you, but Marta just called," she said. "You are meeting her in 35 minutes. She asked if you had done the errand for her. I told her I had no idea what she was talking about."

"I wish I didn't either and, no, I haven't," Susan grumbled. "She knows I am trying to finish this deal. Well, I guess I should just get it out of the way. Tell Wilhelm I will stop by his office at 12:20 p.m. Crap, I'll just go see Wilhelm now. Oh, and leave word that Steven can come up to my office. He's joining us for lunch."

"Will do," Jane said and hung up.

Well, Susan was trying to finish the deal, so just because she took a little break to read the Latin attestation...she hadn't told too big a lie. Oh, well, she'd better go see Wilhelm. She would start by telling him about the clearance, then pop Marta's question and leave. She did not want to do this at all. It could make him feel like Susan and Marta were playing with him. But she said she would do it. She would make it quick.

"Wilhelm, do you have time for an update?" Susan asked as she rapped on his door jamb to get his attention.

"Yes, of course," he said. "I got the signed consents from Eastland, Evergreen and Jameson back to Ms. Wainwright. Are we good to go?"

"Yes, I got an email from Sandra just a few minutes ago. Can you call the real estate and tax groups to tell them? Susan took another step into his office. She saw the look of concern come over his face.

"Yes, is anything wrong?" he asked. Susan rarely dallied after finishing.

"Nope, would you come to my office at about 4:00 p.m., so we can spend a few minutes with Patrick before New York?"

"Of, course," he said.

"Did they get the title straightened out on that Louisiana property?"

"Yes, it was done this morning," he said. "Mr. Mason asked me if I can help him in DC on Saturday morning if our group is done. Should I volunteer?"

"It's up to you—Marta says you have a big day Monday," Susan said. "Always cover your bases—it's okay with me unless the deal blows up and I need you in New York Saturday. Patrick is a good guy, so just tell him I need you here in Chicago Monday, if you have to."

"Thanks," he said trying to figure out if she wanted something more.

Susan was hesitating; maybe she would just leave and tell Marta she forgot about Wilhelm. It was a tossup as to which would be worse–asking Wilhelm or facing Marta. She had told Marta that Wilhelm would be a good catch for the NSA, but she also did not want to be helping–she did still have to be kind of loyal to Peale, Curtis. Well, whatever, she said she would ask the question. "Oh, before I forget, I am supposed to ask you a stupid question for Marta. Is that okay?" She saw him squirm, but then regain his composure.

"Yes, of course, Ms. Graves."

"Um," she was trying to bring herself to ask. "Oh, crap, when did Pete, my foreman, go to Arizona?" Don't ask me any questions, just answer. And, yes I would like to kill the wench for making me do this."

Poor Wilhelm stared at Susan for at least a minute.

"Wilhelm, if you don't know, just say so," Susan said.

"I do," he said. "Pete came to Arizona by train with his family in about 1890."

"Well, that was fun. I will tell Marta you passed."

"I don't understand; she is the one who told me." He truly looked puzzled.

"It's called pulling facts out of what sounds like nonsense," she said as she began to leave. "Also, it's supposed to throw you off when you don't know why I would ask you such a stupid question. Feel free to ask Marta for her motives—I owed her a favor." She looked at her watch—it was 12:25 p.m. It was almost time to meet Steven. Marta would meet them in the Partners' dining area."

"But," he stammered.

"I'll see you later this afternoon. Pete lived to be 92. His older sister, Adele, taught for many years—first in Tucson, then in Tombstone while she was married, and then back in Tucson again when she'd had enough of Tombstone and her husband. When she retired, she came to the ranch where she lived to be 93—she died just before I went to college. She was she was an artist—she did the painting of the kingfishers that hangs over my credenza. She also was my tutor. I do miss them both…and my horse." She got out of Wilhelm's office as fast as she could. At least that was over.

CHAPTER 31

"Susan," Jane said as Susan came back to her office. "You just had a call from Dr. Cahokia. He left a telephone number and asked that you call him back within the next 15 minutes," she said as she handed Susan the message. "He said you would know what he was calling about. I got his number this time."

"Okay, let me know when Steven gets here."

"He just got here a few minutes ago. He's sitting in your office," Jane said. "Also, Marta said to tell you she was on her way to the lunchroom. She asked if I had a message for her. Was there something I was supposed to tell her?"

"Other than that she is way too pushy, no. I just did her stupid errand though, but I can tell her at lunch. Better tell her Steven and I may be a few minutes late for lunch," she said over her shoulder as she went into her office.

"Steven, we just got a message from Dr. Cahokia," Susan said. "He wants us to call him. Jane gave me a number."

"Yes, I know," Steven said. "He just called my cell. I told him you were on your way here and that we would both talk with him then. Why is he still using that stupid name, Susan? Maybe we should ask Marta to have one of her thugs run a background check on Jon. We don't have time to waste on a phony name and misinformation. I still don't like the fact that he said he was going back to Penn because he had classes today."

"You'd have to give Marta his name…. So, have you found anything to be amiss in the documents?"

"No, but when he does this phony name stuff and tells me he is going home to teach a class he doesn't have, I get nervous," Steven said.

"Well, I have a bit of news," Susan said slowly. "It looks like the letter signed by Joham refers to at least two boxes, not one."

"Really?" he asked.

"Yes, come look here—see, it's plural," Susan said pointing to her computer screen. "We may have only one of the boxes that Joham brought with him. Also, three 'Guardians' were with him; the word is *Susceptores*. Should we tell Jon that he should be looking for at least one other box or do you think he is hiding the other one?"

"Well, we need to call him back, now," Steven said. "I want to know what the deal is before we tell him more. Susan, let's see if I can meet him in New York tomorrow. If he took the week off for Spring Break, he can just hop on the train and come to New York."

"See what he says," Susan answered. "We should at least tell him that the box appears to be a Mediterranean wood, and that we have an Israeli and a German lined up as authenticators."

"I thought he was Swiss," Steven interjected.

"He's from Zurich, the German speaking part of Switzerland and his name is Hershel Gruber," Susan said. "It sounds German to me. Anyway, we have enough to do without this nonsensical 'Cahokia' name again. It isn't amusing anymore." She paused and then asked, "You don't think he stole this box, do you?"

"Well, call him, and ask," Steven said. "Oh, I got a short message from Bob—it's a Folsom point, and he thinks it's real."

"Damn," she said. As Susan dialed, she looked at Steven. "There are just so many possibilities here. Occam's razor would say that the hypothesis with the fewest assumptions should be selected. But every hypothesis we come up with has too many alternatives to...," she stopped. "Jon?" she said as someone answered the phone.

"Yes," Jon said slowly. "Is this Susan?"

"Yes, Steven and I are here together. May I put you on the speaker? We are in my office, so there are only the two of us."

"Of course," Jon said. "Steven, I am sorry I wasn't in my office to get your call. I was planning to be there, but I haven't been feeling well," Jon said. "I'm at home today."

"I'm sorry to hear that, Jon. Look, this is very interesting and Susan and I are enjoying the puzzle you have given us. But you have to be straightforward with us—cut out this cloak and dagger stuff. I called your office earlier today because you said you had a class and would be in all day. You can imagine my surprise when I found out that you teach only on Mondays and Tuesdays. So, if we are to update you, perhaps you would tell us how and when we should contact you."

"I understand your concern, Steven," Jon started slowly. "I don't exactly know how to do something like this. As I told you, my real concern is the guy I voted against, damn Angus Pierson. When I found this box in a place it shouldn't be—on the wrong continent with a date that was, to put it mildly, way too early, I got concerned. My biggest fear is not even whether the contents are a hoax—it's whether I have missed something obvious that should tell me someone recently buried the box on my site. And then, the crystal and that damn spear point…."

"Jon," Susan said, "we are having the same problem. We did have a friend look at one of the pictures of the box where you could see the tree rings pretty well. The wood is from the Mediterranean—possibly Portugal, which is where our Joham says he came from. Our expert says that the wood could be a few hundred years old. If this is a hoax, someone has spent a lot of time on it. Oh, and Bob says the spear point is Folsom—but he won't be back until April 23 to give it a good look."

"That's good, I guess," he answered.

"Jon, assuming the box is real, who does it belong to?" Susan asked.

"Well, I don't see that there could be any Native American claim with respect to where or what it is, so I guess it would be the landowner," Jon said.

"So, real or a hoax, the landowner could profit right?" Steven asked.

"Yes, oh I see," Jon said with a little laugh. "Cui bono, right? Who benefits?"

"Indeed," Steven said. "Your colleague may not be the only suspect—it seems like a lot of work for spite. Who is the landowner?"

"It's called Wendelstein Trust, LLC," Jon said. "I was contacted by Mr. Oppenheimer, but he is with a Boston law firm. He put me in touch with the US representative for the owner—his name is Joaquin Samovar. I mentioned him before; he's the man I have been sending emails to. He told me where he thought I should dig."

"Do you know which law firm?" Susan asked.

"Yes, it is Hartley Marin. They seem to be pretty big—like your firm Susan," Jon answered.

"So, is this Samovar an American?" Steven asked.

"I don' know—I have only spoken to the lawyer and Samovar by telephone," Jon answered. "He sounds American. When he said that they wanted to reopen the site, I was so happy, that I didn't really ask too many questions. The funds for work at my old site went straight to the University. As for the second site, that is done as a contract where I am reimbursed directly by the landowner—my first check was drawn on Wells Fargo. It is sort of complicated, but I am allowed to work a certain number of hours on my own time pursuant to a separate contract. Our legal office worked it out with that Hartley Marin firm I mentioned."

"Well, don't worry about it," Susan said. "I probably can find the owner through public records and possibly even who owns the owner if it is indeed an entity. I'll have a search done."

"Why do you want to know?" Jon asked.

"It would be good to know that you aren't dealing with known criminals or enemies of the state or something, Jon," Susan said. "I know you think this box has been in the ground for a few hundred years, but if there is a known criminal involved, I would want to know and so would you."

"Jon, we are both very concerned that this landowner directed you to the second site—petroglyphs or not, it is fishy," Steven added.

"I understand, but the cost?" he asked.

"Not a lot. Steven and I will consider it an entertainment cost. This is an interesting puzzle," Susan said. "Is that okay, Steven?"

"Yes, of course, Susan."

"Thank you," Jon said. "I made the right decision to ask for your help."

"Another question, Jon," Susan hesitated and then continued. "What's your son's role in all of this?"

"My son wasn't at the site when I found the box. I was working with an intern. We were the only ones there. We hit the top of the box in a test trench. The box was light enough that we didn't really expect to find anything inside, so I moved it to the shed we use. We wanted to finish opening the trench by Spring Break, but, because of the box, we ran out of time. We closed up for break, after determining the amount of site contamination we had from the box. We are behind schedule now. As I told you, we had already found a crystal buried by some nut in the northeast quadrant of where we were working. The intern has put up a sign telling the crystal owner to call me if he wants it back."

"Any calls, yet?" Steven asked.

"No."

"And the box?" Steven asked.

"The box was a conundrum," he said. "I had no idea what it was doing there and I was furious because of the delay it caused. The date on the box hasp was unreadable when we found it, as the entire thing was encrusted with dirt. I took it home and forgot about it for a while. As you know, I just cleaned the damn box this last weekend. I needed time to open it without damaging it. I took the stupid crystal home too."

"Does your son know what you found?" Steven asked.

"Not exactly, but I'll get to that. I did tell Father Bartolome that the new site had a couple of intrusions. We were so busy; there just wasn't time to tell Father about the box. And I didn't actually open the box until just before my talk. Um, before I forget, Clay is the friend who told Father that my colleague,

Angus Pierson, knew how I voted. I guess you can understand why I didn't leave the box lying around at the site.

"So?" Steven prodded.

"Last weekend, when I finally cleaned the box up a bit, I saw the date on the hasp, 1307. When I opened it, I glanced at the materials as I removed them, and then locked everything in a file in my closet for safekeeping."

"And?" Steven asked impatiently. "Jon, we are trying to get to the bottom of all of this—the more you tell us, the easier it will be."

"My colleagues all know where we are working. The State of Maine knows where we are working, for God's sake," he said. "My first conclusion was that it was a hoax and that it likely had been directed at me because of the tenure issue. I mean documents in Greek? What would you think?"

"So, do you still believe somebody planted it there?" Susan asked.

"I want to, but, as you said, it is well done. When I looked at the actual documents, I was horrified," he said. "I had no idea why these documents were in the box, why a box with a 1307 date was buried there or how old or real any of it was. I just couldn't be sure that they weren't old. Mind you my Greek is non-existent, but I could read some of the Latin." He paused.

"Jon? Are you still there," Steven asked.

"Yes, well then I got really nervous. If there was something glaringly wrong that I missed and I took it to the University, I would be a laughing stock. That's why I drove over from Bangor, Monday—I thought I would look around the new site to see if I might have missed something. Of course, when I went into the shed to get my trowel, I gave up—that stupid fake spear point was there. So, I thought of you two."

"It's Folsom—and you still haven't told your son?" Susan asked again.

"Well, Monday evening, before I decided to come to Chicago, I mentioned that I found some old material, maybe 1500 or 1600, and that I might send it to a couple of old friends to look at. I may have mentioned that I saw a name on one, but it was a very short call—he usually just says hi and that's it. I told him that they didn't look like they could be too important. Again, I didn't want to get him involved. He has his hands full right now. He is trying to wrap up his work at his old site and get a publication out while he prepares for his move to Chicago."

"Are we the friends?" Susan asked.

"Yes." He paused, and then said, "Last night when I got home from Chicago, my son called again. He doesn't call that often and, as I said, we had just talked Monday night. He had called me when I was having coffee with you, Susan, but I told him I was busy, so I figured he was just calling back to say hi. We chatted for a few minutes and then, almost as an afterthought, he asked if I had seen the name 'Joham' anywhere on what I found. Well, my first thought was that he knew who the trickster was. When I said yes, though, he was dead silent for at least a minute–I actually thought he had gone into a moment of prayer or something," Jon chuckled.

"And?" Steven asked, having no idea what was coming next. He wished Jon was in the room; it would help to see his facial expressions as he talked.

"Father finally said that about a year ago he found a small, plain wooden box at his site down near Popham in Maine. It was in the area where, Susan, I told you my son and others at their site periodically found 'Pilgrim' artifacts. In his box was a small, leather and wood bound book that was like a short diary. It looked to be in Portuguese, so he couldn't read much–but it had that same name on one of the covers."

"Joham?" Steven asked as he tried to decipher what he just heard.

"Yes, well actually it was João A D Ovelho," Jon said. "That was all that could be read. Father had gone off about 20 yards to take a quick nap. He saw a couple of stones that looked as if they had been piled by someone–like a cairn, you know. He dug around the cairn base and found that the pile of stones went down over a foot–the box was under that. I guess João and Joham are similar enough–but with the Ovelho being legible as well, it seems possible that we have the same person."

"What did he do with the book?" Susan asked.

"I asked him if I could see it, but he turned it over to the chief archaeologist for the site when he found it; he hasn't seen it since. It would have gone to the college for cataloging at some point– that would have been almost a year ago. He's going to ask them if he can see his stuff that went to cataloging. There were two other 'fragments' with the small book. He said none of it was in very good shape. Susan, Father found these pieces where the rogue digging was done this year—the bulldozing."

"And did the fragments refer to this João?"

"He thinks the name was only on the book."

"How sure is he?" Steven asked.

"I am telling you what my son said," Jon said. "He found it about a year ago. He said he had thought it was interesting, but not in his area. When I mentioned finding documents buried around 1500 to 1600, he remembered what he had found last year."

"And it was the site near Popham?" Susan asked trying to make sense out of this new information.

"Yes, my son found his 'João' material on Cape Small at the site near the 1607 Popham site. And, that is why I am even more puzzled…. There were French and English colonies in Maine in the early 1600s, but not a specific Portuguese colony. They were exploring the coastal areas, possibly as early as 1472. I found a reference that said João Vas Cortereal found the 'Land of the Cod' in 1472. It's possibly a reference to Newfoundland. A Portuguese explorer mapped the Maine coastline in 1525. He was sailing under the Spanish flag, but this is simply me reading a history book. I have no idea if what I just told you is even main stream."

"The name João or Joham must be common—you just mentioned another explorer with that name," Steven said.

"I think it's like 'John,'" Susan said.

"Yes, yes, like 'John,' it is a common enough Portuguese name. But when you have two or more strung together—the 'A. D. Ovelho,' for example, it's less likely to be a coincidence. Anyway, Father said he would try to retrieve what he found last year so we can compare the signature to see if it is indeed the same. He asked me to send him the document I found, but of course, I left it with you."

"I assume you don't want them back yet, right?" Steven asked.

"No, I need you to make sense of them. Until last night, when Father called to tell me about that small book, I truly thought we had a hoax, Steven. And now, I have a new problem."

"And that is?" Susan asked.

"Father's friend Clay's generally a very sweet man, but sometimes…well, apparently, he's been harassing one of my female interns. She left me a note telling me she lodged a complaint against Clay. So, I called Clay this morning and banned him from my site. I just…." He stopped in mid-sentence.

"Just what?" Steven asked. "Were you going to say something, Jon?"

"I, um, want to know if this really is a damn hoax, and who's involved if it is. I don't want Father showing anything to Clay. As I told you, Clay is a friend of the guy who didn't make tenure. If he buried my box, I certainly do not want Clay to tell him I found it. I…well you understand. Anyway, I did ask Father to keep the name similarity under wraps—hopefully, he will. But, then again, the vote was just in early March—Father found his stuff last year."

"So, are you saying the colleague wouldn't know of Father's find?" Susan asked.

"I'm saying Father found his stuff way before my colleague knew he wouldn't get tenure…."

"Jon, are you still there?" Steven asked.

"Yes, just trying to collect my thoughts."

"That does argue against a hoax involving this colleague," Steven said, not knowing what else to say.

"I don't know if I should say this, but Father's first allegiance isn't to me anymore. I want to keep this quiet until I know what is going on. Father is going to Rome tomorrow for a seminar. He won't be back until around April 25. He said he will check with the college before he leaves, though."

"And when you spoke to him yesterday at lunch, did you tell him where you were?"

"I told him that I was in DC for the afternoon and couldn't talk—I didn't know why he was calling. I know this is stupid, but a hoax…especially, when I just got the grant to reopen my site…. Perhaps I did panic."

"We are trying to help, Jon, so just be honest with us," Steven said. "We have already begun the analysis. I don't know if you will be happy about this, but one document appears to be in medieval Greek—it could be an old fake, but if so, it's very well done."

"Please let us know when you see Father's stuff," Susan said. "It's best to think of this as a hoax until proven otherwise. Um, could a Pilgrim bury your box and then walk a hundred miles to bury the material Father found? I guess a Pilgrim burying both caches is as believable as Samovar burying the caches and then expecting you and your son to find them a year apart. Nobody told Father where to dig, right?"

"No, it was pure coincidence—he wandered off to take a nap," Jon said resignedly. "I guess this new owner could somehow have buried the one my son found first, and then bought this property and buried some more stuff. But we both believe our materials were under undisturbed levels at our sites. Samovar would have to be damn good to pull that off."

"And Dr. Cahokia and your classes?" Steven asked.

"Steven, Susan," he stuttered. "I do apologize. I'm just so worried about my reputation…. Please forgive me. I do hope you will continue to help me."

"Of course, Jon," Steven said. "And we will decide together how to proceed as we get deeper into this. I have one last question, who knows about the spear point?"

"I haven't told anyone. Bob says it's Folsom?" Jon asked.

"Yes, he left a message saying it was real and it's Folsom, but he is now out until the 23rd. He will call us when he gets back. We made no mention of where you found it yet."

"That is perfect. Thank you," Jon said.

They talked for a few minutes about getting Father Bartolome to locate the documents he had found. Then Susan told Jon about the two authenticators they planned to work with. Jon agreed that he would keep their names to himself. He also would come to New York and meet Steven for lunch in the Trustees' Dining Room at the Met. They did not tell Jon about the possibility of more than one box.

CHAPTER 32

Jane knocked on Susan's door just as they finished the call with Jon. "You're five minutes late for lunch with Marta—she has a table. Tell me you did her errand, please," Jane said sarcastically.

"We are on our way, and yes, I did Marta's stupid errand for her," Susan said. "Also, I am staying overnight in New York tomorrow. It's personal travel; get me a room at the Pierre with my own card. Steven will be with me. Oh, would you try to get Steven on my flight?"

"Consider it done. May I go to lunch?" Jane asked.

"Yes, of course," Susan said. "You know you'll miss me tomorrow."

"Thank you for taking such good care of my wife," Steven added. "And me."

"Keep her in New York for a few days, Steven," Jane said as she put her coat on.

Susan looked at Steven as he got up. "Remind me to get a trace going on the landowner."

Marta was waiting at the table when Susan and Steven walked in.

"Okay, first you guys are ten minutes late," Marta said. "Second, which one of you has trivia for me?"

Susan's look at Steven told him he was on.

"How about this?" Steven asked. Without waiting for an answer, he said, "There has always been a controversy over how many nails were used in the Crucifixion. But did you know that Helen, the mother of Constantine, brought all of the nails used on the True Cross back to Istanbul, when she returned from the Holy Land?"

"No," Marta said. "Do tell."

"Well," Steven said, "supposedly, Helen found the True Cross and the nails used to crucify Jesus in Jerusalem. She had one nail inserted in the royal helmet, so that Constantine's head would be safe from his enemies. She had another nail imbedded in the bridle of his horse to fulfill an ancient prophecy of Zechariah, who had predicted that '[t]here shall be upon the bridles of the horses Holiness unto the Lord Almighty.' Where else, Susan?" he asked when he saw she wasn't paying attention.

Luckily she had been listening. "Um, Constantine gave at least one nail to a foreign dignitary, which is supposedly how one of the nails is in the Iron Crown of Lombardy. Helen also cast at least one nail into the sea to calm a storm while she was returning from the Holy Land. Despite there being at least four nails thusly accounted for, people still argue whether there was a nail in each hand and one through the feet or one in each foot—so, three or four."

"Helen tore down Hadrian's Temple of Venus to get to the relics," Steven continued. "Constantine then built the Church of the Holy Sepulcher there. The site is supposed to be Golgotha where Christ was crucified. However, some people say that Golgotha is outside the city wall near the Damascus Gate. That story doesn't come until the 1800s, when someone noticed a rock there that looked like a skull; since one of the possible etymologies for Golgotha is Aramaic for skull."

"Marta knows that Helen took dirt from Golgotha back to Rome, Steven."

"And did she bring the Cross back as well?" Marta asked.

"According to Rufinus, who updated the Ecclesiastical History of Eusebius around 400 CE, Helen found remains of three crosses when she found the nails," Susan said. "Didn't Eusebius say that before Hadrian built his temple, the site had been venerated by Christians?"

Yes, they often built over sacred sites of other religions, so it does give some credence to Helen's claims," Steven started. "There were three crosses, so, in order to find out which one Jesus had been crucified on, she and a priest laid pieces of each cross on a sick woman. The piece that healed the woman indicated it was from the True Cross."

"It's nonsense," Susan snorted. "Eusebius never wrote about the nails or the Cross and he was Helen's contemporary. A Fifth Century historian named Theodoret said Helen found the nails from the cross when she visited the Holy Land in 326 or 327 CE."

"Susan's right, none of this was reported during her lifetime. The first mention of pieces of the Cross is around 350 CE, when Cyril of Jerusalem said pieces of it were everywhere," Steven said. "As Susan said, Rufinus added the story to a new edition of Eusebius around 400 CE."

"Yes, well, John Calvin, a major player in the schism of Catholics and Protestants, said something like 'Jesus could carry the Cross, but if you collected all of the reliquary pieces from around the world, they would fill a ship.'"

"But somebody else said that the sum of all of the known pieces is less than a third of the amount in a cross," Steven said. "Anyway, after Helen finds it, all hell breaks out–the Sassanians take part of the Cross when they capture Jerusalem in 614 CE. Then Heraclius recaptures it a decade later. He takes it to Constantinople and then back to Jerusalem. It stayed hidden away there until the knights of the First Crusade captured Jerusalem. They made the Byzantine Patriarch tell them where it was. Only a small fragment of wood set into a golden cross was left. That fragment was then captured by Saladin in 1187 and was never seen again. Somehow, there are still pieces all over the world."

"There's even a piece in a monastery in Cyprus," Susan added.

"In Helen's defense, people writing during her lifetime said she was quite pious," Steven said. "Eusebius said she wore simple clothes and mingled with the worshipers in the churches she had built in the Holy Land. Eusebius also says that her gifts to the naked and unprotected poor were especially abundant. Our pious Right Wing Christians could learn a few things from her."

"You would expect that from the finder of the True Cross," Marta laughed.

"And, by digging for relics, St. Helen became the Patron Saint of archaeologists," Steven added.

"I've never heard that…did you make it up?" Susan asked.

"I read it somewhere. But to finish, Helen lived into her 80s. Some say her body was interred in the imperial vault at the church of the Holy Apostles in Constantinople. Of course, Constantine built a mausoleum for her in Rome; maybe they moved her when the mausoleum was done. Her body was then moved to Reims in about 849. By 1100, her sarcophagus was in the Lateran Palace. It eventually ended up in one of the Vatican museums."

"Her skull is supposedly in Trier, now" Susan added. "And the Holy Apostles Church wasn't finished until after Constantine died. Anyway, that's more than enough trivia."

"Okay, but what has pulled you away from your deal?" Marta asked. "Oh, did you do my errand?"

"Yes, somehow Wilhelm knew when Pete came to Arizona. He was off a year, but that's probably your fault."

"What is this about Wilhelm and the gauntlet that was set before him? Susan, do you mean old Pete, your foreman?" Steven asked innocently.

"Marta has been obnoxious again, Steven," Susan said. "She was beguiling Wilhelm with stories of her youth in the Wild West and she included me and Pete as two of her characters. You were probably one too."

Before Steven could say anything, Marta piped in "Steven, can you come to New York tomorrow? I found Dr. Gruber; he's in New York now through next Monday on business. We can have dinner with him." She had been saving the news for the right moment—this was perfect timing.

"Excellent—Susan already convinced me to go with her tomorrow."

"You'll come to New York?" Susan asked.

"I'll come along to do introductions. We have a reservation for tomorrow night at 7:00 p.m. at Le Bernardin. He says it's his treat. Do you forgive me?"

"It's a very good start," Susan said. "You will stay for dinner, right?"

"Of course. I'm anxious to find out what you are spending so much time on," Marta said. "And, I did tell Hershel that all three of us would be there. So, may I tell Hershel exactly what you would like for him to do?"

"First, tell Steven who he is," Susan said. "And, you are not totally off the hook, yet."

"Okay, his name is Hershel Gruber and he owns a laboratory called Hoftstein Sciences located in Zurich. It's been around forever–Hoftstein was his mother's father," Marta said. "He has done a fair amount of work for some of our agencies."

"Will he sign a confidentiality agreement?" Steven asked.

"I'm sure he will, but do you really need one?" she asked.

"Marta, we don't know what we are dealing with yet," Steven said. "If this is a hoax, it's well done. Susan is tracking down the owner of the property where the stuff was found. It changed hands in February or March. The new owner let Jon reopen his site after it was closed by the previous owner. He also asked Jon to dig at a specific spot near his old site. That's where he found the box with the documents."

"The new owner told your guy where to find the box? Wait–you said Jon, so it is Jonathan Christiansen at Penn," Marta laughed.

"Yes, damn it and don't sound so smug," Susan said.

"Dr. Christiansen seems honest enough," Marta said still laughing. "His son's a priest you know."

"How the hell did you know that Jon's son is a priest? Oh, never mind."

"Good job, Marta" Steven said laughing. "Anyway, the owner asked Jon to do a little excavating around some nearby petroglyphs," Steven said. "He wanted a brochure for his guests, but it gets better. Jon's son, the priest, also is an archaeologist. He just told Jon that he had found a little book buried near early settler artifacts about a year ago when he was working down by Portland–well over a 100 miles south of Jon's site."

"Don't tell me that it has our 'Joham's' name on it," Marta said.

"Okay," Steven said nicely. "I won't. Susan, you tell her."

"Seriously, there is another document with Joham's name on it?" Marta asked.

"Yes, apparently," Susan said. "Actually, it was João A D Ovelho, so very damn similar. These could be planted by someone," Susan said. "It could be something as simple as a dealer wanting to obfuscate the place where the stuff was found. So the dealer buried stuff in a few places and then told somebody where to look. He, or she, added some real cachet by burying it in the US. But then, either Jon or his son would have to be in on it, because the stuff was found so far apart."

"Father Bartolome, Jon's son, found his stuff last year," Steven said. "Jon found his stuff a couple of weeks ago. Father's piece was in Portuguese and had nothing to do with his research, so he gave it to the chief archaeologist at the site. It was archived at the college that is overseeing the site, so he will try to retrieve it."

"Both Jon and his son say they found their stuff in undisturbed layers; in Jon's case, it was below something that was actually dated," Susan added. "Even so, Jon was worried that one of his colleagues did this as a hoax, hoping that Jon wouldn't catch it. I think we told you, Jon voted against tenure for this colleague, and he knows the colleague wants to get him. But if this is a hoax, it's so well done, that it would be almost impossible for the colleague to pull off."

"Father found his stuff only because he went off to take a nap and saw a cairn," Steven said. "Jon has no contact with his son's site and has never seen the materials his son found. Most importantly, Father found his material and sent it to the college long before Jon's colleague was denied tenure."

"So, what if it isn't a hoax?" Marta asked.

"Assuming the box was buried around the time of the 1307 date on its hasp, it appears that someone brought some very early Christian materials to Maine right around the time of the great purge of the Templars in Europe," Steven said soberly. "Obviously, that is before Columbus and therefore highly unlikely. If it's 1607, then we still have to see what compelled our Joham to leave Portugal with this stuff."

"For some reason, our Joham and his three Guardians were keeping the box safe. We are sort of hoping that he and the Guardians were Pilgrims."

"It will certainly be interesting to see what Father's stuff adds to this," Steven said. "I hope it's a diary of some kind."

"According to this 'Templar,'" Susan stopped mid-sentence. "Actually, we are calling him that only because of the date on the box. Our Joham doesn't say he's a Templar, but he is some type of knight. He was ordered to keep the box and the Guardians safe. The documents had been protected by the Guardians for a very long time, but he doesn't say why or where they're from."

"Susan, you didn't tell me you finished the 'Templar' letter," Steven said looking at Susan. "When did you do that?"

"I haven't finished it yet, Steven" she said. "It's Latin, so it's pretty straightforward, except for some vocabulary. I need more time with it; but Joham seems to say that he took a box from Tomar and sailed to Wales to pick up a guide," Susan said. "It looks like those three Guardians were already in Wales with more boxes, not just the one Jon had. God only knows who these Guardians are, but there seem to be three of them."

"Maybe each one had a box."

"Isn't there just one?

"There could be more, Marta. Before I forget, there may be a 1541 date in the text. That should clearly refute him coming in 1307, but I'll have to see the original. I can't make anything out around that area of the document."

"So, is there any reference to 'Templars'?" Marta asked.

"No and he doesn't even hint that he is a Templar. Unfortunately, the attestation doesn't have a legible date at the bottom. But then, the Templars in Portugal survived the purge that was occurring throughout Europe in the 1300s. King Denis let them reconstitute as the Order of Christ in recognition of their services to Portugal during the Reconquista. Prince Henry the Navigator and Vasco de Gama were members of the Portuguese Order. Some say that Christopher Columbus sailed under their banner. Supposedly, that's why a red cross is emblazoned on the sails of his ships. He was sailing for Spain, though."

"Where did you find that?" Steven asked. "Better yet, when?"

"Last night when I couldn't sleep, I tried to move the date forward to something reasonable and still have a knight," Susan said. "Prince Henry still would have been too early. I did find an interesting tidbit, though. The Portuguese and the Spaniards fought over the Canary Islands, which the Portuguese claimed to have discovered in the early 1300s. But Pliny the Elder, who died in the eruption of Vesuvius in 79 CE, knew the Canaries. He believed Juba II named them. We know Juba II as the husband of Cleopatra's only daughter, Cleopatra Selene. Marta, you remember her tomb in Algeria, on the way to Tipasa."

"How could I forget," she laughed. "The guide called it the 'tomb of the Christian woman.' You had your hands full trying to calm Steven since Cleopatra Selene probably died no later than 10 CE, so it would be hard to call her a Christian even though there was a cross over the door, probably added later."

"Bravo, Marta," Steven said.

"Anyway," Susan continued, "our Joham doesn't seem to be a 'Templar.' But he is a knight, only a few centuries later."

"Go back a second—you said Christopher Columbus sailed under the flag of the Order of Christ," Marta said. "So, the cross we see on the sails of the Nina, the Pinta and the Santa Maria originated with the Templars?"

'Possibly," Steven said.

"Interesting," Marta said slowly, "what have you stepped into here?"

"We don't know exactly," Steven said. "Still want to play?" he smiled at her.

"Damn right Steven, dear—I'll carry your bags tomorrow if I have to. Damn, I'll carry you if I have to."

"Let's get back to the documents, then. At least one of the Greek writers is very upset about the changes being made under Constantine to the religion of the followers of Jesus. Now mind you, what I am reading is in Koine Greek and hence, purports to be written around the time of Constantine. The Latin document Susan just mentioned is supposed to be almost exactly 1000 years later. Susan, did you look at the other one in Latin?"

"No, dear, I still have a real job, remember?" Susan said sweetly. "Also, you only sent me the Joham document. Hopefully, both Latin documents will be almost exactly 1300 years later, like 1607 or thereafter. That would take us into post-Columbian North America."

"I could use your help on the ones in Greek, but given what you just read, you should look at the other Latin document. It is some type of legal agreement and it has been witnessed. There's a lump of something with it, so it may have been sealed originally. We'll call that one the Latin seal document."

"A lead seal?" Susan asked. It wasn't in the pictures Steven sent. She also hadn't seen anything like that at Chase yesterday, but she hadn't looked that closely.

"No, it is a lump that looks like a black wad of wax; it was probably discolored with age. I may be wrong, it isn't attached to the document, which was unrolled," he said.

"Does the seal have the busts of Peter and Paul or SPA–like a Papal seal?" Susan asked.

"Hello, guys, remember me?" Marta asked. "I am still here—what are you talking about? Remember, I am Jewish, if it matters."

"Papal seals, at least in medieval times, were typically made of lead. They were attached to a document with a cord–traditionally, they had 'SPASPE' embossed on one side–for Saint Paul and Saint Peter. The lead seal was called a bulla, thus papal documents became known as papal bulls. So, a 'bull' would be a formal pronouncement. In 1139, Pope Innocent II issued a papal bull that exempted the Templars from tithes and taxes," Susan said. "A wax seal means it's a lesser document."

"The Vatican does seem to be a party, Susan," Steven said. "Hopefully, it won't be some Templar crap."

"There is a Mexican drug gang that calls itself the Knights Templar," Marta said. "Also, I assume you've heard that the Norwegian who killed all of those people in Oslo claims to have revived the Knights Templar."

"That's all we need," Steven said. "This doesn't seem to be a nut job like that, but we have absolutely no confidence that this isn't some kind of hoax."

"Is there any evidence that the Templars came to Maine?" Marta asked. "I know they participated in the Crusades, but Maine?"

"There's no credible evidence that any Templars were ever in the Americas," Susan said. "I mean, the documents that Steven is reading could possibly be real. It's still highly unlikely that a Templar or anybody else brought them to North America in 1300. The best case would be that Joham's Latin attestation was done at least two or three hundred years later than the date on the box."

"No credible evidence?" Marta asked. "Does that mean there is evidence?"

"Steven and I occasionally read the fringe books. They often mix facts in with their fictional theories, so something pops up from time to time. There is a 70 or 80 foot tower above Narragansett Bay near Newport, Rhode Island. Some people say that it pre-dates European colonization."

"Is there any evidence that it is that old?" Marta asked.

"There is a story that Verrazano saw it when he explored the North Atlantic coast around 1520. He definitely was in the Narragansett Bay area. The Vatican even has a map of the North Atlantic that Verrazano's brother made sometime in the 1520s after Verrazano returned to Europe. Supposedly, the name 'Normanvilla' appears where the tower would be, but I think that has been soundly refuted. I think most people believe the tower is the base of a windmill built in the mid-1600s. There are similar structures in England from the same time period."

"So, is there any evidence that Verrazano saw the tower?" Marta asked.

"Not really, but I did find that he was killed and eaten by the Carib Indians on one of his later trips south," Susan answered.

"Susan, Marta should know that Jon's son found his stuff at a site near where Verrazano may have been," Steven said. "Supposedly, Verrazano met a local tribe of Indians in Maine. They were butt-naked, which led Verrazano's crew to call the Cape Small area near Popham Terra Onde di Mala Gente."

"Steven," Marta said. "I'm surprised at you!"

"That's the area where Father Bartolome worked," Susan said when she stopped laughing.

"Oh, God, not looking for butt naked men, I hope," Marta said totally amused by her joke. Steven was laughing as well.

"It's not that funny," Susan said. "To continue, the tower is in a Gilbert Stuart painting done around 1770. The structure is said to be modeled on Templar-associated churches, like the Convent of Christ on the coast of Portugal. Like the Newport tower, those churches have a rounded architecture. At least some, like the tower, have octagonal bases inspired by the structure of the Dome of the Rock on the Temple Mount. That, of course, was the Templar headquarters in Jerusalem. A Sufi mathematical design was used to build the Dome of the Rock in the seventh century. That's what the Templars would have seen on the Temple Mount. Nevertheless, eight sides or not, the tower was probably built by Benedict Arnold's great-grandfather."

"To look like a windmill in England?" Marta asked.

"Yes, but, of course, the Templars were in England for a long time, so the eight-sided structures still could have ultimately come from the Templars.."

"And Wales?" Marta asked.

"Damn, it's 2:30 p.m. already," Susan grumbled. "There are Welsh everywhere. Jefferson thought he was Welsh—I think that was proved with DNA recently. There is a Welsh commemorative plaque in the Washington monument; it's one of the 193 commemorative plaques on the inside staircase. There, a bit of trivia thrown in. I have to see the Big A yet this afternoon. Steven, are you going back to Chase?"

"Yes, dear, I am," he said. "Should I offer to bring Marta with me?"

"Well, since she'll be with us tomorrow night at dinner, I think you should. Marta, do you have time to go with Steven?" Susan asked.

"I would make time if I had to. Right now I'm free until Monday. Steven, do you have time to show me?"

"Of course," he said. "There aren't many documents. I will even show you a picture of the box, but you have to promise to stop telling stories about my wife."

"I will come over after my meeting," Susan said as she stood to leave. "I want to arrange to get some professional pictures of these. And hold Marta to that promise, if she gives it…"

"Susan, I can get a photographer for you," Marta said. "I could probably get someone to come this afternoon if I try now."

"Excellent," Susan said.

"I'm going back to Chase," Steven said. "If we can get the more interesting documents done, we can decide what to show Herr Gruber. Marta, come over after you check on a photographer. I will leave your name with Sarah Adams. Call me if you have any problems."

"Cell?" Marta asked.

"Yes, it works there. Susan, can you see if the conservation center has a way to store parchment safely."

"Good idea." As she left, she called back to Steven, "if Marta gets bored tell her about the spear point."

CHAPTER 33

After a couple of calls, Marta had lined up a photographer to meet her and Steven at Chase by 4:00 p.m. Like Steven and Susan, Marta assumed this was some sort of scam, but she couldn't figure out the angle. Well, if it were, she could call on some of her former co-workers to help sort things out. At least she had caught Hershel Gruber in New York. He could help determine the age for them. That would make for an interesting dinner Friday night.

Marta was happy that they had asked for her help; she had been wondering what she would do for excitement. As Susan said, even just ferreting out a hoax could be interesting. Of course, that huge forgery trial in Israel over the ossuary of James, the brother of Jesus had ended recently. Some respected antiquities experts in Israel had been accused of faking artifacts and conspiring to sell them to museums and collectors. They were acquitted, but no wonder Susan and Steven were nervous about this project. She put on her coat and headed to Chase.

Steven was ready for Marta when she got to Chase at 3:20 p.m.

"I have a photographer coming in half an hour," Marta said.

"That's great," Steven answered. "I can show you the documents as we set them out for the photographer. We have to be out of here by 4:45 p.m. As you can see, there are only 10 pieces. We have two letters and a fragment in Latin, four letters in Greek, a fragment in Hebrew and a letter and fragment in Aramaic."

"I read a little about the James Ossuary Trial before I came over," Marta said. "Are you concerned about something like that?"

"Of course we are concerned," Steven said. "Susan was on a tear last night making a list of possibilities. One is that the guy who didn't get tenure did this for revenge. But he would have to be insane—it's too much work. It's also possible that Jon or the new landowner faked all of this to get rich. You know, Jon gets us to say they're real and then he sells them to the landowner. But we aren't experts and again it seems like too much work. The landowner is a possibility; perhaps he didn't know Jon would take what he found to us. But then again, what do you do with the materials Jon's son found a year ago?"

"Jesus," Marta said exhaling. "Steven, you know, even the publicity of these being fakes might be exciting to someone seeking fame."

"Best not use that word if you are going to work with us on this. Some of the 'experts' are kind of nutty that way."

"You're joking," Marta said.

"No, I'm not," he said, glaring at her over his glasses. "Many of these experts are at religious universities. You know Susan's ranching background has colored her language; I sometimes have to muzzle her. I expect you to help me, not encourage her."

"Sorry," she said. "Please continue, Steven."

"Anyway, there are many more possibilities. Someone could have faked these in medieval times. It might be a good way to get rid of an enemy, if they are found with blasphemous documents. Oh, and it is possible that some Pilgrim brought these over in a box that had been made in 1307, which is the date on the hasp. You know, maybe it's a family heirloom that could make the owner a target of witch hunters. They needed to hide it, so they buried it. Susan keeps coming up with possibilities; this stuff being what it says it is being at the bottom of her list."

"And, what is that?" Marta asked.

"Well, a knight put some very old documents in a box sometime from the 1300s to the 1600s, and then he buried the box in the New World to protect them," Steven said. "Of course, 1307 is interesting because the French King, Philip, arrested the French Templars for blasphemy on Friday, October 13, 1307. Many of them were put to death and the Templar Order itself was disbanded in 1312."

"I thought Susan said it wasn't a Templar...," Marta started.

"As I said, the hasp on the box is dated 1307, but the 'Templar letter' date itself is hard to discern–it could be 1607 as easily as 1307. According to Susan, the author says nothing at all about Templars. So, it's just that coincidental date on the hasp that is a problem," Steven said. "And I'm not sure about sailing from Wales, although it is possible. We did tell you we are getting someone to look at the wood, right?"

"Yes, but what about the documents," Marta asked.

"Well, we'll get Dr. Gruber to date them and I will get David and maybe one of my old professors to help determine what they might be."

"I mean what is the content...did the Templars find stuff like this in Jerusalem?" Marta said.

"The Templars got to the Temple Mount in Jerusalem in the late 1100s," Steven said. "The treasure they supposedly found was hidden there by the Jews as Titus was destroying the Temple in 70 CE. Then, after a cycle of destructions and re-constructions lasting over 1,000 years, the Templars came along and found the treasure that everyone else missed. They then parlayed that wealth to become powerful bankers. They even financed King Philip's wars with England. That was their downfall; the King couldn't repay his debt, so he confiscated all of their wealth in 1307. By the way, Philip had already expelled the Jews in 1306–he owed them money, too."

"So, you and Susan agree; she told me there couldn't have been anything left," Marta said. She still didn't know if Susan was joking when she told her that some Templars escaped to Switzerland, and hence the Templar Cross ended up on the Swiss flag.

"We don't think there was much left," he said. "Titus destroyed Jerusalem and his soldiers ransacked the Temple. You've seen his Triumphal Arch in Rome– the South Panel shows Roman soldiers carrying the Temple's treasures and sacred objects, including a Menorah, in that procession. Josephus mentions the Menorah, too. Then Hadrian completely reworked the Mount in 135 CE and, according to Cassius Dio, built a Temple of Jupiter there. Constantine destroyed Hadrian's temple to rid the Mount of its pagan presence. The Mount got reworked again in 363 CE, when the Roman Emperor, Julian the Apostate, authorized the Jewish people to rebuild their Temple. That project ended when Julian died. And then, finally, the Muslims arrived in 622 CE. They began building the Dome of the Rock and the Al Aqsa Mosque around 685 CE. They had been on the Temple Mount for about 500 years when the Templars showed up."

"So, by the time the Templars got to Jerusalem, everything had been pretty well picked over?" Marta asked.

"Yes, many times. Caches of stray documents and gold treasure are still found around Jerusalem from time to time. They may have found something, but the Templars probably worked their way to riches. You had to donate all your assets to the Order when you became a Templar and some very rich men became Templars. Susan thinks that if the Templars got anything like these documents, it's more likely that they got them as a result of the Fourth Crusade. The Templars weren't among the crusaders who disobeyed the Pope and sacked Zara in 1202 and then Constantinople in 1204. After the sacking, supposedly the Pope sent the Templars and Hospitaliers in to restore order and administrate Byzantium. It was called the Imperium Romaniae Under this Latin rule."

"Why would crusaders sack Christian cities?"

"Zara and Constantinople were on the land route to the Middle East. The Fourth Crusade was financed by the Venetians, who were trading rivals of Byzantium. So, the crusaders sacked the towns and shared the loot with the Venetians. Within a couple hundred years after the sacking, the Ottomans ruled Constantinople. Oops, it's already 3:40 p.m. Here, let me show you the documents while we finish setting them out. Oh, one last thing—Constantine collected as much of the early Christian writings as he could find and put them in his library. It was there in Constantinople waiting for the Crusaders to loot."

The photographer and his crew showed up about five minutes later. Steven and Marta then worked with them to get reproductions of each document and each fragment. They worked fast so that a good set of prints could be sent by FedEx that evening to the Pierre where Steven could pick them up.

CHAPTER 34

Susan found Wilhelm at 3:45 p.m. She had just taken a call from James Jameson who confirmed that Eastland would be a sale. "Well, except for New York tomorrow, we are pretty much done with this one, Wilhelm. Tomorrow will be mostly real estate and we won't get a term sheet for the debt before Monday. The whole thing should be done by mid-May. I may even see a Museum this weekend."

"There's a rumor that you'll take a sabbatical after this deal is over. Is that right?"

"Marta?" she asked.

"No, actually Ms. Krejci said you're retiring," he said.

"Did she?" Susan said rhetorically. Marta must be getting good service out of Wilhelm–it wasn't like her to gossip like that. Well, Susan was leaving, so maybe it didn't matter. She sat looking at her desk.

"I was asked to help on the debt piece of another deal," Wilhelm said breaking the silence. "Mr. Mason told me this morning that you were planning a sabbatical, so you wouldn't need me for a while after this deal. The sabbatical seems more likely."

She looked up at Wilhelm and said, "Marta is hoping you will go to the NSA, so if she gets her way, we'll both be gone one way or another. I am leaving for good, but I think only Jane and Big Mouth know–and you now, because she blabbed. If I could get up the energy, I would do it today, effective as of the end of this deal. They don't lock you out of your office when you announce that you are retiring, so it's just a matter of getting the energy to resign."

"Is there anything that you want me to do?" Wilhelm asked. "In talking with Ms. Krejci last night, I realized that you have taught me a lot. I'm taking your assistant, Jane, to lunch so I can find out how to work with an assistant. People say that she would kill for you if she had to."

"I'm leaving Wilhelm—no need to butter me up. Jane can give you some good tips; I do hope she doesn't have to kill anyone for me—then again, maybe I should give her a list," Susan laughed. "She has me trained very well. I am hoping to keep her with me, did Marta tell you that?"

"Yes, she also told me that you wouldn't be bored in retirement," he said.

She looked at her watch. "Oh crap, I'm supposed to be at Chase now. Take advantage of Jane's wisdom while you are here."

"I plan to," he said.

"I'll see you at the airport in the morning. You probably know that Marta and my husband, Steven, will be on the flight as well. Give me a week to formally announce that I am leaving, will you? Peale, Curtis may have some way it wants to handle this. I am coming back here after I go to Chase, so leave me a message if anything comes up," she said as she put on her coat to leave.

Her cell phone rang as she walked to the elevator. "Yes," she answered without looking, thinking it must be Steven or Marta seeing if she was on her way yet.

"This is Lawrence Taylor, from Peale, Curtis in New York. We found the owner of that property. It changed hands very recently—it was handled by Hartley Marin out of their Boston office."

"Sorry, Lawrence —I thought you were Marta Krejci calling to tell me I'm late. Do you have any contact information for this new owner?" Susan asked.

"Yes, but it's not very helpful. I will email you what we have. It was bought by a US subsidiary of a Japanese conglomerate. It took two days to find that— luckily, certain foreign indirect ownership has to be disclosed."

"Can you find someone at Hartley Marin and tell them we would like to purchase the property?" Susan asked. "It's a family matter. The family didn't think the property would sell, so they were taking their time."

"I will see what we can do," Lawrence said. "Would you mind if I move this to Mark Jones in our Boston office? He has better local attorney contacts in Maine and he probably knows the real estate guys at Hartley Marin who handled the sale."

"Not at all," Susan said. "Thank you for doing this so quickly. Tell Mark to call me with any questions."

CHAPTER 35

Susan got to Chase at 4:15 p.m.

"Susan, you're here!" Steven said surprised. "You are smiling–does that mean you are done?"

"Looks like it, Steven," she said still smiling. "We are doing a sale. So, I go to New York tomorrow for the meeting. We sort things out, and I am done, except for clean up and maybe the debt piece."

"Excellent, we are just wrapping up the photography now–about 15 more minutes," Steven said. "This is Jim, the photographer. He can get good prints out to us by FedEx tonight so that I have them for my meetings tomorrow."

"That's great."

"I'll help Jim finish up then put things back in the safe deposit box. You should tell Marta why documents like these might have been taken from Constantinople when it was sacked in 1204 CE."

"Yes, dear," she said. "Did you hear from Bob?"

"No," he said. "Remember, Bob may or may not be picking up messages. He's not crazy like you. Did you get a conservationist? I don't think these should sit in a safe deposit box for too long."

"Yes, dear, they will be ready for you on Monday." Susan smiled, she always hated the lulls between deals or when major changes were being made and she had nothing pressing. This was different though…as of tomorrow, she wouldn't have much left to do on the deal and then she was retiring. Luckily, Jon showed up.

"Susan," Marta said. "Steven just said you're supposed to talk to me, not daydream."

"Oh for God's sake, Marta, it's pure speculation, but here goes. No, wait; I'll give you a little trivia to pique your interest. The 'Crown of Thorns' was one of the few relics that Constantinople still had after being sacked by the Fourth Crusade. However, it was being held by the Venetians as security for a loan. In 1238, the Latin Emperor of Constantinople sold the 'Crown of Thorns' to the King of France, who then paid off the Venetians' loan. The King built Sainte-Chapelle to house it. During the French Revolution, the crown was moved to the National Library. It's now somewhere in Notre Dame Cathedral."

"Have you seen it?"

"No, we'll have to look for it next time we're in Paris. Oh, by the way, the Loretto Chapel in Santa Fe, the one with the floating stairway, is modeled on Sainte Chapelle. Anyway, Constantine pushed to preserve early writings relating to the Church and Christianity. Constantine's son, Constantius II, founded the Library of Constantinople to amass and preserve not only the Christian material, but also writings from throughout the Empire. One thing you should know is Constantine made himself the arbiter of religious differences. For example, he ruled for the 'pro-Trinity' group at the Council of Nicea and for the 'anti' group later. It is very possible that documents of both schools were being saved at the Library."

"I know the Library of Alexandria had something like 500,000 scrolls," Marta said. "How did that compare to Constantinople?"

"Constantinople had 100,000 volumes, but I don't know how volumes compare to scrolls. Anyway, Venice encouraged the Fourth Crusade to attack the Byzantine Empire, in part because of religious differences. The bigger reason was that Venice competed with Constantinople for trade and Constantinople was a very wealthy city. The crusaders looted everything, including Orthodox holy sites in Constantinople and, of course, Constantine's Library. Since the Venetians were backing the Crusade, part of the loot ended up in Venice and the rest went to Rome and the crusaders. Crap, I need to take this call, sorry." Susan walked to the window as she answered her phone. When she came back, Marta was waiting for her.

"What were the religious differences you mentioned?" Marta asked.

"The 'Roman' Pope wanted to rule over the Eastern Orthodox Pope in Constantinople—they had separated in the first of the two great schisms. The second schism was, of course, Luther separating from the Catholic Church. After 1204, the Greek Orthodox Church was ruled by the Roman Pope and Constantinople had a Latin ruler who was subject to Rome's direction under the Imperium Romaniae."

"So, are you finally done with work?" Marta asked.

"Yes, after New York and some clean up. There are still some issues that we need to work out with O'Keefe Hopper, but it's basically a real estate deal now. Anyway, our documents went from Constantinople in 1203 to St. Catherine's in the Sinai. They stayed there until 1290, when they went to Cyprus by way of Acre—oh, here's Sarah. Geez, when did the photographers leave…?"

"Are you ready for me, Mr. Graves?" Sarah asked.

"Yes, Sarah, here you go," Steven said. "I won't be back until Monday. Have a good weekend."

"Steven," Susan said as they walked out. "I haven't quite finished telling Marta my thoughts. Maybe we should go for a drink or back to our office to talk. Marta, what do you think?"

"How about dinner?" Marta asked.

"Phil Stefani's?" Steven asked. "It's quiet and they have a nice selection of oysters. Susan, see if we can we get in."

"Yes, dear."

"Where?" Marta asked.

"Phil Stefani's—you know, where Riccardo's used to be. It's behind the Wrigley, down the stairs by the statue of Benito Juarez. It's the one with the murals on the wall."

"It's by the Billy Goat, right?"

"Yes. It's on that street level, but it's at Rush and the Billy Goat is at Michigan," Susan answered. "I just got 5:30 p.m. for us on 'Open Table' while we have been chatting. I hate to do this, but I have to go pick up my briefcase at the office. Can I meet you both there?"

"Maybe we should go with you....," Steven started.

"No seriously, I am just picking some stuff up," she said. "I don't want to go in after dinner, since we have to leave for the airport by 5:15 a.m. tomorrow. Steven, order the Kumamoto oysters before they run out."

"Ah, Kumamoto oysters," Marta said. "They are wonderful little morsels. As I told Wilhelm, Northwest Coast oysters first, then PEIs."

"Teaching the little buggar, are we Marta?" Steven poked.

"I'm off—you two have fun," Susan said. "Marta, don't let anyone tell you there are only two species of oysters in the US. Kumamotos are a third, the Crassostrea sikamea species, specially cultivated in the Northwest. West Coast oysters are generally Crassostrea gigas and the East Coast ones are Crassostrea virginicas. Wait for me in the bar by the murals if they won't seat you until I get there," she added as she left.

"No new deals, Susan," Steven yelled after her.

"Trivia?" Marta asked.

"Alexander the Great brought apples back to Macedonia from Central Asia. Apples spread from there around the Mediterranean. The Latin name for an apple is *Malus domestica*, because the evil serpent had Eve bite into one in the Garden of Eden. But, since the Garden of Eden was in the Middle East, there would have been no apples there yet. See you at dinner."

Susan showed up right on the dot at 5:30 p.m. She had her briefcase and was on her cell, but she was there on time. She could see them; they were already at the table and had started on the oysters. There better be some left....

"You're here," Steven said as he stood and kissed her head.

Susan hung up her cell and hugged him. "Yes, and on time as well," she said. "I can see you both waited for me. Marta, what are you drinking?"

"A 'Brooklyn,'" Marta smiled.

"What the hell is that—something you made up?"

"No, it's just a Manhattan, but you replace the sweet vermouth with dry vermouth and a cherry liqueur, actually it's a maraschino liqueur. It's also supposed to have Amer Picon rather than bitters, but I prefer to keep the bitters," she added. "Would you like one?"

"God, no—it sounds hideous. I would really like a Bloody Mary with Grey Goose Vodka, but I better just get a glass of wine. They have the Ponzi here by the glass. I had an A to Z Pinot at Shaw's last night. Both, of course, are from Oregon, which I think has the best Pinot Noirs."

"Let's order," Marta said. "I want to hear more about why you think these documents might be from Istanbul."

"First, I have a Chicago tidbit for you, which I just got from the cab driver. Are you ready?"

"You'll tell us anyway," Marta said.

"Okay, supposedly there is a plaque at 1232 W. Washington that says Mary Todd Lincoln lived there for a while after Lincoln's assassination."

"Did her son put her up there?"

"I don't know; we'll go look for the plaque when we're back from New York."

"Let's finish these oysters," Steven said as he waved the waiter over to order the main course. Susan and Marta ordered the risotto and Steven ordered the papparadelle.

After they finished ordering, Steven said to Susan, "Remember, we are all on an early flight to New York tomorrow, and some of us have a harder time getting up than you do. Now, finish telling Marta why you think these documents might be from Constantinople."

"I thought I did, didn't I Marta?" Susan asked. "I am only talking about the Greek documents—the two Latin pieces are a different story."

"You didn't quite finish—we were just getting to the Fourth Crusade," Marta said.

"Oh crap. Steven, you start, so I can finish my oysters."

"Well, before Constantine, Christianity had no centralized leadership to dictate what Christians believed. There was a lot of overlap among Paganism, Judaism, and Christianity. For example, many aspects of pagan Sun worship, including its iconography, were incorporated into Christian beliefs. Clement of Alexandria described Jesus as driving a chariot across the sky like the Sun-god. Also, about a hundred years before Constantine, Hadrian had started an Antinous 'death and resurrection' cult that spread throughout the Roman Empire. Jesus, of course, went through death and resurrection as well. Go ahead, Susan."

"Christianity likely began as a Jewish sect. As Christianity expanded to convert the Gentiles, it had to drop some provisions of Mosaic Law, like circumcision. For example, Gentiles could become Christians without being circumcised. Paul's letter to the Galatians actually went so far as to condemn circumcision. He said something like 'if you let yourselves be circumcised, Christ will be of no value to you at all.'"

"Steven, did I see you wince when Susan said 'circumcision,'" Marta asked laughing.

"Very funny, Marta," Steven said. "With all of your experience, you could easily have picked the Jews from the Gentiles in those days. Of course, you would have been stoned then, but..."

"Steven," Marta said. "Be nice."

"Have you been bickering since I left you?" Susan asked.

"He started it," Marta laughed. "Go on, Susan, why Constantinople. Actually, first, if 'Paul' condemned circumcision, why is it done in 'Christian' nations like ours?"

"We are not a 'Christian' nation," Susan objected. "That was made clear in 1797 with the Peace Treaty of Tripoli signed by John Adams. It included a clause that said '…the Government of the United States is not, in any sense, founded on the Christian religion….'"

"Okay, but if circumcision is prohibited by Paul, why are there circumcised Christians?"

"It's a very old practice—at least 4500 years," Steven said. "There's a tomb at Saqqara from the Fifth or Sixth Egyptian dynasty showing a circumcision in process. And, of course, God made Abraham circumcise himself, his household and his slaves to show their faith."

"Genesis 17," Susan said. "It comes and goes throughout history. When Constantine came to power, he enacted a law saying that Jews couldn't circumcise their slaves. I just pulled up a survey here that says it is now generally accepted that circumcision is good, health wise."

"Put your iPhone away, dear," Steven said.

"Should I finish Constantinople?" she asked.

"Yes, please," Marta answered. Steven didn't answer as he was now busy with his iPhone.

"First, around 650 BCE, Byzas built a Greek city on the west side of the Bosporus where the Bosporus and the Golden Horn flow into the Marmara Sea. The legend is that the Oracle at Delphi told Byzas to build his city 'opposite the blind.' Chalcedon was built on the east side; its founders were said to have overlooked Byzas' superior location, hence they were 'blind.' Septimius Severus conquered Byzantium in the second century. Like Rome, his city was built on seven hills. Constantine then consecrated Constantinople in 330 CE. Strategically, the Bosporus is important because it connects the Mediterranean Sea with the Black Sea. Troy sits at the southern end on the Asian side."

"On the Dardanelles, opposite the Gallipoli Peninsula," Marta added. "It's one of my favorite movies."

"*Troy* with Brad Pitt or *Gallipoli* with Mel Gibson?"

"I was thinking of *Gallipoli*, but *Troy* was good, too," Marta answered. "And, before you ask, I still haven't read Colleen McCullough's *Song of Troy*."

"Wait, I have two last ones on circumcision," Steven said. "Hadrian's cousin, Aquila, once asked a rabbi why, if circumcision was so important, it wasn't one of the Ten Commandments. I don't think he got an answer. And lastly, the Gospel of Thomas says that if circumcision were useful, God would have made children pop out at birth already circumcised. Anyway, abandoning circumcision helped the Gentiles become Christians. Now, it mostly comes and goes for medical reasons. Susan, go back to Constantinople, please. Dinner's almost over."

"Is the Gospel of Thomas part of the New Testament?" Marta asked.

"No, it didn't make the final cut for the Bible," Susan said. "Actually, a Coptic copy of the text, probably copies from an original in Greek, was part of a stash of leather-bound papyri found at Nag Hamadi in Egypt. The stash was buried around 367 CE. It's a good example of why the letters Steven is looking at might be real. The Gospel of Thomas says that it contains the hidden words of Jesus. It was not accepted as a true gospel by Bishop Athanasius, and, thus, had to be hidden away."

"Athanasius did accept the Book of Revelation for the Bible," Steven added.

"St. Thomas went to India where he and his followers were then isolated from the Church. They are known today as Nasrani Christians. Almost 1,500 years later, the followers of Thomas living in India had a run in with the Portuguese Inquisition; their Christian beliefs were rather different from those of the Pope."

"Thank you, dear," Steven said. "Bishop Athanasius allowed Christians to read only the books that were approved for inclusion in Eusebius' recently standardized Bible. Constantine had Eusebius, among others, pull everything together, pick what they liked and ban the rest as heresy."

"This all relates to the formalization of Christianity from teachings and folklore to a structure with specific dogma and rituals," Susan said. "Eusebius' Bibles became the standard. Those Bibles and Christianity reflect more what Paul, not Jesus, preached. Oh, and Constantine more or less became God's representative on Earth."

"The *Jefferson Bible* is a simple demonstration of what Susan is trying to explain," Steven added.

"Your favorite President, Susan," Marta commented.

"Yes, he is...Jefferson cut everything out of the New Testament except what Jesus said," she said.

"That meant none of the miracles or other fictions survived," Steven added. "What Jefferson ended up with is, as Susan always says, a beautiful philosophy. As for Paul, his teachings were more folklore than philosophy."

"We aren't alone in this opinion of Paul," Susan added. "I think my favorite is a statement by Will Durant."

"He wrote *The Story of Civilization*." Marta said.

"Yep, that's him," Susan said.

"I still have all 11 volumes that we used when we took that art history elective, Susan. You taught me how to appreciate art that summer; more importantly, you told me we didn't have to like the same artists."

"Was that when Susan taught you to ride a horse?" Steven asked.

"No, Steven, dear. I had already known your wife for several months by then...it was the summer after our freshman year. I didn't want to go home to my parents, so we took some summer classes. Susan, what is Durant's quote?"

"'Fundamentalism is the triumph of Paul over Christ,'" Susan said.

"Let's get back to Constantinople and our stash," Steven said deciding that they needed focus again. "I told Marta earlier about the multiple sackings and rebuildings of the Temple Mount."

"Steven told you about Titus and Hadrian, I suppose," Susan said. "We also mentioned that Constantine funded Helen's travel through the Holy Land to look for relics and bring them to Constantinople."

"That was at lunch," Marta said.

"Yes, and Constantine had columns, marbles, doors, and statuary from all over the Roman Empire brought to Constantinople to expedite the building of his new city. He also oversaw the seminal Christian councils in which he gathered all of the bishops together to decide on Church rules and interpretations. The most important one was the Council of Nicea."

That's present day Iznik, Turkey," Steven added.

"Anyway," Susan began again, "because Constantine was consolidating power into Constantinople, he likely would have searched everywhere for material relating to Christianity. We also know that Constantine spearheaded a massive effort to transfer papyri documents relating to Christianity to parchment. Those documents were ultimately kept in the library built in Constantinople by his son, Constantius."

"He also had Eusebius compile the history of the Church," Steven added. "Constantine had Eusebius pulling everything together to ensure that Constantine was given the nod as the ruler chosen by God. Many of the stories that Christians learn today came from Eusebius' *Church History*. For example, that may be the source of the story that Nero blamed the Christians for burning Rome in 64 CE."

"So, there should have been a fair amount of material in Constantinople. There were other pockets, Alexandria and the Sinai, for example. Then, in 1204, along came the Fourth Crusade financed by the Venetians. Rather than going to the Holy Land by sea, they went by land and sacked Constantinople. That's how the Horses of St. Mark's ended up in Venice–they were looted in 1204 and brought back to Venice. They also sacked Zara on the way even though it was under the Pope's protection. Oh, one more thing…there was a copy of Plato's '*Republic*' in that stash in Egypt at Nag Hamadi."

"Could the early conquerors have missed something in Jerusalem, Susan?" Marta asked.

"Absolutely, especially if it's a bunch of old stuff like the Dead Sea Scrolls. Anyway, we mentioned the Library of Constantinople established by Constantine's son, Constantius II. A lot of what was saved from Alexandria was brought to Constantine's library. Like Alexandria, it was damaged by fire several times, but it was the Fourth Crusade that destroyed it–what wasn't burned went back to the West. So there you are."

"So, the crusaders sacked Constantinople to repay the Venetians and crush its trade rival?" Marta asked.

"In part…it also was tied to the first of the two 'Great Schisms' in Christianity. This one began in 1054 when the Eastern Church split from the Roman Catholic Church. Anyway, as Susan said, the Crusaders would have taken anything they didn't destroy back to Rome, or possibly Paris, which was the wealthiest city in the West by the 13th century. They had already started building Notre Dame around 1150."

"When the French king went after the Templars in the early 1300s, the Templars supposedly moved their assets to Scotland, Portugal and Cyprus. So our Joham, being Portuguese, could have had contact with some of those assets. Because the Templars fought for the Portuguese against the Muslims in the twelfth century, the Portuguese king allowed them to re-constitute as the Order of Christ after they were disbanded in 1312. Joham does not say he is a Templar and he is too late, if the box is 1600s. He says only that he is a knight. We don't know where he got the documents or why he was protecting them."

"Steven, we are speculating about documents without knowing whether they are real. We need to focus on that."

"Yes, dear," Steven said.

"One last thing, two of the koine letters reference the Council of Nicea that Constantine convened. We don't know how our knight came to be guarding any of this with the three Guardians. So there's our entertainment for tonight's dinner."

"Damn Portuguese kicked my people out with the Muslims," Marta said.

"I thought you were Czech...oh, I get it. Yes, they did."

Marta sat quietly for a few minutes. "Why did Joham take these to Maine?" she asked Steven.

"Let's hope he tells us somewhere," Steven said.

They finished dinner in silence. After the check came, Susan said, "in the interest of full disclosure, I will mention again that very few Templars, if any, were traveling with the Fourth Crusade—virtually all of them were in the Holy Land waiting for these guys to finish looting. The Pope sent them into Constantinople afterwards to clean up the mess. Steven, the Latin seal document mentions Paris. I need to look at that again. Right now, though, we should go home and pack."

CHAPTER 36

Kat read the email from Utamaro. The company's counsel in Boston, Hartley, Marin, had notified Utamaro that a client of a Chicago law firm was willing to pay a 10% premium plus costs for Kat's property in Maine. The American client had planned to buy the property because the family had lived in the area in the 1700s. The client hadn't realized that someone else was even looking at the property. Had it not been so similar to the story he had just used, he might have chuckled. Was this just a coincidence?

He certainly wasn't going to sell it, yet. Perhaps he would offer them an option to buy the property in six months. It shouldn't take the archaeologist too long to see if anything was at the site; if he didn't find anything, then he would sell it. He decided he would ask his Boston counsel to get more details. Should he send Eisen to meet them? Eisen could attend as a Samovar representative. Kat called Eisen.

"Yes, sir?" Eisen asked.

"How would you feel about going to Boston next week, Eisen?

"May I ask why you want me to go to Boston?"

"I have just received word that someone wants to buy our property in Maine." Kat said. "Our US counsel says it was an unsolicited offer through a firm in Chicago. I may have you meet with the potential buyer to see what you can find out. You could be a representative of our Samovar entity, since neither of us would pass as a real Mr. Samovar. You would simply sit with our lawyers and ask them any questions you might have. New York might be better…I will tell Utamaro that you will meet them in New York."

"I have no problem with either city, sir," Eisen said. "I might pass as a Filipino Samovar. You would come with me?"

"Maybe—not to the meeting though. You could handle that, but I don't think you look Filipino."

"Thank you, sir, for your trust. Any information on why they want it?"

"Like us, an old family connection," Kat chuckled. "I read the property report you gave me. This is not a property that is ripe for development. It's quite a coincidence—everybody trying to buy land that nobody but a family friend wants. I guess we should find out why they really want it. Good thing we came up with the 'retreat' concept."

Yes, sir," Eisen said. "Boston is an extra flight for us."

"They can come to New York. Boston is nearby, so if they don't budge, we will go there—from New York."

CHAPTER 37

The flight to New York landed on time. Susan and Wilhelm went off to the O'Keefe offices and Steven and Marta went off to Peale, Curtis to look at the confidentiality agreement that had come in from Dr. Gruber.

Susan received a text from Steven at about 2:00 p.m. indicating that Marta had someone at Peale, Curtis review the confidentiality agreement for them. Steven had gone over the agreement with Jon at lunch and then signed it and sent it back to Dr. Gruber. Susan chuckled as she read that Steven had Marta do a counter signature as well.

Now, at 2:30 p.m., Steven was calling to tell her how his meeting with Jon had gone. She answered on the second ring.

"So, how is it going?" Steven asked hesitating. He did not want to hear bad news—he wanted to hear that her deal was still a sale.

"All is well, Steven," she said. "We had a couple of structural issues to work out, but it looks like it will be a sale. I have to stick around for another couple of hours to finalize the pricing mechanism. Then, I'm done except that I'll have to work on the debt piece. Oh, and bad news for Marta—Wilhelm is going to DC tonight to help with a transaction there."

"On a Friday night? Did you tell him that he had to go?" Steven asked.

"Of course not! I told him that it was up to him, since he and I are pretty much done with the deal. I will go in tomorrow around 8:30 a.m. to make an appearance and make sure everything is on track. I would have told Wilhelm to ask Marta if he could go, but I am trying to be nice for a few days."

"Yes, well does that mean you have made it almost a full day being nice?" he chuckled.

Susan chose to ignore the bait. "So, you got the agreement done with Dr. Gruber?"

"Yes, of course," he said. "More importantly, Jon and I went over a fair number of things. The only thing that's disconcerting is that his son, Father Bartolome, now knows about the 'Templar' letter. That is where Jon saw 'Joham.' Father Bartolome asked Jon to send it to him, but Jon told him that he was having a friend look at it before he showed it to anyone else."

"Let's call it the 'Joham' letter. Does Jon's son know about the other documents?" Susan asked.

"Nope," Steven said. "I think Jon is afraid that he will lose control; his son might be more interested in the documents than in protecting his father's reputation. Of course, if he hadn't told Father about Joham, we wouldn't know that there was another document with this Joham's name on it."

"Did, um...," Susan stopped for a minute.

Steven waited for Susan to continue. After a minute when he hadn't heard anything more, he asked, "Susan, are you still there?"

"Yes, sorry," she answered. "I was just thinking about an approach for tonight. I guess we would ask Dr. Gruber to determine the age of the 'Joham' letter, so that not too much information gets out about Jon or what he found before we're ready. Also, I would prefer to have David look at the older material with you for language inconsistencies first, but that's only because I don't know this Dr. Gruber. Maybe test this Gruber on the parchment and ink of the 'Joham' letter. We know David can tell quickly if the Hebrew or Aramaic is proper for the period. He probably could verify the Greek too, if you want."

"That's what I was thinking. Let's take a picture of the attestation with us tonight, to see if he's interested. If he is interested, then we will finalize an arrangement. I do need to talk more with David."

"You're pretty chatty today," Susan said. "Anything else?"

"Well, I was saving the best for last," Steven said. "As for the diary that Jon's son found...."

"Yes?" she asked almost to the point of begging for information.

"Jon's son, Father Bartolome, said that the college still hasn't found the stuff he sent in last year. However, there are two things that will interest you," he stopped to wait for a reaction from her.

"Steven, between you and Marta toying with me, I swear—what are the two damn things?"

"Okay, these are good," he said. "First, an archaeologist that Father Bartolome worked with at a Verrazano site nearby has a brother in Lisbon. This 'brother' owns a very reputable antiques store that specializes in memorabilia of early North American explorers. Apparently, when Father was complaining to the archaeologist about the lost materials, he mentioned that some of it was in Portuguese. The archaeologist then volunteered to ask his brother to check around."

"For what?" Susan asked.

"To see if they might have gotten onto the market."

"Steven, are you serious? You mean like they were stolen?"

"Yes, the dealer brother confirmed that there were rumors that a 'journey diary' of an early 14th century Portuguese visitor to North America was on the market. Since American explorers are his specialty, he figured he could get information without being suspicious. Unfortunately, he was told that the 'journey diary' had been sold to a collector in the Middle East, subject to some conservation work being done in London. By the way, the dealer brother scoffed at the date."

"And Father Bartolome thinks it may be his material that has gone missing?" she asked.

"He thinks it's possible," Steven said.

"Okay, it went to the Middle East, but how? Did the college sell it, or was it stolen?"

"They don't know yet, but, the Lisbon brother thinks it may still be with the London conservator. Unfortunately, the person he talked to–well this won't surprise you–his cell phone number doesn't work anymore," Steven said.

"Do we know who the London conservator is?" she asked.

"No, the trail has gone cold as they say," he answered. "The Verrazano archaeologist is at the same college that Father's material has disappeared from. The brothers, Father and Jon all think it is too much of a coincidence that this day journal is floating around when the college can't find Father's stuff. At the Lisbon brother's suggestion, Father apparently advised the college to contact Interpol."

"So, that means Father Bartolome also thinks it is the same material."

"As I said, he thinks it's possible. But what is this stuff?" Steven said almost to himself.

"No idea–what's the second thing?"

"Father Bartolome found his notes. There were three items: the diary; a fragment with a drawing on it that might be a map, but it was too faint for him to make out; and a piece in a language that he didn't recognize–it wasn't Portuguese. None of it was very legible, but he did see the name, João Alvares, and some dates. One was March 8, 1552; the other was October 6, 1608. He also saw 'Tomar.' He recalls seeing other dates, but his notes were sketchy as he planned to finish them later, but ran out of time. It wasn't his area of interest, so he sent his materials to the college and didn't think much more about it until he talked to Jon. So what is this stuff, Susan?"

"Steven, I don't know–but it's consistent with Joham's attestation that I have been reading," Susan said. "And the dates are more within reason for New England. You're still at the Met?"

"Yes, Jon left for Philadelphia about 45 minutes ago. I have to go; I'm having coffee with Dr. Barnes in a few minutes at the little café in the American Wing. See you tonight.

"Okay, 7:00 p.m. at Le Bernardin. I probably won't go back to the hotel before that. I promised James Jameson that I would have a drink with him and his daughter, Seattle. She's at the *New York Tribune Herald* now."

"If he's the buyer, thank him for me," Steven said. "And don't be late."

CHAPTER 38

Susan got to Le Bernardin at 7:10 p.m. Steven, Marta, and a distinguished looking man of about 60, with a full head of silver gray hair, Dr. Gruber she guessed, were already seated. Marta had a glass of wine waiting for her. Susan didn't like to have a cocktail before a meal when she was meeting someone new—so she would order a glass of red—then it would be ready when her entrée arrived. Marta had done that for her.

"Please call me Hershel," he said taking Susan's hand before they sat.

"We have just been comparing our backgrounds Susan, so you haven't really missed anything," Marta said. "I ordered you a glass of the Ponzi Pinot Noir."

"Thanks, I'm glad they have it. I'm sorry to be late. It was impossible to get a cab. Friday night I guess," Susan said. "Steven, have you showed Dr. Gruber the picture yet?"

Dr. Gruber interrupted, and again said "Hershel, please."

"Sorry," Susan said smiling at Hershel. "Steven, have you shown Hershel the picture yet?"

"No, dear. We have, though, taken the liberty of ordering some Chef's Cove oysters and stone crab claws."

"Then perhaps by the time we finish our appetizers you will have forgiven my tardiness, Hershel," she said.

"Already done, Madam," he smiled.

"I was just telling Hershel how we are enamored with the Willamette Valley Pinot Noirs," Marta said. "The Ponzi vineyard is where Susan?"

"It's just west of Portland and the Willamette River in Beaverton. I could live on Oregon Pinot Noirs and Napa Valley Cabs."

"My wife grew up primarily in the western part of the US," Steven added. "You name a place and she invariably knows where it is and has probably been there."

By the time the appetizers had been cleared, Steven was explaining as vaguely as possible, how a friend had given him and Susan the task of determining whether the document he was going to show Hershel might be real. Susan added that where it was found suggested it would be dated somewhere between 1300 and 1600 CE.

"It's definitely parchment, not vellum," Steven said.

"As Steven or Marta may have told you, it was found in a box with a hasp that says 1307," Susan added. "We are leaning to the 1600s end of the range, hoping that the document was put in the box after 1307."

"You say it was found in something dated 1307. Can you tie the date of the document to that date?"

The entrees came and there was a lapse in the conversation as everyone surveyed the presentations. Marta ended the silence. "Hershel told me about one of his last authentication projects" she said. "It was done for a Japanese company—he had done work for one of its principals many times. Coincidently, this recent work involved a parchment document that was possibly medieval as well."

"Yes, it was from about the same time period," Hershel said. "In fact, it was very close in time," he said remembering that the map had a date of 1307 on it. That was an odd coincidence, he thought to himself. Maybe he was remembering the date incorrectly. No, he had seen a lot of documents since he did that one for Mr. Ohno, but he was pretty sure it was 1307; it was on that map segment. The parchment that the map was on was indeed old; maybe as early as 1300, but Hershel had reported to Mr. Ohno that the signature and the 1307 date on the map likely were added a few centuries later. He looked up and saw they were waiting for him to say something more. "Herodotus said that it was common to write on animal skins in his time," he said pausing. "The medieval document I did for the Japanese gentleman was parchment as well," he added.

"Ours cannot directly be tied to 1307, yet," Steven said. "May I ask how you come up with the date for something like this?"

"One uses a number of approaches, as we discussed," Hershel said beginning slowly. "The language itself is a key, as language changes over time. If there is organic material, you might use radiocarbon dating. Of course, the parchment itself and even some inks contain at least traces of organic material. Also, one might look at how the ink penetrated, and interacted with, the parchment. Some of the most difficult ones are the palimpsests; they can have traces of older writing that still gets picked up. You can also do a spectroscopic approach on inks–there you are looking for something that was not commercially available before a certain time. In all of the above, comparison to calibration pieces is important. I like to test as much as possible–the fact that you date the parchment to say 1300, doesn't mean that somebody didn't write on it yesterday. So, what exactly is this parchment you are concerned about?"

"I brought a picture of the piece," Steven said. He was quite happy with Hershel's explanation. "As you will see, it's in Latin. We think that it is an attestation by the author; there is no salutation. As Susan mentioned, there appears to be a date on the piece where the signature is, but it is pretty much illegible. It looks like it could be 1607 to me. But it could also be 1307; as you will see, the parchment looks scraped there. The date is what we are most concerned about."

"It is something of a brief historical piece," Susan said. "The author is reciting that he was ordered to come to a certain place and did as he had been asked. He seems to identify himself as a knight who has sailed from a port in Wales."

Hershel was looking at them. These were upright people and, since Marta was with them, they had to be legitimate. "Does it say where he sailed to?" Hershel asked.

We'll get to that," Susan said. "He recites some battles that he fought in or places where he lived–it's like a little recitation of his history, an attestation maybe. It's just a long page; there are dates in the text, but they are hard to read. Since it is Latin, which even I can read, our only difficulties come from where the document is damaged. Of course, we are not medieval historians. Might this be a common thing—to write out a little history?"

"There is a very famous example written by a historian whom we call 'Le Templier de Tyr'," Hershel said.

"A Templar from Tyre?" Marta asked. "Lebanon?"

"Yes, but he lived on Cyprus. The book was written in the 1300s, but in Old French, not Latin. He, or an aide, wrote a part of the *Gestes des Chiprois* or the *Deeds of the Cypriots*. It's a history of Cyprus up to the time of the author. The exciting part is that he gives a personal account of battles like Acre as well as the dissolution of the Templars in 1312, I think it was. I have actually read it only in translation—I cannot read Old French."

"Well, ours certainly isn't a book, but it has similar content."

"And your Templar was in Cyprus at the time he wrote it?" Steven asked.

"That is the general belief," Hershel said. "But I am anxious—may I see the photograph, please? Is the text clear?"

Steven looked at Susan. He wasn't sure he wanted this to be real. Susan nodded to him, so he handed Hershel a picture of what they were now calling the 'Joham' attestation. It was signed by Joham Alvares Diaz Ovelho.

Hershel stared at the document in the picture. What on Earth was this? He looked at Marta. Then he looked again at the picture and then at Susan and Steven. His mind was racing. He needed to calm himself before he spoke. What should he say, though? In February, Kat had him authenticate a map with a very similar signature. That signature on Kat's map was incomplete as the edge was torn, but the part he could read on the map had definitely been 'Joham Alvar.' However, the signature on Kat's map had been a later addition, but now here was what must be the full name. How could people from a different continent show up with something that had the same person's name?

"Hershel, you look like you've seen a ghost, are you okay?" Marta asked.

"Yes, yes," he said as he pulled a small magnifying glass from an inside pocket. They were right; it did look like a short historical recitation with an attestation at the end. It was indeed dated and, although the date was almost impossible to read, it could be the same as the date that was added on the map. Hershel took a breath and then a sip of wine. "May I ask where you got this? Did you buy it?" he asked. Perhaps someone had put Kat's materials and this on the market, and these Americans bought what Kat didn't.

They looked at Dr. Gruber. "Is there a problem?" Susan asked.

"Well," he said. "I have seen part of this signature before. This document in the picture, did you find anything else with it?" Hershel was worried now. Had he just authenticated something for Kat that was part of a hoax? He had told Kat and Eisen that their document could be 1300 to 1600, but that the signature and the date likely were added recently. That certainly made it seem that a major hoax was afoot. God, he thought to himself, maybe he would be lucky and it would turn out to be a hoax perpetrated in medieval times.

Susan looked at Steven and Marta. She saw Steven's almost imperceptible signal. Marta didn't move. "As Steven mentioned, an old friend, a respected archaeologist, asked if we could find someone to authenticate this," she said. "I cannot tell you much about where or how he came across this, yet. I am not sure whether Marta or Steven told you before I got here, but Steven and I met in graduate school a little over 30 years ago—we were studying biblical archaeology. Our old friend knew our background, so he assumed, well he knew we could at least read Latin. We are leaning toward this being a hoax of some sort as is our friend. When did you see the signature?"

"It was within the last few months, Madam."

"The conundrum, as I guess we can tell you, is that this was found in a box buried under an undisturbed layer with confirmed dating to 1300 to 1600," Steven added.

"Undisturbed? You are sure?" Hershel asked looking almost relieved.

"That is what we were told by our friend—he has been working in the area for many years—his focus is on a much older layer—so he was quite upset at finding this," Susan said. "The 1307 date is on the hasp—we are having the wood dated by an expert. The signature you saw, perhaps you can tell us where you saw it and we can piece things together."

"It was on a piece of parchment I was asked to authenticate. If the original of this picture has the same attributes as the one I saw recently, it probably can be dated to somewhere between 1300 and maybe 1650. That was...well, you may be correct about the hoax element, but perhaps not a recent one. You know, I received a call a week ago from a London dealer I know. He asked if I have seen any documents from the early 1300s. He said he had a client willing to pay top dollar for things like this. I reminded him that I was primarily a conservator and didn't actually deal in works. He then offered me a finder's fee if I found anything."

"This is a dealer you have worked with before?" Marta asked.

"No, but I know of him. He has a solid base of clients, including a couple in Zurich whom I know. He even purports to do conservation work. I wouldn't...that is to say, he isn't always, um...his reputation isn't the best. Look, I am afraid I cannot say anything more. I need to think about this. I have a duty to you and a duty to my other client. I will call that client tonight to get instructions. Of course, I will not disclose the details of what you have shown me."

"We would be willing to meet this other client to compare notes, wouldn't we Susan?" Steven asked.

"Yes, I think so, but we have to confirm it with the archaeologist. Again, he was quite upset by finding this. He is very sensitive to the possibility that it was planted as a hoax, but he cannot explain how it could be buried below undisturbed...well, you understand," Susan said. "Marta what do you think?"

"I don't know why not," Marta replied.

Susan sat for a moment and then asked Hershel, "Is it possible that the dealer or your client is Joaquin Samovar?"

"No," he said. "May I ask why?"

"It's a name we have heard...he supposedly is looking at this type of document as well," Susan said stretching the truth just a little. "I was hoping you might know why he is poking around like that. For all I know, it could be an alias for your London dealer or your client. This London dealer wouldn't be an American in London would he? Mr. Samovar has an American accent."

"I'm sorry, that is not a name I know," Hershel said. "The dealer I spoke with has one of the most embellished British accents I've ever heard—upper crust, you know. Now, let's enjoy dinner. Do any of you come to New York for the Sotheby's and Christies art sales?"

"We all live in Chicago," Susan said. "It's only 734 air miles from here, so we come pretty often." Susan flew so much in the US that she knew the air distance from Chicago to almost any major city—867 miles to Boston, 633 miles to DC Reagan and 1,437 miles to Tucson. "Is your client coming to the auctions?"

"Possibly...he is a collector." Hershel said.

"We come sometimes if there is something we might want," Steven said.

"Do you have a particular interest?" Hershel asked.

"We have an eclectic collection at best. For example, we have antiquities and Islamic pieces. We particularly like the Mamluk period in Egypt," Steven said.

"We also like the American Luminists like Thomas Moran. The Luminists are more like a subgroup of the Hudson River School; they worked around 1850 to maybe 1900. We have only one," Susan added. She looked over to Hershel—he was staring at his glass. "Hershel, are you okay?" she asked.

Hershel looked up and smiled weakly, "It's very interesting. I had a conversation about Thomas Moran with someone in Zurich a couple months ago."

"Speaking of luminescence, Susan has several hummingbirds by John Gould in her office at home—those are my favorites," Marta added. "Gould applied gold foil to convey the luminescence of the hummingbird feathers. He did drawings for Darwin—Susan once showed me Darwin's reference to Gould's work in *On the Origin of Species*."

"Marta and I are bird lovers; the Goulds are pure joy," Susan said. "She's a much better spotter than I, so I collect pictures of them—the birds can't move in those."

"And do you bid at the auctions?" Hershel asked.

"We do occasionally, if something comes up," Susan answered. "It's tough, though. We put in a low bid on a small Thomas Moran piece a while back—it was a little atypical to our thinking. We lost, but it may have been a good thing. A professional forger was arrested a few years later. Small paintings by Luminists were mentioned as one of his specialties."

"Perhaps you are referring to Shaun Greenhalgh and his family. He was busted by Scotland Yard. I think it was an Assyrian relief that got him caught. He should be out about now. I think he only got four or five years. Someone like him scares me more than you can imagine. He was very good."

"And then there was a woman—Morales, but I think she only sold them, she didn't do them," Steven said.

"And, like Al Capone, she didn't pay taxes on the sales proceeds—what a moron," Marta added. "Some of these forgers are damn good. Even the Art Institute bought a fake Gauguin statue—anyone can make a mistake."

The talk was making Hershel uncomfortable—he hated forgers, it made his life so difficult. It was one thing to try to figure out the age of something, but when someone was trying to deceive intentionally, that was too much. And, now who do these Americans mention but Thomas Moran and a forger! After forgers, he hated coincidences. Kat had mentioned the same artist. What was that phrase, 'just because you're paranoid...?'

Susan could see that Dr. Gruber was on edge. It wasn't a good night for him; first, he is upset by their document; then, they bring up forgers. No wonder he looked nervous, forgers must be a horrible problem for an authenticator. She changed the topic and asked Hershel if he had seen the new Islamic art installation at the Met.

"No I haven't," he said. "I understand the Louvre is doing a re-installation as well."

"Yes, it is." Steven said. "When does it open Susan?"

"It already did, I believe," Susan said. "That's an easy flight from Zurich, right? Perhaps you will meet us in Paris for dinner some time."

The remainder of the dinner was amicable. They would all meet for dinner again tomorrow. Dr. Gruber would try to get in touch with his other client before then. He suggested they meet at Daniel for dinner. His treat, since he had to cut the discussion of their project short.

"Are you sure you can get a reservation on such short notice?" Marta asked.

"Yes, Marta. My partner and I have a lot of friends in New York and we are here several times a year. I have my assistant book a table for 4 at my favorite restaurants well in advance. I can always dig up a companion or two to eat with me when I don't have the pleasure of entertaining guests like you. Is 7:00 p.m. okay tomorrow night, as well?"

Susan saw that Marta liked the 'trick.' "It's fine with us, Marta can you make it?"

"Yes, of course. Let me know if you ever need a fourth diner, Hershel," Marta said. "I'll pop up from DC."

The smile on Hershel's face indicated that he might just do that—Marta would dress up any table.

With dinner over, Susan, Steven and Marta headed back to the Pierre.

"Susan, you have to go in tomorrow morning right?" Steven asked.

"Yes, I told Jameson I would be at O'Keefe Hopper by 8:15 a.m. I thought I should, since Marta's boy has gone off to DC tonight. I just need to meet with Jameson and make sure everything is under control as we hand the torch to real estate. It might just be him and me at that hour—the locals won't straggle in by train or limo until about 9:30 a.m. I should be done by early afternoon. If it doesn't blow up, on Monday I will tell Peale, Curtis I am retiring."

"I think I might take a train to Princeton tomorrow morning," Steven said. "Dr. Alberts asked me to come down for lunch. He's being a little mysterious, but he says he can tell me about the leather cover."

"What leather cover?" Marta asked.

"The older documents, not the ones in Latin, were inside a wooden cover that was bound in leather. An insignia was embossed on the front, with 1267 under it. I think it's a date—we only have a picture of it, Jon still has it. I sent a picture to Norman."

"It may be a coincidence, but our Koine copies were finished in 1267," Susan added.

"I'll use the opportunity to ask him if he has seen any other evidence for some of the accusations raised in the letter I'm working on. I have always suspected them, but I had never actually been able to find a document voicing them. That's the main thing I want to talk about. The insignia is extra; he gets a free lunch if he can tell me about it."

"So, that letter supports your theory about the changes to align the Church with Constantine's rule?" Susan asked. She was amazed–for Steven to actually get on a train to meet with their old professor, Norman Alberts, meant he had seen something more interesting than the insignia.

"Yes, meaning that everything is being conformed, Jesus has become God and Constantine has become the arbiter," he said. "Susan, where is that saying, "[A]nd he said unto him, 'Why call me good? Only God is good.'"

"It's in both Matthew and Luke. In Mathew, someone asks what good things they should do and Jesus first says there is only 'One' who is good–and then he says to follow the Ten Commandments." She got her iPhone out. "That's Matthew 19:16 to maybe 20, near where Jesus says 'it is easier for a camel to go through eye of a needle. In Luke 18, Jesus asks 'Why did you call me good?' Then after someone answers, Jesus says 'No one is good except God.' They are used as support by the 'Jesus is not God,' crowd. Why do you ask?"

"One author, Ammonius, is upset about the 'Trinity' language. The author also says Jesus was a teacher, not 'God.' Susan, do you think we could have a mix of real and faked or forged documents?"

"Meaning that the 'Templar' stuff is faked, but the older stuff is real?" she asked.

"Yes," he said slowly. "It's just a thought. Someone might not have known what to do with these early documents. Remember, one of your thoughts was that someone buried these to avoid a charge of blasphemy during the Puritan witch hunts."

"It's possible, Steven," she said. "I mean documents that say Constantine is God's manifestation on Earth," are pretty dangerous. Anyway, if Jon's right that the box was below undisturbed earth at a layer for which he had reliable dates, then we have a box buried at least 400 or so years ago."

"And what if this 'document' that Hershel mentioned somehow got Hershel's client to the site where Jon discovered the box? Then Hershel's 'document' has to be as old as the box unless it was made later based on information from somewhere else. It would support the idea that the Greek materials and our 'Joham' documents were buried by someone who needed to hide them–or keep them safe from someone. Hershel's client would then be Samovar or an affiliate."

"If Hershel is right, and someone changed the date on the map to 1307, how old is the box?" Susan asked. "Hershel said he didn't know Samovar, but that could be a fake name given only to Jon. What do you think Ms. Spy?"

"It is plausible–I was just thinking about how your picture spooked Hershel tonight," Marta said. "We need to check that dealer who is looking for documents from the 1300s. Sounds to me like he somehow accidently let the piece Hershel saw earlier slip away from his shop after he changed the date; now he wants it back. Why the hell didn't I ask Hershel the dealer's name?"

"That's brilliant–and none of us asked him, Marta," Steven said. "Let's make that the first question tomorrow. What I really care about are the older materials. If Alberts doesn't scoff at the text too much, then maybe I will go see David, while Hershel gets us dates."

"It was good to get you involved, Marta," Susan smiled. "Steven, if you are going to see Norman, does that mean you spent some time on the Greek documents today?"

"Yes, I did. Susan, again, if it's a hoax, it's damn well done. Anyway, Norman will meet me at the train station. We'll chat there over lunch and, when I've eaten, I'll get back on a train. I want more than one opinion on this, so I'll involve David and Norman. My thought is you for the Latin pieces, Hershel for determining the age of the documents and David to help me with the language issues with respect to the Greek, Hebrew and Aramaic documents. Especially the Aramaic…damn thing is odd. I will save Norman for special issues, like the insignia on the cover."

"Okay, I'll focus on the Joham document and the wax seal one. Um, can I set an alarm on your phone so that you don't get too engrossed and miss your train?" Susan was chuckling, but she was serious too–it had happened before.

"You do need to be back for dinner, Steven," Marta said. "I would tag along with you, but I am having breakfast with an old colleague. I need an introduction from him for the project I have in DC next week."

"Ladies, I will definitely be back before dinner," Steven said. "You know how I like to eat—and a free meal at Daniel would be hard to miss. Besides, I'm planning to get back in time for a nap."

"So," Susan said thinking out loud as much as anything. "If this isn't a hoax, it sounds like we have a box that was buried by someone in the 1600s—let's use that date for now so we can set aside somebody coming to Maine from Portugal or Wales in the 1300s. The stuff inside is real. One group of documents, those in Greek, Hebrew and Aramaic, is second or third century, one document in Latin may actually be 1300s, and the other is contemporary with burial of the box. So, who buried the box and why?"

"And is the dealer looking for the box, or does he just want his doctored piece back?" Marta added.

"Good question, but we don't have a clue," Steven said. "Susan, if I gave you the photos of the Hebrew and Aramaic fragments, could you possibly get copies made and ship them off to David? He will be in Israel for just a few more days—he goes to Shanghai next Friday."

"We may be able to do it in the hotel's business center," Susan said. "Wait, there is a FedEx office in the O'Keefe Hopper building. I can do it there on my way in tomorrow. Steven, it's two days for international—that's Tuesday, at best."

"That'll do," he said.

"Um, maybe you could get the photographer to send them digitally as well… I'll work on FedEx and you or Marta can call the photographer."

"Jim," Marta said. "Steven, I'll email you his number."

They rode the rest of the way to the hotel in silence.

As they got out of the cab, Susan said, "It would be too much if the piece Hershel saw was one of Father's missing pieces."

"Goo god, Susan, that's something to sleep on," Marta laughed.

CHAPTER 39

"Eisen, sorry to bother you at home," Kat said.

Eisen was stunned. Ohno-san had called him at home on a weekend only one other time. That had not been a good time—Smith-san's wife had died. "What is it, sir?" Eisen asked slowly.

"I just got a call from Hershel," he said.

"Good news, sir?" he asked, not sure what to say. He had no idea why Dr. Gruber would call Ohno-san on a Saturday.

"Not good or bad—just news," Kat said. "Hershel just had dinner with three Americans in New York. They are from Chicago."

"In New York?" Eisen asked. He looked at his watch. It must be after midnight in New York. He sat for a minute trying to guess what the urgency might be. Could it possibly be the Americans who wanted to buy the property? That would be too much of a coincidence.

"Eisen, are you there," Kat snapped. He was edgy today; he was working on his Giotto paper and he was having difficulty with a segment.

"Yes, sir," Eisen said. "It would be humorous if these Americans are the same ones we are to meet in Boston."

"They just might be, Eisen," he said relaxing a little. "And we are not going to Boston to meet any Americans. If Hershel's Americans can meet him in New York, then the Americans who want our property can come to New York as well."

"And are we to meet Dr. Gruber's group, too?"

"Yes, he said they would come to Zurich if that were easier. Anyway, it must be the same group because one of the Americans asked Hershel if he knew our friend, Joaquin."

"Samovar?"

"Yes," Kat said.

"Oh, oh," Eisen said.

Kat knew Eisen was shaking his head slowly, trying to assemble the facts rationally. "Eisen, are you there?" he said again to encourage him.

"Yes, sir, but, why are they meeting with Dr. Gruber? I am afraid I don't quite understand…he doesn't know the Samovar alias, does he?"

"No, he doesn't, but they do. They even said the poor man had an American accent," he said stifling a chuckle.

"And why did Dr. Gruber call, sir?"

"It seems old Daf wasn't sending us off to chase butterflies…they just showed Hershel a document signed by our Joham. He's confused, Eisen." Kat too was confused, but then he thought of poor Hershel being handed another 'Joham' document by the Americans and he started chuckling.

That sound of Ohno-san chuckling worried Eisen, he rarely saw Ohno-san show too much emotion. He did love to laugh, though. It was more of a chuckle, but it could go on for a while—at least he was chuckling now, but Eisen didn't quite understand why. "I am sorry to be dense, but are you saying that Dr. Gruber was just handed a document signed by Joham?"

"Yes, I am," he said and then heard Eisen chuckling as well.

"Poor Dr. Gruber.…"

"Actually, Eisen, it was only a picture of a document. They hadn't actually brought the document with them. Hershel said it was an attestation of some sort bearing a date that could be 1307 like ours, but he said the Americans believe it was more likely to be 1607. He couldn't really tell from the picture, even though it was high resolution. Can you imagine his surprise?"

When Ohno-san and Eisen stopped chuckling, Eisen asked, "Did our Joham say he brought this document to Maine?"

"We don't know yet," Kat said. "Poor Hershel was very upset. After he saw the name and heard the date, he asked them to take the picture back. But they did tell him that it was found in a box with a hasp dated 1307."

"So, is it possible that these are the Americans who want to buy the property in Maine?"

"Yes, but, of course, Hershel knows nothing of that."

"And what did they want him to do with the document?" Eisen figured he knew the answer, but he had to hear it to be sure.

"What do you think, Eisen? They asked him if he could tell them how old the parchment was. As I said, Hershel declined to take the document—I mean the picture of it. Hershel explained that he had a possible conflict and wanted to check with us before he looked at it in detail."

"He was sure it was our 'Joham'?" Eisen asked. That seemed impossible unless it was some sort of fraud and someone was flooding the market with documents purportedly signed by the same person—but that would be so stupid. "How did he know?"

"The signature was pretty close and the date is about the same, except the signature was complete on the Americans' document. The full name is Joham Alvares Diaz Ovelho."

"Oh," was all Eisen could get out this time. He thought for a few minutes then said, "I guess that means we can meet with the American property buyer when we meet with the American 'Joham' group. If we schedule it for New York, maybe you can also preview the American Art auctions."

"That is a very good idea, Eisen. Call Dr. Gruber and Hartley, Marin and see what you can arrange. Tell Hartley it has to be in New York because of scheduling issues," Kat said. "They have a lot of our business—tell them to make it happen. We will pretend that we don't suspect the Americans are one and the same group for now. What I cannot figure out though, is how this American group got a document signed by our 'Joham' with the same questionable date. And what is this box? Has our archaeologist mentioned it?"

"He hasn't mentioned a box, sir. He did find a crystal—that upset him a lot," he added. "If he's now found a box in Maine dated 1307, he's probably more upset than Dr. Gruber. Perhaps I better check on him…I'll ask if there's anything new." Eisen and Kat were chuckling again.

"Good," Kat finally said when he stopped chuckling. "Hershel suggested that we might have a seventeenth century hoax on our hands. I tried to calm him a bit by suggesting that an old hoax could still be interesting. Just to add a little more intrigue, Hershel also told me he got a call from Mr. Prenbryer, the London dealer, a couple of days ago. Seems Mr. Prenbryer asked Hershel if he had seen any materials from the early 1300s recently. He said he had a client willing to pay top dollar for anything Hershel had. Hershel says he told Mr. Prenbryer he would look around."

"Mr. Prenbryer…," Eisen mused. "Should I invite Mr. Prenbryer to meet us in New York as well, sir?" Eisen said chuckling. He caught himself right away, "Sorry, I understand this is a serious matter, sir.

"It's not a bad idea, Eisen," he said chuckling himself. It was rather humorous…a bunch of people running around looking for something that likely was a hoax. But the map apparently had taken them to a box in the middle of nowhere—well, the middle of nowhere in Maine.

"I haven't told Hershel that Prenbryer contacted Daf as well," Kat said. "Or that we suspect him in that rifling of Daf's office. I did tell him that I would prefer that he not tell the dealer anything about us. He said the Americans told him the same thing. I guess we should check again with Margery to see if anything has happened with the investigation."

"I check with her weekly, sir. There hasn't been much. Apparently, Kate Parker, the new assistant who was to take over from Ms. Short, has disappeared. Since nothing seemed to be missing except Ms. Short's calendar, the police don't seem too interested—simply a robber who came up empty handed. With Smith-san gone, Ms. Short is alone except for her sister. I think it helps for her to get a call now and then. How did Mr. Prenbryer come to call Dr. Gruber?" Eisen asked.

After processing what Eisen had just admitted, Kat replied, "Hershel said only that he knew this dealer and he was not one of his favorites. I suppose it's possible that Mr. Prenbryer did sell something to Daf and to the Americans by accident. That would explain why we both have something, but that seems too simple."

"Yes, sir, it does. Smith-san must have bought his pieces sometime in the fall whereas the Americans…"

"I agree. They seem to have obtained their document only recently. I doubt Mr. Prenbryer would be stupid enough to make two accidental sales months apart. I will be here at home until Monday," Kat said. "Besides, I think that Daf would have bought anything Prenbryer had."

"I will work on the meeting in New York, sir."

"It is a weekend. I'm not sure that many Americans work on weekends. We know their friends the Brits certainly don't, although they do work more than the French. I am sure you will find Hershel, since he is German. Start with him, but be easy on him. As I said, he is pretty upset."

"Yes, sir," Eisen replied. "And if he asks questions?"

"I didn't tell him that the map led us to Maine, so I don't have to worry that he will disclose that. That's the enigma—it may be a real map with a fake date added. I will give him no more information until we find out what the Americans want or, more importantly, what they have. He is meeting with the Americans again for dinner. Have him arrange a meeting in New York during the first week in May."

"He is Swiss, sir," Eisen said.

"What?" Kat asked.

"He's Swiss, sir, not German."

"Same difference. Good day."

Eisen sat looking at the phone. At the end of the year, he had been alternating between staring at the wall and at wood block prints done by his favorite artist and namesake, Keisai Eisen. What a difference now. He thought he better track down their archaeologist. He fumbled around on his iPhone until he found the name—Dr. Jonathan Christiansen—he was at Penn. Perhaps this Dr. Christiansen had shared something he found with his fellow Americans. It wouldn't hurt to stop by and visit him. Philadelphia was a short train ride from New York. He would see if Ohno-san thought Mr. Samovar's representative should go there as well.

The phone rang again.

"Yes, sir?" Eisen asked, seeing that it was Ohno-san again.

"Let's plan for you to meet that archaeologist when we are in the States. Maybe we will have Samovar's representative go to the site and see how things are progressing," he said. "We'll have to work that out. We don't want our archaeologist to find out that someone with a name like Samovar is an old Japanese or Filipino man. As I mentioned, the Americans said that Samovar seems to have an American accent."

"They certainly will get a surprise when they meet Samovar."

"Yes, well perhaps Samovar will just send that old Japanese man he knows to meet the archaeologist."

"I think the old Japanese man might enjoy that," Eisen said. "I will follow up, sir." Eisen hung up the phone with a smile on his face.

CHAPTER 40

Richard Prenbryer slammed his phone down—he was not happy. Joshua Borne, his American contact, was coming a week earlier than planned and Richard wasn't ready for him. Josh had lined up a buyer for the map and the diary in the Middle East.

He and Josh had made a small fortune when the last piece they did together was sold to a private buyer in the Emirates. The nice thing was that when their pieces were sold into private collections, especially in Asia or the Middle East, they were unlikely to surface again for many years. In fact, as a rule they would resurface only after the buyer died and his heirs tried to sell them at auction—the trail was usually pretty cold by then. That was the way they liked to do things, but he still needed another week.

Richard had been surprised when Josh showed up at the end of August last year with a little scrap with a map drawn on it, a small diary-like book, and a piece in Welsh. They had been found in the States, of all places. All three were on parchment. The map and the Welsh piece probably dated to around 1500 to 1600. The diary looked older. God knew where Josh found the three new pieces, or, if the map was real, where it might lead.

Nevertheless, there was a big market for old maps hinting at treasure. This map, though, couldn't garner much interest by itself. An old map that pre-dated the invention of longitude in 1775, might have some novelty value, but people generally liked to know what the map was depicting or have an 'x' for treasure.

Even when timepieces had evolved enough to allow longitude to be calculated, the measurements weren't terribly accurate. He had looked it up—Captain Cook used an early timepiece on his 1775 trip to the Antarctic. Cook praised the fact that the timepiece's determination of a day never varied by more than something like eight seconds. That correlated to a distance of two nautical miles at the equator. You certainly couldn't find a treasure without some longitudinal direction, but a two mile-range would still make it almost impossible. This map had nothing.

Josh said they had delayed for a few months while they tried to decide what to do with the pieces. He had finally come to Richard—it was Richard's idea to tie the map to the diary.

The diary also was in bad shape, except for its leather over wood cover, but it had real promise. The pages were parchment, two in Portuguese and the rest in Latin. The name João Alvares was still clearly legible inside the cover and Joham Alvares Diaz Ovelho appeared on a later page. The diary also referenced a couple of dates and the Portuguese city of Tomar, but he couldn't pick out much more because of the condition.

Richard decided to make Joham a Templar knight of the 1300s to give the map a 'story.' The leather cover was fine—his problem was that some of the writing inside the book could still be seen very faintly. He decided to rework the parchment by scraping off as much as he could. He would then use his own ink mixture which had fooled many experts.

He used snippets from an English translation of a history of the Templars written in Old French by 'Le Templier de Tyr' for descriptions. Richard couldn't replicate the Old French, but he could do his 'diary' in Latin. It turned out to be one of his best works—the diary not only looked fantastic, but it also read well. Thank God he hadn't left that sitting on his workbench with the map and the Welsh piece.

As a final touch, Richard had added a date to the 'treasure' map—just the year 1307 with the rest looking worn off. Then he added a partial signature of Joham Alvares Diaz Ovelho to the map, so that it was credibly tied to the little diary that had the 'Joham' name in it.

Richard initially thought the Welsh piece should be sold with the map and the diary, since it also had the Joham name in it. Josh disagreed—a piece in old Welsh that neither of them could read would take too much time to fix and might make the story too complicated.

Richard eventually agreed. Unfortunately for him, the Welsh name, 'Dafydd,' was also in the text. Apparently, that had caught the eye of that Welsh scholar who came into his shop last September just after Josh had brought the pieces to him—the scholar's name also was Dafydd. He knew it was his fault leaving the damn Welsh piece and the map in view on his desk, but who would have expected some damn Welshman to see it. Of course, Richard stupidly told his new assistant it was worthless trash he picked up at a flea market. She thought she had done well selling some trash while he was out.

It had taken Richard months to finish the diary—luckily, it had taken Josh a while to find the right buyer. Now the diary was done and the new map was almost ready. Nobody would really miss that damn Welsh piece and he hadn't doctored it. He did want the 'doctored' map back— it might be traced back to him. And now Josh was coming early and he was out of time.

His prior attempts to reach the Welshman, Dr. Smith, hadn't worked out at all. He had refused to meet with Richard. And now the stupid Welshman had died on top of it—well, so maybe he had been too sick for visitors. Richard had even agreed to let Josh send one of his specialists, aka Kate Parker, to Cardiff to get the map back. 'Kate' thought the Welshman had given the documents to someone, since they weren't among his possessions at the University. All she took was the Welshman's calendar. It turned out that you don't meet with too many people when you are dying—and it was mostly illegible—horrible handwriting, so he had her destroy the original. She did such a crappy job rifling through things during the Welshman's funeral, that the police had been called. At least whoever Josh got to search the Professor's home during his funeral had done an impeccable job. Nobody ever reported a break in, but he too came up empty handed.

The only real lead had come from the Welshman's old assistant; she mentioned to 'Kate' that some things would go to an old 'Asian' friend. Before Kate fled Cardiff, she said she had heard the old assistant ask for Mr. Shikawa at the St. Davids Hotel. So, at least they knew that it was an old 'Japanese' friend. When Richard had checked, there was no one named Shikawa at the hotel. The hotelman hung up on him when he asked if they had anyone who looked Japanese staying with them. The only good news was that Kate hadn't heard anyone talking about a map at Cardiff.

Richard had spent all of this effort on the diary only to lose the map. There was no point having the diary without the map. He decided to try one more time to find the map, thinking he had another week. He needed to find out who this Japanese friend was. Perhaps he would call Ms. Short and offer to pay her for her time if she could find out how he might contact the Japanese friend. Or, perhaps she had the map and figured it might be worth something. But with Josh coming now, he first needed to finish the new map. If he had the extra week.... He called his assistant in; he kept her on so as not to call too much attention to the mess up. What she sold needed to stay as worthless scraps.

"Elizabeth, I have a possible lead on some antiquities that I think a client would like. Find me the phone number for that woman who retired from Cardiff—Margery Short. I think her sister said she would be living in London by now."

"Yes, sir," Elizabeth responded. "I will see what I can find."

This woman, Elizabeth, was at least competent. Josh's Kate Parker had been a complete waste—she had disappeared as soon as the police had shown up. Oh well, Josh had hired her and Josh would have to deal with her. He went back to work on the new map.

CHAPTER 41

Susan was up at 7:00 a.m. She got ready, laid out Steven's clothes for the morning, kissed him on the head and left for O'Keefe Hopper by 7:30 a.m. She set her alarm to call him at 8:30 a.m.; that would give him plenty of time to catch the train to Princeton for lunch. She walked south on Fifth Avenue to 53rd and turned right to head over to Eighth Avenue. It was cold, but not brutally so. She got coffee at Starbucks, and was at the O'Keefe building by 7:45 a.m. The FedEx office in the building had opened at 7:30 a.m., so she got the pictures copied and off to David. She would wait to call Wilhelm in DC until 8:45 a.m., in case he had a late night. She had left O'Keefe before him last night, so that she could have a drink with Jameson and his daughter and still be at Le Bernadin by 7:00 p.m.

Susan's phone rang as she walked into the O'Keefe conference room. It was Wilhelm. That was one of those 'character' points she liked–he called first. It was 8:20 a.m. "Hello, Wilhelm...where are you?"

"DC, I am on my way in to a firm called Hartley, Marin to meet our real estate guys. There's a draft waiting for you in the room we have at O'Keefe Hopper. It's in a folder with your name on it. The edits are mine. Will you tell me if I missed anything?"

"I doubt that you did, but I will call you if anything changes," Susan said. "I had a drink with Jameson and his daughter last night. He's quite pleased with you–he even told his daughter he likes you. So, you know, that's an extraordinary compliment to come from him."

"Thanks," he said.

"Let me know what you think of Hartley, Marin. Their Boston office represents the seller in a real estate deal for one of my clients." She hung up and sat down to look at the draft Wilhelm had left for her. Then she remembered to call Steven—he was up, so she went back to the draft.

When Steven got to Princeton, he found Dr. Alberts waiting for him.

"Thank you for meeting me on such short notice," Steven said shaking Norman's hand.

"Steven, it's always good to see you," Norman said. "I got us a reservation for lunch just around the corner. I imagine you're hungry."

"Yes, of course—and my treat," Steven said. "That's the least I can do to thank you for making time to see me on such short notice."

When they had ordered, Steven said, "I wanted to chat with you about a few things we are looking at, but first I have a question about Morton Smith. You knew him right?"

"I don't want to disappoint you, but if you want to know if it was a hoax, I don't know," Norman said.

"No, I could ask you that on the phone. My question is a little different. I have been looking at some old Greek documents—two letters specifically. I do not know if they are authentic, but because the text is so intriguing, I think it is possible that they are," Steven said.

"Is it the authenticity you are after or information on the topic?" Norman asked.

"The topic, of course," Steven laughed. "Here, I brought a picture of the letter that piqued my interest," he added as he passed the picture to Norman. "It's by one Secundus and purports to be written in 325 CE. Actually, to be clear, this is a copy of that letter which purports to have been last copied in 1267 CE in the Sinai. I assume you got the picture I sent you; it's the insignia from the cover of the folio that this letter was in. The cover also has 1267 emblazoned on it."

"Yes, let's start with that. It's not a symbol you see often, Steven. The serpent was the key."

"That's a serpent?"

"No, Steven, it's a serpent wheel. It's a Gnostic symbol."

CHAPTER 42

It was only 12:30 p.m. and Susan was done. Except for a small issue, it was pretty much a real estate deal now. Susan had coffee with Jameson and on a whim asked if Seattle might be interested in a possible art world hoax. He said she was always looking for stories, so Susan should call her. Ordinarily, she would head for the airport to get on the next plane home. But this time she was staying in New York and was free until dinner. Steven was still in Princeton, so she called Marta's cell.

"Susan?" Marta asked. "It's so early. Why are you calling?"

"Very funny...I'm done for the day. However, now I don't have anything to do until we meet Hershel for dinner," Susan said. "I'm going to the Ruben Museum, unless you have time for lunch."

"Oh, oh, maybe you won't be able to handle retirement," Marta chuckled. "I'm just finishing here—maybe another half hour. Go to the Met instead. We can meet in the Trustees' dining room, how about 1:15 p.m.?"

"I'll be there," Susan said. She hailed a cab as she hung up and headed for the Met. Maybe she would take a nap after lunch, she thought to herself. Then she remembered that she had promised to look at some governance proposals for the Research Center. Sometimes, she liked being on the board of a charity and sometimes she didn't.

Marta was already at the table when Susan walked in. Susan had made a beeline to the Egyptian Wing so she could see the New Kingdom pieces again. She then detoured through the American Wing to see the Tiffany stained glass pieces on her way to meet Marta. Some day she would take Steven and Marta to see the Tiffany panels in the Gadsden Hotel in Douglas, Arizona. Oh, well, she was only about five minutes late.

"The only downside I see to your retirement is that you won't stop by to visit me in the office," Marta said as Susan sat down. "It's a dreary place, you know."

"Well, you aren't poor Marta. You could quit and travel with us—we'll still meet you anytime or anywhere for dinner, you know. And you do have Wilhelm." Susan was toying with having a glass of wine—she hadn't one at lunch years. No, she would wait until dinner.

"Wilhelm and I both need someone we can be seen with. He's a nice man, but in case you haven't noticed, he is too young for me. And as the daughter in a Jewish family, my two brothers get the inheritance—I was supposed to get married and live happily ever after off my husband. I did try twice, but.... Anyway, Wilhelm probably will ship off to the NSA. Then you will retire and I will be all alone at Peale, Curtis."

"Your mother will leave you something, maybe her home in Palm Beach," Susan laughed.

"Just what I need...a home in facelift land."

"Seriously, you know she is very proud of you."

"That's only because my brothers are saps."

"Marta—nobody else's daughter is a beautiful ex-spy. You know she loves that. Ask Steven, she was beaming when you walked in to her party last month."

"Well, I still need the structure of a job, so it'll be a while."

"There is that guy in the DC office whose wife left him. He does ERISA and employee benefits. Nice looking guy...they say he took the divorce very hard. He would have to take me and Steven as part of the bargain. Look him up when you are in DC—are you going tomorrow?"

"Slow, down. How much coffee have you had?" Marta laughed. "And what section did you dally in too long? You were five minutes late. Are you going to give me his name or will I get it through osmosis?"

"Geez, not enough coffee to interfere with a nap this afternoon," Susan said. "I detoured through the American Wing to look at the Tiffany pieces yet again. Actually, my favorite here is the glass mosaic *Garden Landscape and Fountain*."

"I'm still partial to the Tiffany piece at the Field, the *Mermaid*," Marta said.

"Me too," Susan said. "You still haven't been to see the Tiffany panels in the Gadsden Hotel in Douglas, Arizona. You could see the nick in the marble staircase supposedly made by Pancho Villa's horse as he rode it up the staircase, too…ah, let's order."

When they had ordered, Marta said, "You still didn't tell me the DC guy's name, so I can't look him up. Have you heard anything from Steven, yet?" she asked. "Why did he go to see this guy, Alberts?"

"Norman Alberts was his favorite professor at Penn; now he's at Princeton. As you know, I focused on the usurpation of early Christian philosophy by creation of the 'Church,'" Susan started. "Steven went further and argued that the standardization of Christianity, including the rituals and iconography, was pulled from pagan myths and rituals, and hid the philosophy. Constantine capitalized on this and, by working with the 'Church,' secured his supreme authority on Earth. Along the way, they suppressed or destroyed beliefs that were inconsistent. That's why you find biblical texts buried at Nag Hamadi—they were like contraband."

"So?"

"So, Norman is a good sounding board for Steven. He has lunch with Norman at least once a year, anyway. Norman may even tell us what that insignia is, although I'm not sure how. I still haven't seen it."

"And the Greek letters in the box support Steven's research?" Marta asked.

"Apparently," Susan said. "Well, supplement, might be a better word. At least one of the Greek pieces complains about creation of the 'Trinity.' I might add that the concept is not found in the teachings."

"Have you read the letters?"

"I can't anymore. I recognize it when Steven translates it, but I cannot read anything with ease now the way he can. My vocabulary is gone. So, he has to tell me what he sees."

"And, again, he sees support?"

"He does indeed," Susan smiled. "People don't realize that organized religions are mostly made up by men. I mean, can you imagine 'Jesus' living in the lap of luxury with a golden crown on his head. Until Pope John Paul II, Popes were carried in a chair by a bunch of men in red uniforms. Compare that to Mathew 25:35, where the teaching of Jesus is to feed the hungry. Even the Old Testament says something like 'Open wide your hand to the needy and to the poor, in your land.'"

"You know I donated to 'Nuns on a Bus,'" Marta said. "I may be Jewish, but that was a very good and brave thing for them to do."

"It is a good cause. And the guy's name is Cy Steele. 'Cy' as in 'Cyrus' and the Cyrus Cylinder found in Babylon."

"Yes it is a good cause," she said, ignoring the fact that Susan had thrown in the DC guy's name.

"Anyway, 'Christianity' had to be standardized so that it could spread to the masses. So, Jesus teaches a philosophy of good works to a small group, but as new followers join, they have less contact with Jesus and things begin to muddle. It's kind of like that old game, where you whisper a phrase to the next person and that person whispers it to the next, and when you get to the end, the phrase is rarely anything like what it started as. Jesus is no longer there to say yes or no, so it gets corrupted. And then Constantine steps in as ultimate arbiter and gets everything to conform. It may have started with Hadrian or possibly even earlier."

"Didn't Steven mention Hadrian's relative, Aquila, when we were talking about circumcision?"

"He's an interesting character. Aquila worked with Hadrian in building Aelia Capitolina over the ruined city of Jerusalem. He also translated the Hebrew Bible into Greek. Some even say he is the 'Aquila' whom Paul references as the husband of Priscilla, but the dates don't work. Priscilla, in turn provides evidence that women were accepted as teachers of Christianity early in its history."

"So, it wasn't only men?"

"No, the early Church wasn't men only. My guess is that Christianity moved from being a Jewish sect toward Gnosticism. That may be why they found Plato buried at Nag Hamadi. The Gnostic, Marcion, appointed both men and women as priests. But as more converts came in, the power went back to the Jewish patriarchal ways and women were pushed back into minor roles. Mary Magdalene would be a good example. She went from being at Jesus' side to being labeled a prostitute. She is now being rehabilitated by the 'Church,' I think."

"As what?" Marta asked.

"I have no idea. Anyway, Constantine consolidated everything into Constantinople and then standardized the Christian religion by making himself the arbiter of arguments amongst the Bishops. Oh, and he made it clear that God selected him to rule. So, many of the rules for Christians to live by were codified by Constantine."

"It's not surprising," Marta said. "We Jews have standards that allow us to live all over the world, but still identify as Jews because of our rules. Most of us have no idea why...was Constantine a Christian?"

"There is a story that a vision helped him win control of the Western Roman Empire in the Battle of the Milvian Bridge in 312 CE. At midday, Constantine looked up at the sun and saw the Greek letters, Chi, which looks like an 'X,' and Rho, which looks like a 'P,' configured sort of as a cross with a hat on it. Those are the first two letters of the Greek spelling of Christ."

"Like the Cyrillic alphabet, dear. Chi, rho, iota, sigma, tau, but what was the point?"

"I don't remember if the angel said 'By this conquer' or it was written in the sky, but they used that sign on their military standards and shields and won the damn battle."

"Like the old sky writing bi-planes at air shows?" Marta laughed.

"Don't laugh too hard," Susan was laughing now as well. "Remember, God spoke to your Moses, too. And Moses got tablets—just like Joseph Smith of the Mormons, except Smith had to dig for them. Anyway, most stories say that Constantine didn't convert until he was dying. By the way, the 'Chi Rho' symbol has been used at least as long ago as Plato—I think in his 'Timaeus.'

It appears on coinage of one of the Ptolemaic Pharaohs and it was used as an editing mark meaning something like 'This is good.'"

"So he waited until he was dying?"

"Supposedly...I think it was Hendrix who described the conversion as being like 'Pascal's Wager'—why not hedge your bets when you are dying?"

"Interesting," Marta said. "I'll remember that when I'm dying."

"I should mention that a fair amount attributed to Eusebius, was actually added to later editions of his Church History well after he died. Are you bored yet?" Susan asked.

"No and I haven't finished eating either," Marta answered.

"Steven believes that Eusebius helped establish the religious basis for Constantine's authority beyond that of Emperor Worship. Also, the sect of Christianity that he favored used both the Old and New Testaments. That helped because Constantine then had Solomon and David as examples. The end result was that he became Christ's 'King' on earth, with the Roman Empire becoming the agent of God's plan to Christianize the world."

"And Constantine was buried in the Church of the Holy Apostles in Istanbul, right?" Marta asked although she was more questioning herself.

"Originally, the tombs of Constantine and the 12 Apostles were to be in the Church of the Apostles," Susan added. "As we mentioned, some say his mother was there too for a while. Eusebius provides the only description of the Church."

"So, that's why Steven is so interested in the Church of the Holy Apostles. I never quite understood that until now."

"Steven can tell you more—he's the expert. By the way, the Church of the Holy Apostles was important architecturally. It was built in the form of a cross rather than a centralized basilica style. By the 5th century, it was 'the' style. St. John's Basilica near Ephesus has the same design. My favorite is the Church of Saint Simeon Stylites, in the Dead Cities area north of Aleppo. Too bad your spy group wouldn't let you go into Syria with us—the column capitals are the most beautiful I've ever seen. They are modeled on acanthus leaves."

"Maybe someday...."

"Anyway, Constantine pushed for a standardization of Christianity. It happens with all philosophies. You dumb it down and then you convince the followers that they will get something good from it. Like riding a white stallion in heaven—I heard someone say that once. Can you imagine how sore your butt would get riding a horse for eternity?"

"You're really on a tear today. I'm glad my meeting ended in time for lunch," Marta smiled. "Go on."

"I will stop whenever you want."

"No, don't."

"Originally, the beliefs were more like Plato described—when you die, your soul is freed from your body. It then becomes one with other souls that have already been freed on death. That was in his *Phaedo*, right? And Socrates, said virtue can't be learned...Damn, I'm rusty. And, again, Plato's *Republic* was in the Nag Hamadi stash with writings of the Gnostic Christians."

"What's the difference between an apostle and a disciple?" Marta asked.

"I'll tell you in a minute, but to make my point, many people argue that Eusebius borrowed heavily from existing cults in describing Christianity. Mithraism is a good example; the birth of the god, Mithra, was heralded by a comet and attended by magi. Like Jesus, Mithra had 12 companions."

"And the difference between apostles and disciples is what?"

"Jesus chose the 12 Apostles to be with him. Disciples generally came later as followers."

"Are Mathew, Mark, Luke and John apostles or disciples?" Marta asked.

"Only Mathew and possibly John are Apostles, but it's complicated," Susan said as she tried to decide if she could still name all of the Apostles. "You can see their pictures in Michelangelo's "Last Supper," but the list is in Matthew," she laughed. "There is Andrew and his brother, Peter; Matthew, the tax collector; Philip; Bartholomew; Thomas; James, the son of Alpheus;

James and his brother, John, who are sons of Zebedee; Thaddeus; Simon the Zealot; and Judas Iscariot. Is that twelve?"

"Yes, congratulations," Marta said. "But for all I know you made them up."

"Peter's birth name is Simon but it's unclear whether he's Simon the Zealot. He is supposed to be buried in Rome under the Vatican, but the Franciscans found the ossuary of Simon bar Jonah or Peter, in Jerusalem. The ossuary is in a nice little museum at the Church of the Flagellation in Jerusalem. So, Peter's ossuary is in Jerusalem, but his tomb is at the Vatican."

"So, he's buried in two places?" Marta asked.

"Maybe...Constantine scoured the Roman World, which of course, included the Holy Land, to find the remains of the Apostles for his Church of the Apostles. He died before it was completed. When his son completed the church, only relics of Saints Andrew, Luke and Timothy were included. Only Andrew was an Apostle, but then, he was the first one chosen by Jesus. When Mehmed conquered Constantinople in the 1400s, he built the Fatih Camii mosque over the Church of the Holy Apostles. Again the Fourth Crusade is blamed for weakening Constantinople so that could happen."

"God, Susan, some of this is actually beginning to make sense," she mused. "That's the crusade that sacked Zara and Constantinople."

"Steven thinks Constantine or his son likely would have put out an order to find the remains of the Apostles. There would have been good money in "finding' those remains...or at least the ossuaries. Ancient forgeries can be interesting.... Crap, there's my phone. I have to take this call, we have one last issue. Hopefully, this is a call to say it's resolved." When she finished ten minutes later, she looked at Marta. "Are you still eating?"

"I'm done, let's go back to the Pierre and take a nap—it's already almost 3:00 p.m. I promise I won't snore."

"So you were bored!"

"No, I was well entertained, but as you said, a nap would be nice," Marta protested.

"It's not too cold—shall we walk?" Susan asked.

"Twenty blocks?" Marta blurted. "I wish I had stayed at the Carlyle! How's the ankle— can you make it?"

"They are short blocks—I'm just using my cane because it's damp here—it helps to exercise. Do you want to stop at the Carlyle for a drink? I've heard they love you at Bemelmans's Bar."

"Let's just get a drink at the Pierre. Actually, let's skip that, I need my nap. Your room okay? My room's a mess."

"Fine with me."

"You exiled my Wilhelm to DC. I need the company."

"I did not; he went of his own accord. Besides, you can see him in DC tomorrow."

"I will be in DC all week, actually," Marta said as they began the walk back to the hotel. "Wilhelm has to be back in Chicago Monday afternoon. I have lots more questions about our lunch topic."

"Good, ask Steven," Susan answered. They walked silently for several blocks; then Susan said, "Somebody called me an 'apostate' in graduate school because of my thesis. God knows what they called Steven. Anyway, they were wrong; *Merriam-Webster's* website says you have to believe in something first, before you can be an apostate. Steven and I only disagree with Western religious beliefs that have no foundation, so I guess we are just renegades. Of course, we haven't found any with foundations."

"Oh for God's sake, Susan," Marta said, laughing. "You've always been a renegade. God, I tried to tell someone how your friend would bring mammal specimens back from Mexico in her bra…he didn't believe me."

"They were small mammals. She used two small strainers inside; she couldn't build up her front too much or the Federales might have pulled her over for a different reason. Anyway the bribe worked…I think we used to give the Federales $10 at the blockades."

"Bribing was that common?"

"Marta, for God sakes—when Steven and I started practicing in Chicago, you put your filing fee on top of the papers you wanted to file and a $5 bill underneath. If that $5 wasn't there, they wouldn't accept them at the filing window."

"Seriously?"

"Ask Steven. We have five more blocks, and I wasn't the renegade in that story. You'd fit the bill as a renegade, too."

"Damn, it's still cold here…let's go to Tucson soon. You and I and Steven can be renegades among the tumbleweeds."

"Warm renegades," Susan laughed.

They walked the rest of the way in silence.

CHAPTER 43

When Susan and Marta got to the Pierre, they stopped to get Susan a coffee in the bar. Susan convinced them to find her a 'to go' cup and they went up for their nap.

"Marta," Susan hoping she would fall asleep soon. "How often do you wonder why we really bother with all of this? I mean, what is the point?" Crap, she thought to herself, Marta is already asleep.

Susan began thinking maybe she had read too much Dostoyevsky when she was young. She wasn't unhappy, but sometimes she wondered how people could stand living…everywhere you looked, there was such pain…starving children, abandoned animals…and assholes. Dostoyevsky's character, Ivan Karamazov, put it well, "It's not God I don't accept…I do not accept the world that He created…and cannot agree with it." Susan had stopped reading Dostoyevsky after *Brothers Karamazov;* it was his last book anyway. She remembered Steven's assistant from so many years ago—she was an excellent chef, but rarely cooked. As she always said, it wasn't that she couldn't, it was simply that she wouldn't. As for Susan, it had been too long since she had last read *Brothers Karamazov*. She probably couldn't read it in Russian now even if she would. She was ready now to finally fall asleep.

Marta rolled over and awoke. "Susan, have you forgiven me for telling Wilhelm about our little diversions?"

"Do I have a choice?" she asked. "I sure he didn't believe you anyway."

"I am sorry—it was just that… do you remember the first time you took me to the ranch?"

"Yes, of course. We took the old pickup out to the cabin, since you lied about knowing how to ride a horse. We spent the day bird watching. *Doveryai no proveryai*...I wanted to trust you, but I needed to verify that you weren't up to something."

"I didn't lie—I just didn't tell you I had never been on a horse. We went to see the phainopeplas. That night, you showed me how the scorpions fluoresced in black light while we listened to the great horned owls calling back and forth across the canyon. You were so nice back then—making sure I didn't break my neck my first time on a horse! I did at least make it up to you when I gave you the little..."

"Dear God, Marta, that was a very long time ago," Susan said laughing as she remembered Marta's little present. Damn, she was naïve in those days.

"I needed to do something nice in return—and you were such a loner. Do you remember what you said after you tried it?"

"No—we were maybe 18 the first time you were at the ranch—actually, if it was the first half of our freshman year, I was only 17. That was almost 40 years ago."

"We met second semester—legal age, dear. You said, 'we're even,' that's all you said."

Susan laughed. "Well, I did spend most of my weekends with Pete trying to keep the ranch afloat. My dad did love to gamble, and then, when he died, well, he wasn't there to service all the damn debt he put on the land. Pete and I were driving to St. David to take something to one of his pals when I told him we would have to chop up the ranch. We stopped on a hill and watched the freight trains going by down in Benson; that song was right, you probably could hear a whistle blow a hundred miles." She sat thinking; it was an entirely different world then...it ran out on Pete.

"Pete told me he was happy with the cabin and knowing he didn't have to run things anymore, Susan."

"I hope he wasn't telling another tale," she said pushing the old times away. "Anyway, I was scared to death of you. Even worse, I was worried that Pete might have a heart attack when he saw you saunter up—then I would be alone.

He was already in his eighties by then, and Adele died before I met you. And it was my horse, not me, being nice."

"Scared of what?"

"Duh, we were from very different worlds," Susan said as she stifled a yawn. "Good thing my mother was a librarian—I had at least read about your world. Sebastian and I had a bet over whether you would even show up."

"Sebastian," Marta said slowly. "I miss him too, Susan—he bet I would show up, didn't he?"

"Yes, actually he did. 'Always give people a chance to exceed your expectations,' he would say. I would always tell him that meant you should set your expectations near zero. But you did show up—shocked the hell out of me. Sebastian always did like you."

"Susan, I wanted to live in the world you were in."

"You were a very rich Jew in a sorority, for God's sake. Hmm, I guess they didn't know you were Jewish."

"Precisely—some of them were entertaining, but we were all trying to be alike. And there you were sitting in the art section of the library every Friday selling pot with your gimp leg and a cane. Then, when I found out you were from a ranch.... Somehow, you had gotten outside the box and I wanted to be there too. And almost 40 years later, here we are."

"Well, I would never have been allowed in the box—and I was not selling pot in the library. I told you, I may have taken an order or two—but I never sold it in the library. Libraries are sacred places, or at least they should be. Anyway, I did offer to take you out to the ranch, so I figured I deserved whatever it was you had planned...," Susan stopped. She had just remembered something. "You ass, do you remember when you had me bring you a book up on your sorority's sun deck?"

"God, that was funny. I sat at the far end so you would have to walk past all of my sorority sisters sunbathing butt-naked up there. I didn't think you'd make it. You really were a prude."

"I still am, and it was pretty disgusting," she said laughing. "Marta, the fluorescing scorpions couldn't have been when you were first at the ranch. That was February; it would have been too cold for scorpions."

"Yes, you're right, it must have been later," Marta said, but Susan had fallen asleep, so Marta rolled back over and went back to sleep as well.

Susan woke at 5:10 p.m. Marta was still asleep. Steven wasn't back yet and she had no messages from him. "Crap," she thought. "I better call him."

"Hi, we just got to Penn Station," he said when he answered. "I'll be at the hotel by 6:00 p.m."

"Okay, we are eating at Daniel tonight, so I'll lay out your suit and tie. Good meeting?"

"Excellent," he said. "I'll fill you in while we get ready for dinner. Is Marta with you?"

"She's napping. We had a late lunch at the Met after I finished today. Believe it or not, I took a nap today as well. I'll have to wake her, so she can get ready–dinner is at 7:00 p.m."

"Tell her I will see her tonight."

"I miss you," Susan said. "Hey, it's definitely a sale–I am done."

"We'll celebrate, then," he said. "See you in a bit. Oh, so I don't forget, Norman says the insignia is Gnostic, it's called a serpent wheel and it represents the Gnostic messiah who awakens his followers and brings unity. It was used by Gnostics, but he's seen it elsewhere…it was common in Egypt. I wonder if it appeared with the Nag Hamadi stash…oh well, I'll see you shortly."

Susan got Marta up and kicked her out at 5:30 p.m. As she drank her now cold coffee–it was the taste, not the temperature that she savored–she reviewed the materials for the Egypt Research Center. Steven got back to the hotel at 6:15 p.m., so he had to rush to get ready. He sounded quite happy about his conversation with Norman–she was looking forward to hearing more about it after dinner. She had ordered a car, so they wouldn't have to fight for a cab at dinnertime on a Saturday. It would be close getting to Daniel by 7:00 p.m.

They were on time, but Hershel was already there.

"Hello, everyone," Hershel said. "I hope you are hungry." It looked like Hershel had recovered from whatever had spooked him the night before.

"I know I am," Steven said.

"We all are, Hershel," Susan said.

"Well, let me start with logistics," Hershel said. "My client has suggested we all meet here in New York during the first week of May. However, he and his assistant likely will be in the States for about two weeks and then possibly again at the time of the art auctions. As he is retired, he will accommodate any date in that time period that works for you."

"Hershel, you mentioned that you had done work for a Japanese company. Is the gentleman we will meet Japanese as well?" Susan asked. She wasn't quite ready to ask whether he might be part of the Japanese conglomerate that owned the property in Maine.

"Well, since you will figure it out when you meet him, yes," Hershel said. "He's a somewhat elderly man, probably in his mid 70s. He's a retired tycoon."

"Marta, how about May 2 through 5?" Susan said looking at her calendar. "That works for us, Steven."

"Does May 3 work for everyone?" Marta asked. "It's a Friday; I could come up from DC."

"Great," Hershel said. "I will confirm the date. Marta, I have only seen you with a white wine, will it be the same tonight?"

"It depends on what I'm eating, Hershel. I already know what I want tonight, so I too will have a red."

"Ah, let's order then—Susan will you pick the red? Marta told me how you love your reds."

"She implied I was a wino last night because I knew where some of the Oregon vineyards are," Susan laughed. She then checked with Hershel and

Marta on their dinner choices. "I would recommend the Belle Pente—it's an Oregon pinot noir. It should go well with your salmon, Hershel."

After ordering, Marta asked, "May we know your client's name? I assume you have told him who we are."

"Actually, I haven't," Hershel said. "I did not have your permission. I will email you, if it is okay with them. Am I correct that if they authorize me to give you their names, I may share yours as well?"

"Of course," Steven answered. "Also, did you ask you client if he knows Joaquin Samovar. We are trying to tie up some loose ends here."

"I did," Hershel said. "They said they will let me know. I guess that means either they know Samovar or they are trying to figure out why you asked."

"Anything else you can tell us about your client?" Marta asked. "When Steven showed you our piece, you looked so surprised."

"I had just authenticated a small piece with the name 'Joham' on it. The fact is that I believe the name was a more recent addition to the first document. You must admit when people on two different continents each show you an old document that happens to have the same man's name on it, and you have just given one of them an opinion…I'm lucky I didn't have a heart attack. I will be the happiest of all of us when we get to the bottom of this. Let's eat."

"Hershel, I can assure you it will be a very interesting meeting," Steven said.

Steven insisted on picking up the bill. "We will see you in two weeks, Hershel," Susan said as Hershel got into a cab. Susan, Marta and Steven got the next cab.

On their way back to the Pierre, Susan asked Marta, "Have you met Hershel's partner?"

"Why do you think he has a partner—do you mean a male?"

"He mentioned a partner yesterday at dinner. When I thought about it today, I realized that I had possibly met Hershel's partner here a few months ago when I was having a drink with a colleague."

"God, you know too many people."

"Tell him to bring his partner sometime. His name is Heinrich Wells."

"Darn," Steven said as they pulled up to their hotel. "The food was excellent as usual and I know I had the black bass, but I'm so tired, I don't remember what I had for an appetizer."

"You didn't get a nap today, Steven. You had that scallop thing. I would tell you if it was good, but you ate it all yourself. We all had oysters as an appetizer, as well."

"I must have liked it," he said.

"I'll pay for the cab," Marta said as they pulled up to the Pierre.

It had been a very interesting Saturday evening, but they were all beat. Marta was taking the train down to DC in the morning. Steven and Susan were on a flight home at noon.

CHAPTER 44

Monday morning as Susan headed to her office, she got an email from the real estate partner in Boston who was working on the Maine property. "Holy shit!" she said loudly enough for the cab driver to turn and ask if she was okay. "I'm fine," she said to the cab driver. "It's just an email. Thanks." She called Steven.

"Everything okay?" he asked.

"I'm in a cab and almost to my office, so I will need to call you back, but I just got an email from the real estate partner who is checking on the property in Maine," she answered. "Our guy says the owner will be in New York May 1st through 7th. Do you think that's a coincidence? Oh wait, I'm here, let me pay and get to my office. I'll call you in a couple of minutes."

As Susan walked inside, she got three more emails. Two were work-related, but the third one was from Dr. Gruber. The meeting was set for dinner on Friday, May 3 in New York. If more time was needed, they would meet again on Saturday. Katsutoshi Ohno and his Assistant, Eisen Shakura, would be there with Hershel. He indicated that he had conveyed their names to Mr. Shakura and that the dealer in London was Richard Prenbryer of Prenbryer & Co. Susan would ask Marta to see if the dealer was on anyone's radar. Susan saw that Marta was copied, so that might have already have been done.

She called Steven back. "Did you see Hershel's email?"

"Yes, now we know the names."

"Steven, I'm thinking same day for the property owner, right?"

"That should stir things up if they really are one and the same," Steven said.

"We'll see," she said and hung up. "Good morning Jane. Did you miss me at all?" Susan asked.

"Not really, did you miss me?" she asked.

"Yes, can you order me two books by John Hessler? One is *A Renaissance Globemaker's Toolbox* and the other is *The Naming of America*. Do you want to know why?"

"Okay, but again, I didn't miss you."

"The books are about a map made in 1507. Paraphrasing the review I saw, the mapmakers, Waldseemüller and Ringmann, already knew about the Pacific Ocean and the shape of South America, before Spanish or Portuguese sailors sailed around Cape Horn. Balboa wouldn't even discover the Pacific Ocean until six years later."

"Only you would want those," Jane said.

"The Library of Congress has the map—I think it's the first map to show the name 'America.'" Susan went to her office and called her real estate guy in Boston. "I got your email about a meeting with the owner of that Maine property," she started. "New York is fine, if they can make it on May 3–the afternoon would be preferable, as we have an engagement that evening. Have you spoken with the owner or just Hartley Marin?"

"Only Hartley Marin, Susan," he said. "I don't know who is coming to the meeting, but I was informed that it had to be in New York."

"Do you know who owns it yet?" Susan asked.

"It's a Nevada LLC called Wendelstein Trust, LLC. It's wholly owned by a Delaware real estate development company, whose parent is a Japanese company. Wendelstein's manager is Joaquin Samovar, Ltd., a BVI company. There's nothing out of the ordinary, except that they all have the same Los Angeles address on Wilshire Boulevard.

"New companies?" she asked.

"Well, Wendelstein was formed in February, but the others have been around for a while. That's all I know so far."

"Okay, set it up for May 3 in our New York office," she said. "Make it 2:30 or 3:00 p.m."

"They want the buyer's name, Susan," Mark said.

"Everybody wants something," she said. "When you get the name of the person that we will meet, you can tell Hartley Marin our side is Saguaro Capital Group, LLC. I've heard the name, Joaquin Samovar, but I'm not sure it's a real person. I will play, but I'm not going to make up names. They can work for my name."

"They can probably find you that way, if it's your LLC," Mark said.

"There is another LLC before they get to me, so as I said, they can at least work for it," she said. "By the way, did you know that the Tohono O'Odham use their word for 'saguaro' to mean people as well?"

"What?" Mark asked.

"The Tohono O'Odham–it's a tribe living in Southern Arizona and Mexico. The word 'O'Odham' means 'people' in their language. It is also their word for the saguaro cactus," she repeated. "I don't really think Wendelstein wants to sell the property, so we probably won't need you there. They probably just want to know who we are and why we are interested. Can you have them ask for one of your real estate associates in our New York office?"

"Why do you want the property?" he asked.

"For an old friend," Susan said and hung up. She looked around her desk to see what needed to be done–damn, there was the Pagels book, again. She picked it up, and then set it down as more emails had come in. There were two that needed an immediate reply, so she took care of those.

As she was reading her emails, a new one came in from Mark. The meeting would be at 3:00 p.m. on May 3 at the Hartley Marin office in New York.

She called Steven again. "Hi Sweet One, we now have meetings on May 3 with the property owner at 3:00 p.m., and with Hershel and his clients at dinner. I am convinced they are all the same people. I am inclined to ask Hershel to check with his clients to see if he should come to their meeting with us at 3:00 p.m. This cloak and dagger stuff is taking too long. What do you think?"

"I agree, but ask Ms. Spy what she thinks. Also, see if she checked on that Richard Prenbryer. I checked the Internet–he was accused of dealing in stolen antiquities two years ago, but it doesn't say whether he was convicted. His website says his specialties are 'Late Medieval illuminated documents and Roman era Middle Eastern art. He also lists himself as a conservator."

"Late Medieval?" Susan said pondering. "I guess he could be interested in a document dated 1307. Hershel did say that he thought the date on his document might have been altered."

"Yes, he said it was more likely 1607 than 1307–the same problem we have. That doesn't help us with the box though."

"Crap, we may have created a problem for Jon," Susan said. "He has given us something that probably belongs to these Japanese people. Let's go see him."

"Now?" Steven asked.

"No, of course not 'now;' see if we can spend a few hours with Jon sometime this week. Wednesday works best for me."

"Okay, I'll call you back."

"Marta's in DC this week," Susan said. "If I find her, I'll see if she has a problem with putting everything on the table with the land owner and the map owner. They must be the same people, right?"

"It seems like it. Call Marta."

Susan found Marta on her cell. "Do you have a few minutes?" she asked.

"Can I call you back in about 20 minutes?" Marta asked. "And, yes I saw the email and I am having somebody check on the dealer."

"Thanks," Susan said. "I'll be in my office all morning." She hung up. After sitting for a moment, she picked up the phone and called Cy Steele.

When she was done, she rummaged around until she found Pagels' book again. As she opened the book, she saw that the bookmark was from the Singing Wind Bookstore. She felt a pang for Arizona—where else would you find a great bookstore in the middle of a ranch, 30-some miles southeast of a city like Tucson? Her private line rang.

"Hi, Steven," she said.

"I took you at your word," he said. "We have a flight to Philadelphia tomorrow evening from Midway. We'll stay overnight at the Four Seasons. We'll have breakfast with Jon at the hotel Wednesday morning. When we finish with Jon, we'll walk over to see the new Barnes Foundation Museum, and then come home. You can see the Barnes from the hotel."

"That's excellent, Steven," she said. "Is there anything special at the Philadelphia Museum?"

"I'll look," he said. "Jon confirmed that he hasn't met any representatives of the Maine property owner in person. Jon leaves a message for that Mr. Samovar when he needs anything. He didn't mention the box in his last report because he thought it was suspicious and he hadn't opened it yet, anyway. Now he feels he will have to tell him about the box in the report that's due."

"He's probably right, but we need a few days before he does that," Susan answered. "Marta is calling on my cell. Bye. Hi, Marta," Susan said as she answered her cell phone.

"Susan, this Prenbryer guy is a bad one," Marta started. "Sorry, I didn't get back to you when I promised, but I didn't get a call back until just now."

"Forger?" Susan asked.

"He's never been convicted but has been known to have fakes in his possession. He avoided a conviction for knowingly selling a fake document; I think it was supposed to be part of a medieval illuminated book of prayers. He got off by arguing that if the buyer had come back to him rather than Scotland Yard, he would have refunded the 'buyer's' funds. It was the good kind of fake, old parchment, and with touched up or added material to make it desirable."

"Like adding an older date to a real map?"

"Exactly; he also was implicated in a major looting ring that was bringing Coptic documents out of Egypt. Old churches and homes were looted. If he wants the documents that Hershel saw, then they may have been doctored."

"Or, I suppose he could have a buyer lined up for them," Susan added.

"By the way, I decided to re-check Hershel. He's clean—no involvement with this dealer," Marta added.

"That's good news," Susan said. "You're sure?"

"Yes, I just said that," Marta said in her irritated voice.

"I was just kidding. Anyway, we now have two meetings—one at 3:00 p.m. with the property owner and then dinner with Hershel's client at 7:00 p.m. Steven and I are convinced that the Japanese guys, Katsutoshi Ohno and Eisen Shakura, own the property and are Hershel's clients. They probably think we are one and the same as well. We are inclined to call Hershel and have him tell his client we have invited him to the meeting at 3:00 p.m. What do you think?"

"I think 'crap' as you would say," Marta said slowly as she was trying to parse out what Susan had just told her. "Let me think for a minute."

"While you are thinking, the box likely belongs to the property owner since it was found on his property—assuming it hasn't been stolen from somewhere else. We still don't know how it got to Maine or if it's real except that Hershel's people have that map with Joham's name on it. It's possible that the box was put there by this dealer, but then Jon is positive it was below an undisturbed level—at least as old as the 1600s. And now we have his son's stuff to deal with as well. Of course, he could be working with the owner and the dealer, except that we aren't experts. Maybe they are duping Hershel."

"Slow down, throwing all sorts of other things into the mix doesn't help me think," Marta said.

"Marta, maybe these Japanese are as confused as we are," Susan said. "Should you ask Hershel to call his client and tell them we think everybody should be at the 3:00 p.m. meeting. No, maybe I should just have my real estate guy in our Boston office do it. He's checking into buying the property in Maine. He can just say that we think we are also having dinner with them, and if that's the case, we'll all meet at 3:00 p.m. and then go to dinner. You call Hershel separately, but don't scare him. Actually, just tell him you'll be there to protect him." After a minute of silence, Susan asked, "Marta, are you still there?"

"Yes, damn it," she said. "Didn't you have someone try to date the box?"

"Yes, it's Mediterranean wood and it could be a few hundred years old. Since it was only a picture of a section, even though the rings were visible, it isn't definite. The box is small, so when we go to Philadelphia Wednesday, I may ask Jon if we can send it to our friend. Most of the box was covered with a tar of some sort, probably to keep it water tight. It was presumptuous of us to ask for a guess based on pictures."

"Let me think about this," Marta said. "I have a short meeting that I am late for. I will call you when I'm done. Oh, and you still haven't explained why Jon came to you. I need more information on that."

"Me too," Susan said as she started to hang up. "Marta, are you still there?"

"Yes, I am."

"Do me a favor, can you check out Jon's son—something seems just a little odd."

"I checked Father Bartolome when I was looking for Jon...did you find something odd?"

"No, it's just that Jon said his son joined the Franciscans to atone for something and that he and his son weren't that close any more. The last part I can understand, but coupled with his other statement...anyway if you have time. By the way, free trivia—'Bartolome,' aka "Bartholomew,' as in a later Apostle, probably is Aramaic for 'son of a farmer.' 'Bar' is son, and 'talmai' is the farmer part. However, it also may be 'bar' 'ptolome' relating to the rule of Judea by the Ptolemaic dynasty. Ptolemy, of course, was the Macedonian general who became ruler of Egypt around 323 BCE after Alexander the Great died," Susan hung up and called Steven back.

"Did you talk to Marta?" Steven asked.

"Yes, I asked her to check into Jon's son, Father Bartolome."

"Why?" Steven asked.

"As I told her, Jon said his son had decided to join the Franciscans to atone for something. She had a meeting to go to, but promised she would call back."

"I think we may want Jon at the meeting as well, but I'm still thinking about that. I talked with David this morning about meeting him in Shanghai. He's rather excited about what we sent; he got the digital copies from our photographer a couple of hours ago. He will send me a couple of dates in mid-May to mid-June for Shanghai. Do you know where he'll be staying–I forgot to ask him?"

"Near his university, I'm sure," she answered.

"Well, that's a pain. Traffic is horrible these days and you know I like staying on the Bund. Anyway, I'll try to ask him before he goes back to Shanghai."

"Just have him pick a hotel that you like, then get two rooms so he doesn't have to go back and forth in the traffic. Steven, I almost forgot, Martha says the dealer is indeed a bad guy. He's even been implicated in a looting ring operating in Egypt to steal Coptic materials."

"Yikes," Steven exclaimed. "That's not good. Has she told Hershel?"

"Well, I'm an idiot. I didn't ask her…she did say Hershel was clean, though. Speak of the Devil–she's calling again. I'll call you back," she said as she hung up with Steven and picked up Marta's call.

"Susan," Marta said. "Call your real estate guy and have him set things up. The way you suggested is fine. If you get the nod, then I will call Hershel and tell him he is to join us at 3:00 p.m. I have to go."

"Thanks."

"Oh, one more thing," Marta said.

"Yes?"

"Why the hell would they call your Apostle, Bartholomew, 'Nathaniel'? Oh crap, I have to go–another call. Bye."

Susan sat for a minute chuckling to herself, before calling her real estate guy in Boston.

"Hi Susan, I sent off an email to Hartley Marin, but haven't heard back."

"Well, I have an interesting issue here," Susan said. "It seems that the people we are going to meet at 3:00 p.m. are also going to have dinner with us and a third party that evening."

"I thought you didn't know them," he said.

"Well, that's the issue—we have never met either the afternoon group or the dinner group. We are being introduced at dinner by a third party, an art restorer. For a number of reasons, we are beginning to think that the dinner group and the property group are the same people."

"And you want me to do what?" he asked.

"Well, if we are having dinner with Hartley's client and a third party that evening at 7:00 p.m., we should all meet at 3:00 p.m. and then go to dinner. Tell Hartley the third party is an art restorer. Feel free to use my name now."

"And dinner is where, if they ask?"

"Tell them we don't know because the art restorer is setting it up—they can ask him," Susan said. "We think they know him as well. Any questions?"

"I have way too many, Susan. Do you want me to try for our office in New York again?"

"We can go to their lawyers if they push. Let me know how it goes," she said and hung up.

CHAPTER 45

Eisen got a call from Utamaro Wednesday morning. Hartley Marin had spoken with the Americans' law firm. The Americans wanted to meet at their lawyers' office in New York on May 3 at 3:00 p.m. Eisen went to see if Ohno-san was in yet.

"Good morning, Eisen, come in," Kat said. "I just hung up with Hershel. We are on for a dinner meeting with our 'Joham' Americans on May 3. Hershel wants to host the dinner, but you will arrange to pay for it when we know the location."

"Yes, sir."

"Our American dinner guests have names now so you can get me some information. They are Steven Graves, Susan Graves and Marta Krejci. Oh, and they have insisted on knowing whether we know Joaquin Samovar. As Sherlock Holmes would say…'[t]he game's afoot, Watson.'"

"Good, sir," Eisen said almost with glee. "I just heard from Utamaro. Subject to your approval, he is setting up an afternoon meeting for Samovar's representative and the 'property' Americans. It will be on May 3 in New York as well. These Americans want to meet at 3:00 p.m. at a law firm representing them—I think he said it is Peale, Curtis and Blume. Did you tell Dr. Gruber we knew Samovar?"

"Of course not," Kat said. "Let's see how this goes for just a little longer. We still don't know about the dealer or how the archaeologist at our site might be involved."

"Well, I can go to the lawyers at 3:00 p.m. as Samovar's representative and you can go to the dinner, right?"

275

"Yes, I think so." Kat answered with a smile. "Although, it might be amusing if Samovar joins us for dinner. We have a week, so let's see if anything else turns up. Tell Utamaro to set it up at our New York firm at 3:00 p.m. No lawyers are to attend."

"Yes, sir. I will start working on a meeting with the archaeologist. I'm thinking I may try to meet him in Philadelphia on May 2. Is that okay."

"Yes, I doubt there would be much to see in Maine."

CHAPTER 46

It had been an hour and a half since Marta had called Susan. There was nothing worse than waiting, with nothing pressing, so she was fidgeting about her office. She was too antsy to sit down and restart Pagels. Now, she was staring out the window wondering if it was a mistake to quit.

When she had time like this, all sorts of horrors bubbled back up into her mind from places she had stashed them away. It was odd, but people rarely could hurt her no matter what they said; she could always think of even worse things herself. But that horrible feeling of not being able to make something right, would sometimes overwhelm her when she least expected. Like Sunday night, while watching *Sullivan's Travels*...all of the men running to catch the freight train hoping somewhere there would be a job....

Susan looked at her phone wishing it would ring...well, enough of that, she decided. She needed to get busy—if not, that feeling like she was drifting along without purpose, like a tumbleweed, would overtake her again. As a kid, she used to chase tumbleweeds as they drifted along—a good wind could really get them going. But, as you got closer, you realized you didn't want to catch them—they were sticky as hell. She'd have to think about that—maybe you were going somewhere when you chased them.

She reached for her cell phone to find a recording of *Tumbling Tumbleweeds*. She was maybe 5, when she first heard Gene Autry, the singing cowboy, sing it in an old movie being rerun on TV. She loved that song. As she started the recording, her phone rang.

"Susan, it's Marta. First off, you twit! Cy Steel just introduced himself to me—we are having lunch tomorrow. Does that make you happy?"

"I don't know," Susan stuttered as she tried to move back into the real world.

"Well," Marta laughed. "He's very nice and quite dapper. He made me laugh."

"That's good," she managed to get out.

"You okay?" Marta asked. "Not in one of your mopes are you?"

"I'm fine. I was trying to find a recording of *Tumbling Tumbleweeds* sung by Gene Autry," Susan said. She had made it back to reality. "Roy Rogers, whose real name was Leonard Slye, was one of the original Sons of the Pioneers. It was their song, but I'm positive I first heard it sung by Gene Autry."

"What happened to Trigger when the Roy Rogers museum closed?" Marta asked.

"He's still stuffed, but he's somewhere in Branson, Missouri now." She paused and the said, "Cy must be desperate; I just called him this morning."

"Very funny! Did you set things up for the meeting and dinner on May 3?"

"We're working on it," Susan said—she was back to action. "The owner is a Japanese holding company, so, I assume the principals are in Japan. It's 10:30 a.m. here, so it's just after midnight in Tokyo, right? We shouldn't hear anything until at least late this afternoon. Hershel's people are Japanese, too."

"If you get the nod, then I will call Hershel and tell him he is to join us at the 3:00 p.m. meeting. I used to watch Roy Rogers and his wife, Dale Evans, on TV. I liked Sky King and his niece, Penny, too. They must have been reruns from the 50s."

"So you came to Tucson to be like Dale Evans, riding a horse?" Susan laughed. "Or maybe you were looking for Sky King's hypothetical ranch—it was in Arizona, you know. His niece, Penny, could ride a horse, too. Anyway, you beat Dale and Penny and became a spy."

"Sort of," Marta said.

"Well, at least you did something productive for a while—I just helped other people make money. Is Wilhelm's interview today?"

"He should be meeting with them at 4:00 p.m.," Marta said. "Why?"

"I haven't seen him yet today," Susan answered. "We have a call at 1:30 p.m. to wrap up loose ends on our deal. Anyway, I'll call you when I hear more about May 3. Last one, tumbleweeds, the icon of the West, didn't actually get to the US until the 1880s. The seeds probably came in on some ship in the 1800s. They're called 'Leap-the-Fields' in Russia whence they came. Bye." It was time to get back to work.

CHAPTER 47

Eisen called Utamaro's office. He was out at a meeting, so Eisen left him a message. "Tell Hartley Marin to set up the meeting at their office in New York at 3:00 p.m. on May 3. Call me with any questions."

Eisen reviewed some correspondence on routine matters and then began working on airline and hotel reservations. He had just finished getting two rooms at the Peninsula when Utamaro called back.

"Good morning Eisen," he said. "I wanted to catch you regarding a new email I got."

"Yes?" Eisen asked.

"Hartley Marin got a call from the buyer's counsel, Peale, Curtis," he said. "It seems that you and Mr. Ohno may also be having dinner with the buyer and an art restorer. If that's correct, they would like to invite the art restorer to the 3:00 p.m. meeting. Then, you can all go to dinner together."

"Interesting," Eisen said to say something while he thought. "Did the buyer say who this art restorer might be?"

"No, I paraphrased the email for you. The buyer is an entity called Saguaro Capital Group, LLC. It's represented by the Peale, Curtis firm and owned by one of its partners, Susan Graves."

"Let me talk with Ohno-san about this restorer. Oh, and by the way, can you get Human Resources or someone here to do a background check for Mr. Ohno?"

"Yes, of course."

"The gentleman's name is Richard Prenbryer," Eisen said. "He is an art dealer in London. Mr. Ohno doesn't like to talk with dealers unless he knows their background or they are introduced by someone reputable. Please tell them we want them to get enough for us to help a friend of Ohno-san to decide whether to deal with Prenbryer. I would like it as soon as possible."

"We use a service to check backgrounds when we hire in Legal," Utamaro said. "We will start with them if that's acceptable."

"Good. How long will it take?" Eisen asked.

"We can get a quick read in about 24 hours," Utamaro said, hoping he was impressing Eisen. You impress Eisen, and Ohno-san would hear about it. Not that Ohno-san was that important anymore, but he was still the largest shareholder.

"That is perfect," Eisen said. "Ohno-san will be pleased. Please let me know when something comes in."

"I will have them start today," Utamaro answered.

"Thank you, Utamaro," Eisen said as he hung up.

Eisen called Ohno-san. "May I come in, sir? It seems there are some new issues to deal with." Kat gave the okay.

"Eisen, at least you are smiling," Kat said as Eisen entered. He had seen Eisen smile more in the last few months than in many years. "What is it?"

"I have just spoken with Utamaro. He was out when I tried him earlier. Between the time that we talked and when Utamaro called me, the Americans figured out that the people who are joining them for dinner with Dr. Gruber also probably own the property in Maine. They have suggested that we invite Dr. Gruber to the 3:00 p.m. meeting at Hartley Marin. Actually, they didn't name Dr. Gruber; they called him an art restorer. They would like to bring him to the meeting."

"Well," Kat said. "I think this is good—we can get to the bottom of this. Do you agree?"

"Yes, sir, I think I do. I did a quick search just before I called you. Ms. Graves and Ms. Krejci are partners at Peale, Curtis which is the law firm for the buyer. The buyer is an LLC called Saguaro Capital Group, LLC. Mrs. Graves owns the entity that owns Saguaro. Mr. Graves is, like you, a retired businessman. Shall I get Dr. Gruber on the line for you?"

"No, send him an email please," Kat said. "Ask him to call you if he has any questions."

"Yes, sir, and shall I contact the archaeologist?"

"Let's ask the Americans if there is anyone else who should come," Kat said. "This is good Eisen. Hershel and I would have missed you at dinner."

"Thank you sir," Eisen said with a slight bow.

CHAPTER 48

Susan was in her office on Tuesday by 8:30 a.m. Yesterday's call had gone well–the Jameson deal, as it was now called at Peale, Curtis, would close on May 10. She had a bag with her for the overnight in Philadelphia. She would meet Steven at Midway this afternoon for the flight. As she began reading her emails, she saw one from her real estate guy in Boston. It said, "I need confirmation that the art restorer is Hershel Gruber. Call me when you get in to discuss logistics." She called right away.

"Hi, Susan, you should know that neither I nor the Hartley Marin guys can figure out the relationships in your deal. Notwithstanding, we have a meeting for you at the Hartley Marin New York office at 3:00 p.m. on Friday, May3. We need to confirm that the participants at that meeting will not have their counsel with them. Oh, and if Hershel Gruber is the art restorer, he should attend."

"Yes, it is Dr. Gruber," Susan said slowly. "Look, since this is the same group that we are having dinner with, they likely have bios for me, my husband and Marta Krejci."

"Yes, oh I see," Mark said. "That should mean they know that you and Ms. Krejci are Peale, Curtis lawyers."

"Just make sure they know we are coming as principals and not as lawyers. Oh, and the same for them. They can use Hartley Marin's offices, but principals only–and Marta and Dr. Gruber."

"Of course," Mark answered.

"Thanks," Susan said. "Where is Hartley Marin's office?"

"It's on Park Avenue just north of 42nd Street."

"That's good—it's impossible to get a cab around Wall Street on Friday afternoons—at least we won't have that headache. Anything else you need from me?"

"Nope," he said. "I'll email you with a confirmation. Oh, one more thing—I am to ask you if anyone else should attend."

"Crap, tell them there may be one more person they may know as well, but we need to check his schedule—I'll know tomorrow. Thanks," she said. "I'll be on my cell tomorrow if anything comes up. Damn, ask them who else they think should be there. We keep hearing about a Mr. Samovar, but we don't know what his role is. Ask if he will attend, too."

Susan called Marta and got her voicemail. She left a message telling her to invite Dr. Gruber to the 3:00 p.m. meeting at Hartley Marin. She added that she would be in Philadelphia for the next two days and hung up.

CHAPTER 49

Susan and Steven got to the Philadelphia Four Seasons at 7:30 p.m. They were both tired, so they had dinner in the hotel's Fountain Restaurant.

"We should be set for New York on the 3rd," Susan said. "I left Marta a message to invite Dr. Gruber. Tomorrow, we'll ask Jon if he can come to New York. I took a break this afternoon before leaving for the airport to look back at the earliest historians who wrote about Jesus."

"Tacitus, Seutonius, Josephus—who else?" Steven asked while not bothering to look up from his food.

"Pliny the Younger and Philo," she said. "I did a chart in graduate school, but I'll never find it now. So, I organized them in three columns—one for their lives and one for the date of the oldest copy of the writings in which they reference 'Jesus' or Christians and one for their sources."

"Why?" he asked looking up finally. "You know there are only copies left and those were done in the monasteries. And I said Josephus, but everyone is pretty certain that his reference was inserted later by Eusebius."

"Yes, I know, it's the *Testimonium Flavianum*. But your koine materials are copies too. I thought I would start with a chart and then do an analysis to see where I could fit the ones you are reading—both stylistically and then in terms of dates."

"How far did you get?"

"So far, I have only names and earliest dates for them. Your Eusebius says that Philo met Peter in Rome."

"Maybe I can help," Steven said. "I guess it might be good to set this out systematically on a framework of known documents. We also need to search more for the names we are seeing."

"I thought you talked with Dr. Alberts about that."

"I did. Norman had not heard of Ammonius, but he has heard of our Bishop Secundus—he is intrigued to say the least. I guess setting up a chart might be good. Maybe we can get Norman to cross check it and then do a paper with him. Oh, um, did I tell you he knew of Ammonius Saccas, but he's not our guy?"

"So you showed him the Ammonius?"

"No, I mentioned the name and told him about some of the text. Obviously, he wants to see the documents. I told him I would get back with him when I knew more. Are you done eating?"

"I'm ready," she said. "It's hard to believe that a source like Tacitus is only known through a copy made in the 11th century. Anyway, it's too bad about Saccas. Have you seen anything other than the insignia that sounds Gnostic?"

"Well, Norman suggested that Secundus 'leaned' Gnostic," he said. "I have spent most of my time so far on Ammonius, so I won't speculate on our Bishop Secundus."

"Should a Gnostic be a bishop? And the serpent wheel…he said it's Gnostic? I think it's also related to the Catholic baptismal cross which has eight spokes. Anyway, there is some weird stuff there."

"Wasn't there something about the Sufis studying with the Gnostics, Susan? They studied with the Buddha before the Gnostics and with Mohammed after, right?"

Yes, but Steven… Crap, we meet Jon at 7:30 a.m. here tomorrow morning, so we should get some sleep. By the way, my Greek is really rusty. I need to find a primer or something. Do you think we still have one at home."

"We do, but it's on a shelf in the reading room in Tucson," Steven said beckoning to the waiter for the check.

"Oh, crap," she said as her cell rang. It was Marta. "Hello, Marta, still in DC?"

"Yes, until Friday," she said. "Why are you in Philadelphia? Are you visiting Dr. Christiansen?"

"We're having breakfast with him here tomorrow. We don't want him to be surprised if the property owner invites him to New York. Did you talk to Hershel?"

"Yes, he's on board for both meetings on the 3rd. He's relieved...in fact, he is so relieved that he let out that the piece he looked at was a map in bad shape."

"Good job, Ms. Spy! Did you get any more information on this Richard Prenbryer?" Susan asked.

"He is known for handling antiquities, often giving them better provenances than they merit. The problem is, he has been implicated more than once, but has never actually been charged with anything. He's more like a person of interest."

"Does he have any ties to Hershel or the property owner?"

"None that I have found—I told you Hershel is clean. He says your 'property owner' is that 70-plus year old Japanese tycoon, Katsutoshi Ohno, or his assistant, Eisen Shakura, who is about as old. Apparently, Hershel works on pieces from Mr. Ohno's collection of Renaissance Art and materials. By the way, like you, this Ohno loves Thomas Moran. That was the other 'coincidence' that scared the hell out of poor Hershel."

"Really?" Susan asked, surprised. "How do you know that?"

"Yes, really," Marta retorted. "I told Hershel that although you almost faint whenever you see a Bernini, especially *Ecstasy of Saint Teresa* or *Daphne and Apollo*, your real love is Moran and the American Luminists. So, Hershel started laughing. When I asked him what was so funny, he said that Ohno has always wanted a Thomas Moran—Ohno may even stick around New York for the auctions if a Moran comes up."

"Did you make that up?" Susan asked, remembering that she had mentioned Thomas Moran at dinner. "These coincidences make me nervous."

"No, I didn't make it up. By the way, you will be proud of me–I knew that your Bernini was Baroque. More importantly, I went to see the *American Art and the Civil War* exhibit at the Smithsonian. There were a fair number of paintings by your Luminists, especially Church and Gifford. I don't remember any Morans. Hmm, I didn't see that little Frederic Church you like, *Our Banner in the Sky*, either. There's an exhibit at the Library of Congress too, but I'm not sure I will get there on this trip."

"Damn, maybe we'll take the train down tomorrow afternoon. There should be two Morans in the North Lobby on the 2nd Floor of the National Museum of American Art. I know one is *The Grand Canyon of the Yellowstone*. I think the other is *Chasm of the Colorado*. We'll see if this Ohno knows his Morans," she said. "Anyway, I will call you if anything comes up in our meeting tomorrow with Jon. By the way, Frederic Church was a founding trustee of the Met."

"Free trivia, thanks—dinner this weekend?" Marta asked.

"Of course, we can catch up," Susan said. "Um, if you talk to Hershel again, ask him if Shakura speaks English, and, if so, if he has an American accent," she added and then hung up. She looked at Steven and said, "Marta says the Japanese guy likes Thomas Moran."

"That's too bad," Steven said. "Drives the price up."

"Well, if that's all you have to say, I'm ready, except that we have to go back to the Borghese," she said. "Marta reminded me of Bernini's *Daphne*—her hands turning to leaves…."

"Fine, but right now, I am tired," he said getting up. "Let's go upstairs."

"Steven," Susan said as she got into bed. "Who knows you have the pictures Marta's photographer took?"

"Marta knows we have them since she got us the photographer," Steven said thinking aloud. "Hershel knows we have a picture of at least one of the 'Latin' documents because we showed it to him. And David has seen some, too."

"How about Jon?"

"No, it has never come up," he answered.

"We only sent Jackie pictures of the box," Susan said. "Did we get those back?"

"Sorry, yes they came back yesterday, but we should check in with her," Steven said.

"Maybe Jon will let her look at the box," she said. "Anyway, I want to be sure that we have a copy of everything."

"You're worried we might have to give the documents to the Japanese, right?" Steven asked breaking in.

"Yes, they are his unless he stole them. We don't know much about this guy, Ohno. More importantly, we don't know why he bought this property and then had Jon dig right where the box is," Susan said.

"That's true, Susan," Steven said. "At least he didn't tell Jon what to look for."

"He might be a religious nut who will destroy them," Susan added. "Let's get another set of the pictures from the photographer and put them in a box at Wells Fargo. Right now, we have no reason to believe they are fakes or that they belong to someone other than this Ohno."

"It's only Tuesday and we'll be home tomorrow night," Steven said. "I'll go to Wells Fargo Thursday."

"You know, if Jon would let us have the box for a few days, we could run it out to Jackie." Susan said. "And I could pick up that Greek primer. We could check in with Bob, too."

"Good idea. I should see if we have any right to publish on something that doesn't belong to us—we probably need this Ohno's permission. We certainly haven't come to these documents in any bad way. Maybe this Ohno is planning for his own scholar to publish…."

"Get some sleep, Steven," she said. "We'll know soon enough."

"Hershel really said this Ohno likes Thomas Moran? Marta wasn't pulling your leg was she?"

"I didn't think of that, damn it. Now, roll over so I can get closer." He obliged. After thirty odd years, he had only gotten more comfortable. She kissed him and fell asleep.

CHAPTER 50

The next morning, Susan and Steven were at the table at 7:25 a.m. Susan had just mentioned to Steven that perhaps they should take the train down to DC in the afternoon to see the Civil War exhibits when Jon came in.

"Good morning, Jon," Steven said as he and Susan stood to meet him.

"Thank you for meeting me here in Philadelphia," Jon said. "I'm anxious to hear what you have found so far."

"We're hoping you will be pleased," Susan said noting that Jon looked much more relaxed than when she had first seen him in Chicago. That was only a week ago, she marveled to herself. They had indeed made progress.

"We have a fair amount of news," Steven said slowly. He then filled Jon in on his initial thoughts on what the Greek documents might be if they were indeed real. Susan added a few facts here and there, but she thought Steven did a great summary. "Susan, it's your turn, tell Jon about Hershel."

"Last Friday, we met with Dr. Hershel Gruber in New York. We wanted someone who could date the parchment; Hershel came highly recommended by a trusted friend. When we met him, we didn't know that he had done work over the years for a gentleman named Katsutoshi Ohno. We think he is your property owner. Mr. Ohno is an elderly Japanese man who collects Renaissance art." She stopped to look at Jon. He seemed comfortable with what they were telling him. "Coincidentally, Hershel had recently looked at a piece for Mr. Ohno. It was a map with Joham's name on it."

"Of course, Hershel knew nothing of the connection between Mr. Ohno and you," Steven added. "If only you could have seen poor Hershel when we showed him a picture of your piece with Joham's name on it…he looked as if he had seen a ghost."

"It was pretty funny, Jon. And if one coincidence like that wasn't enough, I was jabbering at dinner about an American artist that we like, and lo and behold, it turned out that Hershel's client, the Japanese collector of Renaissance art, had mentioned the same American artist as one of his favorites."

"And no one has mentioned me?" Jon asked when they had stopped laughing.

"Not yet, Jon," Susan said. "We have a meeting and a dinner set for May 3 in New York. They have asked if anyone else should attend the meeting—that may be to see if we know you. Interestingly, no one has asked us how we got what we showed Hershel yet. Of course, we still haven't seen what they have either."

"I suppose they are coming to the US to ask us, right?" Jon asked.

"Yes, they want to see what we showed Hershel, so I'm sure they'll figure out you are the link," Steven answered.

"Anyway, Jon, we do have a couple of issues to discuss."

"Yes?" Jon said getting a little apprehensive.

"We want to be ready for the meeting," Susan said. "Has your son tracked down…?"

Jon broke in before Susan could continue. "The college can't find them. Apparently, cataloging is done by volunteers and there was some mix up. The documents were definitely sent to cataloging, but never made their way into the records. Let me clarify that, three pieces were cataloged, but the description of those pieces doesn't match what Father sent. My son thinks that maybe because they were in such bad shape, that the volunteer might have erred. I'm sorry; it may be a dead end now."

"Could Father's pieces have been stolen?" Steven asked. "We think they may somehow have made their way to Mr. Ohno."

"Stolen?" he asked surprised. "I guess it's possible, but why would someone steal worthless scraps?"

"The three pieces that are in the archives—are they artifacts?" Susan asked.

"No, they are just old trash, basically. Remember, my son's pieces were in bad shape—they may have looked like trash too. Because they were likely 1600s, they weren't terribly important to the Paleo or Archaic groups. Father thinks he mentioned them to the Verrazano guys too, but they didn't seem too excited either. He sent them to the college and forgot about them until now. Anyway, he will be back on Sunday—I'm sure he will get an update then."

"Well, if one of Father's pieces were a map, it might explain how Mr. Ohno knew where you should dig."

"You don't think he had them stolen from the college, do you?" Jon asked.

"We don't know enough yet," Susan said. "If only you had seen the look on Dr. Gruber's face when Steven showed him a picture of the Latin piece with our Joham's name on it." When she stopped laughing again, she added, "Hopefully, we will get to the bottom of all of this on May 3."

Jon sat looking at his hands. When he finally looked up, he asked, "Dare I ask what the other issues are?"

"The meeting I mentioned is set for May 3 at 3:00 p.m. in New York," Susan said. "We also have dinner that night with the person Hershel works for. Mr. Ohno may ask you to come to one or both meetings. By the way, Hershel says Mr. Ohno is rather secretive—we think that his assistant, Kesai Eisen, might be your Samovar."

"Ohno's assistant is Samovar? He sounded like an American."

"I guess Mr. Shakura could have an American assistant named Samovar," Steven said. "We'll have to see."

"I am sure I can arrange some time on a Friday afternoon," he said. "Should I call him?"

"Maybe, but not yet," Susan said. "To be honest, Mr. Ohno only knows we have the one Latin document, the attestation. We didn't say anything more to Dr. Gruber. Since these documents were found on this Ohno's property though, they are his—unless they are stolen property. Then they would belong to whoever they were stolen from. But if they were stolen in the 1600s... Steven, don't forget to tell Jon about the spear point."

"I certainly haven't forgotten the stupid thing," Jon said.

"Remember, only a week has gone by since you came to us in Chicago. We still only know it's Folsom. Bob should have been back yesterday, so we are hoping to hear from him soon," Steven said.

"Damn," Jon said softly. "So, we still don't know if it's stolen?"

'No," Steven said. "Apparently, these Folsom points are pretty common, so they are only worth a few hundred dollars. They also are de-accessioned sometimes if a collection has too many, storage space issues, I guess."

"Well, at least it's out of my hands," Jon said.

"By the way, we were very lucky to get Hershel—apparently, he is extremely busy," Steven added. "Anyway, do plan to be at the meeting on May 3. You should plan to stay for dinner too, so we will get you a room at the Pierre where we are staying."

"You don't think he will be upset that I showed these to you?" he asked.

"You have only tried to figure out what you have found—and, given what they are, whether they are fakes," Susan said trying to reassure him. "As Steven told you, Hershel stopped us from saying anything more because he had seen part of that same name, Joham Alvar, on a document Mr. Ohno showed him. Also, it isn't surprising that this Ohno would use Hershel for a renaissance piece and then this. We had someone check Dr. Gruber. He has an impeccable reputation."

"Is there anything else?" Jon asked.

"We would like to show the box to a friend at the tree ring lab in Tucson this weekend. That date on the hasp is a real pain. As Steven told you earlier, the box is some type of Mediterranean pine and it is definitely old."

It took a while to convince Jon, but he finally agreed. He would meet Susan and Steven in front of the Archaeology Museum at 10:45 a.m. to give them the box. When Jon left, Steven could see that Susan was fidgeting.

"What are you doing," Steven asked.

"Um, I'm checking to see if, instead of taking us to the airport, the driver can take us to the Barnes and then to pick up the box from Jon. And rather than the train, we'll just have him take us on to DC and around to see the Civil War exhibits. You can nap in a car as easily as on the train. We'll fly home out of Reagan."

"Did I actually agree to go to Washington? Oh, never mind. That's fine."

Susan went over to the desk to finish the arrangements while Steven went upstairs to finish packing. They agreed that Steven would call Bob and Susan would call Jackie. They would try to meet with each of them on Saturday.

It was too early to call Bob, so Steven read his emails while Susan changed their airline reservations so that they could leave from Reagan in DC. She then booked two seats on an American flight to Tucson on Friday. She shot a note to Marta telling her that they were going to Tucson for the weekend and thus would miss dinner, unless Marta wanted to join them in Tucson.

CHAPTER 51

The driver had Susan and Steven at the Barnes Foundation at 9:45 a.m. Steven knew Bob was an early riser, so, while they waited for the Barnes to open at 10:00 a.m., Steven called him. Bob would be ready for them at 11:00 a.m. on Saturday.

As they had been to the old Barnes Museum in Merion, they walked through quickly to see some favorites. It was easy, since the inside still looked pretty much the same. They stayed for half an hour and were at Penn by 10:48 a.m. Jon was waiting out front, holding a bag with the wrapped box inside. The bag was just small enough to fit in an overhead bin– that was a relief.

As they drove south to the Smithsonian's American Art Museum in DC, Susan called Jackie. At first, Jackie was reluctant to come out on a Saturday morning to see the box. But, when Susan added that the box hasp had 1307 engraved on it and the box was found in the US buried below a level of undisturbed earth that could be dated to about then, Jackie agreed. They would meet for breakfast at the Arizona Inn at 9:00 a.m. It was close to the University and Jackie's home in the Sam Hughes neighborhood.

They arrived at the American Art Museum just before 2:00 p.m. After a quick lunch at the Courtyard Café, they searched for Frederic Church's *Our Banner in the Sky*. Marta was right–it wasn't in the exhibit. After Susan confirmed that her beloved Morans were still in the 2nd floor lobby, they headed outside to find the driver who would take them to the Library of Congress.

Susan was fidgeting with her phone as they waited for the driver. "Steven," she said as she put her phone away. "I was thinking that we should look at the 1507 Waldseemüller map while we are at the Library of Congress.

"You showed me the book about it, there isn't any detail of coastal Maine."

"Do you know why he picked Amerigo Vespucci rather than Columbus as the new continent's namesake and called it America?"

"Because Amerigo Vespucci determined that it was a separate continent, Susan. I also looked into the 'Island of Vinland, discovered by Bjarni and Leif in company Map,' which is otherwise known as the 'Vinland Map.'"

"Still a fake Viking map of America purported to have been drawn in the 1100s?" she asked.

"Probably…there's our driver."

"After we see the Civil War exhibit at the Library, we'll go see the Waldseemüller map," she said.

The driver picked them up at the Library of Congress at 4:50 p.m. for the short run to Reagan airport. They were home in Chicago that night by 8:00 p.m. with a dinner delivery from Naniwa on its way.

CHAPTER 52

Susan slept in on Thursday until 8:30 a.m. She dragged herself into the office by 9:30 a.m. Jane was waiting for her.

"You haven't retired yet—why so late?" Jane asked. "Never mind, Ms. Krejci is back from DC early and wants to talk to you. Also, Wilhelm has called twice to see if you were in yet. Which one do you want first?"

"Neither," Susan said. "I need coffee. Tell Wilhelm 10 minutes—it would be nice if he would come to me. I'm pooped…getting old you know."

"And Marta?" Jane asked.

"Thirty minutes—she also has to come up here," Susan said. "I want to sit and drink my coffee. If you can't hold Marta off, you'll have to fetch me another cup."

Wilhelm was waiting for Susan when she got back with her coffee. "How did Monday go?" she asked.

"Well, that's why I am here—I have been offered an analyst position."

"Wilhelm—shouldn't you be smiling?" Susan asked. She was about to say 'Marta must be proud,' but realized that might take away from the moment. "With the NSA?" she asked instead.

"Yes," he said. "I'm not used to change, and I guess now that I have an offer, I don't know what to do with it. They want me to start training on June 1 in Virginia. They even have temporary housing for me."

"Well, you grew up in Cleveland and you went to school in Michigan, so you don't have deep ties here. The DC area is a pain, but your job certainly should be interesting. How's the pay?"

"Not quite as much, but then if I don't make partner here, who knows," he said.

"Are they putting you in an interesting area?"

"Yes, I think so. There will be some travel, which I feel I need. Marta said that unless I get shot, I can probably be there as long as I like."

"That's our Marta—I don't know if she has ever been shot at, but I do know she has never been shot." Susan saw a little smirk on Wilhelm's face—she would make Marta pay for her stories one of these days. "I would go for it if I were your age, but I'm not. Any worries?"

"A little, I don't want people to think I'm leaving because I wouldn't make partner, but they won't let me wait either. Also, if I did wait and then didn't make partner, they might not want me."

"Never worry about what people will think—unless you're about to do something bad, of course. Marta is coming to see me in about ten minutes—what does she say?"

"Same as you; I should go for it," Wilhelm said.

"She's been there Wilhelm—she wouldn't say that if she didn't think you would be as happy there as you are here. I guess the real draw is that you will be doing something different. It certainly will look good on your resume."

"Thanks, I think I'm going to do it," he said as he stood up to leave. "By the way, I will wrap everything up here and make it clear right away that I can't take any new projects."

"Try to take a break, before you start. There are some excellent art collections in DC and you can take the train to Philly, New York or Boston to see more. Congratulations!" she said as he rose to leave. Susan got up to get another cup of coffee, but Jane was already coming in with another one.

"Hi, Wilhelm," Jane said as he left. "Susan, Marta just rang and said she was on her way up."

"Okay, um, we're on the morning flight to Tucson tomorrow and then back home on Sunday night. Can you get me a breakfast reservation at the Arizona Inn at 9:00 a.m. on Saturday for three people?"

"Do you need a car in Tucson?"

"No, our car's at the airport. Hello, Marta," Susan said as she appeared behind Jane.

"Off to Tucson, are we?" she asked. "Hi, Jane, I bet you're glad she's back."

"Ecstatic," Jane said as she left.

"We are taking the box to Jackie. And you?"

"Things went better than expected, so I came home," she said. "Did you go to DC?"

"We had a driver take us to DC after we picked up the box from Jon and saw the Barnes Foundation. We stopped at the Library of Congress and the American Art Museum, flew to Chicago from Reagan and were home eating Naniwa by about 8:00 p.m. Come with us to Tucson. You can meet Jackie–oh, and maybe Bob Pitt. We'll come back on the noon flight on Sunday."

"Not if it's at that pace," Martha laughed. "Seriously, though, I would love to come with you to Tucson now that I have a breather. May I?"

"We said we'd have dinner; it will just be in Tucson. Steven will have to stop at El Torero for lunch–dinner wherever you would like. See if you can get a ticket–we are on the morning non-stop tomorrow. We have breakfast with Jackie Saturday morning at the Arizona Inn. While you do that, I need to call Steven."

Marta was already on her cell phone to see if she could get a reservation.

Susan called Steven, but got his voice mail.

"Ah, I got the reservation. So, I guess Wilhelm told you he's taking the NSA position."

"It sounds like a good move for him. Landing deals and all that crap is a pain when you combine it with our prima donnas."

"There's an asshole level there too and it has the same prima donnas," Marta said. "If he's lucky, he may get into something like money laundering. The art world looms large in that arena, so he could have some fun. Did you resign yet?"

"No, I was too tired this week," Susan answered. "I have an appointment with the Big A now on May 6. I was going to send him an email, but I think I can stand him for the few minutes it takes. My deal doesn't close until the 10th anyway."

"I suppose you should do it properly. How are you and Steven doing with the documents?"

"I've been spending my spare time working on the Latin documents so Steven could focus on the Greek. He's been talking with David about the pieces that are in Hebrew and Aramaic. Steven is hoping David has had enough time to look at them, so that he can provide that information as well at the meeting next Friday. Wait, that's Steven."

"Good morning," he said. "Do you have David's number in Shanghai?"

"Try his cell. Anything new from Bob?"

"Nope, I will see you tonight–I want to get back to the documents," he said and hung up.

"So, you picked up the box to show Jackie?"

"Yep."

"But I thought she gave you a rough date from the pictures you sent her," Marta said

"She did; my problem is that damn hasp. Except for that, I think our stuff was most likely put in the box around 1600 by some Pilgrim who buried them for safe-keeping. The Pilgrim then either died or got scared, assuming he knew the contents might be considered sacrilegious. If the Puritans were burning witches, then you probably didn't want an old family heirloom with sacrilegious writings in your possession—especially these, if Steven is correct. If they were heirlooms, the Pilgrim probably just buried them rather than destroy them."

"But the picture I saw shows 1307 on the hasp," Marta said. "Plus, as I recall the box could be that old. And what Pilgrim could read Greek?"

"Thomas Jefferson read Greek and Latin. Maybe the box was buried because whoever had it couldn't read the documents and was afraid of what they might be. Anyway, the box certainly could be that old, it just couldn't be buried in Maine then. I'm hoping Jackie will somehow be able to tell us it's an old hasp on a newer box."

"Can Jackie do that?" Marta asked.

"I don't know. This is neither my continent nor my era of expertise," Susan said. "And then there is this Portuguese man, Joham, who says he put documents in more than one box—so far, we have only one."

"You really think there's more than one box?"

"Yes, damn it, it's plural. But the real question shouldn't be how many; it should be why there is any box at all. Anyway, the best date I found for the Portuguese, other than the early explorers, is about 1658, when some Jewish refugees settled in Newport, Rhode Island. They were Jews of Portuguese and Spanish descent who had settled in the Caribbean when they got kicked out of Spain and then Portugal. Then they got kicked out of the Caribbean. But Joham couldn't be with them—he said he had the documents in Tomar and used a Welshman to get him to Maine at least 50 years before that."

"What if he came with one of the earlier explorers?" Marta asked.

"It's possible," Susan said. "Do you have any time to look at this?"

"Me?" Marta asked a little surprised.

"Yes, you know how to do research. See what you can find—we need to see when and why Joham could have come to Maine. If you find something, we'll have dinner at Hacienda del Sol Saturday night."

"Okay, I'll try," Marta said as she got up to leave.

"Wait a minute," Susan said. "What did you do with Cy?"

"His daughter's wedding is this week end," she said. "I have to be back in DC on Wednesday for a meeting, so we're having dinner Thursday night. I'll take the train to New York the next morning. Who's Bob Pitt, again?"

"He's the archaeologist we know at the museum in Tucson. We sent him the spear point that Jon found at his site. Bob can tell us if it's real and, if it is, whether it was stolen."

"Anything else?"

"Nope," Susan said. "I'm going to ask Steven to come for lunch at 12:30 p.m. You can join us, if you want."

"Sure," Marta said. "So, wasn't Henry the Navigator Portuguese?"

"Yes and he also was Grand Master of the Knights of the Order of Christ, the successor to the Templars in Portugal. I think their headquarters were at Tomar, where our Joham seems to be from. But neither Henry nor Vasco de Gama, a despicable man by the way, went to the New World. There is a Portuguese explorer named João Vaz Corte-Real who was given the name "discoverer of the Land of the Cod" for finding it in 1472. That supposedly is a reference to Newfoundland. The best candidate might still be the Italian, Verrazano, who probably visited New England in about 1524, but he's not Portuguese."

"Nice bridge," Marta said as she headed for the door.

"Yes, that's what I told Jon," Susan said smiling. "Happy trails, Dale. See you at lunch."

CHAPTER 53

Margery's sister, Betty, was visiting at the new flat she had found for Margery in London. It had taken Margery two weeks to get everything into storage before leaving Cardiff in mid-February. Then she spent six weeks with her sister, Emily, in Australia. Emily had moved to Australia when she married 55 years ago. Emily's husband had died six months ago, so she had asked Margery to visit. Meanwhile, Betty had found her the flat. It was only two Tube stations away from her. Margery had moved in on April 15.

"You've been here only about a week, but it looks like you have settled in quite nicely,' Betty said. "It's so nice having you here. I really enjoyed our outing to the National Gallery yesterday. I hadn't been to Trafalgar Square in years."

"Well, it hasn't changed much except for the traffic–thank God for the Tube," Margery said thinking that it really had been a good idea to move back to London. She moved to Cardiff with her husband in 1980. He took a position in the French Department and she went to work for Dr. Smith. They were both gone now, so it felt good to leave Cardiff behind. She always missed London…living there again was proving to be quite nice.

"I remember as children we went to see Richard the Second on the *Wilton Diptych* every so often with Mum– she did love it," Betty said. "It was comforting to see that it was still there."

"Yes, Betty, it was. I still like the right panel the most, the angels' wings you know. It was nice to rummage through Foyle's again, too. I have enough to read for six months, now. More tea?"

"One more cup, please," Betty said. "Then I had better leave."

The phone rang while Margery was getting the tea. "Can you get that, Betty?"

"Hello?" Betty said as she answered the phone. "Yes, just a moment. May I tell her who is calling?" Betty cupped the receiver and said, "It's a man—he says he is Richard Prenbryer. Dr. Smith was one of his clients. Is there something wrong, Margery?" Betty asked, seeing an angry look on Margery's face.

"I'll take it, Betty," she said. "This is Margery. Can I help you?"

"I'm not sure, Ms. Short," said. "I am trying to track down something that Dr. Smith bought from my shop last fall. I understand that he has died, but I have a client who is willing to pay top dollar for it. I was wondering if you might know who took care of his estate."

"Well, I did some of it," she said. "He gave all of his research materials to the University. All of that was handled by the University's counsel. His niece and I only had his home to close up. May I ask what you are looking for? There wasn't much that didn't go to the University."

"It's just an old piece of parchment. It was in pretty bad shape, but it was a family heirloom."

"Something like that would have gone to the University's collections with all of his books and papers. We did an estate sale of his furnishings and personal belongings, but I didn't see anything like that. I'm afraid I can't help you."

"Wait, please don't hang up," he said as politely as he could muster. "I have one more question—two actually. Who would I contact at the University?"

"Oh dear," she said. "I don't really know. I guess you might try the Cardiff Alumni Fund—they handled it, as I recall."

"Thank you," Richard said. "I have one more question. I thought perhaps I could reach his friend, a Japanese man who attended Dr. Smith's Memorial, but I don't remember his name, Shikawa, I think. Might you know how I could contact him?"

"Shikawa?" Margery asked.

"Yes," he said. "I believe so. I checked at the St. Davids, but they didn't have him registered. I guess he had already checked out when I asked for him."

"I have never heard that name and no one named Shikawa was invited to the Memorial, if that helps," she said telling the truth. "If it's important, maybe you can check with the registrar at Cardiff. I cannot access Dr. Smith's contacts anymore as I retired at the end of February."

"Do you think his cell phone is still around? It might have a phone number."

"His cell phone was University property, so it went back to the University," she said. "They probably deactivated it or something like that. He was sort of old school; he didn't much like using that cell phone anyway."

Richard gave Margery information on how to reach him at his gallery and then hung up. What idiotic people, he thought. Not using cell phones in this day and age. Nevertheless, Ms. Short could be leading him on…perhaps he better have someone check her flat.

"Margery, that man called me while you were in Australia. I guess the University gave him your forwarding information—my number until you got back."

"Richard Prenbryer?"

"Yes, his voice sounded familiar when I answered. He called at least twice and then I finally told him that you were on a tour celebrating your retirement and 67 years of frugality. Sorry, I did tell him I would have you call when I heard from you, but then, he refused to give me his name. What does he want?"

"I don't actually know, Betty. His name came up in the context of that Kate Parker issue at the University, but nothing came of it. He's an art dealer of some sort, so it may be that Dr. Smith bought something from him that he wants to sell to someone else now."

"And you are going to see if the Registrar will get this name for him?"

"Of course not," Margery snorted. "Dr. Smith never used the University system—just his memory, scraps of paper and me. Besides, I wouldn't find the name he asked me about—it wouldn't be there."

"Good," Betty said as she got up to leave. "I don't like him—he was very pushy. Are we all set for our 'Agatha Christie' visit to Torquay Friday?"

"Yes, and we are going to splurge. I booked two rooms at the Imperial Hotel from April 26th to May 1. It didn't seem appropriate to stay anywhere else."

"Oh Margery, that's too expensive," Betty protested.

"It's only for a few days. We can afford it, Betty."

"Well, it would be fun to stay at Ms. Christie's 'Majestic Hotel,' Betty said. "I guess we only live once. I will finish reading her *The Body in the Library* on the train tomorrow. I finished *Peril at End House* last week after we decided to go. I think I may switch from Miss Marple to Poirot for our trip. This will be great."

"I'll read *4:50 from Paddington*; may I borrow *The Body* when you finish it?"

"Yes, of course, dear. I'll see you at the station Friday morning at 8:15 a.m."

"Yes, in front of Boots."

It was after 4:00 p.m. when Margery's sister left—too late to call Eisen. He liked to be in bed by 10:30 p.m. She would have to wait a while, so she sat down and began to read the first book of Colleen McCullough's series on the Roman Empire—*The First Man in Rome*. The series started with Gaius Marius around 110 BCE and ended with Augustus and the death of Cleopatra in 27 BCE. Emily had recommended the series as McCullough was an Aussie; she lived on Norfolk Island of all places. Margery was happy; she had at least six thick books to read. She would take *First Man* with her tomorrow as well.

CHAPTER 54

Margery stayed up that evening reading her book until it was just after 7:00 a.m. in the morning, Tokyo time. "Is this Mr. Shikawa?" she asked when he answered his cell.

"Margery, is that you?" Eisen said. "What's this about Shikawa?"

"Hi Eisen, it is me. I got a call a little while ago from your Richard Prenbryer. Apparently, he called my sister, Betty, a couple of times while I was gone–in Australia you know. Cardiff gave him Betty's number as my forwarding information. I left that as I didn't know where I would end up. Betty finally told him I was traveling for a couple of months. He didn't ask for my cell phone number, so she didn't it give it to him. Anyway, apparently he called Betty's house again today while she was having tea with me. Her daughter gave him my new number here."

"And?"

"He is anxious to find a Japanese man whose name is Shikawa. Prenbryer says he is pretty sure that this guy attended the Memorial and stayed at the St. Davids, but the hotel said they had no one by that name when he tried to find him. I assume that means they couldn't find a Shikawa."

"Interesting," Eisen said as he searched for his glasses. He had slept in a bit this morning.

"Did I wake you? Anyway," she laughed, "if you know this Shikawa, tell him Richard Prenbryer wants the parchment document that he sold to Dr. Smith. He has a buyer for it."

"It's a good thing we all look alike," Eisen laughed. "How do you think he got that close to my name and where I was staying?"

"I believe that he is tied to that Kate Parker. Neither I nor Dr. Smith had the best penmanship, so she may have seen your name on my calendar. Did I tell you they found my calendar in a trash can on campus?"

"Yes, you did," Eisen said thinking.

"Anyway, I had your name in it on the January page. Even I couldn't read it very well if I didn't know it was Shakura. Shall I do anything?" she asked. "He makes me a little nervous. Thank God he was too stupid to ask about a Japanese man; by asking about Shikawa, I could honestly say I never heard of him."

"Let me talk with Ohno-san," he said when he stopped chuckling.

"Do you know why he thinks you may have this parchment? Might they be what Dr. Smith had me send Mr. Ohno?" she asked. "I certainly never saw it."

"I'll speak with Ohno-san," he said. "May I call you back on Friday?"

"I will be with my sister," she answered. "We are going to take the train to Torquay to stay for a few days, so call my cell. We leave tomorrow, but we will be back here in London on May 1."

"Oh yes, your Agatha Christie trip…can you tell the police that you will be gone for a couple of days?"

"That's a good idea. I will do that. Thank you, Eisen." Part of her wished he didn't live so far away. But then, she thought as she picked up her book, it was nice to just go back to *The First Man in Rome*, too.

CHAPTER 55

Eisen knew that Ohno-san hadn't come in yet, so he busied himself by finishing the arrangements for New York. He then finished the bios for the three Americans and the archaeologist. 'An interesting group,' Hershel had said. Eisen was a little disappointed that none of them were on Facebook—he approved of that, but it might have been interesting to get some gossipy information on them.

He had two things now to talk about. First, they had to decide whether to invite the archaeologist to the meeting and then, there was this new issue regarding Prenbryer. As he got up to see if Ohno-san was in, his phone rang. "Finally," he said to himself as he picked up the phone. "Good morning, sir."

"Please come in so we can review the schedule," Kat said.

"Yes, sir. Tea?"

"Yes, Eisen."

Eisen came in with the tea and the bios. "Dr. Gruber was right, the Americans are interesting, sir," he said as he handed Ohno-san the bios. "The Krejci woman worked in Congress for a Senator for several years."

"It's the USA, Eisen," Kat cautioned. "That could be good or bad. Was it a 'Tea Bag' no, I mean 'Tea Party' Senator?"

"No, sir. Based on what I've read, she and the Senator seem quite sane. When she retired, she apparently went to the law firm where the Graves woman is. Mrs. Graves' husband is a retired businessman—the medical field."

"Are the arrangements set?" Kat asked.

"Yes, sir," Eisen said. "We will be at the Peninsula. I have us coming in on May 1 and leaving on May 7. We have another issue, though. Richard Prenbryer has found Ms. Short in London. He is looking for a Mr. Shikawa whom he says attended Smith-san's Memorial and stayed at the St. Davids."

"Shikawa?" Kat chuckled. "Could that be you Eisen?"

"Well, sir, we do all look alike, but I always thought our names were more distinctive," Eisen joked. "Not like the Chinese with 100,000,000 'Zhangs.' As usual, our adjoining suites at the St. Davids were booked in my name. I've done the same thing at the Peninsula, of course."

"Is it possible that the Parker woman obtained your name from Ms. Short's calendar?"

"Yes, sir, Ms. Short also thinks that is what happened. My name was on her calendar—the one they found in the trash. She said her penmanship isn't the best. Actually, having seen her writing, I'm surprised Mr. Prenbryer got that close. Apparently, Mr. Prenbryer tried the hotel and when he asked for Shikawa, they didn't volunteer my name as a correction—quite laudable. Also, Ms. Short was honestly able to say that she did not know a Shikawa—she said he was too stupid to ask if she knew a Japanese man. Her question was whether she should give this information to the Cardiff police. The police may contact me if she does, sir."

"So, am I correct that the Parker woman disappeared and they left it at that?"

"Apparently, sir," Eisen answered. "I asked Utamaro's office to do a background check on Prenbryer as a possible dealer we might visit in London with a friend as you suggested. Also, I told Margery to let the police know she would be gone for a few days—she will be traveling with her sister to Torquay."

"Ah, Agatha Christie…," he smiled. "Hershel was told that Prenbryer is a person of interest at Interpol—he didn't quite remember the exact details as it was a couple of years ago. Prenbryer was never actually arrested, though." Kat sat thinking for a few minutes. He did not want his name mentioned—his son would be quite upset if he thought his father had anything to do with Interpol. But this Prenbryer was going to a lot of effort…. "This is too close, Eisen. Call her back, please. Have her tell the police that Prenbryer may be a 'person of interest' and that he must have been involved in the Cardiff matter, since he is now looking for you. She should use exactly the same words that Hershel used with me. If she has to, she may use your real name."

"Yes, sir," Eisen said as he dialed Margery's number. His first words were that he was in Ohno-san's office and was calling at his urging so that she would know he would be curt. When he hung up he said to Ohno-san, "she will call the police."

"Now that we will all be at the 3:00 p.m. meeting, shall we invite the archaeologist?" Ohno-san asked.

"Yes, sir. I think we might as well," Eisen said. "He has to be the common link, don't you think?"

"Indeed," Kat said. "You have talked with him, so you can call him. We don't need to involve Utamaro at this point."

"Am I still a Samovar representative?"

"Of course," Kat said. "If he does know any of the Americans, he probably has our names. You and I are associated with our Samovar's company—technically, one of its parents pays our pensions, so just tell him we were being a little cautious, but honest. But do ask him if it will be okay with his American friends."

"Sir?" Eisen asked.

"In a nice way, Eisen," Kat said. "Tell him we know about the Americans. You are good at keeping people calm. I don't want to suggest that we think he's done anything wrong."

As Eisen was leaving he saw that Kat had pulled out the box of pictures from Daf again. "Ghosts," Eisen thought to himself. He knew them well–they were best visited when you were alone.

CHAPTER 56

It was Friday before Eisen was able to reach Dr. Christiansen. Susan and Steven had told Jon to expect the call, so he wasn't surprised. Jon dutifully told Eisen that his next report would disclose yet another intrusion that had appeared to be purposefully buried at the site, but this one was different. He explained that it seemed to be an old burial–a box with a hasp dated 1307. Because it wasn't Archaic or Paleo-Indian, he had asked two friends to help him discern what it was and why it was where he found it. He even told Eisen that he was concerned that it might be a fake put there to discredit him based on the tenure issue. Jon agreed to bring the document that scared Hershel to the meeting on May 3. He also would bring pictures of the box.

After a little prodding, Dr. Christiansen, whom Eisen was to call 'Jon,' confirmed that his two friends were indeed Susan and Steven Graves.

When Eisen got off the phone, he sat for a minute. He was stunned that something had actually been found. Eisen didn't know what to say when Jon asked if he had expected to find something there, especially after Jon confided that his friends initially thought that the property owner had planted the box there. Jon then reiterated that he found the box under a layer of undisturbed earth. Eisen assured Jon that he also was surprised about finding the box. He promised to ask the owner if there was more information he could tell Jon about deciding where to dig.

Eisen then called Utamaro to check on Prenbryer.

"We have nothing specific, Eisen. He is mentioned several times in connection with some cheap fakes that supposedly originated in Israel; a 'person of interest' as you said. He also is mentioned in connection with some more valuable materials taken from Egypt. Neither of these resulted in any charges. It does seem that it would be unwise to deal with him as there are a fair number of these references—again no charges, though. May I ask, is this something related to Ohno-san's collection?"

"Of course not. Ohno-san advised a British friend who was considering a purchase to check the credentials of the dealer before deciding—that is what Mr. Ohno always does, of course. He decided he would check as well to protect his friend. Thank you," Eisen said and the hung up before Utamaro could ask anything more. He then rang Ohno-san. "May I come in to report, sir? I have spoken with Dr. Christiansen and I have preliminary information on Mr. Prenbryer."

"Yes, please. Come in five minutes."

Kat had been looking at things from Daf's box again. Their three driving trips were marked on an old map of the Western US at the bottom of the box. He chuckled—the map was so old that many of the US Interstates weren't shown—they hadn't been built yet. Kat had forgotten that he and Daf had driven from Los Angeles to Las Vegas in 1973. They spent a night in Palm Springs. Daf said he felt too old there even though he was only in his 30s—all of those not-so-young, over-sexed and over-tanned Americans cavorting around the pool of the motel where they had stayed in Palm Springs—all of them probably dead now. They continued north from Palm Springs through the Mohave Desert to Las Vegas. Daf felt too old there as well, but seeing night turned into day by all of the neon lights made it somewhat worthwhile. They saw a couple of good shows, but Kat no longer remembered who they saw—maybe Dean Martin or Jerry Lewis. They flew back from there; it would have been a little too much of no man's land for them to drive both ways. Luckily, they had already seen the Muir Woods and Yellowstone, or they might never have gone back to the Western US. He was putting the box away as Eisen knocked on his door.

"Come in Eisen. What have we learned?"

"Well, sir, our archaeologist, Jonathan Christiansen, did find something at the site. It was an old box with a hasp that says 1307. He told me that when he found a Latin document inside, he got scared that it had been purposefully buried by an angry colleague who hoped to discredit him."

"A colleague would do that?" Kat asked. "And he actually found a box dated 1307 in the United States?"

"Yes, sir, it's a small wooden box," Eisen answered. "Smith-san would be pleased if it's real."

"Well, it can't be; 1307 is the date on the map, but we know from Hershel that it was added."

"Mr. and Mrs. Graves think it was buried later. The box was below an undisturbed layer. Dr. Christiansen said that the layer suggests it was buried between 1300 and maybe 1650; obviously, it can't be earlier than 1307. He and the Graves think it is at the 1600s end of the range, so it would be buried during their colonization period. The box might be older."

"That's a reasonable possibility," Kat said. "It does seem odd...," he said while trying to get over his surprise that they had actually found something.

"Sir, the box has a metal hasp that says 1307. Dr. Christiansen found it shortly after finding that crystal I told you about. He didn't know what to do because his specialty is Archaic Native Americans, as he described it. As I said, his real concern was that it was buried by a colleague to discredit him."

"And someone would fake this to embarrass him?" Ohno-san asked.

"Apparently, sir. He voted against tenure for a younger colleague who somehow learned how he voted; he was only one of many who voted against the man. I should mention that Dr. Christiansen is in his upper 60s and will retire this year—almost as old as us, sir."

"And the Americans?"

"Dr. Christiansen knew them as graduate students 30 some years ago. My understanding is that they had been Biblical archaeologists when he knew them. I'm not sure how that ties to American Indian studies. The husband's information on the Internet is consistent with him being a Biblical archaeologist—I found a paper he published last year on a topic like that. Dr. Christiansen said he had always trusted them to be properly skeptical, so he went to them. He thought they could determine whether the Latin document, the one the Graves showed Dr. Gruber, buried in a box dated 1307 in the middle of a Native American site in Maine, was real."

"I can imagine he was pretty upset," Kat chuckled. "At least we were warned ahead of time by Daf. This poor man..." Kat was chuckling again.

"Yes, sir." Eisen was chuckling now too. "After years of waiting, he gets back to his site only to find a crystal buried by some New Ager, but the best is yet to come…."

"A box that is a few hundred years too old for settlement in America with a document written in a dead language right where old Samovar told him to dig," Kat was still chuckling. "So he didn't find anything in Welsh?"

"No, sir. I asked him that specifically. He was puzzled by the question, but said there was nothing like that."

"Hmm, so the box probably belonged to the Portuguese man, Joham, since his name was on the document."

"Yes, but the document was in Latin. Dr. Christiansen did say that Mrs. Graves thought that the document could be 1307, which coincidently was the date on our map, but would more likely be 1607. The parchment was somewhat damaged where the date was. As I mentioned, she thinks the box was buried around the time of the Pilgrims—the 1600s. Oh, and she originally thought you might have planted the box to try to sell off the stuff in it for a good price. She can't figure out how else you could tell Dr. Christiansen where to find it."

Kat was chuckling again. "So, we wait until we are almost 80 to get into the forgery business?"

"Not 'we,' sir," Eisen said with as straight a face as he could muster. "She only mentioned you—the property owner." Kat was still chuckling and now Eisen joined him.

"She must respect you, sir—at least she didn't accuse you of burying the crystal." When they had stopped chuckling, Eisen added, "their friend, the Krejci woman, recommended Hershel for determining the age of the piece that was signed by our Joham."

"And that is why Hershel said he almost had a heart attack when he saw it," Kat said chuckling again. "Does Dr. Christiansen know Hershel or Richard Prenbryer?"

"The Graves told him about Hershel, but he didn't recognize Prenbryer. I prodded him a bit, but he was adamant that he has never dealt with any dealers."

"But how did Daf's map lead us to a real box?" Kat mused. "More importantly, how did Prenbryer get the map? I guess we'll find out in New York."

"Yes, sir. By the way, according to Utamaro, Mr. Prenbryer is mentioned as a 'person of interest' with respect to a number of fakes coming out of the Middle East. However, he's never actually been charged."

"Perhaps we will change that," Kat said.

"Since our Joham seems to be Portuguese, sir, I found a reference that said Portuguese sailors were the first Europeans to visit Japan. They got lost in a storm in 1540 on their way to somewhere in China, probably Macao. They shipwrecked on one of our southernmost Islands. Apparently that counted."

"Our meeting in May should be interesting."

CHAPTER 57

Susan worked on the draft opinion for the debt piece and the back-up certificates for almost an hour Thursday morning. She decided to take a break and pulled out the photograph of the Latin piece with the seal attached. Since it was short, she would spend a little time with it before finishing the opinion. She called Steven when she finished. It was already 11:45 a.m.

"Good morning," Steven said. "What's new?"

Susan decided that she would start with Marta and save what she had just seen for last. "Marta is going with us tomorrow, so I gave her an assignment. She has to find the earliest evidence of anyone from Wales coming to America—other than the Captain of the Mayflower, who may have been Welsh. She also has to find a plausible date for Joham to come from Tomar via Wales."

"She agreed to do that?"

"Yes, if she's coming to Tucson with us, she has to work for it. She also wants to meet Jackie—I think Marta is enjoying this."

"So does that mean we will go to Hacienda del Sol?" he asked.

"Yes, if she finds something useful. You, though, have been useful already, so we'll also go to El Torero for lunch. Anyway, I have been looking at the picture I have of the document with the wax seal. By the way, how are things with you?"

"I'll talk with David tomorrow—his cell phone works in Shanghai. He thinks I am correct about the translation I asked him to focus on. It supports my theory about Eusebius cooking up a fair amount of what today is thought of as Christianity. What he didn't cook up, Theodoret, Rufinus and their pals added when they edited Eusebius. Anyway, we have two very angry writers protesting that the Bishops at Nicea are arguing over issues that are not found in the teachings of Jesus. That should make you happy."

"Seriously? So, he's looked at the Greek, too?"

"Just one, we disagree on a few words, but the letter is quite accusatory. Did you find anything interesting in the document with the seal?"

"It certainly isn't a papal bull, but it is signed by an apocrisiary in Tomar," she said. "At least I think that's his title; you know, like a diplomat or a nuncio of the Pope. The date is January 13, 1296. It acknowledges that the three 'Guardians of the Word' have custody of 21 documents and that they are to protect those documents. We only have 10, counting this one and the three fragments. That means there should be at least one more box. The apocrisiary gave his approval for them to stay with the Templars in Tomar."

"What exactly does 'Guardians of the Word' mean?" Steven asked.

"I'm not sure. The documents aren't listed, so I don't even know if our 10 are part of those 21. We may have a separate stash. You know that the Joham attestation specifically says that the three Guardians were with him. He doesn't say 'Guardians of the Word,' though.

"I thought we were pretty much living in the 1600s now," Steven said. "Your date throws us back too far. I mean 1296 in Maine?"

"Two things—first, this 1296 seal document never mentions Joham. Second, I would guess that the title 'Guardians of the Word' could be passed down through the generations—otherwise, if they are with Joham, they are some pretty damn old dudes."

"I get it; you think the three old dudes with our Joham were protecting these documents. But they are successors of the Guardians mentioned in the 1296 piece, right?"

"It's just a thought, Steven. As I said, this one makes no reference to Joham. It could be that our Joham ended up with this box of stuff which the Guardians, or their predecessors, had guarded since 1296. Can you come have lunch? Marta will join us—in the cafeteria, here."

"I'll be there at 12:30 p.m. That's 30 minutes—I better hurry. Bye."

Susan sat for a few minutes looking at the opinion again. She made a few more changes and then called Jane. "I'll have changes to the opinion in about twenty minutes—can you leave Steven's name downstairs, he's coming for lunch with me and Marta. I have a couple of calls to make."

"I thought you died in there—I'll come get the changes when it is time for you to go to lunch."

Jane dutifully showed up at 12:25 p.m. "Steven is on his way up, and you had a call from Dr. Christiansen while you were on the phone. He will call your cell in half an hour—is that okay?"

"Yep, call me if there are any emergencies."

Susan, Marta and Steven had just sat down with their trays, when Steven's phone rang. "It's Bob," he whispered as he answered.

Susan and Marta tried to follow the conversation, but it was too difficult.

As soon as Steven hung up, Susan asked, "What did he say?"

"First, he apologized for taking so long to get back to us, but then he asked that we please not send him anything like this again," Steven said. "So Marta, Susan told you about the stolen spear point, right?"

"She never mentioned that it was stolen," Marta said.

"Yes I did," Susan said. "I also mentioned that Jon found a crystal buried at the site, right?"

"Yes, but you said it was probably buried by some New Age nut. You did not say that the spear point was stolen."

"I did, too. Anyway, we thought the spear point could be a fake, so we sent it out to Bob Pitt—I know I told you that. So, Steven, what did Bob say? Is it stolen?"

"The piece we sent to Bob is a Folsom point made from chert and it is real," Steven said.

"That's nice, but does that mean it's stolen?" Marta asked.

"Well, it actually has an accession number on it. You have to use a black light or something to see it well. Oh, and someone had tried to chip it off. The chipping was done recently. Anyway, Bob is trying to find out whose accession number it is and whether it was de-accessioned—sometimes pieces are sold off when a museum has too many. As I mentioned before, Bob says you can buy these on the Internet for a few hundred dollars. So, he thinks it is a prank or something like that."

"That does sound like a student's prank," Susan started. "Steven, why did he say it's Folsom and not Clovis?"

"He said that Folsom points are usually shorter and a little wider than Clovis points. He started to tell me about the differences in fluting and pressure flaking patterns, but I told him my brain was too tired. He should hear back on the accession number today or tomorrow. Again, it may be de-accessioned. By the way Marta, Susan said she gave you an assignment. How's it going?"

"I have found some information on sailing to Maine," Marta smiled. "Shall I tell you now or wait until tomorrow?"

"Give us some tidbits and then you can regale us over lunch tomorrow in Tucson," Susan answered.

"Okay, Henry Cabot probably was the first person after the Vikings to make landfall in New England. He landed at Cape Bonavista in Newfoundland on June 24, 1497. At least that's where the Canadians put the plaque. More importantly, a Portuguese sailor named Estevan Gomez explored the coast of Maine for Spain in 1524 or 1525. That's right after Mr. Bridge, Verrazano, was there."

"Maine for Spain," Susan repeated.

"But wait, there's more," Marta continued. "There is a legend about a Welsh Prince named Madoc who sailed to America in 1170 and went up the Mississippi River to mate with the Mandan Indians. He never returned to Wales, so it's only a legend. But the legend was important enough to be used in the 1600s as a basis for the British to claim priority of their land claims in North America. Anyway, in 1617, Welsh colonists tried to found a place called 'Renews' in Newfoundland, but the colony failed. What seems obvious though is that by the early 1600s sailing to North America was well established. There was a fair amount of commerce developing, especially with all of the virgin American forests just begging to be cut down."

"So, is it is possible that a Portuguese man went to Wales in 1607 and hired a ship to take him and three others to New England?"

"It is quite possible," Marta said. "The Mayflower took 66 days going west and about 30 days going east. Oh, and one more tidbit, in 1857, a twelfth century Norse penny was found in an Indian archaeological site in Maine. As far as I can tell, it is either a hoax or it was something that made its way to Maine over many centuries of trading among the tribes in the North Atlantic region."

"You've earned your dinner at Hacienda del Sol," Susan said.

Susan's cell phone rang–this time it was Jon. Steven and Marta listened–it sounded like Susan was trying to calm Jon down. She talked with him for a few minutes and then hung up saying that she would call him back in ten minutes.

"Susan, was that Jon?" Steven asked.

"Yes, the Bangor police just called him. He was busy, so he let it go to voicemail. The message says that yesterday someone reported that there were stolen artifacts in a shed at his site. The police didn't get around to going out there until this morning as it wasn't top of their list. They didn't find anything, so they called Jon because his name was on the sign about where someone could claim their crystal. Do you think Bob called the authorities, Steven?"

"No, of course not," Steven said. "He did put out an email today to see if he can find out where the spear point is from by using its accession number. But we haven't told Bob where Jon found it."

"Well, shit. Jon was paranoid for a good reason–somebody must have planted it and then turned him in," Susan said. "Marta, help...what do we do?"

"Tell me the facts," she said.

"Jon gave a talk in Bangor the Monday before he came to see us—he filled in for a sick friend," Susan said. "Bangor's not too far from his site, so he drove over there to poke around when the talk was over. Actually, he decided to look around because he had finally cleaned the box over the weekend and saw the 1307 date on the hasp. It was Spring Break, so no one was there at the site. He went to get his favorite trowel out of a little shed they have there." Susan was laughing now.

"And?" Marta asked.

"And," she said as she stopped laughing, "he found a spear point wrapped in a rag sitting behind his favorite trowel. He thought it was a fake; even if it were real, it couldn't have come from his site."

"Jon gave it to us and we sent it to Bob Pitt at the Arizona Museum," Steven added. "We figured he could sort it out for us."

"That was Bob on the phone with Steven—before I got the call from Jon. Now, the cops think Jon stole it," Susan added, stifling a laugh.

"Jesus guys, this is ridiculous," Marta said. She sat thinking for a moment, and then said, "Jon should call the police and tell them what he found and why he was in Bangor and then at his site."

"About the box?" Steven asked.

"No, of course not, just that he was nearby, so he drove over to look around a bit. But he should tell them that the spear can't be from his site, so he sent it to an expert to see if it was real. He should get the name of a contact person for the Bangor police, so that when Bob tells us where it's from, he can tell the police. He should be clear that whoever called the police, likely was the person who put the piece in the shed."

"Perfect, Marta," Susan said looking relieved. "On that note, I'm going back to my office to call Jon and finish up. We'll see you tomorrow at the airport."

"I'm looking forward to meeting Bob. Maybe I can vouch for the two of you. I can tell him you aren't low life crooks who steal spear points."

"When are you coming home, Susan?" Steven asked. "And, more importantly, what do you want for dinner?"

"I need about an hour to finish up a couple of things. Oh, and I have to call Jon back. Can you make your chipped beef for me?"

"Okay, and bring what you have translated. We'll talk more when you get home."

"Yes, dear," Susan said as she got up. "Marta, thank you."

CHAPTER 58

The ringing of Eisen's phone woke him. He looked at his phone as he grabbed it to answer. It was Margery.

"Eisen, I'm so sorry to bother you, but I thought I should call. The police are here…I got home at 4:30 p.m. from Torquay and found that my flat had been ransacked. I think it was Prenbryer, since whoever broke in took my phone pad. I had written your name and phone number on it when we talked last week. It is gone now. I also told Scotland Yard that I think this is connected to the University incident and that Prenbryer had tracked me down a few days ago."

"You are okay?" Eisen asked.

"Yes, but I am pretty angry at this bloke," she said. "I told Prenbryer I had nothing. I also am pretty angry with the bobbies. I told them I was worried about something like this happening before I left–just as you told me."

"Did they take anything else?"

"Only some jewelry and my iPad, which I had forgotten to take with me on holiday."

"I will see that it is replaced. I am glad you are safe."

"I have to go, Eisen. They have more questions."

"Please call me back when you are done," he said, but she had already hung up. He would wait a while, and then call her.

CHAPTER 59

The morning flight to Tucson landed on time. They picked up their car at the airport parking. From there, it was only 45 minutes to the ranch, but they stopped on the way for lunch at the Dakota Café, since Susan liked their corn bread. El Torero and the sour cream enchiladas would have to wait until tomorrow.

Susan immediately went in search of the Greek primer when they got home. She found the primer and took it and a cup of coffee to the back porch. Before getting too comfortable, she topped off all of the bird feeders hanging from the mesquites. She then sat down to thumb through the primer as she watched the birds come to feed. Marta brought her a glass of wine and sat down nearby.

"Where's Steven?" Susan asked.

"He's checking in with Jon."

"It's already late there. I hope Jon's calmed down. A call from the police has to be scary."

"Did Jon call the police back?" Marta asked.

"I think so—he thought it was good advice," Susan answered. "What did you open?"

"The Ponzi," Marta said. "I figured a nice Oregon Pinot Noir would help you with the Greek—your coffee can wait—you like it cold anyway."

They sat quietly letting the feeding birds mesmerize them. "There's the male cardinal," Susan said as she watched him come to one of the box feeders.

She always felt that her trip was complete if she saw him, although she would settle for his wife or one of the pyrrhuloxias. The lesser goldfinches were all over the nyjer seed feeder. It would be empty by day's end.

"There's a Costa's on the hummingbird feeder," Marta whispered as the sun caught the beautiful, iridescent feathers of his head. She had forgotten how calming it was to sit on the porch, looking out at the mesquites and the birds. A thousand feet away, the Catalina foothills began their rise toward the mountains. It was good to come here every so often.

"They are the only birds that can fly backwards," Susan whispered.

"Hummingbirds?"

"Yes, and they are very smart—the ratio of brain to body size in hummingbirds is significantly greater than other birds. Remind me to make sure we have enough sugar water for them."

Steven joined them. The noise was enough to scatter the score of birds out on the porch, but they'd be back. "I spoke with Jon," he said. "First, he said to thank you for the advice, Marta. He thinks he's now on good terms with the Bangor police."

"That's always a good thing," she said.

"Also, his son got back early from Rome," Steven said. "He checked on the missing pieces and they have indeed disappeared. What he sent does not match what the cataloger recorded. No one knows whether they were thrown out, mis-cataloged or stolen. The cataloger, who was a volunteer, doesn't remember them, but offered to come back to help look—she just quit last month. However, she was there last year as well when a more important piece, a bowl from New Mexico, disappeared."

"So, does that mean the Japanese guy hired her to take them?" Marta asked.

"I don't think so," Steven said. "I just don't see him as forger. Anyway, the volunteer actually recorded what's in the archives; it's just not what Father found."

"Maybe someone substituted what got recorded before Father's stuff got to the cataloger," Susan said. "She then recorded what was substituted."

"Or, maybe she took it because she was working with someone who wanted it," Marta added. "You know, she was looking for things to get for a dealer. She then sends the piece to a guy like Prenbryer to doctor. She replaces the real stuff with trash and records the trash."

"Well, Hershel said that Prenbryer was looking for medieval stuff, not American historical material, so we'll have to see," Steven said. "Anyway, Jon said he told the police he would let them know if he heard more about the spear point. I'm going to take a nap and then continue reading. I want to call David tonight."

"If the date is 1307, that fits Prenbryer," Susan said. "And if the thief only wanted old material to use for a forgery of something else...."

"Good point, Susan," Marta said. "Anyway, I'm going to take a short walk and then stream some *Warehouse 13* when I get back. Can we go to Amber for dinner? I want the strawberry blintzes for dessert."

"Fine with me," Steven said. "What do you think, Susan?"

"I think I am going to try to relearn Greek. Marta, take your cell and a bottle of water, it's pretty dry on the trail–and it's already hot. Oh, and technically, when you fill the little crepes with a fruit or on top, like strawberries, everyone but the Poles calls them blintzes. Amber is Polish, so they are nalesniki. I'm having the white borsht and nalesniki."

"Duh! Any trivia?" Marta asked as she opened the screen door.

"I just gave you blintzes! Oh well, you know *Warehouse 13*'s Farnsworth communicator is probably named after Philo T. Farnsworth, right?" Susan called after her.

"Who?" Marta asked.

"There's a plaque commemorating Philo T. Farnsworth on Sansome Street in San Francisco. It's on the left side on the way north from Broadway. He kind of invented television."

"Jesus, Susan, now that's a good one," Marta called back as she left.

"Grab a bottle of water," Susan yelled after her.

"Water, cool water…," Steven sang as Marta left. "Susan, is Philo, California in the Anderson Valley named after him?"

"Look it up Steven," she said and went back to her Greek primer.

CHAPTER 60

Marta found Susan and Steven sitting on the porch when she got back from her hike. *Indian Love Call* was playing softly in the background. Marta loved that song.

"Hey, Marta, glad you're back." Steven said. "I placated Susan by finding this old recording—we didn't have time to watch *Rose-Marie*, the movie where Nelson Eddy and Jeanette McDonald sing it. We were arguing over tenors again, and decided to switch to a baritone.

"Nelson Eddy was a baritone?"

"Technically, yes," Steven answered.

"Did you know that Slim Whitman became famous twice with *Indian Love Call*?" Susan asked. Without waiting for an answer, she added, "he recorded it in the early 50's and became a star. His rendition also was used in the movie, *Mars Attacks*. It was the song that they played to kill the Martians."

"Now we are discussing how much better the early 1600s are for someone to come to Maine from Wales," Steven said. "It looks pretty good, but you researched this, so you can help."

"Do we still go to Amber tonight?"

"Of course."

"And Hacienda del Sol tomorrow?"

"Yes."

"Well, it does look pretty straightforward—a number of colonies were started along the Atlantic coast. I'll be right back—I need my notes. Steven, get me a LaCroix, please."

"Susan?" Steven asked.

"I still have some of the wine Marta poured and my coffee."

"Okay, I'm back," Marta said. "So, I started with Amerigo Vespucci because he sailed for Manuel I of Portugal around 1500. Unfortunately for us, although he did prove that Columbus had discovered a continent and not the coast of Asia, he was sailing pretty much around the east coast of Central and South America."

"The mapmaker, Martin Waldseemüller named the Americas for him because of that—he was still living when that was done in 1507," Steven added.

"Thank you, Steven. Anyway, it's a while before people start settling in New England, although Verrazano was looking around up there as early as the 1520s. A Portuguese sailor named Estêvão Gomes, or Estevan Gomez, explored Maine for Spain in 1524 or 1525. In 1605, Champlain goes looking for the mythical city of Norumbega, around Bangor. He founds St. Croix and then everyone moves from there to Port Royal on the west side of Nova Scotia in 1605. The English founded Cuttyhunk on an island off Massachusetts in 1605, but it doesn't survive, and then Popham in Maine, which is also known as Sagadahoc, in 1607, but it doesn't survive either."

"Norumbega in Maine?" Steven asked. "Susan, have you ever heard of that?"

"Nope. Marta?"

"It was a mythical city like El Dorado. It appeared on that map drawn by Verrazano's brother in 1529 with the Normanvilla Tower on it that Susan mentioned. No one ever found Norumbega."

"Maybe we'll get Jon to look," Steven laughed.

"Ignore him, Marta," Susan laughed.

"Okay, so the first European settlement in the Americas was Veracruz in 1519. Santo Domingo was the first real colony; it was founded in 1498, but it was on the Dominican Republic side of the island, Hispaniola. It's actually the oldest permanent European settlement in the Americas. The next date is 1565 for St. Augustine, Florida. It's the oldest permanent European settlement in the continental U.S; the oldest one in the West is Santa Fe which was founded in 1607. The first English colony is St. John's, Newfoundland, which was founded in 1583. The oldest permanent French settlement is Tadoussac in Quebec in 1599. Berwick is the oldest permanent town in Maine—it was settled by the English in 1630."

"Anything else?" Susan asked.

"I threw in Arizona for a bonus. The Oraibi pueblo, which Pedro de Tova saw in 1540, was built before 1100. It, or possibly the Acoma pueblo, is the oldest continually inhabited spot in North America. The Tubac Presidio was founded by the Spanish in 1752 and the Old Pueblo of San Augustin del Tucson was founded in 1775. How's that?"

"And Plymouth and the rock?" Steven asked.

"Richard Smith made a map of North America from Cape Cod to Nova Scotia in 1614. He is credited with naming that area 'New England.' Plymouth came in 1620. By the way, the area of Eastern Maine and New Brunswick was named Acadia by Verrazano in 1523. Prince Edward Island, the land of the Malpeques, also was part of Acadia. I saved the best for last, dears. Are you ready?"

"Do tell Ms. Krejci," Steven said.

"Well, the Inquisition in Portugal began in 1536 at the request of King João III. It wasn't finally disbanded until 1821. They did sit in Tomar in 1541. Is it possible that Jon's box was moved out of Tomar because of the Inquisition?

"We need to look at this—Susan, anything in the knight's attestation?"

"No; damn, I wish we had Father's materials," Susan said. "Anyway, excellent job, Marta. We have a reservation at Hacienda del Sol for 6:00 p.m. tomorrow night," Susan said. "I made it yesterday, knowing you would come through."

"I'm going to do some research," Steven said. "The Inquisition is a good lead. Susan, maybe you and Marta can work up a timeline."

"Yes, dear, maybe."

That evening as they were eating their nalesniki, Steven announced, "I just got an email from David. He's having dinner with Mary and her friends in Shanghai tomorrow night."

"More stories?" Marta asked.

"It isn't easy to integrate a lot of facts into something that becomes so entertaining," Steven said. "It's a gift."

"Your wife is pretty good at it too, but a little more honest with the attributions," Marta said.

"David tells some pretty good stories as well. Susan, do you remember when Mary had that huge American guy with her for something."

"Oh God, yes, it was in Beijing; he was bigger than you Steven. She ordered those midget-sized cabs for us to see if you and he would fit; her friend got stuck and couldn't get out."

"There must have been 50 people watching him trying to get out in front of the hotel," Steven laughed. "*Enfant terrible* is what always comes to mind. Thank God I didn't get stuck in that stupid toy taxi."

"Seriously though, since I don't know most of the people in her stories, I focus on the facts," Susan said. "They are all basically true, but she throws them up in the air and lets the wind rearrange them a bit, ending up with a chimera, maybe one that changes color like a chameleon. The parts are from who knows where; then, depending upon who you are telling the story to, it is colored accordingly and it is always hilarious."

"Great, Susan," Marta said. "Mary is a mood ring."

"Or, maybe like shape shifters," Steven said softly. "That's how I think of you, Susan. You're different out here, like you're still on that old ranch."

"That old one is gone."

"Some of it's still here, Susan," Marta said. "Maybe that's why I love it here."

They sat silently for a while.

Then Susan said almost to herself, "As I once told Pete, if I had grown up here in the 1800s, I would have been on the first damn train that came in heading east. Crap, I would have got on just to get to Los Angeles, but that wouldn't have been until 1881 or so. I would always come back, though…for a visit."

"Let's go home—we have to be up early to get to the Arizona Inn on time," Steven said.

CHAPTER 61

Saturday morning Susan, Steven and Marta drove in to meet Jackie at the Arizona Inn. Jackie was waiting for them at the table.

"Jackie, thank you for coming on a Saturday morning," Steven said. "This is our friend, Marta Krejci, from Chicago. Marta, this is Dr. Jacqueline Santanos, our favorite dendrochronologist."

"Hello, Marta," Jackie said. "Isn't this a beautiful place for a Saturday breakfast?"

"Yes, it's one of my favorites," Marta said. "It's hard to imagine that a woman founded the Inn in 1930."

"That was Isabella Greenway," Jackie said. "She started it as a furniture factory to employ old WWI veterans. Theodore Roosevelt was a family friend when she was a young girl growing up in the Dakotas. She went to school with Eleanor Roosevelt and became her lifelong friend. Eleanor used to visit her here in Tucson. I believe Mrs. Roosevelt bought furniture from Isabella's factory for her house in Hyde Park. Isabella became Arizona's first Congresswoman in 1934."

"Our old foreman, Pete, worked for Mrs. Greenway around 1930," Susan said softly–it seemed far too long ago to be possible.

Jackie turned to Steven and asked, "What's so important about this box you have?"

"We sent you pictures of the wood from this box," he said. "We decided we would show you the box, but let's order breakfast first," Steven said as he motioned to the waiter.

After they ordered, Steven unwrapped the box and said, "See how the hasp says 1307, Jackie?"

"Susan, you said it was found in a layer that was maybe 1300 to 1600," Jackie said taking the box. "It certainly could be as old as 1307. The picture was good, but the inner rings were hard to discern. Also, I couldn't tell how the wood was treated at the outer edge. At least you didn't send me a mesquite box."

As Susan and Steven chuckled, Marta asked, "What's wrong with mesquite?"

"It's pretty much impossible to count the tree rings in mesquite," Susan said. They generally are too faint to see."

"By the way, Marta, Andrew Douglass invented dendrochronology at the University of Arizona in the 1930s."

"Actually, Dr. Douglass had been working on the scientific aspects for about 30 years before that," Jackie added.

"I know you're short of time," Susan said. "Our 1300 to 1600 estimate is consistent with radiocarbon dating from remains of a fire in a nearby hearth at the same depth."

"Radiocarbon dates generally work for a period of about 50,000 years ago to maybe 400 years ago, but that's pushing it," Steven said to Marta. "It was developed by the American Nobel Laureate, Willard Libby, in 1949."

"That and the atomic bomb," Susan said to no one in particular.

"And the carbon 14 is radioactive, but carbon 12 is not, so they look at ratios of Carbon 14 to carbon 12…," Marta started. "Crap, Steven–then what? The carbon 14 decays so the ratio changes over time.…"

"A living thing stops absorbing the Carbon 14 from the atmosphere when it dies. If the original ratio is 50:50, and it is now 70:30–you can estimate when the material "died," because you know that every 5000 years, half of the carbon 14 is gone."

"5,730 years," Jackie corrected. Susan tapped Marta's hand as a reminder not to chuckle–Steven hated being corrected.

"Anyway, it turns out that the level of the Carbon 14 isotope in the atmosphere may fluctuate from year to year," Steven continued. "That means that a radiocarbon year may not be equivalent to a calendar year, so you calibrate with tree ring data when you have it."

"Yes, well, as I said, it's almost impossible to do an estimate from a picture."

"The archaeologist who found it says that the undisturbed area above the box indicated the 1300 to 1600 range. It's a little difficult since you disturb a lot of levels and data with the shovel when you bury something. Luckily, as you can see, it is a small box. Anyway, we thought we would bring the box out for you to see the hasp."

"The hasp says 1307. What's the issue?"

"We are hoping the box is not as old as the hasp," Susan said. "Is there any way you can tell?"

"Not easily," she said. "The simple way is to see if the hasp is made of something, or is fastened in a manner, that wasn't used in 1307. Sometimes, it's easy. Like with cast iron—if you can discern nickel plating on it, then its post-1890, because nickel plating wasn't done before that. We sometimes can tell age as well by looking at the nails—they were hand made until maybe the 1700s. Actually, a nail making machine was first used in about 1600, but it still made only one nail at a time." Jackie was now engrossed in the box. She looked at them and said, "This is a very well made box, even if it is pine."

"Ah, here's the food," Steven said.

As they ate, Steven explained that he was more interested in what was in the box, than the box itself. Susan chastised him, saying that she did not want the box to be buried in 1300.

"Susan, the only thing you haven't told me is where you found the box," Jackie said. "Was it really in the US? Ah, these are screws holding the hasp to the wood. Look, the slots on these screws are not quite dead center—that means they are probably hand-made."

"The box was found in Maine," Steven said. "Although someone could bring a 300-year old box to Maine in the 1600s, it would be easier to fit everything together if we could just be comfortable that they used an old hasp on a newer box."

"Well, you may be in luck," Jackie said as she set the box down and picked up her fork to eat. "I can't really tell you how old the hasp is; it would be costly to even estimate its age. What I can tell you is that these screws wouldn't have been used until the 1500s or 1600s. Therefore, if the box was sealed with the hasp in place, then it was sealed well after the date on the hasp. Is that enough for buying me breakfast?"

"So, old hasp, new screw?" Susan asked.

"Yes. Of course, it's also possible that someone made these screws by hand recently to artificially age the box. You know, old wood put together recently with artificially aged screws. Oh, but you said the box was in an undisturbed layer. I guess you probably have an old box and old screws—around 1500 to 1600, and an even older hasp."

Marta looked to Steven and asked, "that's a relief, isn't it Steven?"

"A big relief," Steven said.

"Oh, now I understand," Jackie said. "You were worried that you had a box buried in 1307 popping up in Maine. That would be a conundrum, wouldn't it? You might have one of those Templars escaping to Maine after the King wiped out all of his French compatriots." She was laughing until she realized that they had been afraid of exactly that. "I guess a Pilgrim could have buried it though. Sorry, for laughing—anyway, your screws aren't that old."

"That's bad enough," Susan laughed. "It was buried in Maine, for God's sake."

"Couldn't someone just take an old box to Maine?" Jackie asked. Then she answered her own question, "no, you said it was buried in an old layer. How interesting."

"This is driving us crazy, Jackie," Susan laughed.

"I still don't understand why you three are involved in this?"

"An old archaeology friend from our graduate school days was afraid that someone planted this box as a prank," Susan explained. "The friend's specialty is the Archaic Period for Native Americans in New England–like maybe 4000 BCE."

"Was anything in the box?"

"The box had some very old Greek and Latin documents in it," Steven said. "That's why he asked us to help–to see whether they might be real. The problem is that they might well be real."

"Can you tell Jackie about the Latin?" Marta asked.

"Might as well," Steven said. "There is a document in the box that is in Latin. We think it is dated 1607, meaning that the box couldn't have been buried before that."

"Before you ask, Jackie, the writer didn't say he buried it in 'Maine'," Susan said. "He said 'under the dancing men and moose petroglyph.' That is descriptive of a petroglyph at the site where it was found."

"What happens next?" Jackie asked.

"We are meeting some people in New York next Friday–they seem to know something about how the box got where it is," Susan said. "If you'd like, we can fill you in after the meeting, if we know more. We are going to Hacienda del Sol tonight for dinner. Would you like to join us?"

"Darn, I would love to, but I have to be at a faculty party tonight," Jackie said. "Oh, it's already 10:30 a.m. I need to leave. Do let me know how this goes," she said as she got up. "This is an interesting one."

"Thank you for coming out so early on short notice," Steven said as he stood as well.

"For you, any time, Steven," Jackie said as she left.

"She stood you up," Marta chuckled. "At least we got some good information, don't you think?"

"Yes, I think so," Susan answered.

"Now you two just have me to entertain tonight," Marta said. "Really, though—you don't have to worry about the Welsh coming here and becoming Mandans now, right?"

"That's true, darn it," Steven said. "Now, we just have to figure out how these ancient Greek and Latin documents got to Maine in 1600. That's a piece of cake, right?"

"We also should try to figure out who our Joham is," Susan said.

"And, how the Japanese guys knew where to find this stuff," Marta added. "We could still have a hoax or a theft from Father Bartolome or both."

"Yes, but at least we know the box isn't as old as the hasp," Susan said.

"Are we ready for meeting number two?" Steven asked. "We are meeting Bob at 11:00 a.m."

"Let's hope it's not stolen," Susan said. "We'll call Jon after the meeting."

When they got to the museum, Susan stayed outside for a few minutes to return a couple of calls. As she walked in, she saw Bob coming down the stairs.

"Hello, Susan. Where's Steven?"

"He and our friend, Marta Krejci, are in the shop. Watch your heart, Bob—Marta is an eye-popper," she chuckled. "I'm hoping the view will make up for dropping this on you." Bob stopped laughing as Steven and Marta came out of the shop. Susan glanced at her watch; it was 11:01 a.m. After introductions, they walked up the stairs to Bob's office.

When they were seated, Susan said, "Marta is a longtime friend and colleague, Bob. So, if you have bad news for us, it is okay to tell us in front of her."

"She's an ex-spy," Steven added. "NSA."

"Well, I guess the movies are right," Bob said. "Spies are beautiful."

"Watch it Bob," Steven said smiling. "Marta is almost as tough as Susan."

"Sorry, Marta," Bob laughed. "As I told Steven, it's a real Folsom point. The accession number is one used by Shawmut College—it's in the Boston area. They checked their records and confirmed the accession number, so now we also know it's from Shawmut's archives."

"Let me guess, they use one of those little tag systems, right? You stick a tag in that says 'I have this' and then date it, right?"

"Yes, that's exactly what you are supposed to do," Bob said.

"But that only works if you card people in and out or else, you...sorry," Marta said. "I didn't mean to interrupt."

"Don't mind Marta—as I said, she was at the NSA for quite a while. We have to put blinders on her when we go to some museums. You have to admit, many of them have virtually no anti-theft protection," Steven said.

"Sorry," Marta said again.

"No, no," Bob said. "You are absolutely right, Marta. Most of us have systems now that record who goes in and out—and cameras to see what they're doing. In fact, ours requires a thumb print to open the doors to where our most fragile or valuable items are stored."

"I suppose you are going to tell us not Shawmut," Steven said.

"The area is locked, but about 20 people have access. They still use keys, so they don't know who goes in or out," Bob said. "The area's been covered by cameras for the last two years. However, the cameras where the Folsom points are stored have been out since the beginning of the year. They think this Folsom point must have been taken after the camera went out," he said as he set the Folsom point on the table in front of them. "There was a card in the box showing this Folsom point was checked out, but the person who put the card there forgot to fill in any information. I have known the curator there for years—as you can imagine, she is not happy."

"Crap, then it is stolen," Susan said. "That is not what we wanted to hear."

"It's odd that someone would steal this," Bob said as he picked up the spear point. "It's interesting as a study item and it was almost perfect before someone started chipping away at it—see there?" Bob said as he shined a little black light on where the chipping had occurred. "They removed part of the accession number. But why would you steal it? Steven, I think I mentioned that these aren't that hard to find, even today. And you can buy them for a few hundred bucks. It's just stupid."

"How old is this," Marta asked. It was this was beautifully symmetric, but the fluting was nicer on the Clovis points Susan loved.

"Maybe 11,000 years—Folsom is usually dated roughly from maybe 10000 to 8500 BCE. You're not a Clovis nut like Susan, are you?"

"I've known her since we were undergrads here at the University. She has pulled me and Steven all over the US to see Clovis points and sites, right Steven?"

"Yes, but they are nice," Steven said.

"I didn't say we went with her unwillingly, Steven."

"Bob, I assume they will let you know what they want to do with this," Susan said. "You can certainly send it back to Shawmut."

"They haven't asked for it, yet. The bigger question for them is how to modernize their system."

"Have they found anything else missing, Bob?" Marta asked.

"They won't know until they do a thorough inventory. As I mentioned, they think this piece was taken when the camera was out. Of course, it could have been lifted years ago before they had cameras— it's not a new accession number. How in God's name did Jon get this, again?"

"He found this in a shed he uses at his site in Maine," Susan said. "He's been busy re-opening the site after being gone for a few years. About two weeks ago, he was asked to fill in at a conference in Bangor for someone who was sick. Since his site is just east of Bangor, he decided to spend an hour or two poking around there. It was Spring Break, so no one was there. He found this point hidden behind his favorite trowel; there's no way it could have come from his site."

"Maybe one of his students did it as a joke," Bob said. "It's not good to steal something, though."

"Poor Jon is totally freaked out—he is afraid it is a colleague at Penn who didn't get tenure—the guy somehow knows Jon voted against him," Steven said. "A friend of Jon's son knows the guy. The guy told this friend he was going to get even."

"He thinks the guy really would do this? It's damn childish—no wonder he didn't get tenure. But…Jon's at Penn—how would the colleague get this? Jesus, I thought Jon would have retired by now."

"He wishes he had—he is retiring at the end of the year," Steven said. "You can imagine how upset he is that this is happening now."

Bob was laughing again.

"Um, if you think that's funny," Susan broke in as she quickly looked at Steven.

"Go ahead," Steven said.

"Jon got a call yesterday from the Bangor police," Susan began, but then she started laughing. When she got control, she continued, "They had received an anonymous tip that there was a stolen artifact in Jon's shed. Of course, we had already sent you the Folsom piece, so it wasn't there."

Before Bob could say anything, Steven added, "Wait, it gets better. The police called Jon because he and an intern had found a crystal buried at the site just before Spring Break. The intern posted a sign that said, 'If you want your crystal back, call Jon Christiansen.' That's why the police called him—his phone number was on the sign."

When they all stopped laughing, Bob looked at Marta and asked, "How did you let them drag you into this?"

"It's a nice diversion from the drudgery of law," Marta laughed as she leaned in across the table toward Bob and added, "You're just lucky they didn't send you the damn crystal."

"Damn," Bob said when he finally got control of himself and turned his gaze away from Marta's cleavage. "Susan, you do know I will have to tell Shawmut how I got this?"

"Absolutely, Bob," Steven said for her. "Feel free to give Shawmut my name or Susan's," Steven said. "I don't think we'll have anything else to tell them, though. On Marta's advice, Jon already told the Bangor police about it. Do they know who stole it yet?"

"I don't think so. It's probably some nutty post-doc who's been there for twenty years trying to get his PhD—that can send you over the edge."

"The big question is why it was put behind Jon's trowel," Marta added. "If you stole it, why would you want to get caught?" She leaned over to Steve and said, "There must be two different people."

"Jesus," Bob said, overhearing her. "You are a spy."

"Thanks for meeting us on a Saturday," Steven said laughing. "We're having dinner at Hacienda del Sol tonight. Would you and your wife be able to join us? We would enjoy seeing Anne again."

"I would love to. Let me call Anne and ask her—what time?"

"Does 6:00 p.m. work?" Susan asked. "Just call my cell when you know. Tell her Marta is very entertaining."

They left the museum and walked over to the Historical Society on Second Street to show Marta the maps with the Santa Catalina Mountains shown as the Santa Catrina Mountains. They stopped for a cup of coffee as they walked back to the parking lot.

"What do you think, Marta?" Steven asked as he put sugar and lemon into his iced tea—he always sugared his tea until it was on the brink of being too saturated to dissolve.

"I think Bob's right—they have a light fingered graduate student and a crappy system. But again, I don't see why you would risk getting caught like that. Steven, why didn't you tell Bob about the box?"

"I think we should wait until after we meet the Japanese," Steven said.

"Marta, Steven, it's almost 12:30 p.m. Anything you want to do this afternoon?" Susan asked.

"Lunch at El Torero," Steven said.

"Sit out and watch the birds while I read the book I brought with me. Oh, but it's already 12:30 p.m., and Steven needs to eat. If dinner's at 6:00 p.m., we might as well stay in town, right?"

"Probably should," he said already thinking about El Torero.

They drove the short distance down Stone to South Tucson then over to El Torero on 26th Street. Food there was served Sonoran style, with tortillas almost as thin as a crepe–they wrapped one around a sour cream and cheese filling and then poured their white sauce all over it. Susan had been eating there since she was eight, and of course, she took Marta there when they were undergrads. It became Steven's favorite Mexican restaurant as soon as she took him. Everyone knew them there; within minutes after they sat down, Steven had his iced tea, Susan her coffee and Marta her Pacifico. Then it was the cheese crisp with chilies, the sour cream enchiladas for Steven, queso soup for Susan, and two green corn tamales for Marta. Only rarely did they deviate.

"What book did you bring, that we aren't giving you time to read?" Steven asked.

"One of Jason Goodwin's books," she said. "Not with 'Yashim,' though. This one is *The Gunpowder Gardens*. It's about tea."

"I wish he would write another with 'Yashim,'" he said. "Have you eaten with us at Asitane in Istanbul?"

"Near the Chora Church, Marta," Susan said. "I don't think you've been there with us."

"I've been to the Chora Church with you–we saw the mosaics and the frescos. I don't remember a restaurant there, though."

Next time," Susan said.

"Anyway, Asitane uses old recipes from the Ottoman Empire of the 1830s," he said.

"Anytime you want to go, Steven," she said as they got up to leave. "To Asitane, that is. Oh, wait, I just got an email from Hershel. He's fretting about dinner next Friday. Hershel has a reservation at Per Se, but it's a fixed menu. He wants to know what we think. He says he started with a list of half a dozen restaurants, but can't decide."

"Tell him we just need a quiet place where we can hear each other talk," Steven said.

"Steven, you must have thoughts on this—he wants help."

"Well, we haven't been to Per Se—it's the French Laundry people, right? But I think a menu with options rather than a set meal would be better."

"The current owners of the French Laundry—not the original ones, I think," Susan answered. "Marta, do you remember when we stayed at the Boonville Hotel in Boonville?"

"I do," she said. "It's near Philo in the Anderson Valley. It must have been at least 15 years ago. They were the original owners of the French Laundry."

"Yes, I think so," Steven said. "We drank a magnum of Roederer's that night and I don't even drink. It must have been that drive through the redwoods—of course there were six of us drinking that magnum.

"Susan, is that Philo named after your Philo T. Farnsworth?" Marta asked.

"Ask Steven."

"Don't know, Marta," he said. "Anyway, let's just vote to go back to Daniel— the food is good and it's quiet. You know how I love seared foie gras—they do have it sometimes. Or, we could suggest Milon."

"Steven, be serious," Marta chided. "Poor Hershel is having a hard time. He has to impress his clients. You and Susan can go to Milon on May 2."

"What about something like Del Frisco's?" Susan asked. "They have steak and sea food, and the appetizer selection is usually pretty good. Del Frisco's has private rooms and it's a good location—Avenue of the Americas at about 48th or 49th Street."

"I would prefer 7:30 p.m., if possible," Steven added. "And we have no problem going back to Daniel."

"I'll email him," Marta said.

The cheese crisp came and they ate almost in silence—it was so good.

Halfway through her soup, Susan started chuckling to herself, then looked at Steven and Marta. "It would be pretty funny if Father somehow sent his missing materials to Shawmut as well."

"God, Susan, let's try Jon," Steven said. Jon didn't answer at either number Steven had for him. He left a message for Jon to call so he could fill him in on the meeting with Bob. Susan then sent Jon an email saying "Call us—we have lots of news."

As they finished eating, Susan got a call from Bob—he and Anne would join them at Hacienda del Sol.

"Can we stop at AJ's?" Susan asked. "I need to pick up a pound of Arbuckle's coffee."

As they pulled in to the AJ's parking lot, Marta asked, "Did you know that they first made Arbuckle's just after the Civil War? Arbuckle's was the first coffee company to ship roasted beans out West to the cowboys. The other suppliers were shipping out raw beans that customers had to roast themselves. Shipping pre-roasted beans was the key—the coffee was the same every time."

"Don't get her started, Marta," Steven admonished. "She knows all the damn roasters out here."

"Steven, I didn't know the Arbuckle's history, except that there's an old ad for it in Tombstone's Rose Tree Museum. Oh, and the new guys at Arbuckle's put a peppermint stick in the bag just like in the old days—supposedly, the cook gave a piece of peppermint to each cowboy who helped out at the chuck wagon."

They ended the afternoon by meeting a couple of the Graves' friends for oysters and a drink at Blue Fin. Before heading on to Hacienda del Sol, they agreed not to tell Bob about the box. Bob and Anne were waiting for them in the bar. As it turned out, Anne had recently retired from the US Foreign Service in the Middle East, so she and Marta were the evening's entertainment.

The flight back to Chicago left at noon Sunday, April 28. Susan and Steven parted ways with Marta at the airport in Chicago when they landed. The Graves were in a cab heading home by 6:15 p.m. It was a beautiful evening. The clouds were moving slowly to the East, obscuring the upper reaches of the highest buildings as they floated by. "Steven," she said. "Look at the skyline. My nephew says it's as if 'somebody took an eraser and wiped away part of the buildings.'"

Steven reached over and patted her hand—he was busy reading his emails. Susan picked up her phone and called Naniwa when they got to the Armitage exit on the Kennedy. As usual, the food was delivered 15 minutes after they got home.

CHAPTER 62

The last few days of April flew by. On May 1, Susan was in the office early again to finish a draft of the Jameson opinion. She went to the office kitchen to get her first cup of coffee and there was the damn Big A.

"Hello, Susan. I'm glad you're here—I need cream for my coffee. Do you know where the hell they keep it? It's not in the refrigerator."

"It's in that bin over there, by your left hand. It's those little containers that say 'Half and Half' on top. I don't know why it doesn't have to be refrigerated, but I don't think anyone has ever died from using it, so it must be okay." For once, she hoped she was wrong.

Big A put the cream in his coffee and walked out. Have a nice day, Susan whispered to herself. She walked back to her office, sat down with her coffee and picked up the *Financial Times*. She put the *Financial Times* down and emailed Jon again asking him to give Steven a call as they still hadn't heard from him. Then, as she started to pick the paper up again, she suddenly remembered that Jon had mentioned Shawmut College. She called Steven. She would wake him, but this was important. "Steven, remember when you said it would be funny if Father sent his materials to Shawmut?"

"Sort of," he said.

"I just remembered where I heard Shawmut College—Jon's son, Father Bartolome, did his undergraduate and some of his graduate work there. I think Jon said Father's friend, Clay, is at Shawmut. Clay is the guy who's helping at Jon's old site. Jon said Clay knew about the tenure issue even though he wasn't from Penn—meaning he may still be at Shawmut. Damn it, I even remember thinking 'Clay' was a good name for an archaeologist. What an idiot I am. When Bob said Shawmut, it just didn't register."

"What, why were you...," he was fully awake now. "Oh, the Folsom point is from Shawmut and Father and his friend went to Shawmut. Do you think that is where Father sent his stuff? We are getting old Susan—we shouldn't have missed this."

"Speak for yourself–he told me the name once. I think it was when we first met. I'm not certain that Clay is still at Shawmut, but the similarities...I was going to track Jon down to confirm that he's coming to New York after I got my second coffee and answered some emails," Susan said more to herself than to Steven.

"But if this Clay took it from Shawmut, why would he implicate Jon? And why on earth would he tell the police where to find it?"

"I don't know." She stopped for a minute, and then said, "Maybe Clay gave the Folsom piece to the tenure guy, not knowing he would put it at Jon's site and call the police...that would be a hoot. We need to find Jon and ask him about this–have you heard from him yet? Steven, we need to make sure before we start bad-mouthing anybody."

"It is possible that this is just a coincidence."

"You know that's not likely. Call Jon–the box may now be the least of his worries."

"Yes, dear," he said. "I hope he doesn't have a heart attack or something when I ask him. Call me later...no, wait, maybe that's why Marta said there might be two guys."

"When did she say that?" Susan asked.

"When we were with Bob; maybe you were answering emails," Steven said. "Marta said maybe there are two guys or something like that. I think she meant that a person who took something wouldn't want his theft discovered."

"So one guy steals it and gives it to somebody who hates Jon, but doesn't know it's stolen?" she asked.

"Jesus, Susan, it could be that Clay guy if he's still at Shawmut...find Marta."

Susan called Jane. "Can you find Marta for me? I need five minutes of her time. Oh, and I need a half hour with the Big A next Monday, May 6th. It's something new, not related to a project."

"You're finally going to tell him you're quitting?" Jane asked. "There's already a rumor going around that you are taking a three month sabbatical after Jameson closes."

"Yes, I'm going to tell him I'm done. Wilhelm told me about the rumor."

"He told me, too," Jane said. "He's been taking me to lunch; plying me for info, you know."

"Marta," was all Susan said. Her phone rang–it was Steven again.

"I just got off the phone with Bob," Steven said.

"And?" she asked.

"The Folsom piece definitely belongs to Shawmut, but we knew that. Bob spoke with that Shawmut curator he mentioned—she's in charge of the archives. She did an informal walk through of the area where the Folsom points were over the weekend. She found more of the tags without any information on them, so she locked down the archives and called the police."

"Holy shit, Steven, do they know if it was Clay?"

"Well, Bob says the police got a warrant to search some offices and found two more Folsom projectile points in a post doc's desk drawer. As before, they found blank tags in the boxes where the pieces were from. They expanded the warrant to search the post-doc's home in Cambridge. They found five more pieces there."

"Well, I suppose he could just be studying them," Susan said.

"It gets better, Susan. This post-doc has a cabin near Bar Harbor, Maine. The cabin also has pieces from Shawmut–lots of pieces. There were at least twenty Folsom points there, most with Shawmut accession numbers on them. There also were some nice baskets, including some with accession numbers from a small museum where the post-doc had worked last year. You can imagine how Bob is enjoying this excitement. Did you get Marta, yet?"

"No. Jane is looking for her—I think she's on her way to DC," Susan said. "Did Bob tell you the guy's name?"

"Clarence Duvall, he's the Shawmut post-doc who apparently is a Paleo-Indian kleptomaniac. They can't find this Clarence, though."

"Clarence…?" Susan asked. "Steven, isn't 'Clay' a nickname for 'Clarence?' Maybe we're right; Clay also is the guy who had the problem with Jon's female students."

"Poor Jon, it would be a bitch if it is Father Bartolome's friend."

"Now what do we do?" Susan asked.

"Should we call Bob about Father's missing materials?"

"Wait—Bob doesn't even know about the box yet," Susan answered. "We're also speculating that Father's stuff is missing from Shawmut. Actually, before we get carried away, I should see if this friend 'Clay' is really Clarence Duvall. If so, we need to warn Jon…I can ask him about Father and Shawmut, too. Crap, Marta's calling…I'll call you back."

"Marta, are you in DC?" Susan asked.

"I'm at the airport, waiting to board my flight. It's an hour late already. I have a dinner tonight…with the time change and the flight being so damn late, I'll be lucky to get there in time for dessert. I have meetings all day tomorrow and then Cy for dinner. I'm taking the train to New York from DC on Friday. So, I'm a little grumpy, dear."

"Sorry, do you have a minute?"

"We're not boarding yet; Jane says you have a question…."

"Yes, Bob called Steven today. Apparently, Shawmut has a Paleo-Indian klepto; lots of things are missing. It's a post-doc named Clarence Duvall."

"Okay, and?"

"And, when Steven mentioned the name 'Clarence,' I remembered that Jon's son and a guy named 'Clay' were helping Jon re-open his old site."

"Okay, and?"

"And, today I remembered that Father Bartolome went to Shawmut as an undergrad and did some graduate work there, too. 'Clay,' is a nickname for 'Clarence.' This 'Clay' that Jon and Father know is a post-doc archaeologist at Shawmut, I think. He's the guy who knows the no tenure guy. So, should I call Jon and ask him if Clay is Clarence Duvall?"

"Holy shit, Susan."

"What should we do? Jon will probably call shortly anyway to see how our meetings went. Actually, I'm surprised he hasn't called already. Steven has been buried in the documents and Big A has put me on his damn speed dial. At least Jameson is still on schedule. This Clarence has a small place in Cambridge near the college, and a place near Bar Harbor. Both places had stolen artifacts from Shawmut in them. Oh, and Clarence or 'Clay' has disappeared. The cops are looking for him."

"Slow down—So this Clay or Clarence guy is on the run?"

"Yes, well maybe. It may be that they just haven't located him yet. Oh, we're checking to see if Father sent his missing materials to Shawmut."

"Damn."

"Marta, are you still there?"

Yes, you should confirm that Clay is Clarence Duvall. I would email Jon, so he can't put you on the spot. You can ask him about Father's stuff too. We'll all be in New York Friday. Oh, my flight is boarding. I'll call you when I get to DC—give me three hours."

"Thanks, one last thing—you must be right that there somehow are two people. I can't see this Clay being stupid enough to leave a piece for the cops to find. But if Clay gave it to his friend who didn't get tenure, the 'no tenure' guy may not have known it was stolen."

"Yep. I'll call you when I land."

Susan emailed Jon and then called Steven.

"I'm on the phone with Bob. I'll call you back," Steven said and hung up.

Susan's phone rang. It was Jon. "Jesus, Jon—where have you been?" she asked.

"Susan, please don't tell me Clay is involved in this nonsense with the Folsom point," he said.

"So, Father's friend, Clay, is Clarence Duvall?"

"Yes, damn it, and he's a post-doc at Shawmut. He has a small site on the shore of Frenchman Bay in Maine. He works there off and on, but I think it's mostly wrapped up now."

"Is Bar Harbor near there?" Susan asked.

"Bar Harbor? Well, yes, it's on Frenchman Bay. Why?"

"Clay has a very nice cabin near Bar Harbor that is filled with things he stole from Shawmut's archives and a small museum. He stole the piece you found behind your trowel from Shawmut."

"But why would he do that to me?" he asked.

"Hold on Jon…Steven is calling me on another line; let me hook him in. Steven, Jon, are you both there?"

"I'm here," Steven said. "Hi, Jon."

"Hello, Steven…this is horrible. Susan just told me that Clay set me up."

"Calm down, Jon. We don't know the details yet. Why haven't you called us?" Steven asked.

"I'm sorry, I was in the hospital Saturday and Sunday, but it was nothing serious as it turned out. Then, on Monday, I had to meet with a committee to discuss the harassment complaint against Clay. He did nothing physical, thank god, but it's still inexcusable. He is a good archaeologist—usually very thorough, but I spent all day Monday and Tuesday explaining why I hadn't supervised him better. And of course, I also had to explain why he was there at all, since he isn't from Penn."

"I'm glad you're okay, Jon—we were getting worried. Anyway…." Susan started.

"Damn it," he interrupted. "Now this…In the back of my mind I was thinking that maybe Clay had left it there, but why would he call the police on me? God, I hope he's not trying to get even because of the complaint, there is no excuse for his behavior."

"Jon, if it's any consolation, we think that maybe Clay gave the spear point to the 'no tenure' guy and that he's the one that tried to get you arrested—not Clay," Steven said.

"Angus? Damn him. And Damn Clay for knowing him," he said and then he fell silent.

"Is it possible Clay gave this piece to this Angus as a gift?"

"Susan, you mean…oh, I see. Angus didn't know Clay stole it, so he called the Bangor police to get at me, not knowing it would land Clay in hot water. Where is the piece now? More importantly, what happens now? Damn morons. I hope they both go to jail."

"Bob is sending the piece back to Shawmut. I presume we will all be contacted for information. Hopefully, your son doesn't know about these thefts. Jon, um, did Father Bartolome by any chance send his missing pieces to Shawmut?"

"Oh, God," he moaned. "Yes, the chief archaeologist at the site near where he found them is at Shawmut—Father knows him from his graduate work there."

"I hate to ask, but is it possible that Clay took Father's stuff as well? Where's your son?"

"My son is coming to Philadelphia to stay with me tomorrow night—he'll watch my dog while I am in New York Friday night. He isn't going to like this at all. Susan, Steven, I don't think Clay would take anything that belonged to Father. I also don't think he would try to hurt me."

"Jon, find your son, and tell him what I just told you." She was about to say goodbye, but she hesitated, "um, do you think Clay might be dangerous?"

"He is very cocky, Susan, but I don't think he would be violent. What do I...oh, he's been found out because of the spear point. Damn it, Angus is probably wondering if I have been arrested yet. It's a good thing you sent it to Bob."

"Jon, we think you should tell the Bangor police to call Shawmut. I don't know what they will do in an instance like this, but it can't hurt. Um, you probably shouldn't name that Angus guy, yet, since it's only a hunch. I guess you should talk to Father as soon as possible—it might not be bad for him to stay with you tonight. Oh, and they can't find Clay."

"I'll talk to him, Susan."

"I do have some good news," Susan said. "The hasp may well be 1307, but it was attached to the box a couple of hundred years later, so we likely are dealing with the 1600s. The screws used to attach the hasp were the telltale sign." Jon was still silent. "Find your son and let the Bangor police know that they should call Shawmut," she said and hung up. Susan saw that Steven was still on the line. "It's just you and me dear," she said. "Any news from Bob?"

"We were right, Bob is enjoying the hell out of this drama we have drawn him into," Steven said. "He sent the Folsom point back to Shawmut."

"Remind me to pick up some Frango Mints for Jon—he loves chocolate. Damn, I forgot to confirm New York with him. I'll call him back to check in a while."

"I'll call Jon," Steven said. "You're too busy getting ready to leave for a couple of days."

"Thanks. I have a question—do you think any of us, Jon specifically, or Jon's site, are in danger? I told Jon he should call the police. I assume Bob gave Shawmut our names."

"Does that mean you haven't talked to Marta yet?"

"I caught her at the airport—her plane was late, so she was in a bad mood and short of time. She said she would call when she lands. I also told.... What is it Jane? Oh, for God's sake. Steven, I have to go, Big A is holding. Can you shoot Marta an email and ask her about danger—tell her to call us tonight."

The rest of the day flew by. She had worked through Big A's issue in less than an hour. Wilhelm had come by to tell her that he had given notice. His last day would be May 15. He wasn't going to a competitor, so they had no problem with him staying long enough to help close Jameson. Wilhelm already had a temporary apartment set up for him in DC near the Library of Congress. Susan was almost jealous—she loved the Library of Congress. In graduate school, she had spent almost a month there doing research, but that was eons ago.

Susan was already home when Marta called at 9:30 p.m.

"Sorry it's so late. I had a nice dinner, though—the 1826 House."

"It's late there for you. I don't remember, did we tell you that Father Bartolome sent his missing materials to Shawmut? We asked Bob to convey that message to Shawmut."

"Have they found Clay yet?" Marta asked.

"Marta, we don't know."

"Well, he's probably just a klepto," Marta said. "They usually aren't dangerous."

"We told Jon to call his son and the Bangor police," She added.

"Well, that should do it—I will see you Friday at about 2:00 p.m. Grand Central Oyster Bar still?"

"Yes, we can walk to the meeting with the Japanese from there. By the way, Wilhelm gave notice today."

"Good, you're next. See you Friday."

CHAPTER 63

Richard Prenbryer flew to Paris on Monday morning, April 29, as Josh, his American contact, had instructed. Richard hadn't known that Josh had a 'boss.' So, he was stunned when Josh told him he had to go to Paris to discuss the map issue with this boss, whom Josh called the Clockmaker. The meeting was set for 11.30 a.m. at Les Deux Magots. The Clockmaker was waiting for Richard when he got there at 11:25 a.m.

"Thank you for coming on short notice, Richard. I'm Seth Thomas; you can call me 'Clockmaker.' I picked this place because right now I am thinking you have a lot in common with its namesake."

"Good morning to you as well, Mr. Thomas," Richard said not bothering to disguise his irritation at the comment. The stupid Americans never could spell, so they always thought they were dining at two 'maggots.' It was a far cry from Chinese figurines. "Hemmingway drank here…he borrowed from Ecclesiastes which tells us the sun also rises…,"

"Cut the crap, Richard…or is it Dick?"

Richard ignored him and waived the waiter over. At least the French waiters were quicker that his countrymen. "I'll start with a Bloody Mary and two blue cheese olives. No, make it just a cup of tea, please." When the waiter left, Richard said, "I do love those olives, but for you, Seth, today I'll stick with tea."

"We need that damn map, Richard. If I can't deliver it in Doha by the end of the week, we have to refund the money that secured the purchase—and we won't get paid. I don't know about you, but I don't feel like refunding anything. I definitely want to get paid. It was such a simple transaction…it's hard to believe you screwed it up."

"The map was crap—it only worked because I enhanced it and put a signature and date on it to tie it to the diary."

"Well, not having the piece of crap isn't any damn better! And, you shouldn't have gone all over England trying to get the damn things back. It's too much exposure."

"Calm down, Seth. You bloody Americans swear too much. I wanted it back because I had doctored it. Now listen to me. We do have the diary—it is quite nicely done, if I do say so myself. However, that stupid Welshman died after he bought the map and that crappy Welsh piece. The pieces weren't in his assistant's flat, so the Welshman must have given them to a Japanese friend named Eisen Shakura. It was a pain in the ass to get his name—your stupid Parker woman thought it was Shikuru. Anyway, he lives in Tokyo."

"For God's sake, Richard. The map is in Tokyo?"

"It might be—probably the other stupid scrap too. This Eisen guy attended the Welshman's funeral."

"Why the hell would he take it?" Seth was glaring at Richard now, but trying to stay calm so he could think. "Did he know it was doctored?"

"I'll ask him when I find him," Richard retorted. "Look here, he was this Welshman's friend. I think the Welshman wanted the scrappy piece, not the map. And I think he wanted that because it was in Welsh. He just happened to see it. When he died, maybe this Shakura got the Professor's personal papers. His research papers went to the University so they may be there—that might be good as they may never look at them. The Jap must be a damn good friend to come all that way for a Welshman's funeral."

"Can we get it back?"

"At this point, it's not worth calling any more attention to it—you just said that it was too much already. I did send a check to the Welshman offering to repurchase the map, but it was returned from Cardiff at the time of his funeral. The Jap probably told the assistant, Margery Short, to return my check. Or, she gave it to him and he returned it—I don't know." Richard hated it when he got flustered—he took a breath to calm himself.

"Well, since we have nothing, can you afford to refund all of your initial payment?" Seth asked.

"You already have the diary—and it's a damn fine job, too. And yes, I could refund it, if I had to, but I don't."

"The diary is good," Seth said, "but the buyer is most anxious to get the damn map."

"He'll have a damn map. By the way, I do know that Seth Thomas isn't your real name. I mean, for God's sake, a nineteenth century American clockmaker? I haven't gotten to that yet. And what happened to that worthless Parker woman? Did she tell you anything at all?"

"No, but she won't be a problem, she's staying in your Moors for a while. Listen carefully, if you don't get me the map, you not only have to refund your down payment, but you'll also have to cover my fee and Josh's—that's $4.0 million. You lost the materials, you pay," he said coldly. "Do you have that, Richard?"

"Look, Seth or whoever you are," Richard started as he regained his composure. "When I did the diary, I removed a couple of its pages, and then re-stitched it. I realized I could put a map on a piece of the original parchment from the diary." Richard paused—it had just registered in his brain that the slime bucket Americans were getting more than ten times his fee.

"Richard," Seth started but Richard interrupted him.

"Wait a minute, why am I only getting £200,000?"

"We have something else in the package for the buyer, asshole," Seth responded sharply. "You shouldn't get anything for all of this trouble."

"Another forged document?"

"It's none of your damn business. £200,000 is a lot more than you deserve at this point. What did you remove from the diary? All of it belongs to me, you know."

"Look, Clockmaker, as I said, it isn't that hard to replace the map," Richard started. "There was a page in the diary with only very faint writing on it; I removed it because I couldn't read, but an expert might be able to—the rule is unless you know what it is, don't keep it. But I figured I could scrape it—make it look a little more worn, and put the map over it, the back was blank so I didn't need to worry about something contradictory there."

"How long?"

Richard ignored him. "I knew I could make an even better map than we had. So, I did that and it looks pretty damn good, if I do say so myself. The ink needs to be properly aged into the parchment. So, you can have the map next week. As for the Welsh piece, I should have thrown that out anyway."

Seth sat thinking for a few minutes. "We have another issue. Josh's intermediary has a couple of people who volunteer to serve as catalogers at different institutions—that's a source for materials. If they see something that might be useful, they just catalog a substitute. A lot of the colleges and little museums have very poor systems—and no space for storage anyway. It would be years before anyone ever found out that something was taken—and by then, of course, the volunteer would be long gone. We were looking for 12th to 14th century material for this buyer. This particular 'volunteer' was a graduate student in medieval studies, so when these parchment documents came in, she saw a 1296 date on the diary, so she figured they would work. They were in bad shape, as you know, so she assumed they wouldn't be looked at again for years, if ever."

"So, she pinched them and you had Josh send them on to me?"

"Yes, they were in bad shape, so nobody paid much attention to them when they came in to be cataloged. According to Josh, the researcher who found them was focused on early Native Americans—like 1,000 years earlier—so he had no interest in them. The cataloger simply replaced them with some junk and cataloged the junk. That was over a year ago; no one should have even looked at them again."

"I'm impressed," Richard said. "I always wondered how you came across the items I've fixed or sold for you."

"It's no big deal, pretty simple when you think about it," Seth said. "The cataloger stays for a while after the replacement is cataloged. That makes it look less suspicious if they find the substitution. Then the cataloger moves on. We have never had a problem."

"That's interesting, but my new map...," Richard started, but Seth cut him off.

"Richard, the document switch has been discovered," Seth said. "The archaeologist who sent them in decided that he wanted to see them again, but, of course, they weren't there. Worse yet, he's a Catholic priest and he remembered that our person was the cataloger. Let me correct that, he recognized her name when he was told she had done the cataloging."

"I thought you said your person was just a plant—how would this priest know her? And where the hell is Josh?"

"Josh is back in the States. The cataloger insists that the priest's name wasn't on the material when it came in and that she never would have taken the material if it had been. She knows him because they have common friends or some crap like that. Josh believes the cataloger; the material had a different archaeologist's name on it. It also was completely outside of the priest's research area. Apparently, he had someone else send it in for him."

"So, she took it? And she knew this Priest?" Richard asked. What a moron, he was thinking to himself.

"Did you not hear me, you idiot? I just told you that she had no idea that the material belonged to this damn priest; he's an American Indian specialist or something. She only found out it was the priest when he wanted to see 'his' material again; she recognized his name. Anyway, now the college wants to know if she remembers cataloging this stuff. She stayed for six months after she had substituted the material. Now, a year later, they have tracked her down to ask about the materials she cataloged."

"And, she remembers nothing right? Besides, even if she talked...."

"Even if she talked, Josh deals with her through an intermediary and I deal with Josh, so we are hard to find. I have done a dozen of these with Josh and you alone. This is the first time that someone has ever found the substitution. Even if someone did find it, they probably just figured it was a mix up and moved on—that is what our girl told the college, it must be a mix up."

"Fourteen," Richard said. "Now, I do need a drink."

"What?"

"You've done 14 with me and Josh, Seth. The stuff was crap, anyway. I need a drink." Richard couldn't figure out why this was such a big deal. Of course, it would have been better that it hadn't happened, but he just couldn't see someone spending much time on this stuff. It was in bad shape.

"Shut up! I've done at least 50 of these in the last 10 years, Richard. This time feels different—why would a priest who is an American Indian specialist want them now a year later? And before you ask, the intermediary also says he had no idea that they were taking the priest's stuff or why the fuck it matters."

"So, maybe he just wondered if anyone had figured out what it was," Richard said. "I mean, he is an American, so maybe he thought he should look at his pilgrim history or something. Once they are in Doha or wherever you sell them, no one will have a clue."

"Or, maybe, since you sold the damn things to somebody, they have resurfaced somehow back in the States and the priest has found out. Richard, it takes one hell of a lot to spook Josh, but he, his contact and the cataloger are spooked—particularly the cataloger. As a volunteer, she handles stuff that nobody much cares about. She saw parchments and knew we could give them a new life as something exciting. We find a buyer and everyone is happy."

"What did she actually catalog?" Richard asked. He had just realized how odd it was that shortly after the Welshman bought the two documents, somebody half a world away would be asking about these same worthless documents. But if the Japanese guy had them now, what could he have to do with an American archaeologist who happened to be a priest. "You don't think that somehow…no, this has to be purely coincidental," Richard said. Then it dawned on him that he should not have sent that stupid letter to the Welshman—it could be traced back to him. At least the Welshman was dead.

"Coincidental? I don't think so, Richard," Seth said. "The college contacted our cataloger, because the archaeologist says that what is cataloged isn't what he sent in—he's a priest, damn it, so they are inclined to believe him. Luckily, they all agree that the stuff that's missing wasn't too exciting and that it's probably a mix-up. Josh's intermediary says the cataloger is nervous. She is afraid to ask why the priest wants them, so we are left in the dark here. She isn't afraid to ask for more money for staying put, though. Josh may have to pay her a visit. Damn it, that always gets messy, Richard."

"The diary and the map are going to the Middle East—they won't surface again in our lifetime, Seth," Richard said. "How can anyone trace them to us?"

"Get me the new map, and do not fuck it up," Seth said. "I want it by Wednesday afternoon. I will still be here in Paris. You will get a message tomorrow as to when and where to meet me. You will have it done by then?"

"Wednesday?" he hesitated. "I said next week."

"No, I need it Wednesday; I have to be in Doha this Friday."

"Dear God, that gives me only tomorrow to finish it. So, late afternoon or early evening, Wednesday?"

"If the map is as good as the diary, we may be okay—then we just have to clean up your mess. You have until Wednesday afternoon," Seth said as he got up. His parting words were, "it better be damn good."

Richard sat for a few minutes to finish his tea. He waived the waiter over.

"Your bill has been paid, Monsieur."

Well, that was nice, he thought as he left for the airport. He really didn't like Seth. He promised himself this would be his last job with Seth, especially since Seth had 'dealt' with the Parker woman. Staying up in the Moors… permanently he suspected. He had never been there, but it looked pretty bleak from the pictures he had seen…maybe it would be better for the Parker woman if she actually were dead. He hoped the cataloger would be okay. Oh well, it was her mistake; never be too greedy.

CHAPTER 64

Eisen had just settled in at New York's Peninsula Hotel when his cell phone rang. It was Margery.

"Hi, Eisen. Where are you?"

"I'm in New York with Ohno-san. How are you? Did the police make any progress on the break in?"

"I'm fine," she said. "They caught the man who broke in to my flat. He told them where he had pawned my things, so I have everything back, except my iPad. Apparently, he sold it to someone."

"That was quick. Did the thief have any dealings with Richard Prenbryer?" he asked.

"They don't think so," she said. "The bloke insists he was just looking for flats where people were away. The problem is that my niece stayed here to watch my new cat. She had just taken it to the vet for its shots—she wasn't gone for more than two hours." Margery wondered what Eisen might say if he if knew she named her new cat 'Eisen.' "Richard Prenbryer was not in London on Monday when the break in happened. I guess they are watching him."

"I will let Ohno-san know," he said. "I didn't get a chance to ask before, how was the English Riviera?" Eisen didn't think there was any need to alert Ohno-san immediately, so he talked for a while with Margery. He made a note to pick up a copy of Agatha Christie's *4:50 from Paddington*.

CHAPTER 65

Richard spent Tuesday night analyzing what he had told the police when they asked him where he had been on Monday. Paris was a pretty good alibi, but he was upset that they hadn't said why they wanted to know. He was pretty sure that his man hadn't named him when the police caught him. That old hen, Margery, must have suggested he might be involved. How dare she! The woman had no basis to suspect him, even if it were true.

The flight back to Paris on Wednesday was uneventful. Now he was waiting for Seth at Harry's Bar, where his favorite drink, the Bloody Mary, was born sometime after 1911, when the bar was moved to Paris. He had one, with two blue cheese stuffed olives, in front of him now. Richard liked Harry's Bar. He sometimes would let himself pretend that if he looked over to another table, he would see one of its famous former patrons—Ernest Hemingway or Humphrey Bogart or maybe even George Gershwin at the piano composing *An American in Paris*. Well they were all dead, and he was still very much alive, so it would be a while before he would really see them. Richard sipped his Bloody Mary; he was ready for Seth, the Clockmaker.

As Richard's second Bloody Mary was delivered, Seth walked in and sat down—it was 5:30 p.m. "Let me see it," he said gruffly. "I see you have those damn blue cheese olives you like. They'll kill you some day," he laughed.

Richard handed the map to him and said, "Hello, to you too, Seth. Quite nice don't you think?" The map had indeed turned out nicely, he thought. He ate the two olives as he waited for a response. He did love them—he always ate them just before he took the first sip of his drink. He had just swallowed that first sip when Seth finally spoke.

"Actually, yes," Seth said as he put the small magnifying glass he had taken out to look at the inking back in his pocket. "This is much better than the one you let get away. It's a good thing too. That priest, Father Bartolome, is raising a stink. Apparently, he mentioned the stuff to a friend who now wants to see it. We will not see each other again. I am going to stay in the Middle East for a while."

"What if something comes up? Can I at least reach Josh?" Richard was feeling a little nervous all of a sudden. He took another sip of his drink.

"Not now. You did a very good job on the diary and on this map, Richard. Enjoy the rest of your stay in Paris, albeit short. I have a plane to catch now. This is good."

"Not even a Bloody Mary for the road?" Richard asked.

"No, I am meeting the buyer in Doha on Friday and I have a lot to do before my flight tomorrow," Seth said and then he was gone.

Richard sat for a moment trying to decide if he should order another drink. Seth was right, his stay would be short—he was going back to London tonight. He needed to quit this business, he thought. He had a fair amount set aside. He could live quite well. He looked at his watch and realized he had another half hour to kill.

As Seth left, he nodded almost imperceptibly at a man in a chauffer's cap standing inside the door of Harry's Bar. The man in the cap walked over to the bartender and ordered a Bloody Mary with two blue cheese stuffed olives. He paid cash, took the Bloody Mary from the bar and walked slowly over to where Richard was sitting. "Are you Richard Prenbryer, sir?" he asked.

Richard looked up; it was a man he didn't recognize. "Yes," he said.

"I understand you like your Bloody Marys with these blue cheese stuffed olives," he said setting the drink down. "This is from the Clockmaker."

Richard looked around. He expected to see Seth, but he couldn't find him anywhere in the bar. "Where is he?" Richard asked.

"He is in the car, sir. I am taking him to the airport. Your bill has been paid as it was last time."

"Well, cheers," Richard said as the man walked away. He sat for a few minutes congratulating himself for getting out of a tight situation. He then finished his first drink. There was no way the woman volunteer could tie him to anything—it was Seth's issue entirely. He picked up the drink the chauffer had brought and plucked out the olives. He ate them, one after another—he did love those blue cheese olives. He then took a big sip. It only took a minute for him to realize that something was wrong. God damn Clockmaker, he thought as he grasped his throat. A minute later, he keeled over onto the table—dead.

The 'chauffer' stood watching two buildings away as the police got to the bar—his hat was now stuffed into his pocket. He walked over to ask someone what happened.

"Someone died—they think maybe a heart attack," the person answered.

"That's too bad," the 'chauffer' said and he walked away. When he had walked for three minutes, he called the Clockmaker on his cell phone. "He loved his drink, sir," the 'chauffer' said and hung up.

CHAPTER 66

It was Thursday and Susan and Steven were heading to New York again. They would stay at the Pierre as usual. The plan was to discuss the agenda for tomorrow's 3:00 p.m. meeting over dinner, go to bed and start afresh on Friday, the 3rd. Jon and Marta would come by train into Penn station. They would meet the Graves at 2:00 p.m. in the Grand Central Oyster Bar. They would then walk to the meeting together from there. Jon would stay overnight at the Peninsula courtesy of the Japanese. Dinner Friday night would be 7:15 p.m. at Del Frisco's.

Thursday night, Susan and Steven ate at Milon. Susan would have been happy with just an order of cheese poori and the spicy chutney, but she splurged and also had the lamb curry vindaloo. Steven had the lobster curry shag. It was one of the cheapest meals they had eaten in a long time. The food was still excellent, but this time they were by far the oldest people there. Apparently, as you got older, you were supposed to dine somewhere like the Four Seasons where what you paid for an appetizer could buy two meals here. Steven told her to ignore it and enjoy the food, so she did.

On Friday, Susan and Steven met friends who lived across the Park for coffee before lunch. They had oysters and clams at Grand Central Oyster Bar while waiting for Marta and Jon. Marta got there at 1:50 p.m.

"Is Jon meeting us here?" Marta asked.

"He should be here any minute—he probably was on your train," Steven said.

"So, how was the big date with Cy last night?" Susan asked.

"He really is a nice guy, Susan, and he loves oysters," Marta said. She stopped as Jon had just arrived.

"Jon, this is our friend, Marta Krejci," Steven said as he stood up to greet him. "I know you've heard her name – she helped with the Bangor issue. Are you okay? You look white as a sheet…here, sit down."

"Hello, Marta. I'm sorry, I'm a little shaken. My son, Father Bartolome, called me just as we pulled into Penn Station," Jon said as he sat down. He looked from Marta to Susan and then to Steven.

"It's okay, Jon. I've known Marta since I was an undergrad. Sit down for a minute and catch your breath."

"I just spoke with my son. Before I left this morning, I asked him to follow up one more time with Shawmut about his lost material. I wanted to give you as current a report as possible. When he called, I was hoping it was because Shawmut had found his stuff. Instead, he…." Jon stopped to wipe his brow.

"He what?" Steven asked.

"It turns out that Clay did give the spear point to Angus Pierson, the guy who didn't get tenure. They are friends, as I mentioned, and stupid Clay gave it to him as a birthday present on April 12. I guess Clay never imagined that Angus would hide it at my site and call the Bangor police to implicate me. Clay, of course, didn't tell Angus it was stolen."

It was Marta who spoke first. "At least there's one mystery solved, Dr. Christiansen. Any chance this Angus buried the box?"

"No, none at all. Apparently, Angus was only at my site the day before I gave my talk in Bangor—he went up Sunday for the same Monday conference that I spoke at. But I have some very bad news from Father. The volunteer who made the cataloging error at Shawmut was killed Tuesday afternoon by a hit and run driver near her apartment."

CHAPTER 67

It was Friday, May 3, and Eisen was up early as usual when his phone rang. "Hi Margery, how are you?"

"Well, better than Richard Prenbryer, Eisen," she said.

"What's wrong with him? Did he get arrested?"

"Well, no," she said slowly trying to decide how to phrase it. "He's been murdered. It seems that our Mr. Prenbryer was in Paris to meet someone at Harry's Bar of all places. The police say his drink was poisoned."

"Poisoned? Do they know who did it?" he asked.

"Yes, he was poisoned and no, they don't know who did it. Anyway, the man he met in Paris is just a person of interest. Someone wearing a chauffer's cap bought a drink and took it over to Mr. Prenbryer, but on the way he added enough strychnine to the drink to kill an elephant. It certainly was enough to kill Mr. Prenbryer. They can't find either man. So now, they want me to tell them who Richard met."

"Why would they ask you?" Eisen asked. "Isn't it 'kill a horse'?"

"They're here because I had told them he probably was involved in the break in at my flat on Monday," Margery said. "They want to know what he would have been looking for. I told them again, I believe it was something Dr. Smith had bought from Mr. Prenbryer, but that I never saw."

"Well, it probably was," Eisen said thinking.

"Eisen, they know that you are the Japanese man Prenbryer was looking for. Apparently, they found my note pad with your name on it at Mr. Prenbryer's shop. I guess that means he was behind the break in. They asked if you might have what Prenbryer was looking for. Of, course I wouldn't know. At least Prenbryer won't be calling me anymore. Oh, I think you're right–it's 'kill a horse, but there was enough poison to kill an elephant if you believe the newspaper.'"

"Tell them they are free to contact me."

CHAPTER 68

Susan, Steven, Marta and Jon got to Hartley Marin a few minutes before 3:00 p.m. They were shown into a conference room where Hershel, Kat and Eisen were already waiting.

Marta began by asking Hershel to introduce everyone. "Hershel, you and Dr. Christiansen seem to be the common denominators here." She looked over at Jon and saw that he was still visibly shaken. None of them knew if the volunteer had been killed intentionally. Father Bartolome had promised to update Jon when he knew more.

"Of course, Madam Krejci," Hershel said. He had never met Marta in person until their dinner at Le Bernardin a couple of weeks ago. He had been so upset after that dinner and the one at Daniel, that he hadn't realized how attractive she was. He may be gay, he thought, but he certainly recognized the beauty of someone like Marta. She was a little old for a bauble though, he thought. Her shorter friend, Susan, was a little too bookish. For women in their 50s, though, they were both still pretty solid. Marta would make an impressive dinner companion, if he ever found himself needing to show up with a female. Perhaps he would ask her to pop up to New York as she had suggested. Hershel then proceeded to introduce everyone.

Kat saw that Dr. Christiansen looked rather pale. To put him at ease, he stepped over to him and said, "Good afternoon, Dr. Christiansen. I have been looking forward to meeting you. I understand you are an Early American Indian specialist."

"Yes, sir. I focus primarily on Archaic Native Americans."

"Yes, well I just heard something that might interest you. A restorer, Maria Pustka, has just discovered some dancing naked men wearing feathered headdresses in the background of an old fresco done in 1494 by Pinturicchio. It has been in the Vatican's Borgia Apartments all this time. That's just two years after Christopher Columbus discovered the New World. Experts are saying it may be the first European depiction of Native Americans."

"That's wonderful," Jon said, relaxing a bit. "We believe Columbus actually met the Taino when he landed on Hispaniola, which of course now comprises Haiti and the Dominican Republic. By the way, please call me Jon, sir."

Since Hershel had cleared the approach with everyone in advance, he said, "If everyone would please sit down, we will have Susan lead off by explaining why she wants to buy your property in the middle of nowhere, Mr. Ohno. Then perhaps you would be kind enough to explain why you bought the property in the first place. Susan?"

Susan made sure she had a full cup of coffee. She saw that Eisen was the slightly taller man who wore glasses—so, 'Eisen' equaled 'glasses.' She was so bad with names. She cleared her throat to begin, just as Kat put on his reading glasses. Damn it, she thought, they can both be 'sir.' She began by saying, "I made a short outline so that I could make sure that we covered everything I know—it likely will change as we get into the details, but I will start with this. I have a copy for each of you," she said as she passed them around.

Marta couldn't suppress a chuckle and, as everyone turned to her, she said, "For those of you who don't know Susan, she loves organization. I was just thinking to myself that I hadn't seen her scribbling out any notes, and here they are, with copies for all of us."

"Susan ignored Marta and began her explanation. To begin, we hadn't seen Jon in years when he showed up about two weeks ago with documents from a small box that he had found at a site in Maine. We did graduate work in biblical archaeology at Penn almost 30 years ago—Steven still is an amateur biblical scholar. Before leaving Penn, we took an elective seminar from Jon on paleo-Indians known as Clovis. I have a picture of a Clovis point here on my iPhone, which I will pass around."

"I can't believe there are two of you addicted to using that gadget to look things up," Kat whispered to Eisen in Japanese.

"Since we hadn't seen Jon for so long, we were very suspicious at first," Susan continued. "But then, as we began to read the documents, we got very interested. Nevertheless, we were still uncomfortable because Mr. Samovar told Jon where to dig. You are Mr. Samovar. Right, Eisen?"

"Yes, Madam," Eisen said with a slight bow.

"Well, we thought we would try to flush you out by offering to buy your property."

"It certainly worked," Kat said.

Susan then explained how Marta had asked Hershel to look at the Joham piece, which led to them all being in New York.

She ended by saying, "We had a friend confirm that the box was made from Mediterranean pine that likely was cut down sometime between 1500 and 1600. We had a lucky break with the hasp, which had a clear date of 1307 engraved on it. The hasp was attached to the box with a type of screw that wasn't made until sometime after 1500."

Steven added, "I haven't yet found any linguistic anomalies that would belie the ages of what the documents purport to be. We have ten pieces total. Four are in Greek, three are in Latin, including one which is only a fragment, one is Hebrew, but it is only a fragment, and two are in Aramaic, including one which also is only a fragment. I have been working with a friend in Israel on the Hebrew and Aramaic pieces. Susan, would you describe the two Latin documents?"

"Yes, of course. They weren't as well protected as the other documents. One is signed by Joham. The other piece is signed by an official of the Catholic Church in 1307. The Joham signature is legible, except that the year in the date line is bad. I thought it was 1607, until I saw the hasp. That made me think it could be 1307. Given that we now know that the hasp was likely attached after 1500, my bet is back on 1607. The piece signed by the Church official could well be 1300 or older. It acknowledges that 21 documents were entrusted to the three Guardians. As Steven said, our one box contained only ten pieces."

Very softly, Jon said "Susan, will you mention Father Bartolome and his find? You probably should mention Clay, too."

"Of course, Jon, I think that's the most important piece," Susan whispered back. "Let's hear their side first though." She turned to Kat and asked, "Sir, how did you know where the box was?"

Kat began by saying, "Our story begins with a friend of mine who died in late December of last year. His name was Dafydd Smith and he was a professor of Welsh history at Cardiff University. I met him over 50 years ago at Cambridge." He stopped for a minute, then said to Susan, "I believe your Thomas Jefferson was Welsh," he stopped again for a minute–it still bothered him to talk about Daf. He looked up and saw that Susan was staring at him. "A question, Mrs. Graves?" he asked.

"Sorry, but is it spelled 'd-a-f-y-d-d'?"

"Yes."

"Dafydd's name is in the Latin document we are calling the 'attestation.' It's the one signed by Joham Alvares Diaz Ovelho."

"Ah, then that must be where our paths began to entwine.... What did it say? Was it in Welsh?"

"No, it's Latin," Susan said. "Joham recited that he met 'Dafydd' in a sea town in Wales called Rhos. Dafydd apparently took over as Captain to get Joham and his crew, including three men called 'Guardians of the Word,' to Maine. Obviously, it didn't say Maine–Maine is where the box was found. We think perhaps they were heading for either St. Croix or Port Royal which are somewhat nearby, but got blown off course in a storm. Sorry, please continue."

"Last September, our friend, Daf, was in London with a friend who liked Jewish antiquities. Actually, Daf called them stupid old fake oil lamps, and Richard Prenbryer's shop apparently had some. Daf was bored and so, as he was poking around trying to amuse himself, he came upon a couple of pieces of parchment, one of which was in old Welsh. More importantly, it had his name, 'Dafydd,' in the text. Prenbryer wasn't in the shop at the time, but Daf managed to convince the young woman who was minding the shop to sell them to him." He stopped for a minute, thinking of Daf.

"So one piece said "Dafydd," Steven said. "What was the other piece?"

"It was a map, but I will get to that. Daf sent me both pieces when he died. He also sent all of his notes. Daf said he bought the two pieces only because the one was in Welsh and had his name on it. Apparently, when he began looking at the Welsh piece, he saw that was the log of a Welshman named Dafydd who took Joham and his crew to North America. As there are stories of the Welsh traveling to the Americas in the 1100s, he was of course, very interested. Eisen, would you take over, please?" Kat asked.

"Of course, Ohno-san," he said—old habits were hard to break he thought. "Dr. Smith left instructions for Ms. Short, his long-time assistant, to send the materials to Mr. Ohno. The packages contained the two parchments, one of which was the map, together with a fair amount of research that Dr. Smith had done on the pieces. Most importantly, one of Dr. Smith's former graduate students visited him in Cardiff when he was dying. She was able to enhance the 'map' for him. He stopped for a minute, then asked, "Ohno-san, shall I show them Eilat's enhancement?"

"Yes, do," Kat said. "I believe you will be quite impressed," he said to Hershel. "It is an enhancement of the map we brought you in February."

"This is a picture of the original as Smith-san found it," Eisen said. "And this is a copy of the enhancement Dr. Eilat Shiloh did for Smith-san. The notes were done by Smith-san. Dr. Gruber, of course, saw the original—with the Joham signature that likely was added."

"My God," Hershel said looking at the enhancement, "this is indeed a map. I have seen many, many enhancements, but this is amazing." He handed the enhancement to Marta who then passed it on to the others.

The enhancement was impressive, but Susan was still leery. The map reminded her of Pete's friends and their hand-drawn maps showing how to get to their old mines. The problem was, only they could decipher the maps. Eisen's map showed two dancing men and a moose in a petroglyph. Pete's friends would show similar things. Sometimes it would even show a mark on a rock that the miner had added—no moose though, not in Southern Arizona.

Marta asked, "Eisen, do you know how she did this enhancement?"

"What I can tell you is what we know from Dr. Smith, and from a brief call I had with Dr. Shiloh to ask why she had removed the signature from the map in her enhancement. She explained to me that you can 'see' substantially more 'data' by using advanced photographic techniques such as infrared lighting. She is at Cambridge now. She did this map to honor Smith-san. I'm sure we can ask her for more information. She too thought the signature was a later addition, Dr. Gruber."

"Thank you," Marta said.

"Are those lines intended to show elevations?" Susan asked.

"Yes, madam," Eisen answered. "Dr. Shiloh's enhancement shows the contour lines; she and Smith-san realized they indicated elevations."

"The Turin Papyrus map supposedly is the oldest map depicting topography," Steven said. "It was done around 1150 BCE in the reign of Ramses IV. Like this one, it shows topographical features and distances as well as some geological features. The Turin map showed elevations as pictures. This is more advanced, but it also over 2,000 years later."

"Steven, maps with contour lines were definitely in use by the early 1700s, so this map is plausible, especially since it got them to the box," Susan said. She then turned to Eisen and asked, "this map shows only a little piece of land–how on earth did you find the rock outcropping?"

"Dr. Smith used the Welsh piece and the map," Eisen began. "He used some latitudinal information, the number of sailing days and some indications of distance from the petroglyphs. He and Eilat enhanced the map and then guessed about where it should be. We engaged a map expert in Japan who used a combination of satellite pictures, old maps, Smith-san's information and other methods to find a likely area on the coast of Maine where the map would fit. We were lucky in two ways–one was that the spot in Maine was still undeveloped; the second was that the map showed a rock outcropping with the petroglyph of three dancing men and a moose, complete with antlers."

"I am very surprised it worked," Hershel said.

Eisen turned to Jon and asked, "Is Eilat's enhancement of the petroglyph correct? I sent an agent out to confirm that there was indeed a petroglyph with a moose, but you are our expert."

"There has been some erosion of the image since it was drawn on the map, so hers is better than what you see at the site now," Jon said shaking his head in wonder. "There's no mistaking it though—it is the same. The oldest petroglyphs done in the Machias Bay area—including those at our site, date to about 1,000 BCE," Jon said. "The newest are probably 1600 CE or so. Ours is in between."

"How do you date those, Doctor?" Eisen asked.

"With great difficulty," Jon said smiling. "You need at least a few grams of organic material for radiocarbon dating. So, you look for hearths and things like that which can be dated. Then, you hope that they can somehow be tied to the picture. There are some pretty sophisticated new ways that allow radiocarbon dating with substantially less material, but as you can imagine, contaminants can ruin the results. At this site, we kind of know who was there based on other evidence."

"Thank you, sir," Eisen said. "I must say, Ms. Graves, we shared your skepticism."

"Kat, you brought me the unenhanced map with the 'Joham' signature," Hershel said.

"Yes," Kat said. "My friend only said we might find a small box or boxes. The cartographers found the property, but we didn't want to buy land in the United States if we hadn't at least confirmed the age of the map parchment. It could still be a hoax on old parchment, but we didn't want it to be an obvious one—my dear friend, Daf, was not beyond doing something like that as a parting joke on me. When you gave me an age in the right range, we went forward with the search in memory of Daf. We are quite grateful, Hershel."

"Thank you," Hershel said looking a little embarrassed.

"I must add, Hershel, that I would have enjoyed being at dinner when our American friends showed you a piece with Joham's name on it," Kat added.

"You looked so shocked, Hershel," Marta said. "None of us could figure out what we had done wrong."

Everyone except Hershel was chuckling now—finally Marta reached over and patted Hershel's hand.

"You were very honorable that night," Marta said.

When Kat stopped laughing, he said, "The key for me was that they found the petroglyphs."

"Yes, sir," Eisen said slowly while he composed himself. "I had our cartographer arrange it–I suggested we wanted a picture for your 'friend,' sir. I told him that she had fond memories of sitting by it–and the picture would be a gift to her with the deed. Actually, I wanted to be sure that we were in the right place, since I had recommended the cartographer."

Before Kat could respond, Marta asked "Who is your 'friend,' Kat?"

Susan looked at Marta–was that jealousy she was detecting?

"A person we made up, Madam," Eisen answered to fend her off. "We were using a lawyer from Mr. Ohno's company. We made up a little story that Ohno-san was buying the property for her, so we could 'throw the dogs off the scent' as you might say."

"I didn't want my son to find out that we were on a treasure hunt to the middle of nowhere. So, we needed a 'cover,' Marta," he said winking at Eisen to show him that he also knew some of the American slang. "So, we made up an old lady friend who wanted to repurchase a property that had meaning to her family–we decided she had met me while I was at Cambridge. As far as my son is concerned, I don't know which was worse…a lady friend or a wild goose chase. Continue, Eisen, please."

"To make a long story short, Mr. Ohno bought the land. He funded Jon to see if there was anything near the petroglyphs. Smith-san warned us that the box would not be too big–we thought we had one chance in a million of just finding the petroglyphs. And here we are."

Do you have the box with you, Jon?" Kat asked. "We would, of course, like to see it, at some point."

Jon looked at Susan, so she answered. "As I mentioned, we took the box to the dendrochronology lab where tree ring dating was invented. No, it is more accurate to say where it became a science. Leonardo da Vinci knew that the rings showed age and their thickness was an indicator of climate. Nevertheless, as I mentioned, it was the screws that attached the hasp that were post-1500, so we at least didn't have a pre-Colombian issue. The box and its contents can still be older, of course, as can the hasp."

"And the box, Susan?" Steven prodded.

"Sorry, the box is in the vault at my Chicago office. I was nervous about lugging it around New York. I probably can get it here tomorrow—when we take a break I will see what I can do." She turned back to Jon and asked, "Shall we tell them about you son, now?"

"Yes," Jon said.

"Jon's son is a Catholic priest—a Franciscan. His chosen name is Father Bartolome. He's also an archaeologist who, like Jon, has done a fair amount of Native American work in New England—most of it in Maine. Father's focus is later than Jon's; it's an era known as 'transitional' which would be the American Indians of about 1000 BCE to 1000 CE. Is that right, Jon?"

"Yes. As a favor, Father and his friend, Clay, were helping reopen my old site in their spare time. Susan will tell you about Clay later; neither of them is on your site—just me and an intern."

"About a year ago, during a vacation, Father worked at a site in southern Maine. It's about 150 miles south of where Jon found the box," Susan said. "Jon, can you tell them about your talk with Father?"

"Well, just after I met with Susan and Steven in mid-April, I mentioned to Father that I had found some old parchment," Jon said. "He jokingly asked if I saw the name 'Joham' on it, remembering his find last year. He was shocked when I said yes. As I think Susan said, he had found two scraps of parchment and a little day journal about 150 miles south of us. He thinks that only the diary had 'Joham' on it. So, there are two pieces with Joham's name on them—the diary and the Latin piece from our site."

"And these pieces were found at separate sites a year apart?" Hershel asked.

"Yes, But more importantly, the box with the documents was under an undisturbed layer. Father found his three pieces under a cairn purely by accident."

""That seems...," Hershel started.

"Ridiculous," Steven finished for him. "It gets better. Jon, tell them the rest."

"Well, last year Father sent his 'Joham' materials off to Shawmut College in Boston to be cataloged—Shawmut was running the site. As the pieces were not Native American, he didn't remember them until I off-handedly mentioned that I had found the parchment. After I met with the Graves, Father asked if he could see the materials he sent in to Shawmut. It turns out that they are missing."

"Well, we have only two pieces from Daf," Kat said. "He's missing three, right?"

"Yes. At first, Shawmut didn't know if the originals were lost, stolen or simply mis-cataloged," Susan said. "It gets a little complicated—let me go back to this 'Clay' whom Jon mentioned. His full name is Clarence Duvall. It turns out that he is a kleptomaniac—he stole a lot of material from Shawmut College where he's a post-doc. In addition, Shawmut is where Father's materials that disappeared were sent. Neither Jon nor Father thinks Clay took Father's materials."

Steven stepped in. "Jon found a projectile point in a shed at his site a couple of weeks ago—it was not from his site. He was already upset about finding a crystal and the box, so this spear point was a bit much for him. Susan and I sent it to a museum friend who found an accession number on it—he traced the spear point back to Shawmut. Just as Shawmut was beginning to see that someone had been stealing spear points from their archives, Father showed up to ask for his materials and they were gone as well."

Kat leaned over to Eisen and said in Japanese, "poor man—a crystal, a box and now a spear."

Eisen stifled a chuckle. He wasn't prepared when Kat then said to Susan, "I can assure you Madam that we neither stole the pieces our Daf bought nor buried the box at Dr. Christiansen's site.

Susan smiled, and said, "I will take your word for it. I guess it is a little far for you to travel."

Steven then asked Hershel "Did you tattle on my wife, sir?"

"I merely reported that Susan thought the property owner might have been involved in a hoax," he chuckled.

Susan continued, "We also have another suspect, so you are off the hook for now, Mr. Ohno."

"Thank you madam," he smiled.

"Anyway, Father and Jon realized that they both had Joham material, but Father's stuff had disappeared. Father told a Portuguese archaeologist from another Shawmut site nearby about the missing pieces and the one in Portuguese. His brother is an antiques dealer in Lisbon who specializes in North American explorer artifacts. They asked the antiques dealer brother to check around. Surprisingly, he found that there had been a 'journey diary' of an early 14th century Portuguese visitor to North America on the market last fall. Supposedly, it had been sold to a collector in the Middle East, subject to some conservation work that was being done in London."

"The antiques dealer brother told Father to have Shawmut contact Interpol, right Jon?" Steven asked.

"Yes, Steven. The brother has a good reputation. His customers have included members of royalty as well as business tycoons," Jon said.

"As I mentioned, the person who cataloged Father's materials, offered to help look for them," Susan added. "Unfortunately, Father learned today that she was killed in front of her apartment by a hit and run driver in Boston this week. Steven, Marta, Jon have I missed anything yet?"

"No, Susan," Steven said. "Kat, we think that you and Eisen might have two of the pieces that Father found."

"Do you know how they got from Boston to London—is that why the volunteer was killed? She knew who took them?" Kat asked.

"We aren't sure how they got to London, but we do think that the volunteer took Father's pieces from Shawmut College," Marta said. "Your friend Daf then innocently bought two of the three documents."

Susan was about to continue, but stopped when she saw Eisen lean over to Kat. In Japanese, he said, "Do they know about Prenbryer?"

"Apparently not; you should tell them," Kat said in English.

"There is another death you should know about," Eisen said. "I believe you all know who Richard Prenbryer is."

"Is he the dealer who wanted your materials?" Jon asked Eisen.

"Yes, he is, or was I should say," Eisen said. "Our friend who has been harassed by Prenbryer, she was Smith-san's assistant for many years, called me this morning from London. Richard Prenbryer was poisoned while sitting in Harry's Bar in Paris on Wednesday."

"Do they have any suspects?" Marta asked.

"They showed Ms. Short pictures of three men. She thinks one of the pictures was of Mr. Prenbryer, based on a picture of him that was run in the local paper today. She never met him, except by phone. Otherwise, she didn't recognize any of them."

"So, Kat," Hershel started, "I know Prenbryer was after medieval documents, because he called me. How do you and Eisen know him?"

"We have never met him. He was pestering Daf; he wanted to repurchase the materials Daf bought in London. There were only two pieces–the one in Welsh and the map. There was no diary."

"Could we send a picture of the unenhanced map to Father?" Susan asked. She turned to Jon, "He might be able to identify it."

"I don't see why not," Kat said. "That would solve one mystery."

Susan saw that Marta was making notes. She said to Marta, "Mr. Ohno's materials might be two of the pieces that Father Bartolome found. Prenbryer may have been murdered because he lost them to Daf. That suggests that the hit and run victim also may have been murdered, doesn't it?"

"Yes, I think we should contact the FBI," Marta said loudly enough for everyone to hear. "More importantly, Eisen, your friend in London–is she safe?"

Eisen looked at Kat who nodded. "I don't know–Mr. Ohno had me tell her to notify Scotland Yard after Prenbryer called her at her new flat in London. She did that, but then someone broke in anyway while she was away. She mentioned Prenbryer to the police again after the break-in and reminded them that Prenbryer also had been poking around at Cardiff. As I mentioned, the police came back to question her again when Prenbryer died."

"Could your friend be involved, Eisen?" Marta asked.

"No, of course not, she's 67 years old. She retired when Smith-san died. The two pieces were sent to Ohno-san by Smith-san, not by her. Let me clarify, she sent him three sealed packages that Smith-san had given her; the pieces were in two of the packages. I believe she still doesn't know what she sent to Ohno-san—just that it was probably what Prenbryer wanted back."

"With everyone's permission, I would like to make that call—is that all right?" Marta asked.

"Marta, how do you call the FBI? I mean, who do you call?" Susan asked. She was being brave—Marta never talked about what she had done during her years at the NSA, before she joined the Senator's staff. Susan had always assumed Marta still had contacts and obligations. Well, at least Marta wasn't glaring at her.

"I used to work for our Government and then for one of our Senators," Marta said. "I have a duty to notify a contact if I come across something that might be of interest. I only inform the contact, since I no longer work for our Government. If it's of interest to the Feds, the contact finds out who we should talk with. If it isn't, the contact finds a local law enforcement person for me."

As Marta expected, no one objected. "Eisen, may I have your friend's name please?"

"Her name is Margery Short. She retired and moved from Cardiff to London when Smith-San died. The break in at Cardiff occurred February 1, during Dr. Smith's Memorial that we attended. Apparently, Mr. Prenbryer knew of me—we have speculated that my name might have been on a calendar that was stolen that day. Luckily, Ms. Short's penmanship is quite bad, by her own acknowledgement—so he was looking for a Mr. Shikuru until Ms. Short's flat was broken into. My name was on the notepad by her phone."

"Ms. Parker," Kat said to Eisen.

"Yes, sir. After the Memorial, I went back to the University with Ms. Short to pick up a box that Dr Smith had left for Ohno-san. That's when we discovered that Ms. Short's desk and Dr. Smith's office had been ransacked. Ms. Short called the police, but nothing was really missing except the calendar I mentioned. Also, a new woman, Kate Parker, who was hired by Cardiff to help Ms. Short close up Dr. Smith's office, disappeared that day. She never came back to work. The box was sealed when Dr. Smith gave it to Ms. Short. As it had been opened by the thief, we don't know whether anything was taken from it."

"May I ask what was left in it," Marta said.

"You may," Kat said. "Does that mean you will?"

Susan tried hard to stifle a laugh, but was unsuccessful as Marta shot her a glare that could kill. Eisen's mouth was open—he hadn't seen Ohno-san so relaxed in years. He must be enjoying this. Eisen certainly was, but he was nervous about Margery.

"Yes," Marta said smiling at Kat.

"A bunch of old pictures of Daf and me and sometimes our wives—we took a couple of road trips to your Western States in the late 1960s or early 1970s," Kat said. "We went to San Francisco, the Grand Canyon, Yellowstone, even Las Vegas. Hershel, you may recall that Yellowstone is where I first saw works by Thomas Moran. That was all I found in the box that Daf left for me. As Eisen said, we don't know if anything was taken."

"Thank you, Kat. Eisen, you may want to update Ms. Short," Marta said as she left the room to start making the necessary contacts. She gave Susan a little pat on the shoulder as she left. "Crap," Susan thought to herself—she knew it meant Marta would get even for that laugh.

As Eisen got up to call Margery, Steven said to Kat, "our Marta used to be sort of a spy. She's with Susan now at Peale, Curtis, but, as she said, she still has contacts." Turning to Hershel, he said, "I believe you met Marta in her prior occupation, right Hershel?"

"Yes, but I think I am supposed to say that I cannot answer that question," he laughed uneasily. "I worked mostly for some of her compatriots in Europe," he said. "By the way, Kat, the Graves told me that Thomas Moran is one of their favorite painters. Perhaps a dinner topic tonight...."

"All that travel in the West and you never made it to Tucson?" Susan asked.

"Ah, Tucson, Madam Graves," Kat said thinking back. "We stayed at a beautiful hacienda called the Arizona Inn there. But we were only passing through—our true quest was Tombstone, Arizona of television fame."

"The 'town too tough to die,'" Susan laughed. "Did you actually make it to Tombstone?"

"Yes, indeed," he answered. "I was surprised to learn that Enrico Caruso performed in Tombstone."

"He was at the Birdcage Theatre. I think it must have been in 1906, just after the great San Francisco earthquake hit. The legend is that after the earthquake, Caruso gave a concert in the street to calm the people of San Francisco. He then he got on a train going east, with a stop in Tombstone."

"A beautiful voice," Kat said. "I see we have much in common, but tell me, how do you know Tucson?"

"My husband and I have a home there—it's where I grew up. By the way, you may have noted the old signs that said 'check your guns at the door,' at every bar in Tombstone. In fact, I think Wyatt Earp banned guns in the city limits—except for him and his brothers. They weren't so dumb in those days."

"Our Americans do love their guns," Kat said to no one in particular. "One place in your West that I missed was the Devil's Tower. Have you been there?"

"But, of course," she smiled. "The Native Indians say the rock was clawed by a bear chasing seven Indian maidens who escaped into heaven. You can still see the maidens; they are the constellation that we call the Seven Sisters or the Pleiades, even though only six stars are clearly visible."

"Ah...," was all Kat could get out, wishing that Eisen had heard her comment. He recovered and asked, "Hershel says that you and Steven like the American Luminists like Thomas Moran."

"We do, especially him and Martin Heade," Susan said. "Gifford and Bierstadt aren't bad either."

As Eisen came back and sat down, Kat said, "Eisen and I know Gifford—as does Hershel, now. Eisen introduced him to Gifford at our February dinner in Zurich. Hershel the painter you mentioned was Winslow Homer, right?"

"Yes, indeed," Hershel replied.

"I think of Homer's paintings as being concerned more with action that light," Susan said. "A turn of the century artist, George Bellows, is often described as another 'action' painter, but I think that is tied to his famous painting of a boxing bout. He is more akin to Homer; an example might be *The Big Dory*." Bellows is not a favorite of mine, but he is seen as a bridge between Homer and later American artists like Edward Hopper."

"Hershel, you like modern art, do you know Susan's favorite, Morris Graves?" Steven asked. "He was a contemporary of painters like Arthur Dove and Georgia O'Keefe, mostly in the 1930s to late 1950s. Hmm, I guess that's too old for you—Clyfford Still perhaps?"

"Everyone knows Georgia O'Keefe," Hershel said bemused. "But Clyfford Still.... You know his work?"

"He spent his childhood in Spokane, Washington, where I lived with an aunt for several months," Susan said. "He is one of the few Abstract Expressionists that we really like. Actually, I think he set the stage for the rest of them."

"And you Steven?" Hershel asked.

"Susan and I enjoy many of the same favorites, although I might add Egon Shiele," Steven said. "Eisen, is Ms. Short okay?" he asked as Eisen returned.

"Yes, thank you…her sister is staying with her." He said as he sat down next to Kat again.

"We still have Marta and Jon missing, let's wait another minute for them to return, Steven said.

Kat asked Eisen to show him examples of pictures by Heade and Still. Steven went over to talk with Hershel about ways to authenticate parchment. Susan pulled up her favorite painting by Morris Graves to show Kat and Eisen.

"This is *Blind Bird* by Morris Graves," Susan said as she walked over and handed Eisen her iPhone. It's in the collection of the Museum of Modern Art here, but hasn't been on display for years. He was enamored with Zen Buddhism. It's obvious in some of his titles, like *Consciousness Achieving the Form of a Crane*."

"The painting and the title have a way of touching one's soul—they are things of beauty," Eisen said as he stood. "My first love is Japanese art of Ukiyo-e or the floating world—particularly in the Edo period. Our Japanese author, Asai Ryoi, described it, if I may paraphrase, as "[l]iving only for the moment, savoring the moon, the snow, the cherry blossoms and the maple leaves… letting oneself drift…like a gourd carried along with the river current."

"That's beautiful," Susan said. "One of Steven's favorites is perhaps your namesake, Keisai Eisen or Eisen Ikeda, who does the beautifully clothed women."

"Yes, they are called 'bijin-ga'—the beautiful women," Eisen said. "My father loved his work and thus, my common name is 'Eisen.'"

"I need to consider how your Mr. Ryoi applies to *Ghosts*, my favorite Yoshitoshi series, or *100 Years of the Moon*, which is Steven's favorite."

Eisen started to comment, but was interrupted by Hershel.

"We should get started again—we still have some things to cover," Hershel said. "Everyone sit down, please."

As Eisen sat again, he handed Kat his iPhone with a picture of Heade's *Cattleya Orchid and Three Brazilian Hummingbirds*.

Jon cleared his throat to get everyone's attention. "I have more information… shall I wait for Marta to return?"

"We'll fill her in, Jon," Steven said.

"I called my son, Father Bartolome, during our break to tell him we may have found two of his three missing items. I also alerted him that Susan had just sent him an email with a picture of the 'map' to see if he recognized it. He said again that he does not remember seeing the 'Joham' name on anything but the diary, but he isn't positive. I guess that is good support for your analysis, Hershel."

"He did at least see the name on the diary?" Kat asked.

"Yes, he did," Jon answered. "Actually it was João in one spot and Joham in another. The diary cover was wood with a parchment or leather like material laid over it. The name was inside the cover—the pages also were parchment, but in very bad shape. He reads Spanish—it was close to that, but not Spanish, so he thought, given Joham's name, that it might be Portuguese. Again, he does not think it was on the map. Do you think this London dealer, Prenbryer, added it?"

"It was added, but I can't say for sure that Prenbryer did it," Hershel said. "He does seem to be the primary suspect, though."

CHAPTER 69

"Eisen," Marta said as she walked back in, "I'm glad your friend notified Scotland Yard when Prenbryer called her. That got them more interested, so they followed him in Paris. I mentioned the possibility that Prenbryer had received the materials taken from Shawmut College. My former colleagues appreciated the Shawmut information, but I am not inside anymore, so that is all I know."

"What will they do now?" Hershel asked.

"I don't know. They seemed to know about the missing materials from Shawmut, but not the tie to the hit and run victim—or our kleptomaniac. I did suggest that the person who stole Father's material and the klepto were different people. In fact, we may have a klepto, a nut who didn't get tenure and yet a third person or persons who took Father's stuff."

Susan knew Marta had said all that she was going to say, so before anyone could get a question out, she cleared her voice and said, "Shall we continue?"

"Susan, Eisen and I would be very pleased if you could get the box here," Kat said.

"Um, it would be best for someone to hand-carry it here. Tomorrow would be the earliest...."

"Susan, shall I call Wilhelm?" Marta asked.

"It may seem silly, but I feel I have a duty to my old friend," Kat said.

"We understand, Mr. Ohno," Susan said. "Marta, tell him to have Jane get him a ticket. I will email Jane now to get the box from the vault."

"Thank you," Kat said.

"Well, don't thank us yet—I don't want to use an ordinary courier, it's too fragile. Marta is trying to get one of our associates to bring it."

"We understand," he said. "I will pay for your courier."

"Thank you, but it's not necessary," Susan answered as she sent the email to Jane. "As I mentioned, we apparently have a Portuguese man, our 'Joham,' who made his way to the coast of Maine on a ship that was captained by your 'Daf's' namesake." Susan pulled out pictures of the documents and, after fumbling for a second, set a picture of Joham's 'attestation' down in the middle of the table.

"This is from the box?" Kat asked.

"Yes, and although my Latin is a bit rusty, you can see here…," she paused. She then pointed to a word and said, "Here, Joham refers to himself. And here, he refers to three men; the Latin word is 'guardians.' They came with him. More importantly, the word referring to what Joham buried has the plural ending—it's 'armaria' not 'armarium.' Jon, that suggests that you have not found everything yet."

"Boxes…," Jon repeated.

"Yes, I think so."

"May we see?" Kat asked.

"Yes, of course. Marta, Gentlemen, look here," Susan said pointing again to the word, "doesn't that look like 'armaria' to you?"

"My God, it does, Susan."

"Smith-san was right," Eisen said.

"One more thing—I've been struggling with this clause here for a couple of days now," she said. "I didn't have a map of the site, so it was a bit difficult." She looked around the table and said, "I apologize in advance—I didn't get a chance to try this myself. Reading Latin is one thing, but figuring out geometry in Latin is almost impossible. Can we get a copy of your map enhancement made, Eisen?"

Ten minutes later, Eisen put a copy of Eilat's enhancement on the table in front of Susan.

She had been waiting for this moment—even Steven didn't know what she had found this morning. "Steven, you can help me," Susan said. "If you point to the words in the document as I explain this, then we can get through it quickly."

"Susan, are these directions to the other boxes?" he asked incredulously as he read where she pointed.

"Yes, I wish Joham had just drawn a damn picture. Anyway, the mark on the map for our box is at the intersection of the angle bisectors of an equilateral triangle. Two of the points of the triangle mark the sites of other two boxes. I was puzzled by this language," she said pointing to a spot on the document. "Steven, it's about the Moose's antlers, right?"

"Yes."

"I believe it says the third point is half way between the moose's antlers—straight down, I think."

"Jon, you'll have to confirm this, but as Steven just said, there should be another box at the base of the petroglyph; maybe you can use a plumb line or something. Is that possible?"

"I don't know why not; I would uncover a broader area so we don't miss it... that then could anchor your drawing."

"Excellent...so, let's assume that box is here. Next, you take a compass and do two 30 degree angles from the Moose box point using the bisector, and extend the lines out on each side—the two boxes are supposed to be on these lines. We use this to show the points on these two lines that are equidistant from the box and these are the spots where there should be two more boxes. Is that correct, Steven?"

"Yes, dear, as far as I can tell. Only Jon will know for sure."

"Good job, Mrs. Graves," Kat said as he looked over Jon's shoulder.

"Jon, have you dug near either spot?" Steven asked.

"No, but it would be easy enough. They're only about four feet in each direction from our box."

"But why was the map buried so far away?" Eisen asked.

"It seems to me that our 'Joham' or one of the three Guardians drew the map, because they were leaving the boxes behind," Steven said. "But...."

"May I interject?" Jon asked. Susan turned to look at him; he looked ill. Well no, maybe he was just tired.

"Of course, Jon," Steven answered.

"I've been thinking about that question a lot. Maybe Joham and his men landed on the coast near my site. It may have been a shipwreck. They could have been going to the French colony of Port Royal, which was across the Bay. Perhaps they had a hostile encounter with Indians or possibly the French, so they buried the boxes for safekeeping. I mention the French because they had a settlement on the northern border of Maine by June 1604. They then founded Port Royal in Nova Scotia in the first half of 1605, so they were definitely in the general area in 1607."

"Then what?" Kat asked.

"Well, Father found the map and other materials down by the Plymouth Company's Popham settlement. Popham was established in 1607, it was quite robust at first. In fact, Popham is credited with building the *Virginia*. It was the first ship built in the English colonies. There were some issues, though and the Popham settlers returned to England in October 1608."

"But why didn't they try for Port Royale again," Hershel asked.

"Perhaps they couldn't make their boats seaworthy again. Popham would have been the only place accessible by land. But it may have been abandoned before they got there. This is all speculation, but for some reason, they hid the map, the log and the diary near Popham, expecting to come back or send someone back for them. They erected a cairn over the spot where Father found them buried. As an aside, the Plymouth Company's next settlement, which wasn't until 1633, was at Machiasport, very close to where our box was found. As long as we are in the 1600s and not the 1300s, we have a lot to work with."

"Bravo Jon," Steven said.

As Susan started to ask when Popham was founded, she saw Marta look at her phone. "Anything new?" she asked.

"Maybe," she answered. She then turned to Jon and said, "Jon, I'm not sure if the police have talked to your son yet, but you might warn him that they will likely question him more thoroughly. Eisen, your friend probably has been visited again, too. Oh, and the box will be here tonight."

Eisen forgot that he had turned his phone off when they had come back from the break—he turned it on to see that he had a message from Margery. "Yes," he said. "If you will excuse me, I will return her call now—it is very late in London."

"Actually, why don't we break for a few minutes, so Eisen doesn't miss anything," Kat said.

"Good idea," Susan smiled—even she was feeling the need for a break.

CHAPTER 70

As everyone stood for the break, Susan looked over to see how Jon was doing. She immediately walked over to him. "Jon, are you okay? You look a little peaked."

"I'm just a little tired, Susan," Jon said. "We need to talk...I didn't want to say anything in front of your friend, Marta, until I talked with you. This is my son's cell phone number," he said handing her a piece of paper. "He knows Clay is the Shawmut klepto, but he also thinks Clay knows who killed the cataloger. Of course, I told him your friend, Marta might help him figure out what to do. Can you call him?"

"Yes, of course. Does he know where Clay is?"

"He thinks so. Father's trying to help Clay turn himself in to the police and maybe get treatment. That's why I mentioned Marta to him. I didn't mention her by name, but she certainly had good advice for me regarding that damn Angus."

Susan's phone rang showing the number that was on the piece of paper— it was Father Bartolome. "Hold on, this is your son," she said before answering.

"Ms. Graves, first, thank you for helping my father with the mess we have stepped into. I don't know how we could have handled this without you."

"Your father has brought us a very interesting project. Did you get the picture of the map I sent?"

"Yes, but I'm not sure it's mine. The name is right, but I only recall seeing it on the little diary."

"We are pretty sure the signature was added recently, Father."

"Ah, then it could well be the little scrap. At some point, I would need to see the original to be sure. I have sent you something that may help, but not with that piece. I'm not sure my dad told you, but I remembered that the chief archaeologist at the Cape Small site, always photographs artifacts that are found at his site. He and one of his post-docs are amateur photographers, so it's something he instituted several years ago."

"Well, it's certainly a good idea…hold on a second," she said as she waylaid someone to get Jon a glass of water. "Sorry, Jon doesn't look like he's been getting much sleep."

"He's a tough old guy. Anyway, I found my 'Joham' material just outside of the Cape Small site's perimeter, but I turned it in as that is accepted protocol. I was pretty sure the post-doc would photograph what I found, but I left the next day."

"Are you talking about photographs of your pieces, Father?" Susan asked as she felt her heart racing.

"Yes, Susan. I was in Boston two days ago anyway, so I rented a car and then drove to that site. I can't explain everything right now as I have a wayward friend with me—he's in the men's room right now. It was standard practice to photograph artifacts found at the site. I wasn't sure mine were photographed, though, because I found them outside the site perimeter. I did find pictures of the diary, but not the scraps. I, um, took the liberty of borrowing the pictures. I sent them to your New York office yesterday morning from Portland. Your secretary said you could pick them up there. I hope that's correct."

"Yes, my assistant emailed me a note; my office is holding your package for me. I'll pick it up tomorrow. But why did you send them to me? I'm anxious to see them, but…."

"I borrowed them because I stupidly mentioned them to a friend at the Verrazano site which is nearby. I think that friend is interested in the pictures because it may be an early Portuguese sailor's diary. I wanted you to see the pictures first, because you are helping my dad figure out what we have found."

"He would steal them from someone else's site?" Susan asked before she realized Father might have done the same thing.

"Borrow, Ms. Graves, just like I just did. And my wayward friend had the keys to the shed where they were kept, so I didn't have to break in."

"Is that Clay?"

There was silence on the other end for a minute and then Father said, "Yes, I was in Boston to find him. He had someone get him the keys, since he can't really go to Shawmut himself right now. I understand that you have a friend who might help arrange things for Clay. He wants to turn himself in, but he also thinks he knows who killed Bonnie, the cataloger at Shawmut. He's scared, Susan."

"The hit and run victim?"

"Yes...um, could you tell my dad two things?"

"Of course."

"Tell him that the guy is Darin Carvalho from Shawmut. Also, Clay knows about Joham now. I found him rummaging through your package before I sent it. Ah, here's my friend. I have to go now; we are just now leaving the Amtrak Station here in Philadelphia. Tell my dad his precious pooch will be fed with half an hour. May I call you this evening around 8:00 p.m.?"

"Yes, of course. I'll talk with my friend now."

"Thanks for your help," he said before he hung up.

Susan sat down next to Jon.

"I guess you know now that my son is involved in this mess."

"This Portuguese archaeologist guy—isn't he the one who heard about the diary being on the market?"

"It was his brother, but that doesn't mean he wouldn't kill to see pictures of it... sorry, poor choice of words."

"Where are Father and his friend, now?"

"Friend? Damn it, did he find Clay?"

"I think so—he said it was a 'wayward' friend."

"Well, he better be going back to my house. Father said he would watch my dog." Jon stopped and wiped his brow lightly with a kerchief from his pocket. "I didn't know about the pictures until last night. I was trying to find the right opportunity to tell you, but so much has happened."

"Jon, your son said he was on his way to feed your dog," Susan said. "I know Clay isn't the guy who might steal the pictures, but are you sure he wasn't involved in taking Father's stuff from Shawmut?"

"Father is having a very hard time with Clay being a kleptomaniac, as you call him. They've talked—that's how we confirmed that Clay gave damn Angus the spear as a present. Angus then hid the spear point behind my trowel and called the police. Father said Clay didn't take his material from Shawmut—the stuff was too 'ugly' as Father put it."

"But then who took Father's stuff?" Susan said almost to herself. "Who would…we seem to be back to the cataloger, but she is dead. I guess she still could have taken them…. Jon, Father implied that Clay knows who killed the hit and run victim. He asked me to talk with Marta."

"Can Marta do anything?"

"Maybe, but this Clay sounds pretty bad. I mean harassment, theft…oh, and Father caught him looking through the package that Father sent me before it was sealed. That means Clay now knows about Joham and the diary, Jon."

Jon sat for a minute, then said, "Susan, if this woman, Bonnie, really was murdered and Clay knows who killed her, then aren't he and Father in danger?"

"Father said Clay is scared. Um, he wouldn't be stupid enough to try to blackmail someone with that information, would he? I mean, he does have that nice cabin in Bar Harbor; he had to get the money for it somehow."

"I hope not, my son is with him."

"They need to go to the police, Jon."

"Father will make Clay go to the police. As for the pictures, Father borrowed them for you to see, while keeping them safe. He was going to send them to me, but then he realized that might be a bad idea. Your office is big, so nobody could get to them."

"But if it's in Portuguese...I can read Spanish, but not..."

"Father thinks only the first page, the dedication, is in Portuguese. He said the rest appears to be Latin. There are only about eight or nine pages, including the dedication and the page with just the name on it."

"Well, that will make it easier," Susan said with a sigh of relief. "Father said Clay had the keys to the shed where the pictures were...." She looked at Jon. He was sweating and he did not look well. "Jon, maybe you should go back to the hotel now and lie down before dinner?" Susan asked. "We are far from being finished, so I suspect we'll meet tomorrow as well. You could skip dinner. Rest tonight and then come tomorrow. Steven can call you after dinner to fill you in."

"I am a little tired. Maybe I will skip dinner."

"I need to talk to Marta about Clay," Susan added. "I also need to call my office here in New York to arrange to look at Father's package tomorrow morning. Oh, sorry, Father also said to tell you the guy is Darin Carvalho from Shawmut."

"The guy? What does that mean?"

"His exact words were 'Tell him the guy is Darin Carvalho from Shawmut and that Clay also knows about Joham now.' Does that mean this Carvalho was after the pictures or he was the guy who killed Bonnie?"

They saw Eisen coming back in again. "I don't know," Jon said.

"One last question, did Father know about the cataloger's death before he went for the pictures?"

"Um, she was killed Tuesday; he went to Maine on Wednesday, so yes, he must have, but he only told me today."

Renegades among the Tumbleweeds

"I'll talk to Marta now so I have information when Father calls again tonight. Go sit down. Eisen's here now." Susan patted Jon on the shoulder to try to reassure him. "I need to call Jane."

As Eisen sat down, everyone could see that he looked relieved.

"Susan, I think we are ready to start again," Steven said. She motioned to him that she would be just another minute. He saw that she relaxed as she hung up.

Susan walked over to Jon and whispered in his ear, "It's all set. I can get Father's package tomorrow morning after 9:00 a.m. I will call you as soon as I've seen the pictures." Jon reached up and squeezed her hand in thanks. As she sat down, she saw Steven and Marta staring at her. She turned to Eisen and said, "Sorry, Mr. Shakura, I had a little emergency to tend to."

"No problem," Eisen said, smiling to himself about using a good old American phrase. "There are two bobbies standing guard outside Ms. Short's flat. She has been questioned again." He looked at Ohno-san and said, "She asked me to apologize, sir. They have asked a fair number of questions about why we were in Cardiff." He looked embarrassed as he added, "And why I call her three times a week, sir."

When Kat had stopped chuckling, he said, "It's already 5:00 p.m., and you look like you could use a rest, Jon. Shall we just adjourn until dinner?"

"I think that's a good idea," Steven said. "Is that okay with you, Jon?"

"Yes, I think a nap would do me some good," he answered.

"Eisen, get us a meeting room at the Peninsula for tomorrow. Is 10:30 a.m. okay with everyone?"

"I may be a few minutes late tomorrow, but you can start without me," Susan said.

"We'll move the meeting to 11:00 a.m., Susan," Kat said. "Does that help?"

"Perfect."

"Dinner is at 7:15 p.m.," Hershel added. "Del Frisco's is at 1221 Avenue of the Americas between 48th and 49th."

Kat walked over to Steven and asked, "Would you mind showing us the pictures of what else was in the box? We can go to the Peninsula with Jon." He turned to Jon and said, "My car is downstairs—the four of us can go to the hotel together."

Steven looked at Susan to see what she thought. She nodded to him.

"Mrs. Graves, Hershel, Marta…," Kat said. "We would enjoy your company as well. Our limo should fit all of us. We do need to get you a nap, Jon."

"Thank you for the invitation, Kat," Susan smiled. She knew he had seen Steven's glance and her assent. "I have a few calls to make. Steven, do you need anything from the hotel?"

"No, I will see you at dinner."

As Jon got up to leave for the hotel, Susan walked over to him. "Get some rest, Jon."

She turned to Marta, who had walked up, and asked, "Coming with me?"

"Yes, if you're going back to the Pierre," she said. "I need a drink. Hershel's abandoning us—he's off to meet someone."

CHAPTER 71

Susan and Marta got a cab to the Pierre. Susan sat for a minute, then turned to Marta and asked, "Are we in any danger here?"

"Well two murders that may be linked is always bad for somebody," Marta said sounding irritated. "Otherwise, I don't know enough. What were you whispering about with Jon?"

"You sound a little cranky. Is everything okay?" Susan asked.

"I don't like being on the outside. They didn't have the Prenbryer link to the hit and run or Shawmut. This is a one way street, though. I tell them what I know and they thank me—I only get information if it helps me get something for them. It was my duty to call with the information; now they are just feeding me bits to see if I know anything else—or can find anything to help. At the end, I might get a pat on the head, but I am no better than an informant now, and unpaid at that."

"Marta, you chose to leave...."

"Oh crap, what did you whisper to Jon?"

"I was convincing him to take a nap. It may be selfish, but we are glad you're a civilian again. Steven got used to having you around in law school—we didn't get to see you much between law school and when you went to the Senator's office."

"Seriously?"

"Oh, for God's sake, do you remember when I gave that talk in Jamaica? It had to be in the late 80s or early 90s." You and Steven came down and the three of us drove for over an hour up into the hills to meet Lisa Salmon at her bird feeding station."

Marta was quiet for a minute, and then said, "Let's go back this fall—I guess she has probably died by now, though. She had to be in her 80s when we met her. God, Susan, she filled Steven's palm with seed and the little finches came and landed on each of his fingers to eat the seed."

"And the hummingbirds drank from the bottles we held...I still can't get mine to do that. They just 'buzz' me when they want their feeders filled." Susan had her iPhone out. "It's still there Marta—she did die in 2000 at the age of 96. It's called the Rocklands Bird Sanctuary now. Her nephew is the caretaker. We could stay in Ocho Rios for a couple of nights and drive up each day."

"You're trying to humor me."

"I'm not—on days like today, it would take far more energy than either of us has for humor. Besides, things always change and you move on...," she stopped. The worst changes were when people died, like Pete, her parents, Adele, her horse and now the Bird Lady. Susan hadn't thought of any of them in a very long time. Some things never stopped hurting—it was better to bottle them up and store them away.

Marta was silent for a minute, and then said, "You're right, I was ready to leave. What's the deal with Jon? God, this traffic is bad today!"

"He's not feeling well—you know he was in the hospital last weekend. Now I need to ask you a favor."

"That's an ominous start."

"There's a reporter at the *New York Tribune Herald*," Susan started slowly getting up her nerve. "Her name is Seattle," Susan stopped after letting 'Seattle' out. She had seen Marta's look on hearing the name, so she hesitated, trying to decide how not to irritate her again.

"Who the hell would name a kid Seattle?"

"Her Dad—he's my client and he is making it easy for me to retire. She's young...actually I think she's probably about 30."

"Big deal," Marta snapped.

"Damn it, I'm asking for this, but I have something for you as well, so stop being a bitch. Look, it's still hard for a woman to get an edge," Susan started again. "You and I had no one to help—you know how tough it was. We were just too stubborn to let them ignore us."

"Assholes!" Marta added.

"You just gave your old guys a lead that they might not have found on their own."

"Yeah, we did," she laughed. "What is it you want?"

"I want to give her a lead," Susan said bravely.

Marta was quiet for a couple of minutes. She was about to say something, but when she looked up all she could say was, "Crap, here's the Pierre—let's have a drink at the bar. We have a little over an hour until dinner."

Susan stayed back to pay for the cab as Marta walked in ahead to get a table at the 2 E Bar. When Susan got inside and sat down, she asked, "Damn it Marta, are we being followed?"

"What are you talking about?"

"A stupid black BMW pulled in behind us—I saw it when I was getting out of the cab. Is that what they drive since they stopped making Lincoln town cars? I didn't think much of it, except there were two guys in the front seat. They turned their lights off, but just sat there. Anyway, I waved to them."

"You did what? Are they still out there?"

"No, that's the pisser—they started back up, turned their lights on and drove off after I waved."

"Oh, for God's sake, Susan—it could be anybody," Marta said. "And they don't all drive black cars, either." She went back to moping, then decided to add, "And don't wave to people you don't know!"

"They waved back," she said defensively. "They should drive American-made cars and besides, it might be good to have friendly eyes watching us. You did tell your guys that Clay is Clarence Duvall, right?" Susan was sorry she mentioned 'Clay' the minute it escaped her lips. Marta's glare said everything—she had told 'her guys' about Clay and she was pissed as hell that Susan felt it necessary to ask. "You could have told me," Susan said. "You know I jabber when I'm nervous. Watch the time, so we're not late for dinner. It's 5:40 p.m. now. Dinner is at 7:15, so we should leave by five of."

Within five minutes, Marta had a Cuban Manhattan in hand. It was nothing more than a Perfect Manhattan where rum was substituted for the whiskey.

Susan had opted for her favorite, a Bloody Mary with Gray Goose. She'd have to watch the wine tonight. As Marta was still moping, Susan decided to give Marta a tidbit. "Did you know that on opening night here in 1930, Auguste Escoffier was the guest Chef here? He was over 80 years old at the time!" She saw Marta smile a little.

"Okay, what 'lead' do you want to give this Tacoma kid?" Marta asked. "Does she have any brains?"

"Seattle is smart. I'm thinking about telling her that the hit and run in Boston may be pre-meditated. Oh, and that it may be related to a poisoning in Paris and a theft at Shawmut College. I mean, we have all pretty much concluded that on our own—we wouldn't be divulging any secrets, right? And besides, I can demand that she share anything she learns with us."

"They didn't really say to put a lid on it. You're right, there are too many of us who know most of the pieces," Marta said.

Susan could see that Marta was warming to the idea. Of course, she was now on her second Manhattan.

"She can't name the sources," Marta said. "And we want to know anything she comes up with. She feeds us info and we will reciprocate. And, damn it, are you sure they waved back?"

"Yes, I'm sure," she said. "Now before I call Seattle, Father Bartolome needs your help with something."

Marta put down her drink before taking a sip. "Does he know where Clay is?"

"Damn it, yes. And Father says Clay knows who killed Bonnie, the hit and run victim. Father will bring Clay in, but he wants someone who can help him do that."

"So that's what all that damn whispering was about. Where is Clay?"

"Can you help arrange this?"

"Susan, it's illegal to withhold…"

"Marta," she started, but Marta put up her hand.

"If I call with information on a fugitive, I should get some attention. I can't promise though, Clay won't pull a gun or something, will he?"

"He's with Father, so that won't happen."

"Where?"

"Damn it, I trust you, but I hate having no control…. Oh crap, when I talked to Father, he and Clay were on their way to Jon's house in Philadelphia. Father is taking care of Jon's dog overnight. Um, Father said something to me that Jon and I didn't understand…."

"Well?"

"Marta, Father says Clay is scared; he thinks Clay knows who killed Bonnie. Father also asked me to tell his dad that Darin Carvalho from Shawmut was the guy, but he hung up then because Clay came back. Jon and I don't know what guy, I mean, maybe this Darin is the guy who killed that Bonnie."

"And Bonnie is the hit and run victim? Do you know her last name?"

"No."

"It's 5:55 p.m. You call Seattle and I'll see what I can do."

"Wait a minute…Jon told Father to ask for your help," Susan said. "There is another issue, Marta."

"Let's deal with this one first," Marta said. "Can you reach Father Bartolome?"

"I have his cell number and he's going to call me back tonight around 8:00 p.m."

"Good, call Tacoma."

Susan got Seattle at her desk, she was still at work. She then told her what they knew and answered a few questions. She had hesitated, but then asked her to find out who Darin Carvalho might be.

"Susan, thank you for this," Seattle said. "It will take me a couple of hours to pull down all of the information I need–how can I get in touch with you?"

"I will be at a dinner tonight, so just text me," Susan said. "We are staying at the Pierre through tomorrow night. I have to go to my office here in New York early tomorrow, so should we plan to meet for breakfast?"

"That would be fine," Seattle said.

"I'll see if my colleague, Marta Krejci, will join us, so I don't make any mistakes. Two things–first, please don't name us until we assent. Second, if you tell us what you learn, we will do the same."

Susan hung up and looked at Marta who was still on the phone; it was 6:05 p.m. As soon as Marta hung up, Susan decided to push her a little. "Did you mention that Father Bartolome and Clay could be in danger?"

Marta glared at her, and said, "of course I did. He should be scared if he knows who killed the hit and run victim. You, I and Steven are perhaps the only people of this group who are below the radar unless Hershel mentioned us to someone other than Eisen and Kat. Oh, but now Father knows your name. I guess we think he's one of the good guys, though."

"God, I hope so. By the way, you know that the Lisbon antiques dealer brother suggested they have Shawmut call Interpol, right?"

"My guys told me."

"Does that mean Shawmut did?"

"They must have."

"I hope Jon is okay, he did not look too well. What happens now?"

"Nothing, they may call me as a courtesy or if they think I can get them more information. We'll probably get more information from Seattle than them. Why do you have to go to the office tomorrow?"

"I have to look at a document for somebody." Susan figured it wasn't necessary to mention the pictures now. She would honor Father's request and look at them first.

"Steven will kill you if you volunteered to help on another deal. Anyway, my guess is that this is a forgery ring that has been active for some time. That Prenbryer may be only one of the forgers. Most of the stuff probably is going to the Middle East–the Emirates I would guess. So Interpol is looking at Prenbryer's death and now the FBI will look into this Bonnie."

"And Clay?"

"I believe they will pick up Father and Clay within a couple of hours. With something like this, they may watch things for a while, first."

"They won't bust down the door or something will they?"

"They'll probably surround the house then knock on the door and ask for Father." She saw Susan reach for her phone. "You can't call Father."

"Damn it, this isn't quite…well, I guess it has to be done this way. What time is it now?"

"For God's sake, it's 6:20 p.m., Susan."

"Sorry. Marta, ask them to call Father first, please."

"I don't know if it will help." Marta softened and said, "I forgot to mention that my guys were surprised that we were sitting with Mr. Ohno and that he had us calling him 'Kat.' He's a very reclusive billionaire–he's rarely seen anymore. He was pretty well known as an art collector in the 80s and 90s. He collected renaissance art; that's how Hershel met him. Kat went to Cambridge for graduate school in the early 1960s. He was called home when his father died and proceeded to build the family's company into one of the largest in Japan."

"And Eisen?"

"He's been Kat's assistant since the beginning, I think. Kat's son put him and Eisen out to pasture about five years ago when Kat turned 70. They went, but not happily. And now, here they are in the US."

"So Kat must have been born in about 1938, just a baby in WWII, right?" Susan asked.

"Yes, Eisen might be a couple of years older—he doesn't look it though."

They sat in silence for a while as they finished their drinks. When Susan's was almost gone, she looked at her watch. Marta, it's 6:55 p.m., we need to go. We'll be late for dinner." As they got into the cab, Susan asked, "If these are just forgers, why are they bumping people off?"

"This sounds like a pretty big deal. Whenever millions are involved, they will do whatever is necessary to tie up loose ends," Marta said. They both looked for the black car, but it wasn't there. "Is Jon coming to dinner?"

"I doubt it—he looked pretty pale. Hopefully, some sleep will help."

CHAPTER 72

Susan and Marta were the first to arrive at Del Frisco's. They were right on time at 7:15 p.m. Certain little things like that made Susan happy–not happy, but comfortable that she wasn't upsetting world order.

"I'm Ms. Graves; we are meeting Mr. Ohno and Dr. Gruber for dinner."

"Ah, yes, Madam. I have a message that you are to call your husband. Your host has postponed dinner until 7:45 p.m. We have your party in a private room. I can take you there if you would like."

"Yes, that would be fine," Susan said. She called Steven's cell when they got to the room.

"Hi Sweetie," Steven said. "Sorry I didn't call earlier, but we will be on our way over in a few minutes. We'll have a companion with us, he's a Fed."

"A Fed?" Susan asked beckoning Marta over to her. "What going on?"

"Well, first, Jon had a heart attack just after he got to his room— they took him to the hospital about an hour ago. Someone from the hospital just called to let us know that he is stable now, but they are admitting him."

"So, he's okay?" she asked. "Just a minute, Hershel just walked in." Susan paused to say hello to Hershel and whispered to him and Marta that Jon had a heart attack. "I'm back, Jon's okay?"

"Yes, as I said, he's stable," Steven said. "He called the hotel operator for a doctor just after he got to his room–the hotel called 911. He's been taken to Presbyterian, which I guess is the nearest hospital. Jon had an EMT call my cell to tell me he was going to the hospital. I saw Jon for a few minutes before they put him and his gurney in the ambulance. He gave me Father's cell phone number and asked me to be sure his son knew where he was. Anyway, I cornered a paramedic. She said Jon had them call Father Bartolome while they were still in his room."

"Well, that's good," Susan said. "Should we go to the hospital?"

"Um, no, not tonight–the paramedic said Jon likely would be encouraged to sleep. I also called Father about 25 minutes ago–he seems to know who we are."

"I spoke with him this afternoon, Steven. Jon told him about us and Marta."

"You talked to Father today?" Steven exclaimed.

"I didn't get a chance to tell you. I spoke with him for just a minute–when Jon was looking so ill. Where is Father now?"

"He was getting ready to board the train in Philadelphia when I spoke with him. We can call him tonight to see how Jon is. Father will go right to the hospital when he gets here–I think he expects to be there by 8:30 p.m. Susan," he paused for a minute, and then continued in a whisper, "Tell Marta that the FBI called Father Bartolome to talk about Clay and the hit and run in Boston, shortly after his dad called him. He asked that they keep an eye on Jon. He thinks Jon might be in danger."

"Crap," Susan said. "But, why are they talking to you?"

"They arrived when Jon was being put into the ambulance, so I introduced myself to one of them. He wasn't interested in me at first, but then someone came over and whispered something to him. Now he's coming with us to talk to you and Marta."

"Let me tell Marta the rest."

"Susan, we are on our way over…hold on." Susan heard Steven talking with someone in the background. She couldn't wait, so she whispered to Marta, "The FBI guys talked with Father and they have someone watching Jon."

"Damn, ask them if they are watching Father on the train," Marta said.

"Steven," Susan started.

"I heard Marta, just a minute…," Steven came back, "Yes, they are. Also, an FBI guy named Douglas is coming with us to ask you a couple of questions, so we can still have dinner. Anyway, Kat, Eisen and I will leave in a few minutes, so we'll be there soon. Bye."

"Are they on their way?" Marta asked.

"I guess so," Susan said. "Jon had a heart attack when he went back to his hotel. He's been taken to a nearby hospital. Father Bartolome is on his way up to New York now. I think it's about an hour and half by train to Penn Station, but he's going right to the hospital when he gets in. The Feds called Father about the hit and run victim and Clay, so he told them to watch Jon. Now, they're watching Father, too and they want to talk with us."

"How is Jon?" Hershel asked.

"Steven thinks he's stable, but they're admitting him," Susan answered slowly. "I'm glad he went back to the hotel when he did—you saw how he looked. By the way, Marta—a Fed named Douglas is coming to ask us a few questions—do you know him?"

"They're all called Douglas," Marta said.

"Great."

"I wonder if Kat and Eisen ever thought life would get so interesting when they decided to take up their friend's quest," Marta said, changing the subject. "Hershel, can you get them to talk more tonight?" Marta asked, bringing him into the conversation.

"Why?" Susan asked, hoping that Marta wasn't just on a mission to get more information for her former colleagues.

"Look, from what I was told, Kat and Eisen are pretty much alone in the world. They are old enough that most of their friends are probably dead. Kat is rich enough that he can't just go down to the local Sake bar for a drink. Nevertheless, he decided that he and Eisen would try to fulfill an old friend's whim—on their own."

"Marta, you are human, after all," Hershel chuckled.

"God, I hope not!" Marta objected.

"We had a delightful time at dinner in Zurich. And their English is so good that my accent doesn't interfere with our conversations. It is difficult sometimes when English is the common language and it is spoken with different foreign accents."

"I have not heard Eisen once say 'Kat,' but he seems to like his boss. And he really likes that Ms. Short. He does seem to have a sense of humor, too," Marta laughed.

Susan had waited long enough. "Marta, how are you getting all of your information?"

"My asshole contact...." Marta caught herself, and started over. "She read it to me over the phone. She wanted to know if anything seemed amiss with what they had or if I could add to it."

"Did your asshole contact say who this Douglas is?" Susan asked again to irritate her since it sounded like Mata was told to get more information on Kat and Eisen.

"I told you, everyone is a Douglas," Marta grumbled. "Hershel, I'm sorry this is such a mess."

"Well, I got into this as much because of Kat as because of you. And it's rather interesting how this is unfolding. But, is there any danger here, Marta?"

"I don't think so...maybe cautious, though."

Susan sat thinking for a minute then asked Marta, "But should we be *'Dark Street in iffy part of town'* cautious or *'he has a gun'* cautious?"

"I don't know—more people may be aware of us now because of Father Bartolome and Clay—I just don't know who's out there. I'm a civilian like you. We inform—not vice versa."

"Well, I assume this Douglas will at least tell us if the threat is *'he has a gun pointed at you.'*" Susan saw the pained look on Marta's face. "Never mind," she said shrugging her shoulders just as Marta's phone rang.

"Excuse me for a minute–I should take this call," Marta said.

"Shall we continue with art, tonight, Hershel?" Susan asked.

Hershel had been enjoying the interchange between the two women. Susan was at least two inches shorter than Marta, but he would bet she could give Marta a good fight. Looked like she worked out–maybe carrying all those law books around, he mused.

"Hershel, are you thinking about your Heinrich?" Marta asked as she hung up. "Susan asked you a question."

"Sorry, I was trying to decide which of you would win, if you really got at it."

"We've always been smart enough to stop before we found out," Marta said.

"As for a topic, Susan, I saw Eisen showing Kat a Clyfford Still and one of Morris Graves works earlier," Hershel said. "If you watch Eisen, you will see that he is always feeding information like that to Kat. I wish I had someone doing that for me. They do like your American Luminists. What do you think, Marta?"

"Well, you and Susan are right. We should probably all agree on some safety matters with Douglas, first. We aren't close to this matter, but Kat and Eisen do have the stolen goods in their hands."

"Stolen?" Hershel objected. "Kat's friend bought them from Prenbryer, he didn't steal them. Besides, I'm not quite convinced that Kat's friend bought those two pieces that are missing."

"Sorry, that was a poor choice of words," Marta said. "Prenbryer apparently got the stolen goods from someone here in the US."

"Father wasn't sure about the map when I sent a picture to him earlier...he was confused about the signature." Susan added.

"Before dinner, we should get briefed on whether we should be taking any precautions. I wish I could tell you what's going on, but I don't know. My contact is simply pumping me for information."

"When this Douglas gets here, he needs to tell us whether we should be doing anything," Susan said. "And he will need to do it quickly as Steven will be starving! Father Bartolome certainly got quick action. And remember, Clay may know who killed the hit and run victim."

"We will have Douglas brief us when he gets here," Marta said.

"Also, the box and its contents were on Kat's property—he owns them unless the stupid Templar stole them from somebody 500 years ago," Susan said. "Hmm, I just got a text from Seattle." She looked up to see that Marta was texting as well.

"What?" Marta said looking up.

"Who's your recipient?" Susan asked.

"I'm asking that Douglas be told we want a damn briefing," Marta said.

"By text? Can't anyone with half an f…ing brain read that?"

"Your NSA certainly can," Hershel laughed.

Susan saw that Hershel was staring at her and Marta with an amused look again. "Sorry, Hershel," she said. "Marta and I have known each other since we were undergrads—please excuse our language."

"No problem," he said smiling. "You two are quite a team. May I ask what's in Seattle?"

"More importantly, what does Seattle Slew want?" Marta added.

"Seattle Jameson is a reporter at the *New York Tribune Herald*. The city of Seattle is one of her father's favorites, so he named her after it. Marta was being obnoxious and calling her 'Tacoma' earlier because it's a city near Seattle. Now, she has switched to a long dead race horse—Seattle Slew. He won the Triple Crown in the 70s. I'm afraid we both were being rather childish."

"I wouldn't name a kid 'Seattle.' Now, that's childish!" Marta added.

She looked at Marta and said, "I told you she would tell us what she found. Hershel, we fed Slew some information on the hit and run and Prenbryer so she might get a story. The rule is that she can't disclose us as sources and she has to share anything she learns with us."

"So, has she found anything?" Marta asked.

"Seattle says that the hit and run vehicle was found abandoned. It was stolen about an hour before the hit on Tuesday and an eye witness says he saw the car swerve to hit the victim. The victim's full name is Bonnie Nogueira. She was a graduate student at Shawmut College and had volunteered as a cataloger off and on. They are looking for someone that they think was Bonnie's step brother so they can interview him. A neighbor mentioned him—he's been around for a week or so. Seattle wants to meet us for breakfast."

"I apologize—that is good. I need to use the damn restroom. I'll be back in a few minutes."

"Placing a bet?" Susan asked. "I know the Kentucky Derby is tomorrow, but Seattle Slew's been dead for years. I doubt he's running." Marta ignored her.

CHAPTER 73

Susan had just finished asking Hershel if Heinrich might be the Swiss architect she met on the Crumpton hotel project in New York last year, when Marta returned. Steven and the others arrived just behind her.

Steven took the lead. "Susan and Hershel, this is Douglas. Marta, do you two know each other?"

"No," Marta said curtly. "Douglas," she said shaking his hand lightly. "It's good that you are here—we would like to know if we need to be cautious, and if so, how you will help us do that."

Kat was watching Marta. Seeing a beautiful woman like her in action was great entertainment. He could swear that Douglas almost looked afraid of her. He chuckled to himself—he would be if he were Douglas.

"Ms. Krejci, if I may just ask a few questions, first...."

"Certainly, Douglas," Marta said smiling. Oh, oh Susan thought. She knew that smile; Douglas better be on his toes.

"You have given us very good background information—and I do want to thank all of you for confirming the connection between the hit and run and the murder in Paris. I...,"

Susan cut him short. "That's nice, but could you skip the formalities? I believe Ms. Krejci has told you everything we know—now you tell us, are we safe? If we are, we will want start dinner. And somebody who looked like you followed us to the Pierre this afternoon. Steven, does Douglas drive a black car?" Susan was tired; she did not want to spend time on crap. Worse, she imagined that Steven must be starving, and he got quite cranky when he was hungry.

"Yes, I came with him in a black BMW, dear," Steven answered. "But Douglas wasn't driving."

Marta did love to watch Susan take charge—when she wasn't trying to do it herself. "Douglas, my friend is right, talk to us." She figured she would pay for her comment about no black cars—well maybe they were even. Crap, she couldn't remember.

"Yes, of course, Ms. Krejci," he said.

Now Kat was sure Douglas was afraid of Marta—and Susan too. He looked over at Eisen and saw that he was trying to hide a smile—Eisen was enjoying this. Kat was, too; he was pretty sure that Marta had just winked at Susan—that had to mean trouble for Douglas.

"Ms. Krejci briefed us and everything checks out. We believe you are correct that Father Bartolome's materials did make it onto the market via London. I do have a couple of questions for you," he said looking to Marta for approval.

"Go ahead, Douglas," Marta said.

Douglas' questions mostly related to why they had been interested in Father Bartolome's materials. After about fifteen minutes, Douglas seemed satisfied. He finally said, "As a precaution, we have stationed a couple of people around to keep an eye on things. We believe that you are all too far removed to be in danger, but you should report anything suspicious. Please call this number, if anything comes up," he said passing out a card. "And we may need to contact you."

"Douglas, I told you that we are meeting again tomorrow. Can we get an update from you, then?" Steven turned to Marta, and asked, "Or, will you do that for us, Marta?"

"It will be Douglas, Steven," Marta said. "I will be right back; I will walk Douglas out.

"One minute, Douglas, Marta," Susan said. Everyone turned to look at her. "Why is Jon in danger?"

"Because Father Bartolome is worried that someone may think he told Jon about Bonnie's role in the Shawmut theft, Ms. Graves," Douglas said. "Without your tip about Prenbryer, that would have been too small a matter for us."

"Not because of Clarence Duvall?"

"Not to our knowledge, ma'am; he's just a dumb kleptomaniac as of now."

"One more thing, does Clay really know who killed Bonnie?" Susan asked.

"I'm not authorized to comment," he answered before walking out with Marta.

Kat had been staring at the card Douglas had given each of them. It didn't say much other than FBI, with an official looking seal on it and a phone number—that was it. He saw that everyone except Marta was seated, so he looked at Steven and asked, "Shall we tell Hershel and Susan about our talk?"

'Yes, please do," Steven answered.

"We missed you, Susan. Steven says you have translated most of the second Latin document and can summarize it for us. Of course, we are extremely pleased about the possibility of finding two more boxes—my friend thought there might be more than one as well, but the single mark on the map gave us no hope for anything like what you figured out."

"I'm pleased, too," Susan said.

"We have made a few decisions about analyzing the rest of the materials that Jon found in the first box as well as how we can look for those other boxes," Kat continued. "We have asked Steven to enlist your aid in deciphering the documents. Steven will give us a weekly update and we will meet somewhere in person periodically to discuss progress until he is ready to publish. Dinner will, of course, always be integral to our meetings. Hershel you and Marta will be responsible for those."

Susan looked at Steven. He was smiling. She then looked at Eisen...he was definitely smiling. Even Kat looked pleased. "That is wonderful–I know Steven has probably told you this, but we still aren't quite sure if the documents are real—they could even be ancient forgeries. If they are real and there are two more boxes...," she stopped to gather her thoughts as Marta walked in and sat down. "Even if they aren't real, an old forgery can be interesting, too." She turned to Marta, who had just come back in. Knowing she would catch her off guard, she said "Marta, will you join our dinner meetings?"

"You know I will have dinner with you anywhere," Marta smiled. "What will we discuss at these meetings?"

Steven stepped in. "We have decided to formalize the document analysis process. Susan will be in charge of Latin documents and she and Eisen will help Jon find the other boxes. Marta, you and Susan will be in charge of confirming Kat's ownership of the documents. We do think that Daf's two documents will have to be returned to Shawmut College, if they are indeed what Father Bartolome found. We don't need them anymore anyway–we will keep Eilat Shiloh's enhancement, though. Of course, Hershel will oversee authentication."

"Hershel, is that okay," Kat asked.

"Yes, of course. Might I suggest, though, that we consider contacting Dr. Smith's friend, Eilat? She did such a good job enhancing the map, perhaps she could help with areas of other documents that we can't read."

"Excellent idea–Eisen you will track her down?"

"Yes, sir."

"Our first meeting will be in Shanghai, so everyone can meet David," Steven continued. "He will help me with finalizing translations."

"Here's the waiter, everyone," Hershel said. "Let's order dinner. I have arranged to have two bottles of the 2003 Dunn Howell Mountain Cabernet Sauvignon available for dinner, so order accordingly."

"Bravo, Hershel–an absolutely excellent American wine," Susan said.

For appetizers, Susan, Steven and Marta ordered steak tartare. Eisen followed suit. Kat and Hershel ordered tuna, and Hershel ordered three dozen Malpeque oysters for the table. Susan, Marta and Eisen went for the scallops and everyone else ordered one of the steak offerings. As they finished ordering, Hershel had the head waiter open the Cabernet, so it would be ready when the main courses arrived.

Marta's phone rang as the waiters left. "Sorry, apparently Douglas forgot something," Marta said as she stood and then walked to the corner of the room to take the call.

"Steven, you and Susan also are also in charge of putting together a reading list for us," Kat said. "Eisen and I are anxious to learn more about your research and this era of early Christianity. I'm also hoping that we can expand our knowledge of the Luminists. Susan, Eisen and I have asked that meetings in the States be coordinated with visits to museums with good collections of the Luminists and the Hudson River School."

"The Gilcrease is in Tulsa, Oklahoma and the Amon Carter is in Fort Worth, Texas," Susan said. "Do you want to reconsider?"

"Might there be some of the Heades you mentioned?" Eisen asked.

"Yes, the Amon Carter has at least half a dozen. There also are several Heades at Crystal Bridges, a new museum in Northwestern Arkansas. That's even farther off the beaten path than Tulsa, though."

"We are game, Madam," Kat said.

"You may enjoy the Kimball Museum in Fort Worth as well, Kat–it has a very nice renaissance collection," Steven said.

"Well, then, Fort Worth should be high on our agenda."

"Steven, we will need to help Jon look for those additional boxes."

"I've done that, madam," Kat said. "We will see if he can continue after he is out of the hospital–if he is too frail, we will work something out. I would like to find those other boxes before this gets into the press. Someone already buried a crystal up there. God knows what other vandalism may occur if it gets out that we found something."

"So far, I believe Father Bartolome knows only about Joham,' Susan said. "He doesn't know about the box, though. Also, I doubt anyone could use Daf's 'map' without Dr. Shiloh's enhancement and your cartographers. We'll see what the diary...." Susan caught herself; she wasn't ready to tell anyone but Steven that the diary photographs were at her New York office. "I hope that diary doesn't go back to Shawmut too quickly if it is found. Let's ask Douglas if they have it."

"Perhaps I could tell Douglas that I won't let Susan or Marta hurt him if he gets us at least a photocopy," Steven said.

"Very funny, Steven," Susan said. "But Kat, your friend didn't mention the diary at all?"

"No, he must not have seen it when he was in Prenbryer's shop," Kat said. "He had been dead for several days when I got his first package, so I couldn't ask him."

"Well, for your friend, Daf, and the Welsh, I hope we somehow tie our Joham to the New World in 1307," Steven said as the appetizers arrived.

"He would be stunned if he knew we had actually found a box with documents in it, even if it is 1607. Now, there may be more. I think he was mainly interested in seeing two old friends have one last adventure. Eisen, we've satisfied that one, right?"

Eisen looked at Ohno-san as he tried to decide what to answer. He gave a slight nod, and said, "More so than Smith-san could have imagined, sir. And it's not over yet."

"As Susan can tell you, there are plenty of Welshmen here in the US who would be happy, too. And my favorite poet, Dylan Thomas, was Welsh, wasn't he, Susan?" Steven asked.

"And death shall have no dominion," Susan added. "He's Welsh, but not American Welsh. And the line, I guess it's the title too, is from Paul's Epistle to the Romans."

"Oops, I thought he was American." Steven said. "Susan when will the box be here?"

Before Susan could answer, Marta returned to the table. She stopped at Eisen's seat and whispered something to him. He got rigid at first, and then, when she whispered something else he chuckled quietly with her. As Marta went to her chair, Eisen whispered to Kat in Japanese, "Mrs. Krejci just told me that the bodyguards your son hired are knuckleheads, sir."

"My son hired bodyguards for us?" he asked Eisen in Japanese. "I've never seen any bodyguards."

"Not for us, sir, they are for you and I haven't seen them either. Mrs. Krejci said the Feds saw them tracking us through New York. Apparently, your son hires bodyguards whenever you travel. I have never seen a charge for them, so I was unaware. She apologized for the intrusion…the Feds haven't found any bad guys after us, just your two bodyguards."

This time Kat laughed as well as he nodded an acknowledgement to Marta, who was anxiously waiting for a reaction. He looked around the table to see who was watching. Only Susan seemed to notice as the oysters were distracting Steven and Hershel.

"Marta, you look contemplative," Hershel said, looking at Marta as he finished his third oyster. "Do you have an update for us?"

"Well, yes," Marta said after finishing the last bite of the tartare. "As you know, because of Ms. Short's calls, and then Father Bartolome having Shawmut notify Interpol, Prenbryer was being watched. He went to Paris and then back to London on Monday and then back to Paris again on Wednesday. Because it was very much out of his usual routine, he was tailed to Harry's Bar on Wednesday."

"Did they catch the guys?" Hershel asked.

"They had a surveillance shot of the guy he met and the guy who brought him the drink in Harry's Bar. Witnesses also saw each guy with Prenbryer in the bar. They picked up the guy who brought Prenbryer the drink that killed him last night. He was still in Paris."

"What about the other guy?" Susan asked.

"The guy they picked up has been cooperating. He gave Prenbryer the drink that killed him, so he has the most to lose. The first guy was supposed to fly to Doha yesterday. Apparently, Interpol was working with Qatar to see if they could nab him, but he never showed up at the airport."

"Then he's still in France?" Susan asked.

"Yes, he is an American, so they thought he might have come back here, but as you guessed, they caught him still in Paris. It's a good thing for the first guy that the cops picked him up right away, or he'd probably be dead now, too."

"So, the American is the mastermind?" Steven asked.

"Yes, he calls himself Seth Thomas, the Clockmaker. The first guy they caught said he makes things run like clockwork."

"Oh, for God's sake," Susan moaned.

"Just reporting what I was told," Marta smiled.

"Anything else?" Hershel asked.

"Maybe," Marta started and then hesitated for a minute. "It seems that Jon's son, Father Bartolome, may have a bigger piece of this puzzle." Marta saw the waiters coming with the main course. "Let's wait a minute so we can get our entrees."

Susan had been resisting the urge to try the Cabernet, but could wait no longer and took a sip. "Hershel, I've heard about this Cabernet, but I've never had even a sip of it before now. It is wonderful; sorry, I couldn't wait to taste it."

"It feels odd that we are sitting here having a wonderful dinner while there is an international crime investigation going on and two people have been murdered," Hershel responded. "I don't know what else we could be doing right now, though."

Kat chuckled and said, "You can safely enjoy your meal, Hershel. We have bodyguards, right, Marta?"

"What?" Hershel asked.

"Sorry," Kat said to Susan, Steven and Hershel, who were looking from Kat to Eisen to Marta and back again. "Mrs. Krejci just told us my son hires bodyguards for me. I pay for the travel, but apparently my son adds the bodyguards. They aren't necessarily competent ones, though, since Mrs.

Krejci's group spotted them." He stopped for a minute, then looked at Marta and asked, "Marta, dear, did you apologize to Eisen because our bodyguards were questioned or because they were stupid enough to be seen?"

When Marta recovered, she said, "Sorry, Kat, but you and Eisen and Ms. Short are the most susceptible because of Prenbryer. Under the circumstances, it's a good idea for you to have bodyguards with you."

"So the Shawmut connection was pretty useful," Susan mused.

"Yes, that Lisbon antiques dealer's specialty in early explorers, particularly those who are Portuguese, like João Vas Cortereal who discovered the Land of the Cod, really paid off in tying Shawmut to Prenbryer," Marta said as she winked at Susan. "That apparently got our 'Feds' interested, too."

Susan figured the wink meant Marta had impressed her colleagues with her research on Portuguese explorers. "Have we heard anything about Clay, yet?"

"No, neither he nor Father was at Jon's when they got there. We know Father came here...I assume they are watching the house."

"So, this Prenbryer was the London forger?" Steven asked.

"That's what they think—they will want to see your documents, Kat." Marta said.

"Yes, well then they can show us the diary—have they found that yet?" Kat asked.

"I don't know," Marta answered.

Susan got a call on her cell—it was Seattle. They talked for a few minutes, with Susan mostly listening. "That was Seattle," Susan said as she hung up. She looked around and saw confused looks from everyone, except Marta and Hershel.

"Seattle Jameson is a friend of Susan's who works for the *New York Tribune Herald*," Marta said. "She is feeding us information as well—she knows only my name and Steven's and Susan's.

"Anyway," Susan started, "as Marta and Hershel know, the hit and run victim's name is Bonnie Nogueira. The *Herald* tracked down a guy who says he is Bonnie's step-brother; he was staying with her in Brookline—a guy named Aldo Morales. Aldo says that the victim got several calls from an art dealer last week—she was very upset about the calls. The victim also had calls from a priest. Those also upset her—one was just before she was hit by the car. He thinks the priest told her to call the police. He heard her say 'No police, it's a private matter.' She left before he could talk to her."

"How did he know it was an art dealer and a priest?" Marta asked.

"I asked that…apparently, the victim kept saying 'No, Father.' Aldo said Bonnie's father and her step-father had both been dead for many years so, he figured it must be a priest," Susan answered. "As for a dealer, Mr. Morales said he heard 'but I thought they sold those pieces of clay.'"

"Has the FBI talked to this guy, Morales?" Marta asked.

"I didn't ask her," Susan said curtly. "If Seattle found him, surely they would…wait, now I have a text. There is another guy as well—maybe 40 or 45 years old. He stopped by to see the victim on Tuesday morning and had a heated argument with her. He didn't know that Aldo was visiting—he was upstairs. Aldo heard the name, 'Josh,' and he saw the man. He thinks he could identify 'Josh' if he was shown a picture."

"So, Seth Thomas, aka the Clockmaker, a French guy and now a Priest, an art dealer who may be Prenbryer and Josh," Marta said to herself. "Any others?"

Let me text her and ask. Susan conveyed the question. She got a response two minutes later. "Seattle doesn't think the driver is any of the people you named. She's asking if we know anything about any of these guys. Marta, I see no reason not to tell her."

"Go ahead—I will make sure Douglas knows." Marta was still smarting over whether the Feds knew as much as the reporter. They sure as hell better, she thought.

"Marta, Susan wait," Steven said. "What if Mr. Morales heard her say '…sold those pieces, Clay.' So, he wasn't the art dealer, Prenbryer; he was Father's friend, Clay."

"Dear God, Steven, you may be right," Marta said as she reached for her phone.

"Don't you go giving the Feds Seattle's name," Susan said.

"Jesus, Marta, are we sure somebody is on that train watching Father Bartolome so he doesn't get killed?"Steven yelled. "Sorry," he said more calmly, "If the victim, Bonnie, was talking with Clay and Father Bartolome told Bonnie to call the police and an older man, who might just be on the train with the Father, had an argument with her…Marta call that damn Douglas guy to make sure."

Susan looked at Marta—it was a look of anguish that she had seen only once before on Marta and again it was something happening that neither of them could stop.

"I did tell them earlier, Steven. I have no control over…I will confirm," she said. She didn't even move from the table; she just started dialing.

Susan looked at her watch, and said, "Steven, Marta, the train should have been in about ten minutes ago. Father must be okay. Steven, Marta also told the Feds that Clay knew who killed Bonnie," Susan added. She was pissed— what if Douglas was a numbskull like Kat's bodyguards? She started to say something when Douglas walked back in.

"Why are you back?" Marta asked Douglas as she hung up her phone and stood up. "Tell me that Father Bartolome is okay." Douglas stated to say something, but Marta cut him short with, "I want a yes or no, Douglas."

Kat said, "Good job, old girl."

As Douglas made his call, Steven's phone rang. He saw the call was identified as coming from Father Bartolome, so, he answered.

"Mr. Graves," the voice on the phone said. "This is Father Bartolome. I just arrived at Penn Station. I have spoken with my dad, but he may be medicated, he doesn't seem to know which hospital they put him in. He suggested that I call you. Can you tell me where he is or, better yet, where are you? Maybe we can go see him together."

Steven whispered to Susan, "Someone has Father's phone. Get Marta!"

Susan rushed over to Marta and grabbed her arm. "Steven's talking to Father and something is wrong," she hissed as she let go and motioned for Marta to come with her over to Steven. With her now freed hand, Marta grabbed Douglas by the arm that he wasn't holding his phone with. She put a finger of her other hand to her lips as she pulled Douglas over to Steven as well. Douglas finished saying something into the phone and hung up. "There's a problem," Douglas whispered to Marta.

"We know."

Steven looked at them and put his finger to his lips, then said into his phone, "Just a minute, Father. He's at Presbyterian. I can give you the number that rings in his room, but it is in my wallet–can you hold for a second? I am in a restaurant so if I lose you, I will move outside and call you back. I'm sorry, I'm having a hard time hearing you–can you hear me? Is this a good number? Sorry, I'm going to stand outside–the reception might be better there and it won't be so noisy."

Steven put the phone on mute, and said, "I'm on mute; Marta, Douglas what do I do? This guy says he is Father Bartolome, but he can't be, even though my phone shows the call coming from Father's cell."

"How do you know?" Douglas asked.

"Because Father knows his dad is at Presbyterian and this guy doesn't."

"This may be the guy who was talking with Father Bartolome on the train," he said to Steven. "Tell him you'll call him back when you get outside, then hang up," he said. When Steven hung up, Douglas took Steven's phone to fidget with it as he spoke into his blue tooth with someone.

"Okay, call him back Steven," Douglas said handing the phone back. "Tell him to come here, so you can go with him to the hospital."

Marta hissed, "Not so damn fast, Douglas. These are my friends. Who is this guy with Father's phone?"

Susan added, "My husband is not going to meet some lunatic in the lobby. Damn it, you meet him, you get paid for this."

"Mr. Graves, get him to come here, if you can," Douglas said again. "Tell him you'll go with him." He turned to Marta and said, "We will be listening in now." He then turned to Susan and said, "Before you ask, we have four people around this building and a guard at the hospital."

Steven called the number. "Hello Father," Steven started. "I hope this connection is better. I have Jon's number at Presbyterian for you, but maybe you could swing by and pick me up. I'm at Del Frisco's; it's a restaurant on Avenue of the Americas. Yes, of course, do you have a pen?"

Marta whispered angrily to Douglas, "Where is the real Father Bartolome?"

"Father Bartolome got off the train at Penn Station with the other priest. They gave us the slip there. We are looking for them now. The guy talking with Mr. Graves now must be that other priest if it's not Father Bartolome. We are checking to see where he got on the train...he didn't sit with Father Bartolome until half an hour before the train got into Penn Station."

"Well, you damn well better tell them not to let any priest into Jon's room until we know who the asshole on the phone is," Marta said.

Susan overheard and asked, "What damn other priest?"

Steven was waiving at them to be quiet. "Yes, I do know that the cab line at Penn can be a pain. We have never met–how will I recognize you to tell the cab driver to pull over–do you wear a collar? Yes, well then that should be easy–I can be there in about ten to fifteen minutes. No, it's Friday night; cabs are tough to get all over the city, not just at Penn, Father. Don't go that far north–we will never find each other in Times Square. I will pick you up on the southwest corner of Seventh Avenue and 38th Street. I will have the driver pull over to the curb just after 38th. I will ask him to put his flashers on. Then we'll head for the hospital–it is all the way across town to York Avenue. Call my cell if you don't see my cab in fifteen minutes and I'll tell you where I am." Steven hung up, then looked at Douglas and asked, "Now what?"

"We'd like you to get in a cab and take this guy to Presbyterian," Douglas said. 'We'll nab him there."

Before Susan could say anything, Marta said adamantly, "no, Douglas. That isn't going to happen."

"Ms. Krejci…" Douglas started.

"No, Douglas," she said again. "Neither Father nor this guy has ever met Steven, so it doesn't have to be Steven in the cab."

Douglas raised his finger, gesturing for them to be quiet for a minute; then used the same finger to push the left earbud from his phone into his ear a little more. Thirty seconds later, he said to Steven, "Sir, Ms. Krejci is right–this is too dangerous for you. How are you to recognize this man?"

"He is wearing his priest's collar and his favorite tam–he says it's green," Steven said. "Is Father Bartolome with this guy who called?"

"No, sir, I don't think so," Douglas answered. "We had a man on the train, he saw them leave the train together, but someone shoved our guy and he lost them–it's a Friday night. We are looking at cameras in the station now to trace them."

"The two guys on the train–were they both priests, I mean were they both wearing collars? Yes or no, damn it." Steven said.

"Both men were wearing collars, but neither wore a green tam, sir."

"Then where the hell is Father Bartolome if he isn't with this guy?" Steven asked.

"We don't know, but we are trying to confirm whether this priest is his friend Clay."

"Clay isn't a priest–he couldn't be sitting with his old friend, Father Bartolome, wearing a fake collar." Susan said. "Damn it, Clay and Father were on their way to Jon's to feed his dog when I spoke with Father a little before 5:00 p.m. Except for Jon's heart attack, he would be there still watching Jon's dog."

"Susan," Marta said, "this guy could be 'Clay' if he and Father are in cahoots. If they are both dressed as priests, maybe Clay was to throw the cops off while Father did something–or maybe Father is just trying to get Clay to a safe place before he has to turn himself in."

"While his dad is lying in a hospital?"

Steven broke in, "Find this guy I just talked to, Douglas—he is on his way North from Penn to Seventh Avenue and 38th."

Douglas said something into his cell phone's microphone.

"Damn it," Susan said as she turned her back to Douglas and faced her friends. "It was definitely not Father Bartolome who called Steven. A priest just collapsed and died in Penn Station. It has to be Father. That damn fake priest gave him his last rights, but no one seems to know where he disappeared to."

Douglas looked at Susan, stunned for a minute, but he recovered almost immediately and almost yelled, "How do you know that Ms. Graves?"

"A blog we follow," Susan said as she turned away from him. She then added 'asshole' under her breath. "Apparently, your guys weren't the only ones waiting for a priest to get off that train. Again, if Father Bartolome is dead, the guy who just called Steven is not Clay Duvall, damn it."

"Douglas," Steven said, "What is happening? You have just asked me to get in a cab with someone who may have killed Father Bartolome, so you need to tell us what happens next. Should I meet this guy?"

Hershel asked Susan, "Did your source say how he died?"

"No, just that he collapsed—he was dead at the scene."

"Douglas, was he murdered?" Hershel asked.

"We don't know yet, sir. I'm trying to get confirmation that it was Father."

"They were on the train together—you had plenty of time to be ready," Kat added. "Am I correct, Susan?"

Marta answered for her. "Yes, Kat," she said. She then turned to Douglas and said, "There must have been someone else on the train with the second priest. Friday night or not, you can't lose two priests in Penn Station because somebody shoved your guy, Douglas."

"Yes, Ms. Krejci, I understand your concern. If it's any consolation, Clay Duvall wasn't with Father. They just picked him up at Dr. Christiansen's house."

"I thought you said he wasn't there," Susan said.

"He drove Father Bartolome to the train, then stopped for dinner," Douglas answered. "He just got back…we were waiting for him."

"Make sure they don't hurt the damn dog," she said whispering asshole under her breath again. "Damn it, not with Jon's son dead now."

"Douglas," Steven said, so that everyone could hear. "I told this guy 15 minutes…it's already been nine minutes."

"We have a cab with our driver and our man driving the route south. We also are looking for the guy now along the route from the station…it should be just a minute," Douglas said.

Hershel said, "I would love a drink, but I am anxious to keep my wits. Perhaps we should order some coffee or tea."

"Sounds good to me, Hershel," Susan said.

Eisen got up and said, "Let me find the waiter. Do we know how Dr. Christiansen is? Should we call?"

"I can do that, Eisen," Susan said.

When Susan hung up, Marta came over and said to everyone, "Douglas is talking with the office—he should have something for us in a minute. If they nab the fake priest, I think we can call it a night. How's Jon?"

"Sleeping," Susan said.

Kat looked at Marta and said, "They have the 'Mastermind' and his accomplice in Paris. They have the dead woman who probably took our material from the college. Now hopefully they will get this guy who may have killed Father Bartolome. But this killer isn't Clay or, as Susan would say, the 'klepto.' Is that right?"

"Yes," Marta said

"We don't know who drove the hit and run car," Steven said. "We also know only that Father is dead, not that he was killed–although somebody impersonating him is using his phone."

"And who argued with Bonnie Nogueira?" Susan added. "And I hate to ask, but have we pinned down whether Klepto Clay was the 'he sold the pieces' Clay guy?"

Douglas came over. "We got him," he said. "We picked him up on surveillance at Seventh and 36th and got him in the next block. I think we can safely leave you all alone for the rest of the evening. I know you are all staying in New York for another day–we will be in touch tomorrow to wrap things up."

"Not so fast, Douglas," Steven said. "I have two questions–you're sure it's the guy who called me? Not just someone he gave his stupid hat to?"

"Yes, sir–he had Father's cell phone and he was wearing a collar as well as the tam. More importantly, our guy on the train ID'ed him. And Clay also is in custody now. What is your other question, sir?"

"Now I have a couple more questions–first, who is watching the dog?"

"He's being taken to a kennel, sir."

"Okay, some of us may go to see Dr. Christiansen in the morning–will someone tell him about his son?" Steven asked.

"We are waiting for his doctors to give the okay."

"Okay, then who is this pseudo-priest? Is he the hit and run driver, and, if not, have you picked up the hit and run driver yet? Susan, Marta, Gentlemen, what else are we missing?"

"Have you confirmed whether someone else was on the train with the fake priest?" Hershel asked.

"Did this man kill Father Bartolome or was it natural causes?" Eisen asked.

"They guy we got is Joshua Borne. We are pretty sure he isn't the hit and run driver and we are pretty sure he had an accomplice on the train. He may have been the guy who was arguing with Bonnie Nogueira, the 'Josh' you mentioned Ms. Krejci. We haven't confirmed the cause of death yet for Father Bartolome. It's classified as natural causes, for now. I will try to get answers for you by tomorrow."

Marta shot a glance at Susan to see if she had heard Douglas say that Marta reported in on Josh. Susan had, but she didn't look pissed.

"And, is this Joshua Borne the priest who gave Father his last rights?" Hershel asked.

"Yes, sir, and he is not a priest."

Eisen said to Kat in Japanese. "He must have killed Jon's son as they walked—a needle prick, maybe."

"Yes, there are still a lot of holes in this story," Kat replied in Japanese.

"Natural causes—maybe they mean it was a naturally occurring poison," Eisen laughed and then said, 'sorry, sir, this isn't really a laughing matter."

Kat and Eisen continued talking in Japanese for another minute, then Kat stood up and said, "Excuse me Douglas, but do you really want us to believe that Jon's son, Father Bartolome, sits on the train with this fake priest; then, gets off the train and drops dead? That might be plausible, but then you say that, after giving Jon's son, Father Bartolome, his last rights, this fake priest gives you the slip, takes Father's phone so he can call Steven and get to Jon? And he wasn't even a real priest? Do you think we are idiots?"

"We lost them getting off the train, sir – someone shoved our guy on the train."

Marta broke in, "Douglas, Mr. Ohno is right. It's been a very long day and we all have more work to do tomorrow. You were sent here to 'manage' us. The first thing you do is assess the intelligence of your charges—after you decide they aren't going to shoot you, of course. Either you didn't do that or you erroneously concluded that we are a bunch of damn country bumpkins. We may know things that could help—we gave you several damn leads, for God's sake. Last chance," she said with that look that scared even Susan. "Call now and do it without moving from that spot."

Steven added, "It's simple, Douglas. We want some assurance that there isn't anyone else we should be worried about."

Kat cleared his throat to get everyone's attention, and then said, "This is a violent country; I have bodyguards, sort of, but my friends do not. Ms. Krejci, are we safe or should we fly back to Tokyo? I can arrange for my plane to take us, if need be."

"Tokyo is beautiful at this time of year," Eisen added.

"Douglas, at least confirm that we have protection," Marta said, "and not someone who can lose two priests getting off a train. Now," she said firmly again.

Douglas seemed frozen, trying to decide what to do. He had been told that Marta's continued relations with certain members of Congress made this a big deal. This was his opportunity to advance—he knew it. Had he blown it or was the office trying to make him fail—he had been following orders, but perhaps he should have given more feedback....

Susan decided to snap Douglas back to work. "Douglas, you nabbed a guy who rode the train with Father Bartolome hoping he would drop dead from natural causes so that he could steal Father's phone and kill my husband with these 'natural causes' on his way to the hospital to kill Jon with even more 'natural causes.' You're nuts."

Kat," Steven said laughing, "where is your plane—Teterboro?"

"Yes, and my limo is waiting outside, we'll have my bodyguards go with us." He and Eisen were laughing now; the situation was rather ridiculous.

"Steven, call the nursing station to check on Jon," Susan said. "Maybe he can go with us."

"Give me a minute," Douglas said as he began to walk out again.

"No, Douglas." Susan said with a voice that meant there were no options. "Look, I want to think that Clay is just a regular 'klepto.' But how exactly did this 'Josh' know that Father Bartolome's dad was in the hospital and that Father was rushing to New York to see him? I mean, he had to find a priest's collar, find the poison, and know which train Father was taking. Then he had to find Father Bartolome on the train.…. Something isn't right. We are missing someone, aren't we?"

"Yes, Susan, we are," Marta started.

"Douglas, call from here where we can see you doing it." She turned to Marta and asked, "How do we know that he doesn't just stand out of our sight, does nothing for a few minutes and then comes back with something he made up? Marta, can't we find somebody who knows what's going on?"

"Douglas," Marta said staring him down. "Susan is right; make your damn call from here where we can see you." Marta turned at the sound of clapping– it was Eisen and Kat. She took a bow, then nodded and gestured for a round of applause for Susan, too.

As Douglas made his call, Steven asked, "Do we need more coffee?"

"I do, Steven," Susan said. "Marta, look at this," Susan said handing Marta her iPhone showing a text from Seattle as Douglas hung up.

"Well, Douglas, any news?" Steven asked as Susan passed her phone to him.

"Yes, I think so," Douglas said.

Susan glanced at Marta and Steven who were reading the text she had received. Marta winked at her and then handed Susan's phone to Kat, who held it where Eisen could see as well. They then handed it to Hershel. "Susan's blog says you helped nab the head of an international ring of antiquities thieves and forgers," Marta said.

"Yes, Ms. Krejci," Douglas said looking surprised. "If you can all wait about half an hour, we should have everything arranged."

"Marta, dear, shall I order some port?" Hershel, asked.

CHAPTER 74

Douglas came back to the private room at Del Frisco's 20 minutes later. "Everyone," he said, "Please excuse my interruption, but I have some news. Ms. Krejci, may I report?"

"Yes, of course, Douglas," Marta said.

"The man we picked up, Joshua Borne, was pretty cocky until we told him we had nabbed the big guy, Donald Carvalho, and his assistant in Paris. Carvalho is the one who calls himself 'Seth Thomas, the Clockmaker.' The junior guy, Antoine Clanton, is actually British, but he lives in Paris."

"So, has the hit and run victim's step-brother identified this Joshua Borne?" Steven asked.

"Not yet. We are looking for the step-brother, Aldo Morales, to see if he can identify Josh as the person who argued with Bonnie Nogueira. Josh started cooperating when we told him the Clockmaker said Josh was in charge of their operations. We also will ask the eye witness if he can ID Josh as the driver of the vehicle that hit Bonnie Nogueira. The ID by our guy on the train was to ensure that Josh won't recant."

"And did this Clockmaker actually rat him out?" Hershel asked.

"I am not authorized to answer that, sir."

"Wait a minute," Susan said. "Did you say Darin Carvalho?" She turned to Marta and said, "That's the guy, Marta."

"Mrs. Graves, the man we caught is Donald Carvalho, not Darin."

"We gave you guys the name Darin Carvalho around 5:00 this afternoon," Marta said. "Father said he was the guy and he was at Shawmut. Did he have the name wrong or is there a relative named Darin out there?"

"Could he be Aldo?" Susan asked.

"If he is neither of them, there could still be one or two people out there, right?" Hershel asked.

"Yes, Dr. Gruber, but the driver is most likely a hired thug, not a major player," Douglas answered. "We know about Darin. He is Donald's brother, but we don't know if he's Aldo or if he is involved. Ms. Krejci, I am authorized to tell you that Father Bartolome was poisoned. A poison called aconite was used. We don't yet know how it was administered, but it was a very lethal dose."

"Monkshood," Eisen said and then clapped his hand over his mouth. "Sorry," he said looking at everyone. "I am a fan of mystery novels—Agatha Christie, specifically. She favored strychnine for her murders, but used 'monkshood,' which is another name for aconite, once in a while. It's also called wolf's bane or friar's cap."

"Medea put wolf's bane in a cup of wine to kill Theseus—she failed though," Steven added. "Oh, and Agrippina poisoned Claudius by putting it in a plate of mushrooms."

"You can't be serious!" Hershel said. "Father Bartolome was killed with a poison called monkshood or friar's cap? What is this Douglas, *Death at the Vatican* or something? Eisen, perhaps Ms. Christie will write a new book?"

"From the grave, sir," Eisen smiled.

"And is Clay just a klepto?" Marta asked.

"My understanding, Ms. Krejci, is that he was arguing with Bonnie because he figured out that she had taken Father Bartolome's materials," Douglas said. "He probably figured that Bonnie's theft would lead to the discovery of his own multiple thefts."

"Father Bartolome was going to help Clay turn himself in, when Dr. Christiansen had his heart attack," Susan said.

"Yes, ma'am. Clay says he still has everything except a spearhead that he gave to a friend for his birthday."

"Shawmut has that back already, Douglas," Susan smiled. "So, how did Josh know which train Father Bartolome would be on? Either Clay or someone Clay knew had to tell him," she added. "If Donald was in Paris, then could it be Darin?"

"I will convey the question," Douglas said.

"Before you do, we are curious, Douglas," Kat said. "Father's pieces that were stolen from Shawmut—we may know where two of them are. Do you know where the third piece, a diary, is? We would like to see it."

"I don't know, sir."

"Do you mean you personally, Douglas or the FBI or whoever you are, doesn't know?" Kat asked.

"I don't, sir, but I will ask." He turned to Marta, "I need to report in; they will tell me if you are free to go, ma'am. I know it's late for everyone."

Susan stifled a laugh—Marta hated to be called 'ma'am' as much as Susan did, but she couldn't really chastise this young pup for using it as he was trying to be polite.

"As Mr. Ohno said, we would like to know about Father's third piece—it is a little book. You owe our Japanese friends—they are the ones who helped tie the Shawmut pieces to London."

"I will check, Ms. Krejci. We will want to see those two pieces you mentioned," he answered.

Marta winked at Eisen and said, "They aren't in the US right now, Douglas. We can talk about that later. So, you haven't seen the third piece?"

"I will try to find out." Douglas went over to shake Marta's hand before leaving.

Marta clasped his right hand, and then put her left hand on his shoulder to stop him from leaving. "Anything else we want to know?" she asked, looking at everyone.

Susan hesitated, and then said "Maybe." It had dawned on her that she hadn't yet told Steven or Marta that Father Bartolome sent her pictures of the diary that he had found. Crap, maybe she should tell this Douglas. They should now be able to trace the map and the document all the way from Father Bartolome's site near Popham to Richard Prenbryer's shop and then to Kat's friend and on to Kat. But one of the slimes must still have the diary. Well, in about 10 hours, she would honor Father's request and see the pictures of the diary first.

"Yes, ma'am?" Douglas asked.

Susan refused to look at Marta who was now probably stifling a laugh herself. "First, I should mention that Father saw a picture of one of Mr. Ohno's pieces today; he wasn't sure it was one of those he found. The other is that Nogueira is Portuguese for walnut–in Spanish it's 'nogales,' like the border town in Arizona. Also, Carvalho is a Portuguese surname. She stopped for a minute trying to gather her thoughts. "Father Bartolome thought someone was going to take something from the site where he found his three pieces– and it wasn't Clay."

"We are checking into things… it takes time."

"Um, could this Bonnie be related to the Portuguese archaeologist or is this step-brother, Aldo Morales, more involved than he said? Also, I'm still waiting for you to tell me how Josh knew which train Father would be on and who Darin is. Might he be Aldo?"

"What's the archaeologist's name?" Douglas asked.

"If I knew, then I could probably answer the question myself. I am asking you–the archaeologist is working at a Verrazano site near Popham, Maine for Shawmut College. You should know–it was his brother, in Lisbon, who got the lead on the diary that we would like to see–we told you it was being restored in London. She turned to Steven and said, "I think maybe we should call it a night. We are getting nowhere." She turned back to Douglas and said, "The Verrazano site is not where Father found his pieces."

Kat cleared his voice and said, "Since Eisen and I are the oldest people in the room, we would like to call it a night as well. Perhaps all of the excitement enhanced the flavors, but the meal was wonderful—and Hershel, your choice of wine was superb. Eisen has reserved a meeting room for us tomorrow at the Peninsula—may I suggest we meet there at 11:00 a.m. and talk through lunch?"

"Douglas," Marta said, "you know where we will be tomorrow morning. Please come by and give us an update."

CHAPTER 75

As Susan, Marta and Steven got into the cab, Susan said to Steven, "Maybe we should go see Jon before the meeting tomorrow–I brought him some Frango mints, but I forgot to give them to him today. Don't let me forget to take them tomorrow. Marta, is Wilhelm here yet?"

"Yes, he's staying with a friend. He'll see us at breakfast."

"Good. Steven, I need to stop at my office here before the meeting at 11:00 a.m.–I have a package waiting for me. I would like to be there by 9:15 a.m."

"What the hell is that for? It better be the deal you are working on–your last one, right?"

"Yes, Steven, it is our deal." She didn't want to tell him about the photos with Marta there and in a way, 'our deal' could be this one–well parsed, she thought, but she better tell Steven soon. "I'll go by my office and meet you at 10:15 a.m. at the hospital. We can see Jon and go to the Peninsula from there. Oh crap, we have breakfast with Seattle at 7:30 a.m. Are either of you joining me for breakfast?"

"I will," Marta said.

"Not me," Steven said. "Marta, do you want to come with me to the hospital after breakfast, or meet us at the Peninsula?"

"I'll meet you at the Peninsula, Steven."

As they got out of the cab at the Pierre, Susan said to Marta, "the first Vatican Council was called by Pope Pius the Ninth in the late 1860s. That was the council that declared the Pope to be infallible. Before that, he could make mistakes. Also, you need to find out for us whether Sussman, the butcher, or Katz of Katz's Deli first served pastrami here in New York. See you at 7:30 a.m."

Steven was already half asleep when Susan finished her emails that night.

"Steven, are you awake enough for me to tell you why I'm going to my office tomorrow morning?"

"Yes, if it doesn't change the fact that you are giving notice," he said.

"Do you remember me whispering with Jon this afternoon just before we adjourned?"

"Yes, you did say you would tell me later." He was wide awake now.

"Father Bartolome remembered that there probably were photographs of the diary at the dig house for his old site on Cape Small. He went up there on Wednesday and found them."

"Photographs? But why..."

"The practice at that site was to photograph all artifacts that they found and then send the physical materials to Shawmut. They kept the photos at the site for reference—not a bad idea, if you think about it. Jon convinced Father Bartolome to send them to me. Father sent them by FedEx to my office here in New York. I can get the package any time after 9:00 a.m."

"You're kidding...."

"No, Steven, I'm not. The package was put in the vault or I would have gone over this evening."

"Well, then I'll go with you tomorrow morning."

"I'm having breakfast with Seattle at 7:30 a.m."

"I'll join you by 8:15 a.m.–order me an omelet, some bacon and an iced tea. What do I wear tomorrow?"

"Sport coat, no tie. It's a Saturday meeting. I'll set everything out for you in the morning."

CHAPTER 76

Susan was at breakfast by 7:25 a.m. She was in luck–there was no table with a single woman. She grabbed a copy of the *New York Tribune Herald* and had the hostess take her to a table for four. She had met Seattle only once two years ago in New York. She wasn't sure she would recognize her, so she asked the waitress to bring anyone who asked for her to the table. Seattle showed up just as Marta arrived with Wilhelm, who was carrying a package. Susan checked her watch without thinking about it–7:31 a.m. That's good, she thought. Damn, she wished she could stop doing that.

"Good morning, ladies, Wilhelm. Seattle, these are my colleagues, Marta Krejci and Wilhelm Galianos. Marta, Wilhelm, this is Seattle Jameson. I hope you don't mind, but I have to be at our office here by 9:00 a.m. I can assure you Seattle, if we don't quite finish, you will be well entertained by Marta and Wilhelm."

"Wilhelm, my father is James Jameson–Susan's client," Seattle said. "He mentioned your name last week. You impressed him and that isn't easy. Here's my card, in case you ever come up with something interesting for me like these two ladies have."

"Thank you. Ms. Krejci was just telling me a little about you–the *New York Tribune Herald* is pretty impressive, too," Wilhelm answered. "I enjoy working for your father," he added as an afterthought. Marta had refused to tell him why she needed the package hand-delivered. All she would say was that it was for Susan. She wouldn't tell him anything more last night, so he stayed with his former classmate.

"Can you join us for breakfast, Wilhelm?" Susan asked.

"No, but thank you for asking. I just stopped by to say hello. I'm staying around the corner with a friend from school who lives here. We are meeting for breakfast and then going to the Whitney—he's going to show me some of his favorite pieces. It was nice meeting you Ms. Jameson."

"Thanks, Wilhelm," Susan said as she stood and walked over to him. "Buy your friend a nice lunch or dinner for me," she whispered. "I'll catch up with you on Monday."

"Steven didn't want to come for breakfast?" Marta asked.

"He'll be down in about 20 minutes," Susan answered as she sat down again. "He's going to Peale, Curtis with me. I'm hoping we'll have time to go by the hospital, too and still make it to the Peninsula by 11:00 a.m."

Marta saw that Susan wasn't going to add anything, so she said, "Let's order. Does the 'lady' want only bacon and coffee as usual?"

"Yes, Steven will have his usual, too—a Denver omelet, bacon and an iced tea with lots of lemon, but I'll order it around 8:00 a.m."

"Seattle, before Susan tells you, iced tea was introduced at the Chicago World's Fair in 1893," Marta said. "By the way, Wilhelm is single."

Seattle smiled and said, "Ms. Krejci, I know you worked for Senator Hinderman after you left the NSA. Our files identify Hinderman as one of the few Senators in recent history who was actually qualified to be on the Intelligence Committee. We gave you credit for most of that, though."

Susan caught herself smiling—Seattle couldn't have done a better job of getting Marta to like her even if the little twit did call her a 'lady' in front of Wilhelm. Then she chuckled, it would be interesting if Seattle asked Marta about a date with Wilhelm. She unfolded the *Herald*—it didn't make the front page.

"Thank you for the text messages last night," Marta said. "As I've been bitching to Susan, nowadays, I send info, but I don't get much back."

"No problem," she said as she watched Susan thumbing through the newspaper. "Susan, it's on page C1."

"The 'Arts' Section? Is that where you wanted it?"

"The choice was to be buried in the front or on the first page of the 'Arts' section. They are basically art-related murders, only one of which was here in New York. Anyway, I cannot thank you two enough. We have a few loose ends to figure out, but we think we're close."

"Good job, Seattle. Is there anyone still out there that you think they haven't caught yet?" Susan asked.

"We are missing the hit and run driver," Seattle said. "What about you?"

"The big issue for me is how 'Josh' knew to get on the train to kill Father Bartolome. I mean, Father's dad had a heart attack at around 5:30 p.m. Josh was able to get dressed like a priest, pick up some poison and find Father on the right train to New York. Somebody had to tip Josh off about Jon's heart attack and somebody must have been watching Father. That somebody probably got on the train in Philadelphia so he could tell Josh where Father was sitting when Josh got on an hour or so later." She turned to Marta and asked, "Have either of you heard anything about Darin Carvalho?"

"I haven't. I also want to know whether Clay aka Clarence Duvall, was merely a kleptomaniac who happened to know Bonnie Nogueira, the cataloger at Shawmut, or was more involved," Marta said mostly to herself.

"I hope he's just a klepto, Jon's had enough tragedy for a while," Susan said. "But who else would know Jon had a heart attack."

"Clarence Duvall is a klepto?" Seattle asked.

"Yes, he stole a bunch of things from Shawmut College, but not Father Bartolome's material," Marta said.

"My husband thinks that Bonnie might have said, 'They sold those pieces, Clay,' not 'They sold those pieces of clay.' So Bonnie was talking to Clay, not an art dealer. Clay knew Bonnie from Shawmut and Father knew both of them. We think Clay figured out that Bonnie took Father's stuff. I guess 'sold' could mean that Father's pieces went to London. If Shawmut started looking for Father's stuff, Clay's klepto ways might be uncovered."

"Father Bartolome and Clay were supposed to watch Jon's dog. Clay drove Father to the train station and then got picked up by the police," Marta said.

"I will have our contact talk with Aldo, the step brother," Seattle said to Susan.

"Good luck finding him—ah, here's Steven, right on time," Marta said.

"Hello, everyone—you must be Seattle," he said as he sat down. He patted Marta's shoulder and then leaned over and kissed his wife's head.

"Hello, sir," Seattle said. She was surprised; Steven was easily twice the size of Susan. "By the way, all we could find on Darin is that he's an assistant professor at Shawmut and he's Donald's brother. May I ask, ma'am, were you going to say that Aldo has disappeared?"

Marta said to Seattle, "that's it—you call me or Susan 'ma'am' or 'lady' again and I'll smack you. Steven, you want to stay as a 'sir'?"

"Marta, you shouldn't be so sensitive about your age—you look young enough to pick up a 30 year old if you tried," Steven said with a smile that he knew would get him off the hook with her. "Anyway, the FBI couldn't find him, right?" Steven hesitated for a second and then continued, "You might see if he had a record. Hmm...Marta, Seattle, has anybody compared pictures of Aldo and Darin? Might they be one and the same? Ah, Seattle is a fast texter. Let us know if either of you hear anything."

After finishing her text, Seattle asked, "So, could Aldo have shifted the blame to Clay because he's involved in all of this?"

"I don't...," Steven stopped. He then turned to Marta and Susan, and said, "If Clay knew Bonnie, then he may know Aldo, her step brother; and, since Darin is a Shawmut professor, they must know him too. Clay might have told Aldo that Jon had a heart attack and that Father was going to New York. Aldo then tipped off Josh. We are missing at least one other person...Mr. X, the guy on the train."

Marta reached for her phone and said, "Crap, another text...Let me at least be sure they are looking into that."

"Ask about Darin, too," Susan said.

"Clay is the Shawmut post doc, right?" Seattle asked. "That seemed like a local Boston story, until we learned of the connection to Father Bartolome."

"It may still be, but for the fact that he has stumbled into this bigger deal. I think we are all trying to fit the pieces together," Steven said.

"Jon is very fragile–he had a heart attack when he was with us yesterday," Susan added. "Now, his son has been murdered. He's a good guy, Seattle; do your best to protect him. Did anyone try to ID Morales as the driver?"

"We talked to him as a witness, not as a suspect," Seattle answered. "But you're right–how did this Josh know to be on the train in a priest's outfit? My understanding is that Josh has now confessed to killing Father Bartolome, but not Bonnie. So, is our step brother, Morales, part of this and how does he relate to Darin, the Clockmaker's brother? Did he tip Josh off about Father?"

Susan asked Marta, "Is that asshole Douglas going to meet us?"

"Douglas will meet us at 11:00 a.m.," Marta said. "Josh wasn't the hit-and-run driver; the eye witness couldn't identify him. They don't know if the eye witness was also shown Aldo's picture, since it was done at a police station without them. Oh, and they don't think Clay or Father knew Josh."

"What does Clay say?"

"He's not talking, Susan…he's on suicide watch right now."

"Oh crap, that can't just be because he's a klepto," Susan said. "I'd guess he feels responsible for Father."

"He probably is responsible, Susan," Marta said.

"Ladies, help me go through this," Steven said. "We don't have the hit-and-run driver or the guy who argued with Bonnie unless it was Josh or Aldo made it up," Steven mused. "We also are missing who told Josh to get on the train and who was with Josh on the train, since we know that someone shoved the Fed who was watching Father. Anyone else?"

"Aldo may have been part of the ring because we are missing how Josh knew to get on the train. And Josh, the intermediary, was erasing the trail by killing Father Bartolome," Seattle said, thinking.

"Do we think Aldo could have been on the train with Josh?" Steven asked.

"I would guess probably not," Susan said. "Since Bonnie knew Clay and Father, Aldo may have known them too."

"Logistically, I don't think Aldo could have been on the train, but I'll check," Seattle said as she sent another text message off.

"Clay is damn lucky that Father Bartolome was hiding him until the Feds picked him up, or he might be dead, too," Steven said.

Steven turned to Marta and asked, "Is someone keeping an eye on Susan? What if Father Bartolome mentioned us to someone like Clay or the 'guy,' Darin?"

"God, I do hope Clay didn't accidently tell Aldo," Susan said to no one in particular. "Poor dumb klepto—it would be sad if he accidentally got Father Bartolome killed."

"It would be even worse if he did it intentionally," Marta said.

"Yes, it would...Steven, we need to go—we have two stops," Susan said as she rose from the table.

"Don't forget your cane—it's by Steven's chair."

"Thanks, Marta," Susan said as she finished the last swallow of coffee in her cup. "It's 8:50 a.m. We have to go review something at Peale, Curtis. Do you want Steven to take the package?"

"I can bring it to the meeting, if you want. I'm going to sit somewhere and make calls for a while after we finish here."

"Thanks, Marta."

"Ready, Steven?" Susan asked. "One last thing—who had Bonnie take Father Bartolome's stuff? It wasn't Father because he didn't know it was gone until recently. It wasn't Clay because Jon said Clay didn't know about Father's stuff until recently. Was Bonnie just coincidentally looking for some parchment? Marta, Seattle, let us know if you find anything."

"Oh, before I forget," Seattle said, "a woman who had worked at Cardiff has been found dead–dumped in the Moors, north of London."

Susan and Steven stopped dead in their tracks. Susan turned back to look at Seattle, then steadied her voice and asked, "What was her name, Seattle?"

"Hold on, let me look. She'd been dead for at least a few weeks…her name was Kate Parker," Seattle said. She saw all three of them literally sigh in relief. "Um, did you think it might be someone else?"

"We were afraid it might be," Marta said.

"We do have to go," Susan said as she grabbed her cane. Steven was ahead of her–off to get them a cab. "We'll settle up for breakfast later, Marta," Susan said.

"I texted my person to check on Aldo and Darin," Marta said.

"Me too," Seattle called after them. "Who's Douglas and who did you think Kate Parker was?" Susan heard Seattle ask Marta as she and Steven left.

CHAPTER 77

The doorman got Susan and Steven a cab right away. As Susan stood waiting for the doorman to open the cab door, she noticed a man in a brown sweater in the cab line behind them. 'Brownie' had come in to breakfast with Steven. He sat at the table behind them. She figured it was just a coincidence that 'Brownie' was now waiting for a cab–he hadn't been at his table when she left. Oh well, now he was behind them in line.

Susan hadn't seen any of her black car guys outside. Maybe 'Brownie' was the guy assigned to them–or maybe he was just a stranger waiting for a cab. Or, maybe it was Mr. X, but she shrugged that off as it was unlikely that he would know them. She didn't see 'Brownie' when she and Steven got out of the cab at her New York office. Four black cars, each with a driver, were waiting at the curb, though. As there was only one person per car, she figured they were waiting to take the local partners home or to a meeting. Marta was right–those cars were everywhere.

"Okay, now what?" Steven asked as they stepped off the elevator after clearing security.

"First, we're stopping at the mailroom," Susan said.

As they waited for Father's package, Susan asked Steven what documents he had looked at.

"I've looked at all of them, but I have only read two thoroughly…ah, Susan here's the package. I'll carry it. Thank you, sir," he said to the mail clerk. Susan led him back to an empty room with a large conference table that they had passed on their way to the mail room.

"Open it; let's see what we have," she said as he set the package down on the table. "There should be at least two pages in Portuguese."

"I'll hand the pictures to you as I unpack them—tell me if you see anything exciting," he said as he opened the box. "Susan, here's a note from Father—read it to me as I set these out."

"Father Bartolome's note says that there are two sets; one is large format and the other is printed on regular sized paper."

"Yep, there is a second, smaller-sized set of pictures. I'll set those aside."

"Steven, he says that the two Portuguese pages were attached to the insides of the front and back covers. The other five pages were written on both sides, for a total of ten pages, but the last page was blank on the back. There also is a picture of each cover; the front one should have an emblem embossed on it...it's probably that damn serpent wheel. He says these should be returned to Dr. Nielsen at Shawmut. That's it, damn it."

"Let me find that cover with the emblem...oh, oh, here it is. Take a look, Susan."

"Crap, this is that same Gnostic symbol, the snake wheel...I thought I was making a joke. The problem is that its symbolism seems more philosophical than Gnostic."

"It doesn't have 1267, though," he said.

"Can you read anything, Steven? Are the pages legible?"

"We'll know in a minute. These first two must be the front and back that he says are in Portuguese; I'll set them aside. Luckily, there isn't much on them, well, I take that back. We at least have João A D Ovelho on one and Joham Diaz Alvaro Ovelho on this other. It's just as Father Bartolome remembered. I can't really understand the Portuguese," he said as he set the pages aside.

"We're in luck—the rest of these pages are in Latin. Aha!"

"What do you see?" he asked as he set down the third page.

"There are some dates, November 11, 1552, being the first one I see; it also says Joham Diaz Alvaro Ovelho in the text. The pages don't seem to be quite in order. Sorry, the page with Joham's name is a right page. See, the binding is on the opposite side along the edge there.

The left page says João A D Ovelho and 1292—that's not good," he said. "And here's a 1267."

"Um, 1267 is when the last copy of Jon's stuff was finished and it's on the insignia," Susan said. "And isn't 1292 the date of the cover letter that says that's when the copies were done?"

Steven gave a little whoop. "Susan, 1267 and 1292 are okay, this is a brief history of two guys with slightly different spellings—look at the dates and the names," he said. "The guy with the older dates is João not Joham."

"You think João is an ancestor?" she asked.

"Yes, I do, his name is here again, but this time with 1308," he said pointing to a spot on the page. "And look here, our Joham was born in Tomar in 1552—it must say November 11, like the date on the back cover, but it is too faint."

"The last entry is 1608, at some place I can't read, is that an 'S,' Steven? I can't read the month or the day either. Father was right; this thing is in bad shape."

"This is the last picture," Steven said.

"Here where it says 'João A D Ovelho,' we have September 28, 1253, and March something in 1315. That's 62 years—it could be his lifespan, but then he couldn't write the last date, could Joham…." She stopped to see if she could figure it out.

"It looks like two, no three different handwritings. If you look at the 1 and the 5 in the numbers, they are different in 1253 and 1315, which must have been added later. We have two guys, João and Joham, who are about 200 or 300 years apart," Steven said slowly. "And we have a third person who added the 1315 date."

"You may be right; that would let Joham come to Maine in the 1600s. Steven, read this down here—Joham's three Guardians were killed on April 13, 1607 by…what's that word?"

"I don't know, do you think it may be the name of an Indian tribe? It would fit the context. This is something Jon may be able to help us with."

"I'd better call and check on Jon," Susan said. "Can you take a picture of that word with your iPhone? Maybe we can distract Jon by asking him to decipher it. Steven, we'll need to leave here in no more than fifteen minutes if we are going to stop by to see him. Can you carry this when you re-pack it?"

"Yes. Call Jon, then help me pick through this for a few more minutes."

"Okay, but this segment, the one with what may be the Indian tribe, says that Joham is left to guard the boxes because the 'Guardians of the Word' were killed. So that confirms that 'Guardians' and 'Guardians of the Word' are one and the same." She sat staring at the words. "Whoa, here's a word for Kat and Eisen; it's Dafydd, I think he's still alive with Joham. But why did you come to Maine?" she asked. She sat for a few more minutes and then called the hospital.

"How is he?" Steven asked.

"Jon took a turn for the worse last night—maybe they told him about Father. Anyway, they've given him a sedative, so no visitors. It's only 9:50 a.m., so we still have over an hour before we have to be at the Peninsula." Susan was staring into space.

"Susan?" Steven asked.

"Let's go by and leave the chocolates and a note. Do you think he has relatives?"

"I don't know," he hesitated. "You're right; we'll drop off the chocolates. Let's just spend another half hour and then we'll go."

"Okay. So, we've got the same symbol on this and the stuff from Jon's box. We also know that the 'Guardians of the Word' died in Maine. So Joham, who is from Tomar, goes to Wales in 1605, where he picks up Dafydd and the three 'Guardians of the Word,' who guard the boxes. We have João from 1253 to 1315. It says 'Tomar' here and 1303 or 1308 at the end and then I can't read what is here—it should be another location."

"The 1292 cover letter indicates it should be Cyprus; actually what they call the Kolossi Castle; it's near Limasol."

"Oh, it's 1303, and it's Paris…crap, you can't sail to Paris."

"We know that Joham has three Guardians and three boxes with him when he sails for Maine. Here, see, you're right. It says João got the boxes in Paris and he took them to Cyprus. João gave them to…ah, he gave them to the Guardians there–no, it says they had them there. In 1604, Joham has the boxes, but he doesn't say where he got them. He also doesn't tell us what's in them."

"He says the 'Paris' boxes that he picked up were sealed, Steven."

"Well, damn it, he should have opened them so he could tell us what's in them."

"Steven–look here…does that say what I think it says?"

"Just a minute," he said.

She decided she couldn't wait, "Steven, Joham says that João's boxes were taken to Paris from 'Imperium Romaniae' in 1207," Susan said. "That's the post-Fourth Crusade name for Constantinople or Byzantium, right? Crap, it's already 10:15 a.m. This is painfully slow…it's so hard to make out the letters."

'Let's keep at it for at least a few more minutes. So we have three boxes. Two go from Constantinople to Paris, then to Tomar, Cyprus, Wales and finally Maine. Our box goes from Constantinople to the Sinai, then Acre, Cyprus, Wales and Maine. I guess it's time to go, right?"

"Yes, but I think our box was in Tomar, too. We should send these large format pictures to my Chicago office. I can't copy them here anyway. At best, Father borrowed these from that Cape Small site–I will have to return them at some point. We'll keep the small set for now."

"This may be the…," Steven stopped in mid-sentence. "Oh, I see; if we have them with us, we may have to give them up–we have no right to them. That's fine; we can show everyone the small pictures."

"I need to find somebody to tell me how to send this to Chicago. I don't how it works here."

"Send it FedEx…that's how Father Bartolome sent it to you."

"Okay, um, I'm back at this line—the one that says 1207 for Paris. Your 1292 cover says that your documents were taken to the Sinai around 1203 because of Zara, right? Steven, I think these Guardians had gathered a stash of controversial early Christian documents. Come read this…am I right?"

Steven stared at where she was pointing for two full minutes, and then looked at her. "I think maybe so," he said softly.

"Could these have come…I mean, if these were taken and saved because they were…. Steven, I think somebody was protecting evidence of teachings before Nicea."

"It's not exactly full blown Gnostic, though Susan. What I've seen is arguably just a simple philosophy…more like what Plato says Socrates argued. For example, virtue is from within, it cannot be taught or developed from rules of the Church."

"Sounds like Thomas Jefferson, too," she started and then saw the time. "Steven, we have to go. We'll talk in the cab."

They had packed everything up, written a short note for Jon and arranged to have the package sent to Chicago by 10:30 a.m.

"I put the small set and our notes in your Met bag," Steven said as Susan turned off the lights. "I'll carry it."

"Put these Frango mints in, too—I have my cell phone, cash, ID and a credit card in my pocket. Crap, I have Douglas' card, too—a lot of good that did." They headed for the elevator.

They were deep in discussion as they headed out into the plaza in front of the building to get a cab at the curb. Susan stopped for a minute to check the time on her phone. As she looked up after finding it, she saw 'Brownie' again—he was coming from the shade of the building at a fast pace and heading directly for Steven.

"God damn it—he wants the pictures," she thought as she thrust her phone back in her pocket and gripped her cane with both hands. She started to move between Steven and 'Brownie.'

"Steven—look out, he has a gun," she yelled. Her cane, a Walgreen's special made of metal, was in the air. As 'Brownie' turned to look at her, she brought her cane down hard on 'Brownie's' lower arm, knocking the gun out of it. While he stumbled to pick up the gun, Susan brought her cane down on him again. 'Brownie' fell to his knees. Steven kicked the gun away and then pinned 'Brownie' down with his entire weight. He was holding the bag with the pictures far off to the side. 'Brownie' had never been able to touch the bag.

The commotion had caught the attention of several people. A cop came running over to them. He yelled, "Freeze, all three of you."

"My name is Susan Graves—I just came from my firm, which is in this building here. My husband is the man holding the crook down," she said pointing to Steven, who still had Brownie pinned on the ground. "The guy on the ground may be a murderer." She had pulled Douglas' card out from her pocket as Steven pinned 'Brownie.' She handed it to the cop. "Tell whoever answers that number we think we have Josh's partner, 'Mr. X'," she said. "Can you help my husband, please?" More cops were coming over to them.

A man in a dark suit was now standing by the cop. She hadn't seen where he had come from. He flashed a badge and said to the cop, "I have just made that call, sir. You can give the card back to Ms. Graves." Two cops were now helping Steven brush himself off—he was okay. Handcuffs had already been put on Mr. X and the gun was in a baggie.

"Just like in the movies," she thought.

CHAPTER 78

It took almost an hour to sort everything out. Steven and Susan were surprised at how much of that time they spent standing around waiting for someone to talk to them. The police seemed busy, just not with them. At one point, Steven asked if 'Brownie' was Josh Borne's partner, but all he got was a maybe. Finally, someone came over to them and said that they could leave. Without any fanfare, they walked over to the curb and got a cab to the Peninsula. Susan had called Marta just before 11:00 a.m. to say that they had a little bit of a hold up, but should be at the meeting by 11:30 a.m.

They walked in at 11:35 a.m. As everyone turned to stare at them, Susan realized they probably looked rather disheveled. Steven did have a smudge on the right knee of his pants and on an elbow of his jacket.

Steven held up the bag, and said, "Anyone want to see pictures of Joham's diary?"

"What the hell happened to you two?" Marta asked.

"We got Mr. X arrested," Susan said as she sat down. She got up immediately; she had forgotten to get a cup of coffee. With coffee in hand, she went back and sat down again.

"My wife saved my life. She beat the crap out of Mr. X with her cane when he tried to take these pictures from me," Steven added as he pulled the package of pictures from the bag.

"They're pictures of Joham's diary," Susan added.

"Mr. X had them?" Hershel asked.

"No, Father Bartolome retrieved the pictures from his site in Maine on Wednesday," Susan said. "The chief archaeologist always photographed all of the artifacts found at his site before shipping them off to Shawmut. Father thought that they probably had photographed his stuff too, although technically he found them outside the site's perimeter. Father was right; Jon convinced Father to send them to my office here."

"That's why you went to the office," Marta said sounding miffed. "I wondered why Steven wasn't more upset. Oh, and that's how Father Bartolome knew about you—I couldn't figure out who told him. Damn it, that's what you were whispering about with Jon."

"Yes, sorry but Jon said Father Bartolome wanted me to see them first... now I have."

"Those are the pictures?" Kat asked.

"Only a small format set; we sent the large format originals to my Chicago office, Kat," Susan said. "Father Bartolome borrowed them from the site, so they will have to be returned. I couldn't make large format copies in my office here; so we'll have them done in Chicago before they go back to the chief archaeologist. Marta, where's Douglas?"

"He called at about 10:50 a.m. to say he would be here at Noon," Marta said. "And he asked why we thought that Aldo Morales was Bonnie's step brother. I came close to saying Seattle told us, but instead I told him you would know."

"So, Steven, how did Susan save your life," Hershel interrupted.

Steven and Susan then described their encounter with Mr. X. At the end, Susan told Marta to thank the guys who had tailed them to the Pierre. But for that, she wouldn't have been watching that closely for a tail. She would have missed 'Brownie' entirely. They then called the hospital to check on Jon again. The news was better—they could perhaps visit later in the day.

"We have been busy admiring Joham's box and now we have pictures of Father's materials. Eisen ordered the buffet set up over there so we didn't have to waste time ordering," Kat said. "Susan and Steven should get some food, and then, while they eat, they can take turns telling us what's in the diary."

"We had only a short time with the photos, so we can't tell you a lot," Susan started. "We definitely have two people, João and Joham, who lived about three hundred years apart. We think two of the boxes went from Constantinople to Paris in 1207. We think all three boxes were in Cyprus by 1292. For some reason, Joham took all three boxes and the Guardians to Maine in 1607. They sailed from Wales though, so we have a gap between Cyprus and Wales. The diary is only five two-sided pages; two pages are Portuguese, six are in Latin and two seem to be blank or too faint to read—I can get a written distillation out to everyone within a week."

"We still don't know why these documents were saved together and why they were with our Joham—again the authors of the oldest documents, the Greek ones, are upset with the changes being made to standardize Christianity under Constantine," Steven said. "We do not know why Joham took them to Maine or why the three Guardians were with him."

"We do know the Guardians died in Maine," Susan added.

"That is what Daf thought, too," Kat said.

"Susan, Daf?" Steven prodded.

"Yes, of course. Kat, Eisen, I have a piece to show you," she said as she set out the picture. "Here, it says that the three Guardians have died. And here, Joham says he and Dafydd have survived."

"That's worth a trip half way around the world, isn't Kat?" Hershel said.

"Indeed so," Kat said.

"The Guardians had a nice stash of documents," Steven said. "I have been working mostly on the Greek documents, but I still can't say for sure that they aren't a hoax. It's interesting because first, of course, there is the issue of whether they are old, and then, even if they are old, whether they might be an old hoax. Hershel, I'm sorry I didn't bring them here, but they are so fragile. Even I am working from pictures."

"Could I come to Chicago for a look?" Hershel asked.

"Of course, let's pick a date."

"Susan, I am overjoyed," Kat said. "Eisen," he said as he turned to look at him, "I don't think we ever expected anything quite like this."

"I think even Smith-san would have be overwhelmed."

"But," Kat said turning back to Susan, "why are you and Steven so excited that these documents are critical of the Church?"

"Well, in many ways, organized religion is inconsistent with the teachings of Jesus and the historical record," Susan said. "There also are scholarly arguments that a lot of what became the 'Bible' was picked up from pagan religions. So, when you find writings by people alive at the onset of Christianity and those people are objecting to how the Bible was being standardized under Constantine, it is exciting. Of course, popping up in Maine wouldn't be your first choice."

"The Church supported Constantine as arbiter in exchange for his support of Christianity. As a result, there was picking and choosing from what competing sects believed," Steven added. "Those who lost, like the Gnostics and the Arians, were discredited. Some were able to preserve their beliefs by hiding them. A collection of Gnostic writings were put in a jar and buried in Nag Hamadi in the Fourth century CE. They weren't discovered until 1945. These guarded documents that we have found aren't Gnostic, but they may also have been hidden because they are inconsistent with the standardized Church."

"There also are arguments relating to the relation of God to Jesus," Susan said. The Arians believed that Jesus was in some ways subordinate to God. The 'Trinitarians,' whom Constantine ruled for initially, believed in the Father, the Son and the Holy Ghost who always co-existed. This was one of the early mini-schisms in Christianity; it happened in 325 CE."

"I know from my art studies that Eastern and Western orthodox split in 1054 CE; that was Rome vs. Constantinople. The second one is what?"

"It's when Martin Luther, John Calvin and others broke from the Catholic Church somewhere around 1520 to form the Protestant Church—it's known as the Reformation," Susan answered. "There is a verse in the New Testament, in Romans, that says that the just will live by faith. Luther felt that the Catholic Church's practice of selling indulgences to get to heaven, violated that verse. It's kind of funny, the Catholic Church doesn't sell indulgences anymore, but now Protestant televangelists do. They are always saying send us a check and you won't go to hell."

"Anyway, Kat, maybe tomorrow there will be time for us to better described what we've seen that is so exciting. I'm actually a little beat," Steven said as he sat down. "By the way, do we think Jon's site is okay?"

"Good question, Steven," Kat said. "Marta, shouldn't we secure our site in Maine?

"I think it would be prudent to do so immediately," Marta answered

"Actually, I made a temporary arrangement," Eisen said shyly. "I couldn't sleep last night–I remembered Jon's story about people using bulldozers to look for artifacts. So, I found our bodyguards and got their company's information. Someone should be there by 1:00 p.m. today to begin a watch. Monday they will begin surveying the site for recommendations. I hope you don't mind, sir. We can remove them just as quickly."

"Excellent, Eisen," Kat smiled.

"May I ask for your advice when we see what they propose, Ms. Krejci?"

"Of course, Eisen, here's my card," Marta said thinking again to herself that he was kind of cute.

Eisen turned to Kat, and said in Japanese, "I thought I should get something in place, given that it is the States and someone already buried a crystal up there. I had them agree to charge us directly. I indicated that they would be terminated immediately if word of this got out."

"I'm pleased that you got someone up there."

"The bodyguards were very helpful, sir." They both chuckled.

"Marta, do you think the police will mention us to the press?" Susan asked.

"Well, you did try to kill someone with your cane," Marta laughed. "I'll see if I can find someone–it may be too late, though. Did you give your name to anyone?"

"Just the police...Steven, that's right isn't it?"

"You did call Seattle—that's when they threatened to take your phone."

"Crap," was all Susan could get out.

"Where's Douglas?" Steven asked.

"He'll come tomorrow morning," Marta said. "I guess we now know he's busy figuring out who Susan whacked."

"Ladies and gentlemen," Hershel said, getting everyone's attention. "Since Steven and Susan look beat, I suggest we adjourn as soon as everyone has finished eating and meet again tomorrow morning before everyone goes home."

"That does sound good," Susan said. "Steven?"

"Yes, of course, then Susan and I can review a few things before we continue our discussion," Steven said. "How about getting together tomorrow for breakfast at 9:00 a.m.? Susan, can you get us this room again—with plenty of bacon?"

"Yes, dear," Susan said.

"One more thing, Steven," Hershel said. "Could you also arrange for me to meet David?"

"Well, I am planning to see him in Shanghai in a couple of weeks. He looked at Kat and Eisen and said, "Maybe we can pin down a date for our next meeting. Would Shanghai be okay?"

"We would like to meet David as well," Kat answered. "May we keep the box today?"

"I think we want you to safeguard it in Tokyo—after all, it came from your property," Steven said. "I would like to keep the documents for a few days so that I can finish checking the originals against the pictures we have."

"But of course, Steven," Kat said.

"Perhaps then we should get the documents to Tokyo, too…."

"Eisen, will you take charge of arranging for these to be moved professionally and then properly stored?"

"Yes, of course. I will start the process immediately, so that I will be ready for you, sir."

"Good, to allay any fears, the originals are presently being kept for me at a friend's conservation facility in Chicago under a controlled environment. Susan and I also need to get everyone a reading list."

"Then, we are adjourned until tomorrow," Kat said.

"I want to go to the Met for a couple of hours," Steven said turning to Susan and Marta. "Either of you want to join me?"

"I'm off for a nap," Marta said. "Susan, I asked the question—I'll text you if I hear anything."

"Steven, meet me at 2:00 p.m. in the restaurant in the American Wing—I have some emails to return. Damn it, look at that dent on my cane. Wait, email me that picture of the name we couldn't decipher. I'll print it for Jon."

As Susan walked out with Marta, she asked, "Wilhelm won't be a damn Douglas, will he? Is Douglas going to show up tomorrow morning?"

"Wilhelm's going into the research group for now. That's where I spent my time until I was about 30, and then they sent me out," she said. "Douglas will come tomorrow morning to brief us. Cy is coming up tonight to have dinner with me."

"That's great; will we see you at breakfast tomorrow?"

"Of course. Aren't you going to ask me where he's staying?"

"No, you'll tell me at some point. Have fun."

CHAPTER 79

Steven had Susan check on Jon as they left the Met. He was now able to see visitors for short periods, so she and Steven went to see him.

"Hey, Jon—we brought you a little box of Frango mints. You look a lot better than you did yesterday," Susan said.

"I heard everything is over," he said. "I got a short briefing this morning. Have my guards left, yet?" he asked.

"They're still mulling around out there," Susan said. "Maybe someone forgot to tell them they could go home."

"Any news on Clay?"

"No, Jon, not yet," Steven said. "We need you to get out of here. Kat wants you to look for those other two boxes. By the way, Eisen put guards up at your site."

"Susan, did you get the pictures?" he asked.

"Yes, Steven and I looked at them this morning and then sent them to my Chicago office. We'll make large format copies there and then return them to Shawmut. It's two men, Jon. One is João and one is Joham. They give a very short history of how they helped guard the documents."

"We'll all meet again in Shanghai in a couple of weeks," Steven added. "David, our expert for the Hebrew and Aramaic texts is there. We'll hook you in by Skype for the meetings if you can't travel by then. Right now, though, you need to get your strength back."

"I should be out in a couple of days."

"Good, we'll need your help in deciphering the Joham documents. I can read the Latin, but I think you are going to be much more familiar with his travels in Maine—we may even have an Indian tribal name or two."

"Of course," Jon said. "I'm anxious to get back to work."

"We're so sorry about Father."

He was at peace with his life, Susan. I will miss him, though."

"Time's up," a nurse said as she came into Jon's room. "Dr. Christiansen needs some rest, now."

"We'll stop by tomorrow, Jon. Here, I have a picture for you...maybe tomorrow you can tell us if it's an Indian tribe."

CHAPTER 80

Sunday morning, Susan was up at 7:00 a.m. to look for coffee and a copy of the *New York Tribune Herald*. She grabbed her phone and headed for the hotel restaurant. She had a text from Seattle, which said "sorry for the publicity; the pictures are from a reader's iPhone so, we had to use them; got you in action." Susan picked up a copy of the newspaper in the restaurant. A couple of pictures of her, Steven and 'Mr. X,' aka Joseph Beria, were there on the front page. One shot had her whacking Beria as Steven swung the bag away; the second had Steven with Beria pinned down. She let out a sigh of relief–they were described only as 'two unidentified people' in the picture caption and the body of the article. She would have to thank Seattle, and maybe Marta.

She went into the restaurant, ordered coffee and continued reading the article. In the bottom half of the article, she saw mugs of Josh Borne, Seth Thomas, and Bonnie Nogueira. The police had found the hit and run driver–a 'young thug' was all they said. There was a nice little blurb about Father Bartolome… at least he wasn't part of the ring. It was hard to read about Father knowing that he was now dead. It would be even harder to decide when to show the article to Jon.

Susan sat for a minute. Who the hell was this Joseph Beria? As she read, she started chuckling to herself. He was a 62 year old American. He owned the Hippolyta Gallery on Madison Avenue near the Whitney in New York until 2003, when it closed after investigators found several objects in the gallery that had been illegally imported from Turkey. Like Richard Prenbryer, Beria had the objects on consignment, so he somehow wasn't charged. The article said he was selling an estimated $10 million a year now by finding pieces for private collectors. Apparently, Beria would be out of business for good this time.

She and Steven had been to Beria's Gallery a couple of times when they were young, but the pieces had all been out of reach then, thank God. She was pretty sure that they had never met Beria himself until yesterday. He would have been far too busy for a couple just out of law school. Her phone rang–it was Steven.

"Where are you?"

"I'm down in the restaurant having a cup of coffee and reading the paper. Do you remember the Hippolyta Gallery by the Whitney?"

"It closed years ago. The owner was pretty full of himself–didn't he go to jail?"

"Not then, but he will now. He's the guy I whacked and you sat on," she laughed. "By the way, you're famous, Steven."

"In the *Herald*?" he asked.

"Yep, we're in a picture on the bottom of the front page. Luckily, they only named the armed robber, Joseph Beria."

"I guess we got even with the snooty bastard. Do they say what his role was?"

"Not exactly, but the gist of it is that Beria would let Seth, the Clockmaker, know what his clients wanted. Seth would have Josh work with his network, which included people like Bonnie, to find something that might be suitable. Then Richard Prenbryer or another conservator in the ring would doctor it to order. Beria and Seth handled the buyers, mostly in the Middle East, for the dressed up goods. It seems so damn simple, Steven. Except...," she stopped.

"Except what?"

"Why did he come after us? I'm thinking maybe he was the guy on the train with Josh since Seattle confirmed it couldn't be Aldo because of when they met with him. But we weren't involved in...crap, Josh actually called you, didn't he? But what was Beria after?

"It had to be the box or the pictures, right?"

"Well, he couldn't know about the box, so he had to be after the diary pictures. Either Father or Clay had to tell him that they were shipped to me."

"Then you think Clay tipped Beria off?" Steven asked.

"Damn it, yes," she said. "So that bastard got Father killed and almost got us as well. Father sent the pictures to me because he thought someone would take them. It had to be either Beria or Aldo who was after the pictures. But does that mean Clay was part of the ring or just an ass."

"See if Marta or Seattle has found anything on that step brother, Aldo Morales, or that Darin guy."

"Good idea," she said. It was hard to believe that Jon had come to Chicago less than three weeks ago. There wasn't anything they could have done to stop Father Bartolome's murder. It wasn't until Bob found the tie to Shawmut and Steven realized that 'Clay' was a reference to Clarence Duvall that everything started to unravel. But why did this Beria come after them… she texted Seattle.

"Susan, are you there?"

"Yes, I was just texting Seattle and thinking about Father," she answered.

"I think he was a good guy, Susan. I just don't know about Clay, though. At least those klepto movie stars don't get their friends killed. Anyway, Clay must have told Father that Bonnie Nogueira had doctored the catalog records and stolen his material. Maybe Father was trying to stop things or he figured that Bonnie was in danger. Come upstairs."

"I'll be right up." When she got to the room, Steven was sitting on the bed reading one of the documents. "What are you looking at?"

"These pictures of the documents Marta's guy took aren't too bad. I'm looking at the Ammonius letter again. The author says they've stolen the death and resurrection of Christ from Hadrian's Antinous cult, but there is a little chunk missing right where I need it. The author also has a litany of new Church practices that he says are pagan."

"I assume you mean Antinous drowned in the Nile and thereby became a God."

Renegades among the Tumbleweeds

"Yes, as I said, death and resurrection, like Jesus, who died and was resurrected."

"But anyone who drowned in the Nile became a god, Steven."

"Well, you are reborn when you are baptized too. Anyway, the Antinous cult spread throughout the Roman World under Hadrian."

"We still need to figure out whether these documents are even real, Steven. If they are, I guess we'll have to worry about the Church coming after us next."

"Beria's missing friend will probably get us first, dear. Why did Beria want to shoot us, anyway?"

"You just convinced me that he would shoot us to get the pictures," she said. "The problem is that the diary pictures were stored in a shed that probably was locked. I know Father got a key from Clay, but who gave it to him? It must be that guy I have to send the pictures back to."

"Susan, maybe Father talked to Aldo Morales, the step brother, about saving Bonnie. The step brother might have made up the 'someone' who was arguing with Bonnie. We still haven't heard anything from Marta or Seattle about that Darin guy either."

"So we are right; they still don't have everyone, damn it," Susan said. "I'll talk with Marta, if she makes it to the meeting. Cy was here in New York at least for dinner last night, so I'm not going to call her…I'm not that brave."

"Well, if she doesn't want us dead, she can focus on the missing guy. Susan, do you think anyone outside our little group knows about the box?"

"Jon is the weak link, Steven. I doubt he would have said anything to Clay, but he may have said something to Father Bartolome when they talked about Joham. But if Beria were after the box, then…no, it's the pictures, not the box that ties them to the murders and the theft. So, you're free to focus on the box."

"I'm making progress, but we still don't know why these were collected. David and I are pretty sure that they are old, and of course, Hershel says the map is at least 400 or so years old. But they may have been touched up in medieval times when they were copied. If they are as old as they purport to be…well, this Ammonius letter, it's the Alexandrian bishop writing to Hosius of Cordova."

"He's got a lot to complain about, since Hosius was one of Constantine's anti-Arian advisors," she said. "Are all three critical of the Council of Nicea?"

"Ammonius definitely is critical. He also says Constantine isn't a Christian and way too much from Hadrian's Antinous Cult is being incorporated into the new religion. The second one, the anonymous one from Rome, says that whoever copied the letters of the disciple Paul, couldn't read Greek—he says the translation has the teaching all wrong. It's short, but succinctly says that only the words spoken by Jesus himself are words from God. It's interesting, Susan. The writer is blaming the translator, not Paul. This third one, Secundus, only says that Constantine is not, and cannot be, God. Oh, and he wasn't chosen by God as God doesn't do that—that means that there is no 'divine right' to rule."

"That's a pretty sensitive issue if it's coming up then. I mean, just by way of example, Julius Caesar traced his lineage back to the Goddess Venus. I guess divine right is a little different—it's more like 'God put me in charge, so shut up.' Divine right has been used by kings and rulers for eons; but I didn't think it was formally embraced until the 1600s. Didn't GW say that God chose him for President?"

"Bush said God told him to invade Iraq, too."

"Well, 'divine right' comes from 1 Peter 2:13 and Romans 13:1. Actually, it's clearest in Romans—it says the powers that be are ordained by God. That's a good argument for war—God ordains Catholic kings and Protestant kings; they have at it and He sits back and watches."

"Susan, this is serious. Um, I've been waiting to tell you this, but I talked to David yesterday while I waited for you at the Met. We have a significant issue with the Aramaic pieces."

"That little fragment and the letter?"

"Yes, I was going to tell you at dinner last night, but you looked so tired… actually we were both too tired. I didn't have the energy, and I hadn't quite finished thinking about them."

"What is it, Steven?"

"Well, you know that the Eastern Orthodoxy regards Constantine as being equal to the Apostles." He stopped for a minute.

"Yes, they even use the term iso-apostolos for him," she said. "And he did build the Church of the Holy Apostles where he planned to have himself and remains of the Apostles entombed."

"He was to have six Apostles on each side of him. And you know about the Talpiot Tomb which is in a suburb of Jerusalem."

"Yes, they found 10 ossuaries there, but only about half had names on them. I don't remember all of the names, but the one you obviously want me to say is Jesus, son of Joseph or *Yeshau bar Yehosef*...so?"

"There were six with inscriptions. Another one was Judah, son of Jesus *Yehuda bar Yeshua*. That's why they say it may be the tomb of Jesus' family."

"Steven, get to the point, it's getting late."

"Well, I told you I thought the Aramaic letter was written to Eusebius in 338 CE, right?"

"Yes, he died right around then...339 CE, I think. Maybe the letter gave him a heart attack."

"Susan, this isn't funny. David says it's actually only a reference to Eusebius; the letter is written to an aide of Constantine's son, Constantius II. The aide had been a student of Eusebius. Obviously, it's written after Constantine's death in 337 CE. We can't read the writer's name, but he is writing from Jerusalem."

"That's a bummer...," Susan said, looking at her watch.

"Not really, Susan. The letter relates to completion of the Church of the Holy Apostles by Constantius and the interment of Constantine there."

"Steven, just tell me, what does it say? We'll be late for the meeting."

"Well, damn it, it's seeking confirmation that four of the ossuaries that his son, Constantius II, ordered for the Church will be accepted when delivered. David says the.... Susan, stop laughing, I am serious. So, it seems that a tomb of Jesus and others was known during the time of Constantine."

"Steven, I can guess what's coming and either David was pulling your leg or you are pulling mine. I mean, everybody and his uncle would be after us," Susan said. "This is just too…what does Norman think?"

"I haven't told Norman, but David wants me to bring this letter to Shanghai as soon as possible," Steven said. "Damn it, if these letters are real, people will say we are two amateurs who don't know what we are doing. At least David is an expert. Besides, if the Franciscans can have St. Peter's ossuary in Jerusalem, then why couldn't there be more."

"Steven, help me, here; the letter talks about ossuaries being delivered to the Church. Does it actually give names?"

"No, except it does say they have sent someone to Hierapolis to fetch the body of Philip and to Edessa for Thomas. I mentioned the Talpiot tomb, but these four ossuaries probably aren't from there. There is no mention of Jesus, the son of Joseph. But then, there shouldn't be, since it's only the Church of the Apostles."

"Steven, that's interesting…you know Marco Polo said that Thomas died near Chennai in India, but most of his relics, including his bones were sent to Edessa around 230 CE. I believe he saw them there. So, the fact they knew where to go to get the ossuary or whatever is impressive. I think that Thomas' remains ended up in Italy in the thirteenth century."

"Yes, well, the letter says that the four are ready, more or less, for delivery, they are fetching two more and they will have the other six within a year. Don't laugh…as I said, David helped me with this. I want it to say something else, but isn't a long letter. I'll talk with David again tomorrow night. I want to go to Shanghai by the end of next week, could you join me? Oh, the scrap has names of the Apostles on it."

Susan sat for a minute looking at Steven; he truly seemed serious. "I have my closing May 1. I guess you would be safer there. Um, doesn't this letter suggest that these may all be old fakes? Anyway, damn it, we have a bigger issue, Steven. You know someone else likely is still out there."

"What is it, Steven?"

"Well, you know that the Eastern Orthodoxy regards Constantine as being equal to the Apostles." He stopped for a minute.

"Yes, they even use the term iso-apostolos for him," she said. "And he did build the Church of the Holy Apostles where he planned to have himself and remains of the Apostles entombed."

"He was to have six Apostles on each side of him. And you know about the Talpiot Tomb which is in a suburb of Jerusalem."

"Yes, they found 10 ossuaries there, but only about half had names on them. I don't remember all of the names, but the one you obviously want me to say is Jesus, son of Joseph or *Yeshau bar Yehosef*...so?"

"There were six with inscriptions. Another one was Judah, son of Jesus *Yehuda bar Yeshua*. That's why they say it may be the tomb of Jesus' family."

"Steven, get to the point, it's getting late."

"Well, I told you I thought the Aramaic letter was written to Eusebius in 338 CE, right?"

"Yes, he died right around then...339 CE, I think. Maybe the letter gave him a heart attack."

"Susan, this isn't funny. David says it's actually only a reference to Eusebius; the letter is written to an aide of Constantine's son, Constantius II. The aide had been a student of Eusebius. Obviously, it's written after Constantine's death in 337 CE. We can't read the writer's name, but he is writing from Jerusalem."

"That's a bummer...," Susan said, looking at her watch.

"Not really, Susan. The letter relates to completion of the Church of the Holy Apostles by Constantius and the interment of Constantine there."

"Steven, just tell me, what does it say? We'll be late for the meeting."

"Well, damn it, it's seeking confirmation that four of the ossuaries that his son, Constantius II, ordered for the Church will be accepted when delivered. David says the.... Susan, stop laughing, I am serious. So, it seems that a tomb of Jesus and others was known during the time of Constantine."

"Steven, I can guess what's coming and either David was pulling your leg or you are pulling mine. I mean, everybody and his uncle would be after us," Susan said. "This is just too…what does Norman think?"

"I haven't told Norman, but David wants me to bring this letter to Shanghai as soon as possible," Steven said. "Damn it, if these letters are real, people will say we are two amateurs who don't know what we are doing. At least David is an expert. Besides, if the Franciscans can have St. Peter's ossuary in Jerusalem, then why couldn't there be more."

"Steven, help me, here; the letter talks about ossuaries being delivered to the Church. Does it actually give names?"

"No, except it does say they have sent someone to Hierapolis to fetch the body of Philip and to Edessa for Thomas. I mentioned the Talpiot tomb, but these four ossuaries probably aren't from there. There is no mention of Jesus, the son of Joseph. But then, there shouldn't be, since it's only the Church of the Apostles."

"Steven, that's interesting…you know Marco Polo said that Thomas died near Chennai in India, but most of his relics, including his bones were sent to Edessa around 230 CE. I believe he saw them there. So, the fact they knew where to go to get the ossuary or whatever is impressive. I think that Thomas' remains ended up in Italy in the thirteenth century."

"Yes, well, the letter says that the four are ready, more or less, for delivery, they are fetching two more and they will have the other six within a year. Don't laugh.…as I said, David helped me with this. I want it to say something else, but it isn't a long letter. I'll talk with David again tomorrow night. I want to go to Shanghai by the end of next week, could you join me? Oh, the scrap has names of the Apostles on it."

Susan sat for a minute looking at Steven; he truly seemed serious. "I have my closing May 10. I guess you would be safer there. Um, doesn't this letter suggest that these may all be old fakes? Anyway, damn it, we have a bigger issue, Steven. You know someone else likely is still out there."

"Who?"

"I don't know, but do you think Beria knew Father Bartolome? Also, even if Beria was the last of the ring with nothing to lose, he shouldn't have risked coming after us with a damn gun. He had to want the diary pictures, but just because they incriminated him and his pals?"

"That's a pretty damning piece of evidence; we'll ask Ms. Spy. In the meantime, we need to work on these documents."

"Whatever, but keep the Aramaic stuff with David quiet for now. Put your shoes on...we have to be downstairs in 10 minutes. I'll check with Seattle, too."

When Susan and Steven got to the meeting, they found everyone poring over the *Herald* article.

"Your young friend did well," Hershel said to Susan. "Her name is on the article."

"And they didn't name us," Susan said.

"Gentlemen," Steven said. "Are we ready to wrap things up until Shanghai?"

"Yes, and Chicago for Hershel," Kat said. "Eisen was on the phone with Ms. Short for over an hour this morning giving her all of the details. He probably can recite the entire *Herald* article by now. The article ran in London too, so Ms. Short had her paper in front of her for reference. I imagine the conversation about the poison took a while–both Eisen and Ms. Short are Agatha Christie buffs. Steven, Hershel, if I ever am found poisoned, do remember that Eisen loves Agatha Christie."

"Where is Eisen, Kat?" Susan asked.

"He is arranging to have Dr. Christiansen transferred to Tokyo. Marta checked for us–Jon has no real family left. Now, she's helping Eisen. We will stay here in New York until Jon is well enough for us to get him to Tokyo– supposedly it will be only a couple of days. Eisen also has someone escorting the dog to New York, so the dog will come with us. Jon's a bit young, but we'll have him join our 'Old Men's Club.' Besides, after all of this excitement, Eisen will need something to keep him busy."

"As Eisen said, Tokyo is beautiful this time of year." Susan started to say something else, but Marta walked in with Eisen. "Marta, can I talk to you for a minute?" she said as she walked over to Marta.

CHAPTER 81

"What's up, Susan?" Marta said.

"I just got a text from Seattle; it's in response to one I sent her about an hour ago. I said I thought Beria was after the diary pictures."

"Maybe he just wanted to shoot you, Susan. God knows I've wanted to at times. Beria did have a silencer on his gun."

"But why would a 62-year old art dealer run out into the plaza to shoot us. Either he was a bad aim and needed to be close to hit us or he wanted the pictures because they tie everything together. Here, read her answer," Susan said as she handed Marta her phone.

"So, you told Seattle you think the step brother, Aldo Morales, is involved? Crap, Seattle says Aldo has disappeared and he is Darin Carvalho, that damn assistant professor at Shawmut. Nice college, Susan…it's full of crooks."

"You already knew Darin was at Shawmut. She also says he's the Clockmaker's brother, not Bonnie's step brother."

"Damn, they can't find him?"

"Nope. The thing is—Jon said Father went to get the pictures because he thought someone might take them. This Aldo or Darin guy is the only one we don't know anything about. I'm going to give Seattle a call…." She looked to the table and saw that Steven had started without her.

"I thought Father got them so he could send them to you."

"His dad talked him into that. Have you heard anything about Clay?"

"I will see what I can find out," Marta said. "More importantly, I want to make sure we still have guys around you."

Susan stepped outside to call Seattle. Seattle answered on the first ring.

"Susan, I was just going to call you—is your spy friend with you?"

"Yes, she's making sure we still have protection. My cane already has one dent in it—maybe it'll get another. Wait, Marta's back—I'll put this on speaker. Can you hear us, Seattle?"

"Yes. You called, so go ahead," Seattle said.

"Well, here's the deal—Father called me on Friday afternoon. He had gone to his old archaeology site on Wednesday and retrieved pictures of his pieces that were stored there. He thought someone else would be after them, too. So, he sent them to my office here in New York. I didn't tell anyone because Father asked that I look at them first, which I did yesterday morning."

"And you think Beria knew you had them?"

"The site was locked, so Father inferred that Clay had someone get them the keys. Aldo Morales, whom we now know is the Clockmaker's brother, Darin Carvalho, is at Shawmut," she started. "He may have fetched the keys for Clay. Father found Clay rummaging through the package before it was sent to me. Maybe Clay confirmed the pictures were there for Aldo/Darin—there just isn't anyone else. Jon also knew Father sent me the pictures—that may be why Father asked that Jon be protected at the hospital. What's so funny?"

"My father said I would like you," she answered.

"Anyway, Clay may have told Aldo/Darin the package was sent to me. Since Aldo/Darin was tied up as a witness in Brookline on Friday night, Beria must have been on the train with Father and Josh Friday night. I saw Beria a couple of times Saturday—he sat at a table behind us at breakfast yesterday at the Pierre and he left when Steven and I did. He was in the cab line behind us and he was there in the plaza in front of my office when we came out—ready to shoot us."

"You really think it was these pictures?" Seattle asked.

"What else could he be after?"

"And you think Beria was on the train with Josh and Father Bartolome?" Marta asked.

"My guess," Susan said. "It sounds like Clay alerted Darin, who then told Beria or Josh."

"Damn it," Marta said.

"Marta, Seattle, I don't think Father knew either of them. Also, I know Darin didn't drive the car the killed Bonnie, but Father said he's the 'guy.' That must mean he hired the thug."

"We need to get this new information out."

"Seattle, I need to ask you to wait until I make a call," Marta said.

"I'll give you 15 minutes, Marta," Seattle said. "Starting now."

CHAPTER 82

Susan walked back in to the meeting. "Gentlemen, I think I can give you a chronology based on the diary photos we got yesterday—up to a point. Steven and I cannot make out the last years...Hershel, I know you could get the dates for us if we had the originals, but we don't. Not yet anyway."

"I'll certainly try if we do, Susan," Hershel said.

"Steven?"

"Go for it dear," he said. "As usual, gentlemen, I'm not sure when she got time to do this."

"Okay, I set it out here," she said passing out copies of a hand-written page as Marta walked back in. "We have four pieces that tell us something about the history of our documents. Even so, we cannot get all the way to sailing from Wales, but we do get close."

"You have the Latin attestation, the 1292 letter, the diary and what?" Hershel asked.

"We have a second Latin piece that sheds more light—it's a legal document with a seal; it is older than the attestation."

"As a reminder, we have the two Latin pieces, the 1292 cover, three Koine Greek letters, an Aramaic letter and three scraps, for a total of 10 pieces," Steven said. "Susan thinks there are 21 documents in the three boxes, but we don't know if it includes our 10."

"We don't know what's in the other two boxes, but I will get to those in a minute. Briefly, an unnamed person wrote the 1292 cover letter in Cyprus. It says that the documents were taken from Constantinople to St. Catherine's Monastery in 1203, to protect them from the Fourth Crusade. The crusaders sacked Zara, a Christian city, as they were heading to Constantinople. They anticipated similar looting of Constantinople, so somebody gathered our letters and took them to the Sinai. Copies were made at St. Catherine's Monastery; those were finished in 1267. They were moved to Acre in 1290, then on to Cyprus in 1291. Steven, we may want a Medievalist to look at the Latin...some of the word phrasings are difficult."

"Perhaps I can help...Eisen, please put Mrs. Graves in touch with Florencio's graduate student, Dr. Boccioni," Kat said. "Where is Zara?"

"It's in Croatia; it's also known as Zadar," Steven answered. "Lest we think our crusaders were men of God, Pope Innocent III, threatened the crusaders with excommunication if they attacked Christian cities like Zara, but they attacked anyway. Zara was a trade rival of Venice, and Venice financed the Fourth Crusade, so they sacked Zara to repay their debts."

"Probably got all the Jews on their way," Marta commented.

"That's it for our documents," Steven said. "The Pope was so upset with the sackings that he installed the Hospitaliers, Templars and Cistercians as 'protectors' of Byzantium under his rule. He sent them because they didn't participate in the sacking," Steven added. "There is an unclear segment in the Latin seal document that suggests that some documents were taken from Constantinople to Paris by one or more Guardians—that is where there is a reference to Imperium Romaniae. I believe those materials are in one of the boxes we have yet to find."

"We aren't sure how our documents got to St. Catherine's, but it has always been a major repository of early Christian documents," Susan continued. "For example, the Codex Sinaiticus was supposedly found there in the 1800s. Anyway, the copying at St. Catherine's was finished in 1267. As I mentioned, the copies went from St. Catherine's to Acre in 1290. Now, it may be a coincidence, but you should know the Templars lost Acre in 1291 and retreated to Cyprus. The Templars were given sanctuary at Tomar, Portugal when the French King finally prevailed and Pope Clement dissolved the Templar order in 1312. Actually, they became the Knights of the Order of Christ in Portugal.

"Are you saying the Templars took these?" Marta asked.

"Marta, we're just giving you plausible dates—there isn't much information. Oh, and we are not talking about our two Latin pieces. Also, we believe that our Joham was a member of the Order of Christ in Portugal."

"As you can see on Susan's sheet, we have a couple of new dates," Steven added. "Susan, you might as well finish."

"Okay, João says his uncle took our documents from St. Catherine's to Acre in 1290. João then took them to Cyprus in 1291, but we don't know who wrote the cover letter in Cyprus in 1292. João also picked up two boxes in Paris in 1305; he, or someone with him, took those boxes and the Cyprus documents to Tomar in that year. The last date we have before the New World is 1540, when "three boxes" were taken from Tomar back to Cyprus. This may have been because in 1536, the Portuguese Inquisition was formally established at the request of King João; he's no relation to our João. In 1541, Portugal established a Court of Inquisition at Tomar. That's all we know until Joham sails from Wales with Dafydd. The section where 1541 to about 1599 should be is illegible, but I think that Joham made a trip to Port Royale during that end of that period."

"We are hoping those other two boxes will help," Steven added.

"We also may be able to get more from the diary pictures and the Latin seal document, after we spend more time with them," Susan said.

"We still have a lot of work to do before Shanghai, but I guess that's a perfect teaser to adjourn on," Steven said. "Susan, Eisen, is it Friday, May 24 for Shanghai, now?"

"Yes, Steven," she said as she turned and smiled at Eisen. "Is that correct, Mr. Shakura?"

"Yes, Mrs. Graves," he said with a wink.

CHAPTER 83

Susan met with the Big A on Monday, May 6. Her last day would be June 30. She would use the time to finish Jameson, which was still closing on Friday, May 10. She also would transition her clients to others in her firm. The police still hadn't found Darin Carvalho.

Susan sent out Father's large format pictures to be copied that same morning. When the originals and copies came back on Wednesday, May 8, she and Steven compared the two sets to make sure that no data had been lost in copying. By Thursday morning, she had the large and small format originals packed up and ready to go back to the archaeologist as Father Bartholome had requested. As she sat looking at the still unsealed package, she decided to call Steven.

"Good morning, I have a question," she said.

"Well, I'm awake now, so what is it?"

"I'm ready to send these pictures back, but I thought I might call the archaeologist first and see if he has any raw data for the pictures…it would be nice if we could enhance that area where Joham should have said where he was before he went to Wales."

"See what Marta thinks. I'm surprised that no one has asked for them."

"Maybe the note that Father left at the shed just said his 'friend' would return them. It's also possible that no one has been up there."

"Or, someone may have taken the note. Has anyone asked Kat for Dr. Smith's two pieces?"

"I don't know. I think they're leaving today for Tokyo with Jon. I'll call Marta."

"By the way, would you mind if I go to Shanghai May 20 to spend a couple extra days with David? Oh, and Hershel is still in New York. He wants to come here Saturday. Is that okay?"

"Fine, I'm going to call Marta, now. Um, you'll have to entertain Hershel; my closing is now Monday, May 13." Susan sat for a minute after hanging up with Steven, and then called Marta.

"Yes? Did you call to ask if I hate being in DC?" Marta asked.

"Since I caught you in a good mood, did Cy stay with you in New York?

"Jesus, today's Thursday—that was almost a week ago."

"Just kidding, I really called because I'm sending Father's pictures back to Shawmut. However, I'm thinking that the archaeologist might have kept the raw data for the pictures. I'm going to call him, unless you think it's a bad idea."

"They aren't Father Bartolome's pictures."

"And you are a bitch today…is there a problem if I call him?"

"No one has contacted you yet about returning them?"

"No, Father said he left a note saying that his friend would return them. So, maybe he didn't leave my name or maybe no one has been there."

"You said Father had a key right?"

"Yes, Clay obviously couldn't go to Shawmut, so he found someone to fetch it for him; maybe it was the Shawmut guy, Darin Carvalho. I do have to send the pictures back, though."

"Well, go ahead then; it's better than him sending the cops to get those pictures from you."

"He'd have to find me first…I'm kidding, they're going back today. By the way, is there any news on this Darin guy?"

"Susan, I wish I could tell you, but I don't know."

"Crap."

"When are you going to Shanghai?"

"Steven is going Monday, May 20 and I'm going on Wednesday, May 22. The meeting isn't until Friday, May 24. We'll meet Thursday evening for dinner."

"I'll go on your flight. Have Jane get me a ticket, so we can sit together. Where are we staying?"

"At the Peninsula, I guess I should have Jane get you a room too. I'll call you if anything comes up." She hung up and then tried Dr. Nielsen. His secretary informed her that he was on vacation until the week of May 20. She arranged to call him Wednesday morning, May 22 at 9:30 a.m. Boston time.

CHAPTER 84

Hershel came to Chicago Friday afternoon. They had dinner that evening at Gibson's, pursuant to Hershel's request. They finalized a plan for conserving Kat's documents and the documents from the box, subject to Kat's approval. Hershel and Steven spent Saturday cross-checking annotations that Steven had made on the photographs that were taken at Chase.

They confirmed with Kat that Steven would take the originals to Shanghai. From there, Hershel would take them on to Zurich for proper conservation. Steven and Eisen had contacted Eilat Shiloh and convinced her to come to Shanghai. Hershel would work with her to see if they could enhance any of the areas that were illegible. Susan then called Artemisia Boccioni, Kat's medieval specialist. Dr. Boccioni would work with Susan to confirm her translation of two sentences in the seal document.

The week flew by. Jameson closed smoothly in New York on May 13. She was back in New York on Friday, May 17 for the closing dinner and home helping Steven get ready for Shanghai on Saturday.

As Steven got ready to leave on Monday, he said, "Tell Mary that David, Hershel and I would like to have dinner with her Tuesday night–David will email her a location."

"Yes, dear. She's going to pick me up at the airport Thursday night. Will you tell her that Marta will be with me?"

"You're too chicken to tell her?"

"What do you think?"

"That'll be a fun ride." He laughed.

"By the way, I asked Kat's medieval specialist to help translate that section of the seal document that I showed you. I'm convinced that it talks about the Sufis."

"Kat has a medieval specialist?" Um, you didn't mention Sufis, may I see?"

"First, it's that woman who is helping him with a paper he's doing. Her name is Artemisia Boccioni. Second, he told me to contact her when we were in New York. And third, I did show you and you ignored me. They aren't named, but to me, it clearly is a brief recitation of Sufi thought. I'll email the text to you, now go or you'll be late for your flight."

Wednesday morning, Susan called Dr. Nielsen. She introduced herself as a friend of Father Bartolome and his father. After they talked for a while about Father Bartolome, Susan asked, "Did Father tell you he was looking for pictures of some parchment he had found near your site last year?"

"Well, yes. I didn't remember his materials, but I told him he could go look. That was back around the end of April. If we took pictures, they would still be in our storage shed there. The artifacts themselves would have been shipped back here to Shawmut. Father had a Shawmut friend pick up the keys to the storage shed. I got the keys back by FedEx a couple of days later. Did he go up there?"

"Yes, have you been to your site lately?"

"No, we closed it in mid-November; we don't plan to reopen it until June 1. Why do you ask?"

"Father borrowed the pictures and sent them to me. He wanted me to look at them in connection with a project he and I were working on with his dad, Jon Christiansen."

"I've never met Dr. Christiansen, but he is well-respected. How is he doing after all of this?"

Susan told him about Jon's heart attack and added that he still planned to retire at the end of the year. "As for your pictures of Father's materials, they are sitting here on my desk. I have them ready to go back to you, but I was wondering if you might have raw data for any of these pictures?"

"I keep that here in my office—may I ask what you are looking for?"

"There's a small area on the third page that we can't read. We think the parchment is old, but that the writing is relatively recent."

"Like a forgery?"

"Maybe, but it also may be that somebody just used old parchment to write something. These are pictures of Father's materials that were stolen. As far as I know, the originals haven't been found."

"Those pictures would have been shot using a separate chip, since they weren't relevant to what we were working on," Dr. Nielsen said. "The chip should be stored in a miscellaneous folder, which is nearly empty. If we kept it, it'll be easy to find."

"Thanks...um, you might want to send the local police over to check your shed. Father sent me the pictures in part because he thought someone might steal them. As I said, the stuff that Father sent to Shawmut last year is missing. It was probably stolen and then doctored up in London for sale overseas. Father was afraid that the thief might know about your practice of taking pictures."

"The local police drive by every week, but I'll call them and tell them what you said. Can you give me your contact information, please?"

"I'm sending you an email with it, now. Did Father's friend, Clay Duvall, pick up your keys?"

"No, but I've heard about our now infamous kleptomaniac. It's too bad about him. I heard about his suicide. At least everything that Clay took will come back to Shawmut."

"Clay committed suicide?" Susan asked, stunned. "I hadn't heard that. When was that?"

"Gee, I think it was maybe a week ago. It was a big deal in our local paper because of Shawmut. The paper said that he poisoned himself. I guess he was out on bail. Anyway, Clay's friend, Darin Carvalho, got the keys," he said. "The rumor here is that Darin's in trouble too and he has disappeared. Is that right?"

"Shawmut's been pretty popular with the reporters lately," she said as she processed the information. "Darin's brother, Donald, apparently was the leader of an antiquities forgery ring. He's in jail in Paris, I think. I just sent you an attachment with a picture of the segment I need. My assistant will send you the tracking information when your package goes out later today."

"I have a little time right now, so I'll see what I can find."

Susan looked at her watch—it was already 9:25 a.m. in Chicago. She had talked with Dr. Nielsen for almost an hour. She sealed the package, walked out to Jane and asked her to send it to Dr. Nielsen. Jane would send the FedEx tracking information as well. She picked up the phone and called Marta's office. Marta didn't answer, so, when she knew Jane had time to get back to her desk, she called and asked her to find Marta.

Susan sat at her desk looking for the card from the FBI. Just as she found it, Jane came in. "Marta is packing; she said to call her only if it's really important, otherwise she'll see you at the gate," Jane told her. "Also, Steven is holding for you."

"Damn, it's only 9:35 a.m., and she doesn't need to leave until noon," Susan said. "Put Steven through…it's late in Shanghai."

"I know you're busy getting ready to leave, but I thought I would check in," he said. "Anything new?"

"Well, three things—first, I spoke with Dr. Nielsen and he is checking to see if he can send me a better picture of that diary segment that is totally illegible. I'm hoping to get it before I leave for the airport at noon. How are things there?"

"We just had dinner with Mary…between her and David, Hershel and I were well entertained. So, Dr. Nielsen might have something?"

"Yes, he keeps the digital stuff at Shawmut. That's probably good, because the second thing is it that Darin Carvalho, the Clockmaker's brother, picked up the keys to Nielsen's shed for Father."

"Have you told the FBI about this?"

"I was just about to call them, when Jane said you were holding. I'll call them when we hang up. The third thing is that Dr. Nielsen says that Clay committed suicide last week while he was out on bail."

"Why didn't we hear about that?"

"Beats me…I'm going to call Marta about Darin anyway, so I'll ask her."

"Well, I'll be quick, so you can call the FBI about that Darin. The sooner you're here, the better. Anyway, David just told me that I'm right. The Aramaic scrap is a list of the ossuaries that aren't ready."

"Oh crap, Steven…."

"I know…call the FBI. I will see you tomorrow. I miss you."

As Susan picked up the phone to call Marta, an email from Dr. Nielsen came in with a photo attached. She had her bags at the office, and didn't need to leave for the airport yet, so she opened the file. Almost the entire segment was legible. She thanked him by email and said to let her know if he wanted a translation. She printed the enhancement. Jane came in as she was packing up.

"Marta's on hold, can you pick up? She's pissed that you didn't call."

"Marta, dear, thank you for calling," Susan said feigning politeness as she picked up the call. "Who do I call to report that Darin, the missing roommate or whatever he is, got the keys to the shed for Father Bartolome?" Susan asked.

"Damn it, how do you know?"

"I finally reached Dr. Nielsen—the pictures were in his shed. Dr. Nielsen hasn't been out there since November. Darin picked up the keys for Father. They were sent back to Dr. Nielsen by FedEx."

"Damn. Call the FBI. Do you still have that card?"

"Not Douglas…."

No. it will be somebody else, do it now—I will see you at the gate. I have to finish packing and make some calls; I have a mini-crisis to attend to. Call them now."

"One more thing, did you know that Clay committed suicide?"

"No, I'll see what I can find out after I pack. Call the number on the card, now."

Susan picked up the card and called the FBI. An hour and 15 minutes later, she was totally irritated and ready to move to Shanghai. But she had been able to convey the importance of the information. She would ask Marta to call them and make them be nice to poor Dr. Nielsen.

Susan stuck the FBI card in her pocket and finished packing as Jane came in.

"Your car is downstairs."

"Thanks, see you in a few days." Susan read the email from Dr. Nielsen as she rode to the airport. He had written out the letters he saw for her. She compared it with the photo he had sent with it. By the time she got to the airport, she knew it by heart.

Susan sat down at the gate. She had 30 minutes until they boarded and there was no sign of Marta.

She then re-read the text in the picture sent by Dr. Nielsen and noted corrections to four words. "Damn," she said as she composed an email to Steven. As she finished, Marta called her cell.

"Where are you?" Susan asked.

"Susan, I have a big issue in DC…I can't go to Shanghai. I'm heading to Midway to get a flight to DC."

"Well, that's a bummer."

"Did you call the FBI?"

"Yes, of course. Unfortunately, now they are going to make Dr. Nielsen miserable for a day as they question him about his colleague, Darin Carvalho.

And Nielsen just did me a big favor, too. Can you call somebody and make them be nice? They also tried to get me to cancel this trip."

"Well, that's stupid. You're probably safer in Shanghai."

"That's what I told them."

"Look, I'll see what I can find out…call me when you land."

Susan got on the plane and settled in with a cup of coffee. She then made a couple of calls and finished her email to Steven. Her email said:

> Our Joham made at least three trips to the New World; he was searching for a place to resettle the Guardians. He went in 1602 and then again in 1604, both times on a French ship as a member of the crew. In 1607, he had the Guardians with him. This time, he was going to Port Royale as we thought, but the storm pushed them to the western shoreline of what is probably the Bay of Fundy. The Guardians took the boxes from Tomar to Cyprus in 1539. They sat in Cyprus with the Guardians from 1539 until 1545, when they were moved first to Casnewydd in Wales (it's probably present-day Newport) and then on to Scotland. The Guardians and their boxes moved to Cyprus because of the Inquisition in Portugal as we expected, but I don't know why they then moved from Cyprus to Wales or to Scotland and then back to Wales. The boxes and the Guardians were definitely in Wales by 1599. They stayed there until Joham took them to Maine via shipwreck in 1607. I believe they went to the New World to be far away from religious persecution. James VI was King of Scotland until March 24, 1603, when the crowns of Scotland and England were unified and he became James I. You may recall that after Constantine's 50 Bibles, one of the next great Bibles was the King James Version sponsored by James I, himself. See you in about 18 hours.'

CHAPTER 85

Susan landed in Shanghai sixteen hours and ten minutes after boarding. Because of the time change, it was Thursday evening. As she had no checked bags, she continued past customs down the escalator. She didn't see Mary anywhere.

"We should have stayed at the Portman Ritz," Susan grumbled to herself. She knew there was a Starbucks next door to the Ritz and she needed coffee. Of course, the Ritz was at the end of Nanjing Road and the Peninsula was on the Bund. As Susan reached for her phone to call Mary, she saw her coming.

"I brought you a Starbucks Grande Latte, with an extra shot, of course."

"Excellent, thank you," Susan said laughing. All was okay now—she had her coffee.

"We will meet Steven and David for dinner tonight at the Peninsula. We need to go—sorry I was late. The traffic is horrible. There's the car. Let's go."

Mary and Susan laughed all the way to the hotel—recounting stories of some of their more adventurous travels.

Steven came over to greet Susan and Mary as they walked into the restaurant. "Long trip, huh?"

"Yes," Susan said, suddenly feeling tired.

"Steven, are you having seared foie gras again tonight?" Mary asked. "He can't get it any more in the US, so he comes here to have it every night. We are a free country—nobody will tell us we can't eat foie gras."

"Oh, for God's sake…foie gras every night, Steven?" Susan asked. He just smiled.

When they were seated, Mary asked, "Is that the cane you killed the man with?"

"I didn't kill him…I just whacked him to his knees, so Steven could sit on him," Susan laughed, showing Mary the dent where she had hit either Beria or his gun.

David, taking Mary's lead, added, "Is it really the famous New York cane?"

"She could have killed the damn crook," Steven laughed. "He was 62 years old."

"You whacked an old man?" When she finally stopped laughing, Mary asked, "Are these guys in jail, now?"

"Four of them are—two in Paris and two in New York," Steven said. "There also are four dead—one somewhere in England, one in Paris, one in Boston and one—a good guy, a priest, in New York. One is missing—at large as they say. Oh, and there was a kleptomaniac. They let him out on bail, and he killed himself."

"Steven said they even killed a priest—that's pretty bad. You should stay here—that guy who's missing may come after you," Mary said seriously.

"He shouldn't have a grudge against us—his friends only got nabbed because they were dumb. And we never met the guy—he disappeared right after seeing that all of his buddies got put away."

"You never know," Mary said, "tell her David."

"Shanghai's a very safe place, Susan," he laughed. "Very nice, too, especially since your husband put me up here at the Peninsula for our meetings."

"Well, we'll see—Darin Carvalho has to find us first."

"Anyway, you will always be safe here, Susan. Steven and David told me a little about what you are working on. I guess it's like when that TV show said they had found that Jesus guy's tomb."

"We didn't say it was real, Mary," David said.

"Won't you get into trouble with your religious fanatics in the US? They seem to hate everybody."

"Only if you aren't one of them," Steven smiled.

"You Americans, too many guns and too much religion…you should read your Constitution."

"I'm Israeli," David protested.

"Do you kiss that Roman Wall and do that head bobbing thing?" Mary asked as Susan sat back laughing. She had missed Mary.

"She has a point, David," Steven said as they finished eating. "I think we all need to get some rest. Mary, can you stop by tomorrow and meet the others?"

"Maybe, I have to think about meeting Japanese. I would like to meet Dr. Shiloh, though. Susan, I will call you. Good night everyone."

"You sure you don't want to stay here? We'll get you a room…."

"No, I have things to do yet tonight."

When Steven and Susan got upstairs, Steven said, "I got your email. Did you bring the piece from Dr. Nielsen? Can I see it?"

"Yes, the picture. I'll show it to you in a minute. I got your email. I'm all ears. First though, I did talk with the FBI. They don't get too excited when you tell them things. I thought the tie between Father and Darin Carvalho was a big deal, but then maybe they already knew that this Darin got Father the keys. I also told them I had the pictures from the shed at one point, but sent them back to Dr. Nielsen."

"But that means this Darin may be looking for us, damn it. Thank God you're here."

"Why us?"

"I guess we could testify, but since we've never seen him, we couldn't identify him," Steven said.

"And why did the asshole kill Father…couldn't he just use Dr. Nielsen's keys to get the pictures himself instead of giving the keys to Clay?"

"Maybe he and Clay didn't know why Father wanted the keys…that damn Clay must have figured it out after Father got the keys. I guess he must have told Darin that Father had the pictures after he saw them. Anyway, you must be exhausted."

"A little, but tell me what you found, while I find what Dr. Nielsen sent me. Is Artemisia here? I want her to confirm a short segment from the Latin seal document."

"She came in with Kat."

"Good. Steven, we may have almost the whole story—or at least Joham's story," she said as another wave of exhaustion hit—damn, she was getting old.

"So, give me a summary," he said.

"Can't you just read my email?" she said as she stifled a yawn.

"It's better when you tell me—you add things."

"Joham was a member of the Knights of the Order of Christ—he says that the Guardians had been in Tomar since before he was born, but that they, the Guardians, had lived in Cyprus before Tomar and then again during the Inquisition. They also were in Jerusalem at some point. Joham first went to Wales in 1599, when he took a man with him to study with the Guardians who were already there. So, the Guardians are some type of special group; you had to study to be accepted. Apparently, that new guy had become one of the three, when Joham came back to take them to the New World. That's about it for the diary. Here, just read my email."

"I did, but I like to hear you, because you add little tidbits."

"If I can stay awake…anyway, the important thing is that Joham made three trips to the New World before he took the Guardians with him. He went with Champlain in 1603 and 1604 as a crewmember. Then he made one more trip in 1606 on a French ship; he was with a man he calls a friend of the 'Guardians.' As you know, 1604 is the year that work was begun on the King James Version of the Bible; the Hampton Council where the revisions to the standardized Bible were first discussed, was in 1602. Of course, he sailed with Dafydd ap Talog on that last journey."

"That's great, but I'm not sure I understand."

"Look, St. Croix, as you know, is an island in Northern Maine; it was then the l'Acadie territory. It was settled by the French in 1604. I think there was a plan to move the Guardians and their boxes to the New World—that seems pretty obvious. But by the time he tries to return with them in 1607, St. Croix had already been abandoned and everyone had moved on to Port Royal in Nova Scotia. He says Port Royale. So, where are you with your Aramaic letter?"

"It's a confirmation that Constantius or one of his assistants ordered ossuaries with the names of the 12 original apostles on them."

"So, is Judas Iscariot one of the names?" she was sure Steven was teasing her.

"No, it's Bartholomew. The ossuaries are for the 'Church,' which I assume means the Church of the Holy Apostles. The Aramaic fragment is a copy of part of the list from the letter. I think we have the 'smoking gun' I've been looking for...Divine old Constantine was all set to buried by his son, Constantius II, in the Church of the Holy Apostles amid the Apostles in their ossuaries."

"Oh crap—really?" Susan asked.

"Yes, but Susan you look like you are ready to fall over—let's go to bed. We can continue at breakfast."

"Okay," she said as she was drifting off to sleep. "It only says 'church'? What's the date of the letter?"

"It has to be the Church of the Holy Apostles, but it isn't named. I told you before, the letter is dated 338 CE, shortly after Constantine died. Let me help you there," he said as she sat on the edge of the bed.

"Thanks," she smiled; at least her shoes were off now. "His son finished the Church of the Holy Apostles when Constantine died, right?"

"Yep, Constantine planned to be buried among relics of the Apostles, but as for the Apostles, only St. Andrew is known to have been found and buried there. It is the Church of the Holy Apostles, and we are pretty sure that Constantius ordered ossuaries or relics for all 12…Susan, are you awake?"

"I think so, um, Andrew was the first Apostle chosen by Jesus, you know. Oh, I almost forgot, there might be a history of the Guardians and their orders in the second box…the original guys were from Egypt," she said as she put her head on the pillow. "They had to be Gnostics; there is something about them teaching the Sufis who then taught those who came to the Holy Land… that's mentioned in the seal document. Obviously, some of that is what I asked Artemisia to confirm."

"Egypt?" Steven asked. "Are you asleep, Susan?"

"Almost…there's also a relic in one of the boxes. I think it's a lock of Mary Magdalene's hair. Is Jon here yet?"

"I didn't know until Kat showed up yesterday, but Eisen took Jon back to the US Monday. He felt well enough to go home and look for those other boxes."

"That's good," she said then fell asleep.

CHAPTER 86

Friday morning, everyone met for breakfast at 8:00 a.m. to go over the agenda. Susan reported on what might be in the second box. Hopefully, there also would be a third box, but she had seen nothing that mentioned what might be in it. After some discussion about Jon and Eisen being back in Maine, they adjourned. They would meet again at 11:30 a.m., when Dr. Shiloh would join them.

She walked over to talk with Artemisia. "Did you have any luck with that segment that seems to talk about the Sufis? I hope you can clarify it for me."

"Yes, you were close. It says the 'soul of Jesus was steadfast and pure.' My specialty is of course, Medieval Latin and Greek, but my understanding is that those words are consistent with early Gnostics. Is that correct?"

Yes, the early Gnostics believed they were able to transcend the material world. The Sufis are similar."

"You have another specific question, then?"

"Well, here it also seems to say that they taught the Sufis who in turn taught those who went to the Holy Land. My question is the words that I believe mean Sufis, the mystic branch of Islam. It doesn't say Sufi, but I believe it says something like "the mystics of Islam who learned from the Gnostic, Simeon." That's a good description of the Sufis. Is that what it says here?"

"Why yes, of course. It's difficult as the word 'gnosis' as used here is in Greek as is the sentence that follows it. The rest of the document is Latin, of course. There are a few words that I will need to consider…I understood the Gnostic reference, but there is another here that is similar. Dr. Shiloh might be able to help because some words are too faint. Do we have the original here in Shanghai?"

I think my husband or Hershel should have it. It's going to end up in Zurich for conservation." Susan said.

"It does say they learned to find an inner knowledge from Mithra. Mr. Ohno said the documents would be interesting," she smiled.

"I need to digest this during the break. I may have more questions, is that okay?"

"But of course."

Susan decided she would take a break to clear her thoughts before the 11:30 a.m. meeting. She headed for the old French Concession for a walk along the shaded sidewalk of one of its tree-lined streets. She stopped at a bookstore along the way to where she knew there was a Starbucks. There on the English language shelf was a paperback copy of *Brothers Karamazov*. Susan bought it, feeling at peace for once. As she walked on to Starbucks, she realized she hadn't checked her emails since the night before…she really was at peace, she mused.

Susan ordered a Grande Latte with an extra shot. While it cooled to a drinkable temperature, she looked at her phone. She had a voicemail from Jon and about 30 emails. She listened to the voicemail…"Susan, call us as soon as possible." Jon's message said.

She looked at her watch—it was 10:30 a.m. in Shanghai, so maybe it was too late to call Jon on the East Coast. "Oh, crap, he did just leave it less than an hour ago," she thought. "I'll just call him."

"Hello, Susan is that you?" Jon answered.

"Yes, sorry did I wake you?"

"No, no, I'm glad you called. Eisen just left a message for Mr. Ohno too… how soon are you coming back?"

"Well, unless you found another box, probably not for a few more days. I just got here last night."

"We did…there is more in Latin, can you come back? Steven and everyone else could stay and you could start on the Latin for us. Eisen got you a flight, there's one at about 7:00 p.m. from the Pudong airport tonight; he's also holding one for tomorrow at 11:30 a.m."

"More Latin? Um, you found another box?"

"Yes, while we were in Tokyo, Eisen had someone refine your diagram. We had a contractor help with platting and there it was…we just got down to it this morning."

"Are you serious?" Susan asked.

"Yes, and there are another five documents in Latin. We'll meet you in New York…Eisen said he would get rooms for us at the Pierre. Oh, and we've added more security—one of the cameras showed some people near the shed Tuesday evening, and the lock was broken…."

"No more spear points, I hope," she laughed.

"No! We would like you to come back."

"Let me call Steven; actually, we'll reconvene in 40 minutes. I'll talk with everyone then."

"You can come back, then?"

"Yes, I think so…can I call you in an hour or will it be too late?"

"Yes, call me. Oh, and the FBI was at our site today. Eisen showed them the surveillance pictures, but they wouldn't say anything. Eisen called Marta; she'll come up from DC tomorrow."

"Oh, for God's sake…I need to head back to the hotel for the meeting. I'll call you shortly."

CHAPTER 87

Friday night, Susan was on a flight from Shanghai to New York. Everyone else stayed in Shanghai to wrap up the meeting on the first box.

Marta, Eisen and Jon were waiting for Susan landed in New York.

"Hi everyone…so, did you bring the new stuff here?" Susan asked.

"We did," Jon said. "You must be tired, though."

"Not really, but I am hungry…maybe we could get a bite at the hotel and talk about what you found. I slept on the plane a fair amount."

"Excellent," Eisen said. "I'll call the driver…we're all staying with you at the Pierre. Marta said it's your favorite."

As they rode to the hotel, Jon and Eisen explained that the second box had been exactly where the map and the directions had indicated. The third box, though, would take some time as there was a clump of seven trees that would have to be cleared.

"I guess you didn't find any bodies, right? Kat said his friend thought that when the Guardians were killed, Joham buried them near the boxes."

"Ohno-san asked me the question, already…no bodies," Eisen said. "Our friend, Smith-san, thought they were killed in a battle at the site. Our Joham buried them nearby. Perhaps they will be by the third box."

"So, we'll use pictures here at the table," Jon said. "You can see the originals tomorrow."

"This is the one we want you to look at," Eisen added handing her a picture.

"There is definitely the word you showed us that you interpreted as 'Guardians'," Marta said. "Susan, Jon and I could pick out a tiny bit of the Latin…we think it says the original Guardians were appointed by Constantine himself to care for these documents."

"Dear God," Susan said, looking at everyone. "Marta, I think you're right; it says that they serve Constantine to 'protect the central truths of the religion as time erodes men's memories.' Constantine himself entrusted them with the documents, with the understanding that they will seek out the truth wherever it may be found. Um, this here more or less says they are also charged with adding documents that 'enlighten' if the ultimate truth is found within and thusly 'we' understand the documents that are to be kept."

"What does that mean?" Jon asked.

"Damned if I know," Susan answered as she stared at the words in the picture. "Steven's documents are dated just before and just after Constantine's death. These words are like the Gnostics, with a good dose of Sufism added to it. The Sufis may have tutored the Templars. Of course, they were charged with being Gnostics among other heresies when they were disbanded in 1312 CE. As Marta can tell you, some say that the Dome of the Rock is based on a Sufi mathematical design. Templar churches used the same design."

"If I may," Eisen said, "my fellow Japanese approach religion somewhat this way…we may say Shinto or Buddhism, but in actuality, we combine elements of nature and spirits of our ancestors, which we call kami, with an attempt to attain insight into being or enlightenment. Shinto itself is very ancient; it means the way of the gods."

"That's something like syncretism, Eisen, where you combine the best of everything. Before I forget, Dr. Alberts, Steven's old advisor, said the insignia on that cover to your documents was a Gnostic symbol for unity or awakening.… Do you have pictures of anything else?"

"Two more, Susan," Jon said as he handed her another. "The other three documents aren't in as good condition, so pictures would be meaningless.

"Well this one must be later…this third sentence says something like "even as Moses led his people from Egypt and Mohamed led his people from Mecca, so also will others be led to their enlightenment. Were there any relics in the box? The attestation said that there was a relic, a lock of Mary Magdalene's hair."

"We saw nothing like that," Eisen said.

"Maybe it's in the box under the trees, then."

"Maybe," Jon said. "Here's the other one. We can't tell if this writer is a male or a female, or two separate people. See, here it's Hypsicratea and there it's Hypsicrates."

"Hypsicratea? Seriously?"

"Yes, see there," Jon said handing her a picture of the new piece.

"Hypsicratea…Jon, it's the historian who was the sixth wife of King Mithradates VI of Pontus, a kingdom on the southern coast of the Black Sea," Susan said. "She also fought as a man, called Hypsicrates, with Mithradates against Pompey. She somehow ended up as a historian for, and a slave of, Julius Caesar, but he ultimately freed her. None of her historical works are known to have survived. It would be a big deal if something she wrote is among these documents."

"Like our female samurai warrior, Hangaku Gozen. There is a woodblock print of her by Yoshitoshi," Eisen said.

"Yes, in fact Eisen, Hypsicratea was from the Caucasus region which, like Pontus, is possibly the land of the Amazon warriors of Greek myth."

"Susan, before we get too excited, is there any opinion on whether these are real, yet?" Jon asked.

"No, Jon. All I can say is they have found nothing to disprove it yet. As you would say though, absence of evidence…"

"I hate that phrase," Jon said.

"Any news about Darin, Marta?"

"They got him, Susan. Eisen and Jon thought I should be the one to tell you. Oh, and I dumped Cy."

"Yahoo," Susan said. "Bedtime."

NOTES

All dates in this book have been conformed to the *anno domini* dating system as modified by the more recent movement to use CE and BCE. The 'A.D.' system is attributed to Dionysius Exiguus who, in 525 CE, began using it to identify date on which Easter would fall. He pegged his system to what is referred to as the incarnation, birth or beginning of the life of, Jesus, with *anno domini*, being year 1, there being no Year Zero in the system. Notwithstanding, scholars generally now believe that Jesus was born some time before the death of Herod the Great in 4 BCE, thus making the *a. domini* designation off by a few years.

Although modern Japanese names traditionally comprise a surname or family name followed by a common or given name, in this book the names of Japanese characters have been conformed to an English format, with the common name coming first. Hence, Katsutoshi Ohno technically would be Ohno Katsutoshi in Japan.

ABOUT THE AUTHOR

Working as a corporate finance attorney for over 30 years, Hewitt Freiburg made enough money to seek and study archaeological mysteries and wonders all over the world. This first novel draws upon those years of travel and study. Hewitt lives in Tucson and Chicago.